FATE

Also available from Millennium
Imperial Light

Mary Corran

FATE

MILLENNIUM
An Orion Book
LONDON

The right of Mary Corran to be
identified as the author of this work has
been asserted by her in accordance with the
Copyright, Designs and Patents Act 1988.

First published in 1995 by
Millennium
An imprint of Orion Books Ltd
Orion House, 5 Upper St Martin's Lane
London WC2H 9EA

A CIP catalogue record for this book is available
from the British Library

ISBN: (Csd) 1 85798 273 8
(Ppr) 1 85798 433 1

Typeset at The Spartan Press Ltd
Lymington, Hants
Printed and bound in Great Britain by
Clays Ltd, St Ives plc

PART ONE
Auguries

Prologue

Billowing white smoke issued in gusts from the pit, then sank to lie heavily just above the dark marble of the floor, writhing leadenly in thick, impenetrable clouds, obscuring sight.

Lykon, Dominus of Darrian, the ruler and the luck of his people, was sweating despite the cold as he held his small wriggling daughter in his arms, an awkward and unaccustomed burden. Barely a year old, she was a dark-haired, dark-eyed child, whose expression suggested she did not greatly care for her present surroundings. Lykon waited, clearing his throat, sharing her opinion.

'Stand closer,' advised the other man present, an elderly priest garbed in a white robe. 'Nearer the pit.'

Lykon complied, shivering, for the marble hall was chill, as if the stone itself exuded cold. The long, high building seemed to him unnecessarily large for what it contained, which was only the deep pit, wide and long enough to contain a human form, and behind it the vast statue representing Lady Fortune, her balanced scales held out at shoulder height, the chiselled features stonily impartial as befitted one of the capricious Fates. Sunlight entered the hall through narrow slits in the walls several feet above his head, but Lykon felt, as he had on other occasions, that they made little impression on the oppressive darkness. At thirty-two, he was a tall, well-built, man, aware that his sensitive face displayed his feelings too openly; he knew the old priest had already registered his present uncertainty.

This was the third of his children Lykon had brought to the attention of the Oracle of Venture; for neither of his sons had the auguries been favourable. It was painful for him, remembering his own far distant ancestor who had first stumbled on this place, who had slept and dreamed on this same hill-top and found his dreams came true, to have to stand and await the Oracle's verdict.

'On what day was the child born?' inquired the priest.

'The first of the new year, at the first hour.' Lykon saw the elderly priest nod approvingly in recognition of the omen, for it was lucky to be born when both moons, Abate and Aspire, were new, attracting good fortune to the child. He stared towards the pit and hoped, fervently, that the Fates would be kind to his daughter. That she had survived her first year boded well; none of the children born to his lady after their second son had survived more than a month until this one, and they had both feared their luck was spent. The child's survival to her present age had given them new hope.

'And what is her name?'

For a moment, Lykon did not hear the question, all his attention centred on the coiling smoke. A cough drew him back. 'Vallis,' he answered hurriedly. 'We named her Vallis, after my ancestress, wife to the first Dominus.'

The priest nodded again, permitting himself the luxury of an austere smile. 'A most worthy choice,' he opined, but Lykon was no longer listening.

'Draw nearer, Hawk.'

The new voice issued from the pit; disembodied, it held an inhuman quality, neither low nor high, harsh nor soft, but cool and clear, reminding Lykon, for some reason, of the sound of snow falling on the sea. He swallowed at the unaccustomed form of address and took a step nearer.

'Show me the child.'

Lykon obeyed, drawing down the woollen blanket in which Vallis was swaddled to reveal her face, which was round and showed surprisingly strong features for so young a child. His daughter stared up at him, but, seeing a familiar figure, decided not to cry, though her chin wobbled ominously.

There was a small sigh from someone in the hall. Lykon waited, unable to breathe for the fear clutching at his heart.

'For you, Hawk, I say nothing.' There was more than a hint of dismissal in the voice, as if Lykon's destiny were of little interest or importance. *'But to this one . . . '* There was a pause, then a sharply indrawn breath which was almost a hiss; then the voice came again, louder and more confident, as if reciting words already familiar:

'The scales of Fate are finely poised;
The Jackal balances the Bear
Till one shall rise and one shall fall.
Then, shadowed child of earth and skies,
In whom is fortune favoured most

4

By blood, by birth, by name – though yet
Bright plumage dimmed by mask of grey –
Cast off your shroud; break wide the shell.
Spread wings that never felt the breeze,
And as the Lady of the Hawk
Return the Jackal to his lair,
The Shadow to its rightful bounds.'

Involuntarily, Lykon clutched the child too tightly, and she emitted a sharp squeal of protest.

'She is your luck now, Hawk. She holds what you have lost. Guard her well – ' Abruptly, the voice broke off. Lykon turned to the priest, who was now staring at Vallis with a look approaching awe.

'What does it mean?' Lykon asked anxiously, understanding only one word in ten of the Oracle's prophecy. The Bear was a reference to Darrian, if he remembered correctly, and the Jackal was Amrist the Conquerer himself, Overlord of the Dominion which controlled most of the known lands. The Dominion must be the Shadow. But the rest of the prophecy made no sense to him. What was the mask of grey? What the shroud?

The priest shook his head. 'I cannot be absolutely certain, Lord Lykon.' He coughed apologetically. 'Sometimes these things are not clear, even to those of us who serve here. We rely on repeated usage of common terms to be sure of their meaning – such as Bear for Darrian, and Jackal for Lord Amrist of Javarin. I would judge,' and he looked down at the slate he held, on which Lykon could see a few hastily scribbled lines, 'that the Oracle is warning us there is to be a change in the balance of luck between ourselves and the Dominion. Perhaps in our favour, perhaps not. But the rest refers to your daughter here. First that she is your child – the emblem of your lady's clan is a serpent, the symbol of your office is the hawk, that is the meaning of "child of earth and skies". I do not understand "shadowed" here.' He looked worried, then brightened. 'For the rest – perhaps we shall face Amrist and his Kamiri in battle, and we shall be victorious. For make no mistake: this child has the gift of good fortune, for herself and for us all in this land of Darrian. She is the true heiress of your line. That much I can tell you.'

Lykon wondered what the priest was keeping from him; there was something furtive in the old man's expression that warned him the reply was rather less than the whole truth. Yet he had no power to command the man to speak; the priests of the Oracle held to no political allegiance, just as the Fates answered to no man, nor woman, bestowing their fortunes as they saw fit. And, as ever, the Oracle's prophecy was ambiguous, except in the matter of his daughter's luck: his own, Lykon knew, was draining away, or so his personal diviner warned him. The man had the gift for seeing the lines of fortune for a man or woman as did few others of his calling, although he had been oddly hesitant in his reading of Vallis. With some unease Lykon recalled the man's rare unwillingness to commit himself. Yet he could not doubt his fortune was reborn in Vallis; *she* would balance the scale with Amrist where he could not, and their land would be safe. Relief surged up in him. Nothing else mattered. He hugged his daughter, lying peacefully in his arms, oblivious to her new importance. She smiled back, her dark eyes wide and serious.

'I will keep you safe, my daughter,' Lykon whispered. 'Whatever happens, you must live.' He was hardly aware of his surroundings, his earlier apprehension dissipated, so that he no longer saw the dark hall as threatening, but as a theatrical effect deliberately engineered by the priests to enhance the power and standing of their Oracle in comparison with others in the Dominion; it was only a trick, if an effective one.

In the courtyard outside, his lady waited with their retinue. With a nod to the priest, Lykon made for the doorway, his steps lengthening as he considered the good news he had to break to them all. He could barely contain his relief that he did not, after all, have to warn them that Darrian, too, would soon become part of the Dominion; now the land and its fortunes were, through the person of his daughter, preserved from Amrist's armies.

At the entrance, on impulse, he turned back, blinking in the sudden glare of winter sunlight on white walls. Vallis gurgled contentedly, echoing her father's mood.

All that concerned him was that he held in his arms the luck of Darrian.

Summer, four years later

Asher looked up at the sky and thought there was a storm coming; the day was so very still. There was no breath of wind to stir the leaves on the trees in the orchard, nor the hedgerows, nor the blades of corn in the fields; even the birds that usually hovered hopefully over the growing ears of wheat were nowhere to be seen, their raucous calling silenced.

She gathered the eggs in her basket, reaching with a practised hand into the loose straw in the hen house, noting how few there were to be found. It was all of a piece with the rest; the cows' milk was either sour or dried up, there were rainstorms just before haymaking. The whole country was going *wrong*, as if all the good fortune that had favoured Darrian over the centuries was draining slowly away; or at least that was the tale in the village. Hens scurried about her ankles and skirts, squawking frantically as she continued to search their nesting boxes, pecking irritably at the grains and grit strewn on the ground.

With a sigh, Asher shut the gate of the pen and carried her filled basket across the deserted farmyard, past the stone haybarn and the dairy and into the kitchen of the square two-storey farmhouse at the rear. The coolness of stone was welcome after the heat of the day; no one in the north of Darrian built in any other material because of the rare danger of firestorms in spring: even one every ten years could devastate a holding or village. But it was summer now, and that peril was past. Asher wiped her brow with the back of her free hand, feeling the sweat on her hairline.

'Mother?' she called, for the big kitchen seemed dark after the glare outside, and so still that at first she thought it empty.

A grey-haired woman stood motionless, her back to the hearth at the far end of the room; her hands were clasped together, her gaze fixed on a high point somewhere on the wall to her left, where hung pots and pans and heavy strings of onions. Her thin, high-boned face looked pinched and tight, as if she were struggling to hold back tears. On a normal day she would have been busy with any two or three of the hundred tasks that filled her life; instead, to Asher's astonishment, she was doing nothing. The kettle still steamed away over the dying embers of the fire, but no preparations were underway for the evening meal, although it was well into the afternoon. There were none of the usually savoury smells of baking bread or simmering stew in the kitchen; the larder door stood shut, and the surface of the huge wooden trestle table that took up a third of the space in the long room was bare, still gleaming whitely from that morning's scrubbing.

'Mother?' Asher ventured again. She put down her basket, suddenly frightened.

Father. It was her first, instinctive, thought. Something has happened to Father. But even as her heart began to pound, painfully, in her chest, she could not bring herself to voice her fear, which was fear for herself as well as for him. She knew a moment's apprehension that had nothing to do with her father, which warned her to take care and say nothing, not to precipitate disaster.

'Mother – what is it?' Her voice was sharp in her anxiety, but the woman by the fire did not respond, although normally she would never have permitted her daughter to speak to her in such tones.

The door which led into the main part of the house opened, and her father came in. Asher started, but, for a rarity, he paid her no heed, going straight to his wife and wordlessly putting his arms round her; she relaxed against him with a quavering sigh, burying her face against his chest. Asher could not remember, in all her thirteen years, seeing her so frail and vulnerable; but even as the thought came to her, she knew that if her father was unharmed, then whatever was wrong was serious indeed. She stiffened, looking down at the eggs and counting them again, concentrating on the smears of earth and straw sticking to the shells, on their different colours and shapes, her mouth unpleasantly dry.

'Asher.'

Her mother spoke her name. Asher found she was growing angry, hating to be shut out, the only one who did not know what was the matter, as if she were a child still.

'What?' she asked rudely.

'Asher, come here.' Her father released an arm and beckoned her to join the circle. Stiffly, she obeyed, filled with a deep wariness, no longer quite so sure she wanted to be party to their knowledge, as if *knowing* was a danger she had to fear.

'Asher,' he began awkwardly, 'you're old enough to be told.' He stopped, and she read in his eyes, the same deep brown as her own, that he would have given anything to keep his news from her. She was conscious of the weight of his hand, of the brown calloused fingers – proof of nearly fifty years of hard labour on the farm – grating on the bare skin of her forearm. It was summer, and she wore only a thin shirt with short sleeves above her calf-length skirts; a child's dress, not a woman's, showing her ankles and the lower part of her legs. Did he see her, then, as only a child?

Her father cleared his throat and continued: 'A messenger arrived in the village this morning. From the capital; from Fate.'

'What did he say?' She sounded grudging and cross, and hated herself for it. She knew her father loved her, his only child, and she adored him; it was only that at that moment she did not want him to speak.

Her father shook his head, looking suddenly weary and much

older than his sixty years. 'The city of Omen has fallen and the south is taken. The Dominus has submitted to Amrist. We are – Darrian is – now part of the Dominion.'

For a moment, the words did not sink in, as though spoken in a foreign tongue, without meaning for her. Asher felt herself as brittle as the thin ice that covered the water barrels in winter, as if she might break at the least pressure.

'What will happen now?' she managed to ask. 'To us?'

'The word is hostages will be taken from the cities and villages, to ensure the peace. Not us,' he added hastily. 'There're only the three of us and the hired hands, and they'll want farmers to farm; even the Kamiri need food. Amrist will put in his own governors, they say, but otherwise there'll be few changes. The Dominus has agreed a higher tribute, so we'll not be subject, only a tributary. He's won us so much independence.' He rubbed the skin of her arm with his thumb, trying to reassure her. She wrenched herself away, ignoring his distress.

'So long as we can pay!' she said shrilly, understanding dimly how little that freedom would prove to mean.

Her mother spoke suddenly, her voice dull and without inflexion.

'Omen was utterly destroyed. The city walls torn down, the buildings burned and crushed.' She left Asher no choice but to face the reality, offering her no false images of hope; she had lost a young cousin and her two children in the city. 'The people were slaughtered like cattle. It no longer exists.'

Her father absently stroked his wife's grey hair, seeking to soothe an anguish he could not relieve. 'That's why the Dominus asked for a peace, Asher,' he said softly. 'His luck was gone so we could not win, and he could bear no more deaths.'

'They didn't have to fight. They could have surrendered. Why did they fight if they were going to lose?' Asher was unsure why she felt so strange and unlike herself, filled to the brim with rage. 'What was the *point*?'

'Keep your voice down!' For a moment, her mother was her old self again, glaring at her daughter. 'When the Dominus sent to ask, the Oracle prophesied Omen had a chance for victory. If the city's people had won, we'd still be free, and Amrist and his Kamiri would have withdrawn from Darrian. You know that. I remember telling you myself.'

'Then the Oracle is wrong!' Asher was glad to have found an outlet for her inner turmoil, something real to attack. 'The prophecy was a lie!'

'No.' Her mother lifted her head in reproof; her eyes were red-rimmed, but she was back in control. 'I forbid such talk! It's not for you to mock the fall of fortunes. The Oracle of Venture is never *wrong* and cannot lie; it follows the lines of Fate and speaks only what it sees. But no Fate is so certain it cannot be altered by even so small an event as a sneeze. The people of Omen spent their lives to give us a chance of freedom; they failed, but they tried, and we must honour them for it.' Her expression was rigid. 'And all hope is not lost. The Oracle has given us another chance.'

'What chance?' Asher demanded mutinously. 'The grey men are *here*!'

'You know perfectly well, Asher,' her mother said sharply. 'Vallis, the young daughter of our Dominus, will bring us good fortune. You know what the Oracle prophesied for her – *she* is our hope.'

Asher began to scowl, more at her mother's tone than her words, but she noticed an odd look cross her father's face. Her mother saw it too, and her eyes kindled with life.

'What is it, Erward? What are you keeping from us?'

Asher's father cleared his throat uncomfortably, refusing to meet her gaze, and his hand dropped from her hair. 'Just a rumour, wife, nothing more.'

'What is this *rumour*?' Asher saw her own explosive anger reflected in her mother's face at the obvious evasion. 'What is it, Erward?' her mother asked again. 'Or are you afraid Asher and I are too frail to bear more ill tidings?' Her eyes flashed a challenge. She was his equal in the affairs of the farm and beyond, and he knew it.

With a sigh, he gave in. 'No, wife. Never that. It was only –' and he shrugged, incapable of explaining to her his instinct for secrecy '– that it's a rumour, not yet confirmed.' He looked at Asher, hoping she would understand and share his desire to protect his wife from further pain, but she only stared stonily back. 'There's a tale that young Vallis has gone missing; that she disappeared from the palace in Fate at the same time the news from Omen reached the capital. They are saying it's because of the prophecy, that Amrist has had her spirited away so she can do no harm to him.'

There was a moment of frozen silence during which Asher saw her mother's face grow blotchily white, the veins on her cheeks and forehead standing out vividly.

'But Erward – surely it's possible the Dominus himself sent her away, for her own safety, to protect her from Amrist?' Erward merely shook his head.

'Then it's all a lie!' Asher was shouting again. 'The Oracle's a lie, and the Kamiri won because they were stronger, and fought better! It's true. Our luck has *gone* and nothing will bring it back!' It was so obvious she could not believe it was not plain to them. She suddenly wanted to cry, to vent her unhappiness on the two people she loved most in the world. 'It isn't *fair*!'

She turned and fled towards the door leading into the yard; as she passed the table her hand brushed against the basket and it fell to the floor, the eggs breaking in a sticky puddle of yolk and white and shell.

'Asher – you come back! Come back and clear up this mess!'

She ignored her mother's angry summons, guiltily pleased with herself; she would not worry about averting the bad luck that came from spilling food. Such things had never troubled her; they were no more true than the Oracle, and the Kamiri had won, and Omen was gone.

She ran across the cobbled yard and took the first path to meet her feet past the barn, stumbling on the rough grass and ruts of dried mud where wagons had gone by. She ran past the hayfields, hesitating briefly at the trail that led to the village, and at the other, which would take her across the common to the great house of Kepesake and her friend Callith. For a moment she was torn, unsure which way to go, with an odd feeling that some unspecified outcome hung on her choice. But Mallory, Callith's elder brother, was home from his last voyage, and she was suddenly shy of intruding on their family reunion, newly aware of the distance separating herself, the daughter of a farmer, and Callith, daughter of an influential and wealthy merchant clan. Until this leave, Mallory, although five years older than she, had been almost as much her friend as his sister, but there was something different about him this time, as if he had crossed some invisible barrier and changed from friend to man. Asher did not feel at ease with this new Mallory.

As she still hesitated, her father's voice reached her, calling out angrily, and she carried straight on and the anxious feeling passed. A farm-hand called out a greeting from the ditch he was digging, but she ran on, with the energy of misery, until she reached her favourite secret place, a hollow ash tree with twisting roots that bordered the narrow river running through the farmlands. She threw herself down on the dry mud and grass, hot and panting for breath, wishing she could cry.

After a time she recovered sufficiently to sit up, and her breathing grew easier as she stared, stony-faced, at the play of

11

sunlight on the slow current of the stream. She thought of the changes coming to the farm. She hated change, especially that in her own body, the budding breasts that were sore to the touch, and the new, monthly nuisance her mother told her would be hers for most of her life. Her mother had said she should welcome her new self, but Asher wished, with all the angry passion of her heart, that life would stand still. She wanted everything to go back to the way it had been, before the tribute ships bearing Darrian's gold sank in the storm the previous month on their way to Javarin, drowning the good fortune of the land with them; before Amrist had invaded and stolen their luck away.

Even if her father was right and they were left in peace to carry on their work, the grey men would come and rule them; they would take the grain the farm produced, the coins they earned, with everything else. She knew what had happened in other lands taken by the Kamiri over the last half-century; it had been the subject of village talk for the past year and more. The Kamiri were slave-makers, brutal and vicious; they killed for pleasure, on the turn of a card or the dice. Or that was what was said.

Only Saffra is free now.

Saffra, the strange, frozen country to the north, a land of mountains and snow, a society where, it was said, the women ruled equally with the men, all together with no one man to command them. The Saff were safe, protected by an invisible barrier none could pass unless the Saff allowed it, using a magic they alone possessed. They were rumoured to own powers of the mind far surpassing those of any diviner, so that they could read not only the lines of Fate but even the hearts of men and women. Asher remembered a Saff girl she had seen once, tall and thin, with white hair and very fair skin. They were an alien people, too, but different from the Kamiri, for they were peaceful and despised slavery, refusing to trade with nations of slavers. Which would leave them isolated now. Gorm to the east, Asir, Baram and the rest; they were all countries of the Dominion, ruled by the grey-skinned men of Javarin and subject to their law.

The Kamiri were unnaturally tall, too, like the Saff; Asher had heard it argued that they must share some bloodlines in common, despite the differences in the colour of their skin. But where the Saff were revered for their wisdom and gentleness, the Kamiri were universally hated and feared, even if some men admired their strict military discipline and blind obedience to orders, which they said was courage.

Asher considered what her mother had said about the Oracle,

and about Vallis. She's wrong, Asher told herself angrily. Everyone knew the prophecy but Asher had always thought it silly, doubting one small girl younger even than herself could be the bearer of so much good fortune, even if she was the daughter of the Dominus. Vallis would be five now, but she had two elder brothers. She was only a child, and a girl child at that. 'Unlucky to be born a woman,' the saying had been repeated to Asher too often for her to question its truth, even if her own observation had not affirmed it.

She drew in an angry breath. Even Mallory had begun to look at her as if she was a girl and of little account, or that was how he made her feel. Why had he changed? Or was the alteration in herself, that now she was growing into a woman she was somehow no longer a person? The thought brought a stab of misery. But what did it matter? If Vallis had disappeared, and their good fortune with her, then it was all a trick, a lie.

They say the Oracle can't lie, but it can. As proof, Omen is lost, and Vallis too. She burned with furious indignation. What was the good of prophecies, if nothing could be done to avert the disaster they claimed to foresee? Why had the Oracle not divined the sinking of the tribute ships and given warning? Then the subsequent invasion might never have happened, for the gold would have reached Amrist and Darrian would have been safe.

Asher trembled with the force of her rage, swearing to herself with the most solemn oath she knew she would never be taken in again; even the village fortune-teller was false, a liar. What of the diviner who had looked into her own future when she was a baby, and foreseen she would live and be lucky? Asher sneered mentally, her lips firming in a thin, determined, line as she deliberated, recalling occasions her friends had told her results of consultations with a visiting diviner. Sometimes the forecasts had been right, but they could just as easily have been lucky guesses as *seeing*. There is no way to divine future fate, she told herself coldly. She would not believe her life must follow one straight line from beginning to end, that there were no choices save those the Fates had already decided for her. She was Asher, and she would do whatever she wanted. She wished, with real passion, that she could be like Mallory and go away to sea, and knew a futile resentment because it was impossible. Women were not permitted to be sailors, or to work on board ship in any capacity, even as cooks. *They*, whoever *they* were, had decreed it was unlucky! Asher bit her lip and hated everyone impartially.

Slowly, as the day drew towards its close and the stillness grew heavier, her turmoil died down, as if in coming to one small decision she had reasserted some form of control over her life. Asher was forced, reluctantly, to feel guilt at the way she had treated her parents, knowing it was not their fault Darrian had been invaded, that they were all to be slaves to the Kamiri in fact, if not in name. It was only an illogical conviction that they were old and should somehow have been able to prevent it happening, which had made her treat them as if they were the enemy. She sighed aloud, realizing she would have to go back and apologize; they would be hurt, as well as angry.

'Is anything wrong?'

The unexpectedness of voice and question startled her, and she whirled round, only to find Lewes standing by the ash tree only a few paces away. He was the nearest neighbour to Harrows Farm, six years older than herself, but at Carling's he farmed only a modest hundred acres to their three hundred; she liked him well enough, but the fair good looks which made her friends cast longing looks after him Asher thought insipid, and she had never cared for the patronizing note in his voice when he spoke to her. She was wary of him, for he was said to have a mean temper, although her father, who liked him, always said that was only because of the mole on his forehead.

'No. Why should there be something the matter?' she said, haughtily because she was still cross with the world. She jumped to her feet, newly conscious of the way the thin material of her skirts clung to her long legs. 'And I've got to get back to the farm, it's late.'

'You've heard the news then?' Lewes displayed no remorse at breaking into her privacy, although he must have been well aware this was her secret thinking-place, where she hated to be disturbed. He leaned lazily against the trunk of the tree, muscular tanned arms crossed on his broad chest, his teeth very white in his sun-browned face. Sunlight glinted on his dark blond hair, turning it to a rich gold, and Asher saw he was laughing at her.

'Of course.' She was poised for flight, not wanting to talk to Lewes, least of all now. His unblinking regard made her uncomfortably conscious of her dusty skirts, of her braid of hair – as fair as his own – which had become unravelled and now lay in tangles down her back, and of her dirty face. Lewes always had that effect on her, as though he judged her on her appearance, not as a person with thoughts and feelings of her own.

'Don't worry about it. I'll look after you. Don't be afraid, my pretty.' Lewes smiled down at her, as if, she thought touchily, she was a child, or a dog which could be soothed by a pat on the head. Asher found herself growing red, and was furious.

'*You*?' she said, putting as much scorn into the word as she could. 'What can *you* do? And anyway, I'm not afraid.'

The smile did not falter, but became fixed and ominously still; Asher was made aware that she had, unexpectedly, succeeded in stinging Lewes' enormous self-conceit. She hesitated, not liking the look in his eyes; she wondered if she should say she was sorry, because there was something frightening about him as he stood watching her. She opened her mouth, then shut it stubbornly. Lewes should have left her alone; it was his own fault if she had angered him. She turned away, hesitated, then moved off at a run in the direction of the farmbuildings, wishing she had not met him.

He was no longer smiling. He watched until she was out of sight, frowning a little, as though a problem troubled him, but not too deeply. Not far away, a falcon hovered on the air with wings spread wide, beady eyes searching the cornfields for movement. A water-rat plopped into the slow-moving river at Lewes' feet. He stooped and picked up a stone, shying it at the beast, but he missed, and the stone splashed uselessly in the water.

He began to whistle as he made his way back to his own, less fruitful, fields, his good humour quite restored. He, too, had come to a decision as he sat beside the river.

Asher was right. It was a good place to think.

Chapter One

Fourteen Years Later

The violent storm of the past three days had finally blown itself out, and there was now only a gentle easterly wind coming in from the sea as Asher ran lightly up the steps leading to the inn. A powerful stench of fish pursued her, hardly surprising since she was near the fish market, and mingled with other, more penetrating, odours from blocked gutters to either side of the steps. The steep lane was unexpectedly dark, clouds obscuring the stars, and Asher swore as her foot slipped on some carelessly flung refuse and she almost fell back down the long flight, barely catching a window ledge in time.

The ground levelled out on to a flat cobbled space which in turn widened into a narrow street, and she was glad to see the lights of Carob's tavern spilling out from half-opened shutters ahead. Ignoring the main entrance, Asher moved to the left and pushed at a narrow door set just below an inn sign depicting a large silver fish.

Once inside, she took a quick look round the room, and felt an instant stab of disappointment: Mylla was not there. The scattered tables and benches of the women's room were only sparsely occupied, mostly by poorly dressed women in well-worn aprons, although a few silent children were still in evidence. It was late, and the mothers with small babies had already left; Asher wondered whether she should go herself, for it seemed pointless to wait the short amount of time remaining until curfew.

'Can I get you something?'

The voice belonged to Cass, a slave from neighbouring Gorm, a small, dark-haired woman of thirty or so, with bright vivacious eyes and tiny hands. She was busy gathering up empty pewter tankards, piling them on a tray, but looked inquiringly at Asher as she worked.

'Is there a message from Mylla?'

Cass shook her head. 'Not yet, but there's still time. Sit down. You look tired.'

'I am.' Asher sank on to a bench, leaning wearily back against the wall. Without being asked, Cass brought her a tankard of ale, which she sipped slowly. As ever, her gaze slipped to the crescent-shaped scar branded on Cass's left cheek, the mark identifying her as slave; that Carob, Cass's owner, treated her more as a young relative than a possession did little to alleviate the shame Asher always felt at the sight of the mark. The rising number of slaves in the city was yet another of the indignities imposed on them by the grey men, a visible sign of the slow but inexorable weakening of their limited autonomy, won from the Kamiri at a high price: the tribute weighed more heavily each year.

The room smelled of fish oil from the table lamps, as well as spilled ale and cheap coal, but the sum total was more appealing than its components. Trade was stable rather than brisk, for it was a cool spring night at the dark of the moon. At the next table sat three women, rather older than Asher's own twenty-seven years, gambling heavily on the outturn of two twelve-sided dice; one had a high pile of copper coins in front of her. A little further away, two very young women were taking turns to pick fortunes from a pile of dominoes; Asher heard a squeal of pleasure from the darker of the two, a pretty girl in a red dress, as she uncovered her selection.

'Five-four – *a lucky speculation!*' Her companion scowled, making her rather plain face actively ugly, then selected her next piece, which she threw down in disgust.

The taproom was warm, although the fire had died to mere embers. Asher kept her eyes on the door, but could feel an easing of her tension as she drank more ale and listened to the low murmurs of good-natured conversation around her. It was pleasant to sit still for a change, and she refused to contemplate disaster, or the long walk ahead. Cass's neat figure in a blue dress of good thick wool whisked efficiently from table to table, collecting coins or depositing ale, a smile for each customer.

'Give it back. It's *mine!*'

The shrill complaint came from a small girl who had been sitting beside the hearth, playing quietly with a stuffed toy of indeterminate species while her mother talked to a friend. Her brother, a year or more older, had grown bored with sitting and the lack of attention, and his thoughts had turned towards destruction. He was holding the toy perilously close to the sinking flames, watching his sister with gleeful malice.

'Dora, Dora, won't have it no more'a!' he chanted.

His mother roused, lifted a thin hand in protest, but was too far away to seize either boy or doll. Asher looked at the little girl, a plain-faced child, too pale and scrawny for good health, expecting to see her eyes fill with tears of frustration. The boy, too, was waiting for some such reaction. Unlike his sister, he was solidly built, rounded cheeks flushed with the heat of the fire and the expectation of easy triumph. Asher supposed that his mother – a worn-looking woman in a much-mended dress – gave him the best of the food and kept little back for her daughter or herself; old customs were hard to break. The booksellers near the slave market still sold copies of a fifty-year-old treatise encouraging parents to feed their daughters only meagre fare, so they would fit the fashionable mould of small, slender women with tiny hands and feet.

The girl, to Asher's surprise, did not bother to appeal to her elders for help. Instead, she rose to her feet, and, in one swift movement, threw herself at the boy head first, butting him heavily in the stomach. He gasped and swayed, reaching up a hand to the mantel for balance, and his grip on the toy loosed. Instantly, the girl snatched it away, retreating to her patch of floor, hugging her prize to her thin chest. The boy took a menacing step towards her, but she raised her left hand, pointing with a curious gesture; the boy jumped back, fell, and his right hand touched the metal grate in the hearth. He yelled, rubbing at a reddening spot. His mother rose wearily to her feet and made to comfort him, glaring at her daughter as though the incident had been all her fault.

Well, well, thought Asher, amused; a talent for ill-wishing was rare, but obviously useful to those who had it. She raised her tankard and drank a silent toast to the small girl. She, at least, had learned to take care of herself. Which was fortunate, since apparently she had no other defender.

The door from the outside opened and Asher looked up hopefully, but it was only Carob, her bulk completely filling the narrow doorway. She might have been anything from forty to eighty; in the six years Asher had known her she had not changed at all. Her sparse white hair was drawn carefully over a pink scalp, above a round face that bulged but did not sag, and her tall figure – taller than most men – did not stoop. Her skirts were large enough to make three for Asher, reaching a modest length just above her ankle-boots. She carried two wooden buckets of cheap coal, lifting them lightly as she tramped over to the fire and placed some of the larger lumps on the embers.

'It's a cold night,' she observed in her gruff voice, to no one in particular. 'There'll be rain before dawn.' She straightened, then came across to Asher's table. 'You should be on your way,' she said accusingly; round eyes of a pale blue reinforced the suggestion. 'The first bell'll go soon.'

'In a minute,' Asher agreed. 'You're a kind inn-keeper, Carob. Not many would feed the fire so close to curfew.'

She sniffed. 'It's cheap!'

Asher grinned at the dismissive tone. The inn-keeper hated to be thanked.

The door to the outside was suddenly slammed back against the wall and the wind rushed in, filling the room with blasts of cold, damp air; several of the oil lamps went out at once. Asher shot up from her seat as three grey men marched in, two of them holding thick leather leashes attached to the collars of a pair of Kamiri scent-hounds. The cosy taproom was transformed instantly into a place of chill, cramped confinement in which the women and children sat frozen in awkward attitudes, unwilling to move and draw attention to themselves.

'Your papers.'

It was hard to distinguish any difference between the grey men; close to seven feet tall, as was usual among the Kamiri, all were broad-built, with dark grey hair and paler grey skin. One, however, sported a beard, his companions only moustaches, and it was the bearded guard who had spoken. Although his words were not addressed to her, Asher fumbled at her belt pouch for her identity papers.

The three took their time as they went round the tables, inspecting each proffered document with exaggerated care; they seemed to be drawing out the time until curfew, hoping to find anyone who failed to obey the decree of the Kamiri governor of Venture to carry identity papers at all times. Someone had had the sense to close the door, but Asher was cold, resenting the intrusion bitterly. This was another freedom being eroded, that they could not even sit and drink in a public tavern without interruption. She watched the guards angrily; their common uniform of heavy loose jackets lined with fur over grey trousers and boots further detracted from any individuality. Their southerly Javarin homeland was far warmer than the northern port of Venture; she knew they detested the cold, and was glad of it.

'You. Who owns you?'

The bearded guard stood in front of Cass, dwarfing her. His harsh accent as he spoke the unfamiliar language made the question deeply offensive, and Asher must have moved for Carob placed a warning hand heavily on her shoulder.

'I do,' she called out calmly.

The guard swivelled in her direction, dark eyes surveying the inn-keeper's bulk with mild interest. 'Show me her papers. For what was she branded?'

Carob heaved herself up. 'See for yourself,' she said, handing over two folded pieces of thick paper, both bearing the city seal. Cass coloured, but stayed very still as the Kamiri's large hand came down on her face, a long grey finger tracing the crescent scar. Asher's temper rose, loathing the man for his arrogance, his assurance of an innate superiority. She knew Cass had been branded for theft in her Gormese homeland, when she was only a girl, but she had always refused to explain or defend herself. Asher, recognizing a pride similar to her own, had never thought the less of Cass, nor doubted some miscarriage of justice.

One of the scent-hounds came to snuffle at Asher's feet, a large, ugly beast with a reddish-brown coat of thick, unkempt hair and an oddly flat face from which sensitive nostrils protruded at an unnatural angle. Bred to the pursuit of fleeing slaves, it was the size of the snow-leopards inhabiting the north of Darrian, but it lacked the grace of the feline; the thick neck and solid hind-quarters bespoke force, not cunning. Surreptitiously, Asher tried to kick it away, but it appeared to have found an interesting scent on her left boot and would not be deterred.

'Your papers.'

A moustached guard was holding out his huge, grey hand to her. She passed over her papers, taking care no part of his smooth skin should come in contact with her own, her loathing for the grey men making her unable to tolerate even the thought of touching him, as if he were some venomous reptile. She held her breath; her identity papers were a good forgery, but a forgery nonetheless, and she was always nervous of letting them out of her possession.

The man read with deliberate slowness, passing a finger across her name, age, status, occupation, and place of residence. The paper was stamped with the demonfish seal of the city, the genuine one, supplied by a woman who worked in the Records section of the administration, but the guard continued to hold the paper out of Asher's reach, a grin visible under his moustache. She sensed his unspoken contempt for a member of a subject race

– in fact if not in name – so visibly inferior in physique, so obviously inferior by nature of her sex; the Kamiri respected only military force. She wanted to snatch the paper back, but common sense warned her not to try. She shifted uneasily in her seat, enduring the speculative survey of the guard, whose gaze moved down from her face to take in the rest of her body in the loose-fitting skirts and shirt she favoured, the collar high and concealing. The Kamiri kept slave-women in their compound for their leisure hours, but had been known to resort to consorting with free women; Asher bore the inspection silently but with rising fury.

Grey men or Darrianite – they're all the same, she thought contemptuously. All that matters is what *they* want, how *they* feel. Her experience of men had left her with a low opinion of the majority, and her work in the city served only to confirm her prejudice; but it was a subject she did not wish to contemplate at length, and when the Kamir finally returned her papers she replaced them in her pouch without comment.

It seemed an interminable length of time before the guards were satisfied with their investigation, but a dozen women and children hardly represented a major threat to their authority and they departed languidly, leaving the door open behind them in a final show of contempt. Carob moved to shut it with a slam, then gestured to Cass to gather up the empty tankards.

'Best get going,' she said loudly to the assembly. 'Curfew's coming any minute.'

Two young women who had been playing quietly at cards, and the second pair who had been occupied with domino fortunes, rose and gathered their cloaks, taking their departure with a smile of farewell for Carob and for Cass, obviously regulars. Asher sighed, knowing there was no point in waiting any longer; this was the third night she had come to Carob's without result. Mylla would have been back now if everything had gone smoothly. There was always a risk in the escort of escaped slaves to Saffra, but Mylla had done the journey many times and knew the route well; it was not the first time her return had been delayed, but she had never been so late before.

'Can I help, Asher?' Cass asked, seeing her anxiety. 'Any message you want to leave?'

'I don't think so, but thanks anyway. I'll be here again tomorrow.'

'Anything you want, Asher. Remember that,' Cass said intensely, touching the brooch she wore on the collar of her tunic, a seven-pointed star, its apices shaped like tiny flames. Asher wore its twin, identifying both to those who knew of its existence as members of the women's group, pledged to offer help to all women, slave or free.

'Is Essa any better?' Carob came across to join them; her lapel, too, sported a star, which looked incongruously tiny against her massive form. 'Tell her from me she's been ill long enough!' But the gruffness of her manner did not disguise her look of concern, and Asher only nodded.

'I haven't seen her this morning.' As ever, it struck her how very improbable was the friendship between Carob and Essa, the taciturn and the talkative; yet it was these two who were the co-founders of the self-help organization, each in her different way a force for change in Venture. What they had begun as a simple means to help poor country girls who came to the city in search of work had expanded far beyond their original intent. The invasion and later attempted rebellion in Venture had opened up quite different possibilities to the women, and it had been Carob, not Essa, who had seen quite how much could be accomplished now that the women had access to city seals and papers.

'If she's well enough, tell her I've a girl of sixteen from a village in the south that needs a maidservant's place,' Carob said briefly. 'She'll need papers too; there's been some trouble at home.'

'I'll deal with it if she can't.' Asher remembered how she had come to Essa six years before in her own time of trouble, first as supplicant, sent by a cousin who had had dealings with the employment agency, later becoming an active member of the group at Essa's request, a challenge she accepted willingly, remembering how she had found a home, and friendship, among the women of Venture. Runaways to the city were uncommon but not unknown, and she felt a special interest in such girls and took a certain pleasure in flouting the law by hiding them under new names, away from whoever pursued them.

'You should be going,' Cass advised quietly, looking towards the door.

Reluctantly, Asher took her tankard across to the table where Cass was gathering the empties on to a wooden tray and put it down. 'Not ready for a trip north yet?' she asked with a grin.

Cass smiled back. 'I think I'll stay. For a while longer, anyway.' It was a standing joke between them, although Asher wondered what loyalty it was that kept Cass a slave in Carob's inn where she might have been a free woman in Saffra.

'You'll be here tomorrow?' Carob asked softly.

'I suppose so.'

'Easy enough to have an accident on the road – a lame horse or bad weather. Mylla'll be here soon.'

'I hope so.' Asher wrapped her cloak, a drab brown affair, around her shoulders, and tied a dark-coloured scarf over her mid-brown hair; it was safer to look shabby when out late at night in the old quarter. 'Good night, Carob, Cass.'

'Take care,' Carob called after her.

It was she who had thought of providing a women's room in her inn, a place to come after a long day's work, or simply to get out of cramped rooms where there were too many children underfoot. There was nowhere else for women to go without escort, or where their children would be welcomed. Venture was unusual among the cities of Darrian, having lost a higher percentage of its menfolk to the internment camps both at the time of the invasion and after the riots which followed two years later; there were many working women, often with young families, and no one else seemed interested in providing for their leisure hours. Carob provided the setting, clearing a small room previously used as a private parlour for the purpose. At first her male customers had protested vigorously, invading the room and shouting insults at the women, but Carob had been firm. Her tavern served the best beer in the old quarter, the poorest section of the city, and what she said went – or the men did. It had been as simple as that, in the end.

As Asher stepped outside, she found herself wishing the inn were not quite so far from the hostel in which she lived. Elsewhere in the city, roads and pathways were paved or cobbled, but in the old quarter they were composed of beaten mud and the mounds of refuse which accumulated in an area where too many people lived in too close confines. She shivered, lifting her feet to avoid the worst of the messes, but it was hard to see; it was the first day of the fourth month, and both moons were new and dark. The sky was overcast with the promise of rain, and the sea air felt damp; cautiously, Asher descended the steep steps and hurried in the direction of the main cross street which would take her to the south of the city and her own lodgings.

A sea wind tugged at her cloak and she gathered it round her, trying not to breathe too deeply as she passed an open ditch into which something had evidently crawled and died some time ago. Voices reached her from the tall tenements as she walked past: babies screaming, a woman crying, other voices raised in argument. Asher wondered what the lives of their owners were like, feeling a rare pang of loss for the home she had left behind, for the different sounds of a country night; for a moment she imagined she could smell damp earth and dusty grain, until a powerful stench of fish brought her back to her present surroundings.

She kept a wary eye open for robbers as she walked, but there were still a few other people about, for the first curfew bell had not yet tolled. She was safe enough, although the shadowy doorways of the tall, squalid tenement buildings offered many a haven for the thief.

She had only got as far as the slave market when the first bell boomed from above the law courts, the sound spreading out towards the city walls, and she cursed under her breath; there was still some way to go, and to be caught out after curfew meant two days in the city jail or a heavy fine she could ill afford. She quickened her pace, oblivious to the changes in her surroundings which would have told her, if she cared, that she had left the old quarter well behind. The street she traversed was wide, and paved, and lights shone from behind shutters of two- and three-storey buildings which were still terraced, but well maintained. The houses were broader, the gutters running clear; the air itself proclaimed the increase in prosperity.

What was that?

She whirled round, thinking she heard an echo of her own footfalls. Her soft leather boots made little sound in the empty street, but she was sure the other steps had sounded heavier, somehow different. She was often out alone after dark, but it rarely made her nervous now, although when she was new to the city it had terrified her; she had learned to take obvious precautions over the years and, despite some unpleasant encounters, she had never been robbed or assaulted in the streets. It was unnerving to find herself a prey to fear where normally she felt herself invulnerable.

The sound came again, quite distinctly.

There was someone there – but where? Asher stopped again, looking back, but there was no one in sight. She hurried on, telling herself she was a fool but listening, nevertheless, for the tell-tale scuffling of another presence.

She reached the tall Treasury building, its familiar double doors firmly shut and barred, each marked with the eight-tentacled demonfish, the city's symbol; eight was regarded as a lucky number, marking the days in a week from the quarter of Aspire, the larger and beneficent of the two moons. Asher had, six months previously, been promoted to the rank of chief clerk at the Treasury, at a salary of ten gold pieces a year; it was five less than the men were paid for the same job, but it was three times the wage of a domestic servant, and Asher knew she was lucky to have it.

She started to run as the second bell began to toll. Now she was sure she could hear sounds of other steps in pursuit, but she did not stop and look back, afraid of being caught by the guard. She felt the first drops of rain on her face, then the skies opened as she reached Scribbers, the residential quarter where she lived. Gratefully, she headed down the narrow street that led to the hostel, panting for breath as she turned into the blind alley to the left and slowing her pace as the building came in sight. She reached it and rapped loudly on the heavy door with the metal knocker, hoping someone would hear her quickly, for she thought she heard footsteps behind her.

Nothing happened. She waited impatiently, knocking again, staring up at the narrow frontage of the hostel. It had once been an inn with quarters for guests of modest status visiting the city, and extended back much further than was apparent from its modest façade, where the gate which had once led to the stables was now permanently locked, the stables converted to living quarters. It still sported a sign designating it the Inn of the Waxing Moon, but everyone knew it was home to forty women, and they still had occasional trouble with gangs of rowdy youths or young men who saw the barred door as a challenge and made periodic attempts to break in, as if doing so in some way gave proof of their masculinity to one another.

The door was opened at last by a tall, blonde woman, older than herself, who made no attempt to hide her disapproval.

'Asher – where *have* you been?'

'Sorry, Margit. There was a bit of trouble at Carob's.' She slipped inside, and the other woman carefully relocked and barred the door. Margit was a plump, graceful person, with a long expressive face which was almost beautiful, and she, too, wore a seven-pointed star on her tunic.

'You're very late. You're lucky not to have been caught by the guard.' Margit looked upset. 'Did Mylla come?'

Asher shook her head. 'No. I think something must have gone wrong; she should have been back two days ago, at the latest.'

'Perhaps she's been delayed by the weather.' Although several years younger than Asher, Mylura, or Mylla as she was known, was most commonly chosen to escort the escapees to the frozen land north of the border; she had an uncanny ability to avoid the

Kamiri guard who patrolled the road. She always said she could *smell* them. Unlike Asher, however, Margit did not seem overly concerned by the younger woman's non-appearance.

'Is everything all right here?' Asher asked, a little irritated by Margit's nonchalance.

'Essa wants to see you. She's better tonight, no fever, and she ate some supper.'

'Good.' Essa owned the hostel and was its oldest inhabitant. When she was a young woman and newly married she had set up an agency specializing in finding employment for women and girls in domestic service, which was how she first had dealings with Carob. When her husband died she had sold their home and bought the inn, then derelict, turning it into a hostel for single women, knowing how scarce was such accommodation in Venture. It was she who chose the residents of her hostel, though not all the women who lived there were members of her private group; as she often said, some companions she chose for practical reasons, others simply because she liked them.

'Go on up,' Margit advised. 'You're the last in, so no one need keep door-watch. You look tired.'

'Thanks a lot!' Asher walked past the older woman and on into the common room.

Most of the other inhabitants of the hostel were still up, talking, or sewing, or making candles, and Asher greeted various friends as she passed through the room. The large hall had once been the main taproom of the inn, and still contained the benches and trestle tables with which it had originally been furnished; the women had added various items of their own, and it was now a cheerful, homely place. A fire glowed in the hearth, and tallow candles in sconces on the walls provided more light. Bright-covered cushions added a further touch of colour, and, with contributions from all of the women, Essa had bought a silky red and gold rug, imported from Petormin, the most easterly land of the Dominion, which now lay luxuriously on the polished-brick floor before the hearth.

At the far end a door led on to the stairway leading up to the two floors of private rooms. Asher went through and took the steps two at a time, wondering what Essa could have to tell her; there had been a steady stream of visitors for Essa in her illness, bringing small gifts as well as a regular supply of information.

Asher knocked at Essa's door which stood at the rear of the building, next to her own, and looked out over the stableyard.

'Come.'

The voice sounded much stronger than for days. Asher obeyed the summons with a lifting of the heart; Essa's high fever had worried her greatly.

'Margit says you're much better,' she observed, perching herself on the end of the bed.

'Do you like my present? A gift from clan Formin, no less,' Essa replied, stroking an unfamiliar blue blanket which covered her narrow figure with an unexpectedly sensual gesture. Asher stared, for the moon-pattern edging proclaimed it a costly gift, out of place in its plain surroundings, bestowing on the square room an elegance out of keeping with the austerity favoured by its owner.

'It's beautiful. Why such generosity?'

'I think they want another cook. They've lost the last four I sent them – the third told me no one but a madwoman could work there for long!' Essa laughed. 'Would you bring me my candle, please? Margit put it out of reach in case I fell asleep before you came in.'

Asher got up and lifted the heavy candlestick from the wooden chest and placed it on the table beside the invalid, the cheap tallow candles which were all Essa ever used smoking slightly. Everything in the room was serviceable but plain, the bed, the flat-topped cupboard, the chest; Essa had been a rich widow, but had given most of her wealth away after she bought the inn and converted it into the hostel, claiming others – single mothers, widows with large families, deserted women and children – needed it more. In a city that lauded the family and expected women to be provided for by fathers or husbands, it was forgotten how many had no family, through ill luck or because none would own them. Margit, Asher knew, was one, for her family had turned her away when she was pregnant with her employer's child.

'You do look better,' Asher observed. 'How do you feel?' She divested herself of cloak and scarf and sat down again, glad of the colour in her friend's face. Essa was close to sixty, and had looked much more during her illness. Now, however, her blue eyes were alight with amusement, and she had lost the air of apathy so unnatural to her active spirit. With her silver hair neatly plaited and wound about her head, she looked very like Asher's own mother, a strong woman, capable, with a durability of spirit displayed in the sharp eyes and firm expression.

'Oh, I'll be back on my feet in a day or so. Whatever you may say,' she added, seeing Asher's reproachful look.

'We'll see. You were quite ill, Essa.'

'And you're very late tonight. Was there trouble?'

'Not really. I was at Carob's, and the guard came just before curfew. Playing their silly games. I was out after the second bell, but I was lucky.'

Essa frowned. 'Really, Asher! You must be more careful. And I take it Mylura did *not* come?'

'No.'

Essa's lips curled in the indulgent smile Mylura's name often invoked. 'Never mind, she'll turn up soon.' Asher wondered in exasperation if she were the only one genuinely worried; no one else seemed to doubt Mylla's safe return. 'Give her till tomorrow night. She's never failed us before, and I don't suppose she will now. I never knew anyone as capable as Mylla of looking after herself.' She shot Asher a shrewd look. 'You worry too much.'

'I know. A bad habit.'

'It suggests you think no one but yourself capable of performing the simplest task,' Essa observed reprovingly. 'We work *together*, Asher, remember that. You're far too young to carry the weight of the world on your shoulders!'

'Yes, Essa,' Asher agreed solemnly, managing to keep a straight face.

The older woman smiled, reluctantly. 'Oh – wretch! You're young enough to be my daughter after all,' she protested, adding more soberly, 'I sometimes think you take far too many risks. When Carob and I began, we only meant to provide a service no one else cared to; we had no interest in politics, only in helping young girls who needed friends.'

'But would you go back to that, if you could?' Asher asked, hiding her dismay. 'When we can do so much more?'

'Oh, no,' Essa assured her hastily. 'Not when every day I see slaves mistreated, and there are times it makes me very angry to see how my girls are misused and underpaid, and I think it a wonderful thing to be in a position to help people like you, Asher.' She paused, perhaps remembering their first meeting, then went on: 'It seems strange it should be the invasion which has given us so many chances to do more than simply provide a few coins or a bed or baby clothes, but it's true; with so many men gone or in the internment camps we women have gained a great deal. Your post at the Treasury, for example.'

Asher nodded. 'I know.' It was an old discussion. 'Margit said you had news.'

'Indeed, I had several visitors today. The first – Derna, one of the Administration clerks, you know – tells me it's certain the Dominus is dying. Poor man, his luck has deserted him to the full now, though he may linger another year, they say. He had another seizure when they brought him the news that Colum was dead.'

'To have lost both sons must be hard,' Asher agreed. 'But he's been a sick man since the invasion.' Colum, the younger son, was rumoured to have died in a fall from his horse, but no one in Darrian believed the story; the Kamiri had every interest in seeing Lykon's children dead and his line eliminated. His family had ruled Darrian for fifteen hundred years, since the Oracle of Venture had named Lykon's distant ancestor the first Dominus, and their fortunes were so deeply entwined with those of the land they ruled as to be indistinguishable.

'The balance of luck is unsettled. It's Lykon's daughter who should concern us now; it's more imperative than ever she be found, Asher. Otherwise Amrist will place his henchman on the throne, and we will never be free of him!' Essa spoke urgently. 'A dreadful imbalance entered our world when Amrist rose to power; wherever he goes, he seizes the good fortune of conquered lands for himself. Already the Kamiri are draining our own country dry – of our gold and our luck.'

'I know.' A shadow crossed Asher's face. 'I keep the tribute returns in the Treasury, and it's clear there'll be a shortfall in Venture this year. The import of slaves keeps wages too low, and they pay the women little enough as it is. A tenth of nothing is still nothing. Our merchant councillors will be unhappy at the amount they have to make up, but it can't be helped. And it can't go on much longer, or even they won't have the resources to pay.'

'And if we can't pay the tribute, we become a subject people,' Essa finished bitterly. 'Already the Kamiri whittle away at the few freedoms we still have. If we in Venture fail to raise our share of the tribute, there's no city in Darrian which can make up our shortfall. If we fail, the Kamiri won't merely send governors but take all power from the city councils, and reduce us to virtual slavery, as they did in Asir and Gorm. Amrist has never broken a treaty, but he must have known he could not bleed us this heavily for long. When we can no longer pay, we lose everything.'

'He can afford to play a waiting game. Who would Amrist choose, if the Dominus dies before the girl Vallis is found?'

'There's a cousin – Ensor – in the internment camp to the south.' Essa closed her eyes in recollection. 'He's the obvious choice, and a bad one for us; he's a fool, and after fourteen years as hostage, no doubt a Kamiri tool as well. No. I know you won't agree with me, Asher, but I think we should try to look for this girl ourselves; we have as much chance of finding her as anyone.'

'You know what I think: that it's a waste of our time,' Asher objected, without much hope. 'There are resistance groups, political organizations in all the cities of Darrian, but here in Venture only *we* try to care about what happens to ordinary people on a daily basis. Let the resistance look for Vallis; we've more than enough to do already. No one has ever found any clue as to where she might be. She could even be dead.'

'No.' Essa's denial came instantly. 'The Oracle has said she still lives.'

'And so you believe it?' Asher could not quite keep the cynical note out of her voice; she had never forgotten her feelings of betrayal on the day she learned of the invasion, nor her sworn promise to herself. Alone among the women of Venture, the city of the Oracle, she had never sought its advice.

'The Oracle does not lie.' Essa stated the fact much as Asher's mother had once done, leaving no room for argument. 'The girl is alive, and since that is so, she can be found.'

'But not by us,' Asher countered. 'Remember why you and Carob joined together in the first place, and what we try to do. Remember how stretched we are for funds because no one on the city council cares what happens to a few women and slaves with no money and no influence! Do you think the resistance would lift a hand to help us? Of course not. They would say we must suffer in a greater cause, as if people's lives were unimportant and politics all that mattered.'

'Perhaps so.' Essa sighed. 'But I want us to try to find Vallis, even if it does take valuable time. I'm sorry, Asher.' But the apology did not negate the order; there was steely determination beneath the courtesy.

'But you *have* tried. You spoke to her nurse years ago, when she came back to live here, because you'd known her when you were girls. And she knew nothing,' Asher protested. 'It's not that I don't agree she must be found, Essa, only that I don't see what *we* can do that no one else can.'

'She is our only hope.'

'All right.' Asher sighed, accepting defeat. 'Very well. I'll let Carob and Cass know, and Margit.'

Essa lay back against the pillows, looking wearied, and Asher stood to pour her a cup of water from a pitcher standing nearby. 'Drink this,' she ordered. 'You should always drink plenty of liquids when you've had a fever.'

Essa took the cup and drank, then handed it back. 'I am better, but a little tired, I admit. I shall be glad when I can get back to my agency, and spare you that burden, at least.'

'It's no trouble. Margit helps too, and Sara, and some of the others.'

'But you're tired, too, and tiredness makes you careless. Margit tells me that only yesterday you almost forgot and brought a bunch of ivy into the hostel. That was foolish, as you well know, and would have brought ill luck down on us.'

Asher made a gesture of impatience. 'I'm sorry.'

'It's not enough to be *sorry*,' Essa went on irritably. 'I have never envied you, Asher, even though occasionally I think it would be pleasant not to have to worry about attracting ill fortune by some small chance action. For you, it seems the Fates themselves are a question of belief, and you choose to deny them for reasons I cannot understand.'

'If I'd been born blind, why should I believe in sight?' Asher demanded in turn. 'My identical twin brother died when we were born, but no one has ever been able to explain to me why that should make me different. Why should the circumstances of my birth make me now immune to the twists and turns of the Fates? They say it makes you favoured, a child of Fortune, to begin life with such a piece of luck, but my life has not been so easy and so blessed that I believe that either. That's why most of these charms and signs seem pointless to me, wishful thinking rather than Fate.'

'You know that's not so, Asher. You've seen for yourself how charms and wards can help or harm. And even you credit how fine is the balance of fortune in our land.'

'But charms and wards have physical properties, just as a telescope helps you see further, or magnets attract iron. And I can accept a natural balance of good and ill fortune, that Darrian has always been lucky because the climate is good, the soil is fertile, and we have metal to mine and people to work the land, and I can see that these advantages may be stolen from us, and some of them lost forever. I can believe that people are born more or less fortunate, for I can see that myself. But not that the caprices of the Fates rule all our lives, nor that they dictate all we do, that it's all decided from the moment of our conception. And I don't believe it is possible to tell the future.'

'I won't argue with you tonight, I'm too tired. Just remember, it's not safe to be visibly different. You're still in hiding here, after all.' But Essa must have seen she had said enough, for she did not elaborate on the topic.

'I should leave you to sleep. It's late.' Asher got up, trying to disguise her irritation, but Essa put out a hand to stop her.

'Asher, I'm sorry for being tiresome, but please don't go yet. I've more news for you.'

There was a strong note of pleading in her voice and, unwillingly, Asher sat down again. 'What is it?'

'I know you don't like to be reminded of the past, but I must tell you.' Essa looked at her anxiously. 'Asher, I had a visitor from the old quarter. She told me three of Mallory's ships arrived today. He's here.'

'I see.'

Asher got to her feet and turned away so Essa could not see her face, filled with a jumble of wildly conflicting emotions. Part of her would be happy to see Mallory again. She had known him all her life, and they had been friends for most of that time; but part of her wished he had stayed on his ship and never come to land. She had known he must come, but not that the confrontation would take place so soon.

'What are you going to do?'

'I don't know.'

'You could resign your post at the Treasury,' Essa persisted. 'Otherwise you're bound to come across one another, and from what you've said, he must recognize you. He'll be second on the city council once he takes his brother's place.'

Silence ensued. It was not the easy silence between friends but a separation, which had its roots in a day six years in the past, a day Asher would not think of, would not remember. Feelings long suppressed threatened to rise up, but she fought them down. The past was dead. 'It won't be necessary,' she said distantly.

It was left to Essa to break the coolness between them. 'I always wondered you didn't know Councillor Kelham, the elder brother, when you were young,' she said tentatively. 'Surely you must have seen him occasionally?'

'Only once or twice, and he never paid any attention to me; he was twelve years older than Callith, and seven older than Mallory. He spent most of his time here, in Venture.' Asher maintained a semblance of calm. 'I was sorry when he died, he was a good and honest man. But as the eldest of his clan, it fell to him to take his place on the council when his father retired to Kepesake, while Mallory travelled and maintained the trading links overseas.'

'Your friend's very successful, they say. Only the Chief Councillor's luck is more proverbial. His ships come safely to port, and always find favourable winds.'

'At least he'll be able to afford to remain on the council – not like Councillor Cavan.'

Essa nodded. 'Last year's tribute ruined him. But he's no great loss. I sometimes wonder if wealth should be the only criterion for membership of the Council of Twelve.'

Asher shrugged. 'What other choice is there? Who else can be relied on to make up the tribute shortfall but the rich? And who else has such a strong interest in maintaining our autonomy? The Kamiri don't care where the gold comes from, but if it ceases, the merchants lose everything. Whereas we have little left to lose. Except the rest of our freedom.' She gave a bitter laugh.

'Perhaps.' Essa steeled herself. 'So. What will you do?' she asked again.

'*I don't know*! Mallory won't hurt me. His coming is an inconvenience, but no worse. He wouldn't expose me as a fraud.'

'Are you sure?'

There was only a brief moment of hesitation. 'Yes. He's not my enemy.'

Essa looked relieved. 'Then I'm glad. And sorry to have been the one who had to tell you.'

'It doesn't matter.' Asher forced a smile. 'Good night. I'll see you tomorrow evening, when I get back from Carob's'

'Good night, Asher. May Lady Fortune favour you.' But Asher was already halfway through the door, and Essa sighed.

Asher unlocked her own door, blessing the good salary which allowed her to afford a space of her own so she did not, as so many of the other women did, have to share her quarters. Tonight, she could not have borne the casual presence of a room-mate, nor any other impingement on her private thoughts.

The room was dark and she paused, waiting until her eyes had accustomed themselves sufficiently for her to find the candlestick and light the stub. She wondered if she had the energy to perform her usual checks, or if she dared leave it, just for once; after all, Essa had been in the next room all day. But she could not. There were too many incriminating documents which would, by their mere presence, ensure at best a lengthy term of imprisonment if they were discovered by some unfriendly hand.

Shutting and locking the door, she moved to the cupboard that held her few clothes, the three dark-coloured divided skirts of the working woman which changed according to season, the tunics and underclothing, boots and sandals. They were all as she had left them. Her room was similar to Essa's in its lack of adornment, for what spare funds she possessed were all donated to the use of the group; apart from her clothes, she had only a small chest containing her few personal belongings. She opened the lid and counted the spare seven-sided brooch, the necklace made up of flat silver moons which had belonged to her mother, two scarves and sewing materials. No one, as far as she could judge, had moved them during her absence.

Lastly, she pushed the chest aside and lifted the loose floor-board underneath, revealing the cache in which she kept a little silver, blank forged travel passes and identity papers, for use by escaping slaves, and her own papers: the real ones, which bore her true name and place of origin, unlike the ones she carried, which named her only Asher of Venture, born to that city. They were still there, untouched.

I wish . . .

She was too tired to clarify the thought. She moved the chest back into place and went across to the narrow bed, but instead of lying down she changed her mind and opened the wooden shutters of the window to the right of the bedstead. She shivered as cold air filled the stuffy room, but the cold was preferable to her thoughts; she stared out on to the empty stableyard at the rear of the hostel.

Why now? she thought rebelliously. Her life was full, intensely satisfying. She had work she enjoyed, and an existence she had spent years establishing. Why should Mallory come back *now* to upset her hard-won peace?

Six years ago, she had been reborn. The Asher of the past, the Asher of Harrows Farm, was dead; she had killed her herself, joying in her destruction. Asher of Venture had no links with that younger self. Except for Mallory, appended her treacherous mind. If she had believed in such things, she might have thought a malign Fate pursued her, to bring Mallory to Venture, to place herself in a position where she must meet him or change the whole direction of her life once more, giving up all she had built.

I can't, I'm needed here. It was reassuring to be certain that, at least, was the truth. But in any case, there was nowhere else for her to go; she knew of no other organization like Essa's in any other city, no other group which would accept her into its midst, provide her with a new identity and home and friends.

Memories of the distant past forced themselves upon her, not all of them painful. She had been a happy child of loving parents who had never allowed her to feel for an instant they had rather her twin brother had lived when they were born. She had been educated to a far higher level than her village friends, a gift for which she blessed her family often, for it had given her a freedom few women possessed by allowing her to earn her living through other than menial labour. But those happy memories were tarnished by that other remembrance, the shadow on her life which had led to her flight, and which bound her to Venture and Essa and the other women; for they were all she had, now.

I've changed, I'm not the same person Mallory knew. Will he really recognize me? She was thinner than she had been, and her thick hair, worn in a long plait, was now dyed a mid-brown, disguising its natural wheat-fair colour; but her features had not altered. Her eyes were still the same hazel, her looks very much her father's. It was impossible to believe he would not know her again. Lacking siblings, she had adopted Callith and Mallory as her own sister and brother; she had missed them both dreadfully when she first came to Venture. But that time, too, was long in the past.

We may meet at any time.

The thought held an unreal quality. She wondered what she would tell him when they met; the truth, or only a part of it? Shame flooded through her. It was not that he was incapable of understanding *why* she had run away, but whether she could ever bring herself to explain how she felt, tainted by an evil no one could forgive, not even him. Only forgetfulness had brought her peace; now, even that was at an end.

She lost control over her thoughts; they crowded in on her, bringing pain in their wake. Shakily, she sat down on the bed, clutching the cloak she had thrown down earlier much as the little girl in Carob's had clutched at her ragged toy.

It was a long time before cold forced her into action, and she undressed, undoing buttons with numbed fingers, then huddling under the blankets, still shivering. She did not dare to sleep. She knew that if she did, she would dream.

We may meet at any time.

The thought recurred often as she lay awake, in the dark, aching for the coming of day and the end of the long night.

Chapter Two

The parlour faced east, catching the morning sun, but neither light nor the restrained opulence of the decor could improve the atmosphere between its three occupants, which was chill in the extreme. Mallory, glancing from his sister-in-law's ominously quivering lower lip to the seeress' impersonal regard, wondered whether it might not be wiser to make some excuse and retire; then realized, with rising irritation, that he had already left it too late.

'If you order us to go, we shall of course do as you command,' Honora said icily, blinking back the threatened tears. 'But I know nothing about the running of a country estate, and all my family are here in the city.'

'It was only that I thought a stay at Kepesake might be good for your sons,' Mallory said patiently, for the third time that morning. 'I have no desire to separate you from your family, and of course you are welcome to remain here.' Could his brother really have been happy with this weeping woman? It seemed unlikely, although Kelham had never said anything to suggest discord between them. Yet she appeared genuinely grieved by his death, and he knew her to be a good mother to his niece and nephews.

'Kirin is too young to serve the clan, but he should be here, learning what is necessary,' Honora continued shakily. She was a conventionally good-looking woman, fair, who had kept her figure despite three successful pregnancies; the daughter of a rival merchant clan, Mallory saw she had every intention of protecting the interests of her elder son, a boy of only eight, against imagined depredations.

'Honora, Kirin will take his place, as we have all done in our time, when I judge him capable of shipping out on a long voyage, which will not be for another five years at least.' Mallory's patience was wearing thin; he was not accustomed to having his orders questioned, least of all by a woman. 'For the moment he is best suited to the company of his tutors, learning the languages and mathematics he will need if he is ever to take his father's place.' He hoped the last comment would be enough to satisfy her.

She rose to her feet, her features strictly composed as she dealt her strongest card. 'Very well, I agree. But here, in Venture. He needs the comfort of familiar surroundings at present, now that his father is dead!'

Mallory stood politely as she made her exit, allowing her to have the final word. In a month or so he would make the suggestion again, and she would comply; he needed someone at Kepesake now that Perron, his younger brother, was to take his own place, travelling with the fleet, dealing with their agents overseas. The estate had an excellent steward, but it was bad policy to have no member of the family in residence. He sighed. Far more than Honora, he wished Kelham had not died so untimely. He had no desire to live a settled existence in a household with another man's woman and children; he could only be grateful that those same children were still young enough to be confined to the nurseries.

'You will find it harder than you imagine to persuade her.'

He gave the seeress a startled look; she had sat so silently he had temporarily forgotten her presence. 'You think so, Oramen?' he asked uneasily.

'She believes that if she remains here, she will be able to safeguard the future of her sons. She is quite certain you intend to usurp Kirin's rights, and will immure her in the country until you remarry and have sons of your own.' The seeress had a surprisingly beautiful voice, a rich contralto at odds with her appearance. She was a strong-featured woman, with a wide jaw and unconventionally short hair, black streaked with silver; her extreme thinness and deep-set eyes gave her an air of authority which had always impressed Mallory favourably. She had served the clan well for over fifteen years, and he valued her opinion.

'What do you suggest?' he asked seriously.

'Do you ask me as seeress, or as a member of this household? Because my answers will be different.'

He considered. 'For the moment, as one of the clan.'

'Then leave her be.' Oramen spoke more acidly than was her wont. 'Try to see matters from her point of view. She may inconvenience you, but she has taken your brother's death to heart, and will bear you ill-will if you force her to leave her friends and family so soon.'

'Do you really think me so impervious to her feelings that I would send her away just to suit myself?' But, prudently, Oramen made no response, and Mallory shrugged and his smile faded; she was, after all, in his employ. 'Then I shall do as you suggest. But tell me, in your other capacity, where should I direct the *Endeavour*? To Javarin, or Petormin? Which would be the more favourable?'

The seeress' manner altered perceptibly at the appeal to her professional talents. 'I will consult the omens, master. Is that the ship you wish your brother Perron to captain?' Mallory nodded, although he still found it hard to see his youngest sibling in his own place; Perron had been a dreadfully sickly boy for the first ten years of his life, even if he was now large and hale. 'Then I shall ascertain the optimum sailing date at the same time from – when – one or two months?'

'My thanks.' He sipped at the cup of thin ale served in the household for the morning meal, comparing it unfavourably with the stronger brew served on board ship. Oramen took her leave, nodding a brief courtesy, and he was alone. Grateful for the respite from feminine company, he stood and walked across to the windows fronting the balcony and looked out, over the city and down towards the harbour.

Kelham, what have you done to me?

He had arrived in port only the previous afternoon, having made good speed from the Islands of Ishara to the south, but already he was depressed by the change in his circumstances. As a second son, it had been left to him to captain the merchant fleet, to be the active member of the clan while Kelham performed the civic duties in Venture and organized the inland distribution of their trade-goods. At thirty-two, he had spent most of the last seventeen years at sea, a masculine albeit solitary existence that suited him well; there could be only one captain of a ship. His good fortune had enabled his clan to maintain its wealth and prestige while others failed, their ships broken in storms or commandeered by the Kamiri to transport troops from place to place. As he looked out over the city, Mallory felt an unnatural depression settle over him, perceiving it as his prison; he could only hope the mood was the forerunner of some good news, as custom would have it.

The house and gardens of the clan had been constructed on high ground in the west of Venture among others belonging to the merchant-venturer caste, and gave him a full view of the city, from the maze of the old quarter to the north-east, through which flowed the River Sair, sweeping east past the deepwater harbour to the shallower inlet beside which stood the warehouses of the clans, then inland once more to Scribbers in the south. Directly below his viewpoint lay the square of civic offices at the centre of the city, an impressive collection of buildings constructed during the height of Venture's affluence fifty years before. Mallory, however, regarded the whole with a jaundiced eye, having no love for the urban life, the teeming streets and noisome air. He had no ties to bind him to Venture, for, other than Honora and her children, the remainder of his family and friends were spread far and wide across the Dominion; Callith, his favourite among his relatives, lived in Fate, Darrian's capital, with her husband and sons. He had, of course, enjoyed female companionship in other ports, but none of the women who had shared his bed had he been attached to in more than a purely physical sense, and he had paid them off without much regret.

What must be, will be, he thought resolutely, but was glad when a knock at the parlour door offered a disturbance. The arrival was a plump young man of about twenty who had been his brother's personal clerk; he came nervously into the room, as if he expected Mallory to bite.

'If you please, master, the Chief Councillor is below, asking to s-see you.' He spoke with a slight stammer.

Mallory smiled, trying to put the clerk at his ease. 'Thank you, Pars. Tell him I will be with him shortly.'

The youth ducked his head eagerly and sped off on his errand. Mallory followed at a more leisurely pace, descending the two flights of stairs to the ground floor where his private office was situated, both flattered and surprised Avorian should pay a visit so soon. He had met him casually on a few occasions, and been much impressed by his astuteness regarding both mercantile and civic affairs; he was by far the wealthiest man in Venture, and his good fortune was proverbial throughout the Dominion.

Avorian stood as he entered the office, holding up a hand in greeting. He was a man of about fifty, of striking appearance, as tall as Mallory, with a high brow and patrician features tempered by eyes the same warm gold as his hair; he looked much younger than his years, the few threads of silver-white at the temples barely perceptible. His physique was still as powerful as Mallory's own, a reminder of the years spent at sea in his own venturing days, but, behind the evident strength of character, the narrow lips were unexpectedly generous, as though the integrity for which he was famed was allied to a capacity for humour.

'Councillor Mallory.' A warm smile accompanied the words. 'I am pleased you arrived safely, and so soon. May I present my companion?'

For the first time, Mallory saw he was not alone, but accompanied by an attendant dressed from head to foot in black. There was something odd about the man, and it was a moment before Mallory realized that it was neither his round figure nor deformity which made him so remarkable; it was simply that his puffed-up face and protruding eyes gave him a close resemblance to a toad.

'I should be pleased,' he said, politely averting his gaze.

'Then allow me to present Lassar, my diviner.' The odd man bowed, but kept his eyes on Mallory's face, bright black eyes meeting blue; the diviner licked his lips, accentuating his resemblance to the amphibian. 'I apologize for the intrusion, but I go nowhere without him, as you may have heard?' Again, a smile invited Mallory to have pity on this minor, if costly, eccentricity; a personal diviner was an expensive luxury.

'Indeed.' Mallory found himself warming to the older man; there was a lack of pretension about him rare among the wealthiest clans. He wondered what were Lassar's particular talents. 'Please, be seated. How may I serve you?'

Avorian complied, although Lassar remained standing behind his master, looming over him like some dark beast of legend. The two men presented a startling contrast. 'Why, at first I want only to make your better acquaintance,' Avorian began pleasantly. 'And to welcome you to Venture, and warn you of some of the difficulties we face in Council at present.'

Mallory inclined his head. 'I'm very grateful to you. As you can imagine, I feel like a landed fish at present.' He remembered, suddenly and irrelevantly, that toads were said to represent wealth, longevity, and money-making; small wonder Avorian had chosen Lassar for his diviner.

Avorian seemed to have caught the errant thought, for he looked amused. 'Perhaps I should begin with the subject of tomorrow's session,' he suggested. 'It concerns the tribute, due in a matter of weeks. Are you familiar with the situation?'

'I know very little of Venture's affairs.'

'Then let me tell you that this year there will be a significant shortfall in the city's contribution; considerably greater than last, when the amount was only ten thousand gold pieces,' Avorian advised. 'You are aware that Amrist will seize on any shortage to curtail what little freedom we still possess – indeed, he has always believed it would be only a matter of years before we would accept the inevitable and become a subject people. Venture has always paid a large share of the total, by reason of our wealth which is second only to that of Fate itself. However, I have a proposition to put before the Council which I think may interest you.' He paused, waiting for Mallory to make some response.

'Please continue.' Inwardly, he sighed, wondering if this was how his time was to be spent henceforth, the boredom of city politics. Outwardly, however, he displayed every show of interest; which became more genuine as he listened to what Avorian had to say.

Asher paused as she crossed the main street leading from the north-west of the city down to the docks. For the first time in weeks the skies were clear, and a misty sun shone down on the city, silvering the grey stone into an illusion of beauty. The air felt fresh, not salt, and for some reason Asher saw the world as wider and brighter than usual. She wondered if she dared go down to the harbour to look at the ships, for she enjoyed watching the activity on the quays, then remembered the tide was on the turn; sailors and fishermen often refused to put to sea if they encountered a woman on the way to their boats. Regretfully, she restricted herself to shading her eyes, trying to make out some of the different ships in the harbour.

To the north, along the river, she glimpsed three two-masted boums coming downstream above the Sair Gate, doubtless carrying freshwater fish and timber as their cargo; Venture served a thriving and populous area, unlike the two other major but more southerly ports of Darrian. In fact, the city was fortunate in many ways, with a sheltered deepwater harbour, a navigable river, rich tied lands, and being a greater distance from Javarin and thus less plagued by demands for ships to transport Kamiri troops and provisions than either Refuge or Prospect. The city's inhabitants attributed these positive factors to the presence in the citadel of the Oracle, the premier augur in the Dominion, on the peak of the hill halfway up which the walls of Venture extended, but Asher was more inclined to credit human common sense and pure luck.

Where were Mallory's ships? She turned her gaze due east, out to sea. The grey-green waters inside the harbour were deceptively calm, but there were still white-crested waves further out. The recent storm had brought many ships to port, but she could make out Mallory's leopard pennant flickering in the breeze from three of the foremasts; it would be one of those which had brought him home. Avorian's wolf pennant was also much in evidence, and she counted five of them all together; she had met the Chief Councillor twice since being told, privily, of his extraordinary generosity in offering to make up the whole of that year's tribute shortfall, for it was her task to estimate the total deficit. She still had a week's work on the figures before presenting her estimates for his approval, and her conscience smote her for the delay.

Asher had known little about ships until she came to live in Venture, but Essa, Mylura and Margit had since enlightened her ignorance, and she could now identify most of the different types in the harbour, from the colliers which plied the northern waters, to the old-fashioned ship-rigged carracks, to the much faster caravels with square sails on all three masts, a lateen only on the mizzenmast. In the sunlight, they displayed a mass of bright colour, many sporting painted figure-heads, often female figures depicting Lady Fortune, the most capricious of the Fates, or dogfish, the imaginary creatures half-dog, half-fish, which were said to disport themselves in the southern waters near the Isharan islands. Most were in shades of gold or blue, the lucky colours, and some ships even bore coloured sails to attract good fortune on their journeyings.

A shout alerted her to move out of the way as a loaded cart rumbled past and down the hill towards the shipbuilding yards, and Asher saw with regret that it was time to be on her way. With a last look at the harbour, at the three tall watch-towers which had so signally failed to protect the city – had, in fact, never played a more significant role than guarding against pirate raids – she set her steps north towards the Treasury and the day's work.

The four buildings housing the various civic offices, which comprised Administrative and Licensing, a Record Office, the Civil Law Courts, and the Treasury, had been constructed in separate sections around a central courtyard. Each consisted of a large two-storey rectangle built from the local pale grey stone, but were distinguished by means of their external decoration, so that even the illiterate had no difficulty in telling one from another. Their architect had arbitrarily selected an unrolled stone scroll to indicate Administration, carved above the lintel; for Records, an incised clerk seated at a desk, pen in hand; for the Law Courts, an impressively carved hawk to represent the authority of the Dominus; and for the Treasury – where his imagination seemed to have run dry – he had decreed an immense version of the city seal. The demonfish spread its eight tentacles to the points of the compass, as though asserting the full extent of its powers; everyone in the city and tied territories fell within its scope, whether for tax or tribute.

As she entered the building by a door at the rear, Asher found herself joined by two colleagues of her own rank, Dart and Stern.

'Fates, I feel terrible!'

Asher turned to look critically at Dart, who normally sat at the desk to her left; sweat beaded his forehead, and his complexion was a pale shade of green. A year or so older than Asher, his pitted skin, broken veins and unhealthy pallor suggested a life-style involving too much strong ale and not enough sleep. His promotion to one of the four chief clerks was due to his ability to add a column of figures accurately and twice as fast as anyone else; in other areas of his life, however, he was less reliable. 'Late night again?' she inquired.

He nodded, then grimaced. 'My head's killing me.'

'Another all-night gambling session? How much did you lose *this* time?' sneered Stern, the eldest of the four, a ferret-faced widower of middle years, whose disposition had long been soured by an incapacity to rise further in the service of the city.

'Next year's wages,' Dart said lugubriously, massaging his aching temples. 'My luck was well out.'

'Why do you do it?' Asher asked. She found the compulsion incomprehensible, particularly since Dart had a wife and three young children to support. She wondered how they fared when he lost.

'Pleasure. After a day in this place, even losing money feels good!' Dart exhaled deeply, causing both Asher and Stern to move away. Both his breath and his person exuded a powerful stench of ale.

They were joined by Tara, the fourth member of the quartet, a quiet woman of indeterminate years who was efficient but shy, and rarely spoke; in silence, the four passed into the main hall of the Treasury.

Some thought had gone into the interior design. Long windows of tinted glass broke up the walls, admitting daylight in rainbow patterns; the floor was of yellow marble with a pattern of contrasting black concentric circles. The effect was impressive, if rather too dark unless the double doors were open, and the hall was often exhibited to visitors to Venture as proof of the city's status and civic pride.

Asher made her way to her desk at the rear of the hall to the right, where the four chief clerks had a clear view of everything that went on. Other banks of desks littered the floor, from the dozen accounts clerks to the right of the entrance, who checked assessments or notarized proofs of wages, to the equal number of cashiers to the left, who took payment. To Asher's right sat the records clerks, whose function was to accept and record receipts of tax and tribute paid and cross-reference them with the Administration to ensure no one escaped payment. It was a somewhat tortuous process, if effective, although Asher privately questioned whether the bureaucracy necessary to make it work might not cost more than the evasions it existed to prevent.

Margit, sitting at a cashier's desk, waved a friendly hand to Asher as the double doors were unlocked by the Treasurer, a short, fussy man with a bitter tongue. Although it was early, there was already a trickle of men and women through the entrance, and Asher watched them, lifting her eyes from the column of figures she should have been adding. Bother Venture, she thought tiredly, aware of having already made one mistake. Her mind felt dull from lack of sleep, and she found it impossible to keep her memories sensibly buried; whenever she relaxed her guard, they rose up to haunt her, arousing feelings best left undisturbed.

'Watch her!' Dart whispered from her left. 'I'll bet you a silver she's trying to get out of paying.' Asher looked in the direction in which his pen was pointed, and saw a young woman carrying a baby stand swaying in the doorway. 'Brought the baby to gain sympathy!' He snorted his contempt for such a manoeuvre.

'Perhaps she has no money,' Asher answered coldly. Indeed, as she continued to watch the girl, she thought it more than likely. She was so emaciated it was a wonder she found the strength to carry the child; her arms were stick-thin, her cheeks mere sunken hollows in a white face hidden by a wave of black hair. She seemed dazed and confused, blinking dark-circled eyes as if she had no idea where to go. Dart grunted and went back to his work, but Asher found herself unable to look away as the woman – no, girl, she could be no more than sixteen or so – started as one of the accounts clerks called to her. She crept over to the desk and began to speak, holding out her papers in a skeletal hand. Asher relaxed the breath she had been holding and looked away.

I wonder who she is? The raggedness of the girl's grey dress suggested she lived in the old quarter, perhaps by Fishermen's Quay. It was unlikely she earned good wages, not with a small child to care for.

'See, what did I tell you?' Dart said softly. 'Watch her!'

Asher did not reply, seized with an unwelcome sense of foreboding as the girl moved away to the cashiers, arms held stiffly round the swaddled baby. There was a determination in the way she directed her steps which spoke of a desperation Asher had seen before, born of hopelessness so unrelievable it made life itself a drudgery. She stood up.

Something is going to happen, I'm sure of it. She had discovered it wiser over the years to pay attention to her mind's rare subconscious forewarnings of disaster.

The girl was standing in front of Margit, holding out her stamped paper wordlessly, but no coins were forthcoming in payment; instead, she lifted up the baby and balanced her on the desk-top. Margit reached out automatically to steady the child, thinking the girl needed to free her hands, but instead she stepped back, away from the desk, speaking in a shrill voice.

'Here. Take her.' She spoke loudly enough to disrupt the other business in the hall. 'Take her,' she repeated vehemently. 'She's worth at least the sum I owe; and if she's not, I've nothing more.'

Asher was close enough to hear Margit's reply as she tried to soothe the mother. 'There're six more weeks before you have to pay,' she said gently. 'I can't take your baby, you must know that.' She held it out to the girl. It was very young – perhaps a year old. It did not cry, nor show any displeasure at the treatment it was receiving.

'They say children her age fetch a gold piece in the slave market.' The girl held her arms rigidly against her sides. 'She's a good child. I've no money, only her.'

Margit, encumbered by the baby, could only look around desperately for help, but the other cashiers made no move to come to her assistance. Asher felt in her pocket, thinking to pay whatever sum was needed and take the girl away from the scene; but she was already too late. Seeing her offer refused, she spun round and ran towards the open doors. People moved aside to let her pass, not wanting to attract ill luck by hampering a mad-woman. But by the doors she stopped.

To their right stood a chased metal cylinder with a slit cut in the lid to take coins offered as voluntary contributions to the tribute, thought to bring good fortune to the giver. The girl, in stumbling against it, had evidently heard the dull clanging that indicated its contents.

'Don't try to break it open now – wait till tonight, when there's more in it!' called out one of the cashiers, trying to make a joke of it. Several people laughed, but Asher felt more strongly still a sense of impending and inevitable disaster rushing toward the girl.

'*No – don't touch it!*' She brushed aside a large woman who stood in her path as the girl knelt, feeling with desperate hands for the opening mechanism of the cylinder. The guards by the doors made no attempt to stop her as she began to rock the box, slamming it violently against the wall, oblivious to the shocked faces round her.

'*Stop her, don't let her!*' Asher was still ten feet away, too far off; there was nothing in her mind but dread. The tribute box, like the vaults deep beneath the hall which held the tribute funds, was protected by more than human guards; the councillors of the city, having little faith in human nature, had ordered other guardians more lethal and less corruptible to be set in place over the city's gold. These were hex-wards, rare stones which acted like magnets on iron, except that these drew down disease, blindness, or worse misfortune on those who came in contact with them, unless they possessed protection.

The girl was crying, tears streaming unchecked down her cheeks, but she released the box, which came back to stand on its base, still rocking slightly. It's not too late, Asher thought in relief, then saw at once she was mistaken. A pale blue spark sprang from the box and attached itself to the girl's fingers, then flitted lightly along her arms and up towards her face and neck. For a moment, her thin features were illumined in blue fire, before the flame flickered and went out. The nearest guard spat in quick aversion.

Asher reached her side, but it was already too late for the girl. She knew it too; her expression changed from despair to disbelief, then to a desperate fear. Her hands came up to her throat as her nails clawed at the skin; no sound came from her, but her mouth opened, as if she would have spoken a protest, if she could. Through her thin dress, Asher should have been able to see the rise and fall of her chest, but she did not seem to breathe at all.

Asher knelt beside the girl, trying to grasp her wrists, and heard a hiss from somewhere behind her, but it was no time to consider her own safety. The girl doubled over, trying to breathe, and began to knock her head on the floor, face scarlet, mouth open in the appearance of protest.

Let her die quickly, Asher urged silently. She had never seen the ward in action before. She had witnessed enough pain to know living was not always preferable to death, but it was clear from her struggles that the girl wanted to live. Her body arched in long, jerking spasms, until at last it ceased and she lay full-length on the marble in a parody of sleep.

'Ah, no! No!' Margit held the baby close, keeping its head buried against her breast so it should not see its mother. A guard ventured a kick at the girl's body, but when she did not move he stood back, scratching his head uncertainly. The bustling figure of the Treasurer, drawn from his inner sanctum by the commotion, came forward.

'Remove her,' he ordered the guards disgustedly. 'Take her to the burning grounds! Send a messenger to the address on her papers. And get rid of that infant. The Treasury is no place for babies!'

Asher, seeing Margit too shocked to move, put an arm round her shoulders and urged her to the rear of the hall; she was crying quietly. 'Come along,' whispered Asher. 'We'll take her to the washrooms and see she's clean. Perhaps her family will come for her when they know her mother's dead.'

'If there were anyone, she wouldn't have given the baby to me,' Margit said passionately.

'Then we'll find a home for her.' Asher drew Margit out of the hall and through a door to the right of the passage behind. 'That's why you and I wear these.' She touched a finger to the star on her tunic. 'We know where to look for a foster-mother.' But although Margit brightened at the reminder, Asher herself was filled with bitterness.

Essa would say I was being silly, taking too much on myself. But she wasn't here. Why had she not paid closer attention to her instincts when she first saw the girl? Was it possible she could have saved her? Asher shook herself mentally, accepting re-criminations were useless. Their first concern was the baby; they would need money for her keep, for food and clothing. That was something she could attend to; was, in fact, her responsibility.

'Do you know how much she owed, Asher? Fifteen coppers, that's all. A tenth of her year's wages.' Margit kept her voice low so as not to disturb the child, but it shook with emotion. 'She worked as a laundress for some of the houses down by Fishermen's Quay, and that's how little they paid her. What's fifteen coppers to the council? Why shouldn't they pay her share?'

'You know the arguments,' Asher said wearily. 'They would say her father or husband or brother should pay, and if she has no family, she should not have encumbered herself with a child.'

'As if there was always a choice!' Furiously, Margit laid the baby down on the floor and unwrapped her. Asher let her be, knowing Margit herself had once borne a child when very young, the result of a casual rape by her employer in the house where she had been a servant. The child had died in its first year, and Essa had rescued Margit, offering her a home and enough teaching to enable her to earn a living where such events could not recur; but she, who adored children, had never forgiven nor forgotten.

If they would pay us as much as men, they might value us more highly, Asher thought angrily, not quite sure who *they* were. Then we'd contribute a larger share of taxes and tribute. But they argue that because we bear children we should be supported by our menfolk, so they pay us poorly, and now, with so many slaves coming to the city, they keep our wages even lower, and the council is pleased because running the city with our labour costs them less.

Margit's thoughts must have been running along the same lines, for she burst out: 'They *know* how many women work, and how hard it is to bring up a family alone. Why don't they help us? Why is it that they would rather spend money on a new bridge over the river than on us?'

'Because they can work out how much revenue a bridge will bring in tolls,' Asher answered stiffly. 'You know what they say – there are more important issues to be dealt with first: the tribute, the city. And so long as the council believes mothers and children to be financial burdens, they'll continue to put us last. That's why we exist.' Again, she touched the brooch on her lapel. 'To put women first.'

Margit picked up the baby and stroked its back. 'I'm sorry, I didn't mean to take it out on you. But it makes me so angry, and we help so few.'

'That's all right. Will you take her now?' Silently, Asher agreed with Margit, but they could not work openly; not when some of the women's actions broke city law, and help to escaping slaves was an open act of revolt against the invaders.

Margit nodded. 'You'll get the funds for her? A gold piece, I should think.'

Stifling her reluctance, Asher agreed, remembering how little they had in reserve. 'I'll see you tonight, and give it to you then.'

As she made her way back to the hall, she had to stand aside as the Treasurer passed, accompanied by the Chief Councillor and his diviner. Avorian favoured Asher with a friendly acknowledgement, much to the Treasurer's disapproval and her own astonishment.

'Mistress Asher – I hope to see you soon, in a week I think we said?' he asked pleasantly.

'Yes, Chief Councillor. I'll have the assessments ready for you.'

'Excellent. Come to my house at mid-morning.' He waited for her concurrence, then carried on through the hall. Asher hesitated. If she asked him if he knew the full extent of suffering in the city, would Avorian help? He would understand how the tribute had impoverished women most of all, the very people who could afford the least. But, reluctantly, she knew he would not; from his perspective, paying the tribute was a political necessity, while alleviating the plight of the women was not. It was an evil truth that the city was more important to him and the other councillors than half its citizens.

She returned to her desk and opened her ledger, feeling a dark depression settle as she did so. Turning to the list of names of men employed in maintaining the civic buildings, she picked up her pen with a hand that trembled.

Stop it, stop being a fool! she told herself angrily. Business was going on around her as if nothing had happened; death was not so uncommon in Venture, and no one had known the girl. It was the personal element that made such events tragic rather than mere spectacles. She dipped her pen in the glass ink-stand balanced on the edge of her desk and took a few deep breaths to calm herself.

She had purposely left some spare lines at the bottom of the list, where she began to inscribe a name chosen at random. She herself was to pay the men that evening, and she could abstract whatever sum she wrote in. One gold, three silver, and eight coppers. That was a feasible sum and should be sufficient to pay for the care of a child for a year. She experienced no guilt at what she was doing; she only embezzled funds in cases of desperate need, and the care of a child easily qualified. The women needed funds, and it was for her to find them, and to evade detection.

Even prostitution was hardly an option now. The merchants imported slaves whose services belong wholly to their masters; far more profitable than free women. That many of the merchants who were also councillors held such investments removed any sense of wrong-doing as Asher concluded her task and picked up her blotter, touching it to the line.

She was disturbed in her abstractions by an awareness of being the focus of someone's attention. Warily, she looked up and caught sight of Stern watching her.

'Do you want something?'

'No.' Stern continued to stare, a small smile creeping around his thin lips.

Uneasily, she bent her head, selecting the ledger dealing with the tribute totals, forcing herself to concentrate as she compared the takings to the previous year's, calculating shortfalls from various districts for Avorian. Her mind, however, was racing from speculation; she neither liked nor trusted Stern.

She reached out her right hand to return the quill to the ink-stand, her attention far away. Her fingers knocked against the glass, and she felt it move; too late, she tried to catch it, but it eluded her grasp and fell, smashing on the floor an instant later.

Someone gasped. It was Dart. He had risen to his feet, sheet-white. *'Death,'* he whispered. 'To break glass means a death. Another death . . . ' He began to murmur words of protection under his breath.

Asher sat, stricken into immobility. Everyone was looking at her, watching her. One of the boys whose job it was to keep the floor clear of dust came across and began to sweep up the mess, smearing ink and shards of glass everywhere. Asher got up to join him, trying to appear deeply concerned as she collected together a few sharp pieces, and saw Stern observing her, again with that same curious gleam of interest.

Had he guessed?

Someone came with a replacement stand, and Asher put the broken glass down on top of her desk. She tried to return to her work on the tribute figures, but felt shaky and off-balance. Slowly, her panic drained away, but her normal self-possession seemed to have deserted her; it had been a day of disasters, and, unfairly, she blamed Mallory for the whole. It was the knowledge of his arrival which had made her careless; and made her, for a painful moment, doubt the value of what she was doing with her life. Her helplessness in the face of tragedy dented the sense of purpose and satisfaction she was accustomed to feel in her work with Essa, as if she were only scratching at the surface of what needed to be done.

Stop it. Every single person is important; that's the point. How would you have felt if Essa and her folk had turned you away? Would that have been unimportant?

Pretending to an application far from her capability at that moment, she ignored the occasional curious stare that came her way and attempted to work, but it was hopeless; images of the girl's hideous death confronted her, with others equally un-welcome.

Mallory, why did you have to come back now?

She seemed all at once to be losing control over events in her life. What would happen if he were to walk through the doors now? The thought obsessed her. For six years she had deliberately never thought about him, nor about anything else in the past; now, she could not seem to dismiss it, or him, from her mind, as if she were a silly infatuated girl.

Shut up, Asher!

With a supreme effort, she forced herself to concentrate on the figures in front of her. They danced about on the page, eluding her best efforts.

By the time the Treasury doors were shut and barred for the night, she had failed to make any headway at all.

The wind had got up again, and the door slammed to as Asher entered Carob's. The tavern was far noisier than on the previous night, but Carob beamed at her and pointed to a small table in the left-hand corner, the only one not already occupied. As Asher sat down, Cass appeared, bearing a brimming tankard.

'There's to be singing tonight,' she informed Asher with a grin. 'That's why we're so full. But Mylla's not here yet.'

'It's early.' Asher managed a brief smile. 'I'll enjoy the music. Thanks, Cass. It's been a long, long day.'

'I thought you looked tired.' Cass surveyed her critically. 'Is there anything else you want – some supper? There's a good fish stew in the kitchens.'

'I couldn't, thanks.' Her insides felt too knotted with tension to accept food. Asher looked about the crowded room, noticing in the opposite corner a slender woman with a lute on her lap. She was tuning it softly, obviously preparing for her turn.

'Then you just sit and relax. Say if you change your mind about the stew.' Cass moved away, giving her a sharp backward look.

Several of the faces Asher remembered from other nights were present; the dice-players were at their usual table, and further away a garishly dressed fortune-teller was doing a roaring trade with her cards. The small girl and her brother were in evidence by the hearth, their mother one of the party waiting to have her future told, but this time the boy had brought along his own amusement, and was engrossed in the destruction of what appeared to be a wooden model of a ship. He fed broken pieces into the fire, watching them burn with a contented expression. Spoons clattered on plates and voices rose and fell with the tankards.

The warmth and friendly atmosphere began to have their

effect, and Asher felt the tension in her neck and spine unravel as she listened to the cheerful conversation around her. The woman with the lute began to sing; she had a high, pure voice, and played well. It was not a song Asher knew and she was content to listen, although most of the other women joined in, humming along with the tune if they did not know the words.

I think I could go to sleep right here. Asher closed her eyes briefly. The room was growing hotter, even a little stuffy, but the music acted as a soporific, and when she next opened her eyes the singer was calling for a pause, and a familiar figure was making its way over to her table. Asher jumped to her feet, her weariness temporarily deserting her.

'*Mylla!*'

A tall, thin young woman of about twenty, with dark hair and dark, thick brows, waved her free hand; the other held a stick on which she leaned heavily as she hobbled to the spare stool at Asher's table. She wore a short tunic over loose trousers which suited her length of leg, although they earned her many disapproving stares from the older women in the room; Asher wished she cared so little for convention, for Mylla seemed not to notice the looks directed towards her.

'If I don't sit down, I'll fall down!' She promptly fell on to the stool, grinning broadly. 'Been waiting long?'

'Four nights! What happened, Mylla? I thought something must have gone wrong.'

Mylura shrugged her shoulders. 'My horse stumbled and I fell off and twisted my knee. It hurts like blazes, but there's no real damage.' Her keen eyes went to Asher's face. 'You weren't really worried, were you? You know me – I always turn up in the end.'

Asher nodded evasively. 'Did it go all right? No problems?'

As if by instinct, Cass appeared, bearing more ale and a large plate of stew which she deposited in front of Mylura, who winked and began to eat, with a smile of apology to Asher. 'I haven't had a bite since yesterday – too many grey men on the road,' she announced between mouthfuls. 'I swear there're more of them than ever. We have a hard time getting to the border, I can tell you!'

'Is the network still intact?' Thanks to Essa's contacts outside Venture through her agency, it had been relatively simple to build up staging posts where escaping slaves could hide on their way north. The smallholders who were the women's main helpers seemed to revel in having some means to oppose the Kamiri invaders.

53

Mylura made a face. 'Not quite. You remember the holding in Stenbrook – Kerwin's place? About forty miles south of the border?' Asher nodded. 'I was wary when we got near it. It *smelled* wrong, if you know what I mean. I went on ahead to take a look, on foot, and it was crawling with Kamiri. So we carried straight on.' She paused, her usually expressive face studiously blank. 'I stopped on the way back. It'd been burned to the ground. Someone must have informed on him. I've arranged a new bolt-hole further west, so don't worry about that. I'll draw a map so you know where it is.'

'I'm sorry.' Asher shivered, sharing Mylura's anger. The collaborators who betrayed their own people to the invaders were worse than the grey men themselves; but it was a subject too close to her private thoughts to speak about, even to Mylura.

'I have, however, some news for Essa – and you, too, might be interested,' Mylla continued, changing the subject. She mopped up the remaining gravy on her plate with a thick piece of bread. 'But first, tell me what's been going on here. You look like death before it's been warmed!'

'It has been a little fraught.' Asher detailed Essa's illness and the events of her day, while Mylura listened closely.

'What happened to the baby?'

Asher's face clouded with disgust. 'We found the girl's father at the address on her papers; he said to give the baby to the orphanage.' Her voice was bleak. 'Do you know, Mylla, it was *his* child. He didn't even seem to care about his daughter, let alone his . . . ' She stopped.

'But you found someone to take the child?'

'Yes. Margit knew a woman who'd recently lost her own baby, and we're paying her an allowance to take this one. She's to be paid monthly, at Margit's insistence, to make sure she keeps the child alive and well.' It was a cold-blooded arrangement, but they had discovered over the years that some women would pocket the coins and leave the babies in their care to die, claiming sickness or accident rather than the truth, which was that they were starved to death.

'You got the money the usual way, I suppose?' Asher nodded. 'You should be careful, Ash. They'll catch you one day.'

'Can you think of an alternative?' They let the subject drop, knowing there was little choice; the underground was perpetually short of funds, not least because the women earned so little and neither the poor mothers they aided nor the slaves they helped to escape could contribute to their coffers. 'But you said you had news?'

Mylura smiled importantly. 'I do.' She leaned forward confidentially. 'Do you remember the fuss about the woman who escaped from the internment camp near where you came from? The wife of some military captain or other, who managed to get to Saffra after the invasion?'

'Of course.' It had been the main topic of the gossips in the markets for at least a week.

'Well, she was there.' Despite the injury to her leg and the long journey, Mylura seemed positively to crackle with energy. 'I don't know how she got to Saffra, she didn't use our network; she was ill from exhaustion when I saw her. But the Saff asked me to talk to her, she seemed to want to tell someone something, and they picked me, in case it was a message I could carry.'

'And what was it?'

Mylla glanced round to see if anyone was listening, then turned back to Asher. 'She was wandering in her mind, poor thing, most of the time; she'd been in that camp for years, and looked like a skeleton. But she did say something.' She paused, then went on in a whisper. 'Ash – she said something about there being a girl in the camp, a girl who was important.'

'Just that?' Asher asked doubtfully, but with a sinking heart, remembering her conversation with Essa the previous night, about which she had, as yet, done nothing.

Mylura's eyes glowed with excitement. 'Couldn't it be, Ash? It'd be an ideal hiding place. Don't you think it might be Vallis?'

Asher frowned. 'But Mylla, it doesn't sound likely. I don't want to curb your enthusiasm, but surely, if she was in a camp, she'd be dead by now. Amrist has every incentive to have her killed, like her brothers.'

'But only if he *knows* she's there.' Mylura seemed no whit dismayed by Asher's negative response. 'What if the Dominus had her hidden there all along? And, yes, I know he's dying. They'd heard it in Saffra – don't ask me how! I never understand them.'

'Did this woman say anything else – what the girl looked like or her name?'

'No. Just that she was important; she had it on her mind that someone should know about her.'

'It's a very slim lead, Mylla,' Asher said slowly.

'But better than nothing. This could be the clue we need.' Asher only shook her head, not certain why she felt so strong a reluctance to involve herself in what would surely turn out to be a wild goose chase. 'Think what it would mean if we found her.' The younger woman's fervour was contagious, and Asher fought to suppress a surge of answering excitement.

'We can't just leave it, Asher.' Mylura regarded her steadily. 'What is it? Why don't you want us to be involved?'

'I suppose – because I don't believe it will make any difference if she is found,' Asher said honestly. 'I don't believe in the prophecy of the Oracle, and I don't think we should waste our time and our small funds on something which will help no one. Why can't we simply pass this piece of information to your cousin Jan, and let him tell any of the resistance groups he talks to?'

Mylla frowned. 'You're wrong, Asher.' But she was puzzled rather than annoyed. 'The Oracle isn't a question of belief; it simply *is*. It's as if you still thought the world was flat when it's been proved it's round. I've never understood you in this. What is it you don't want to believe, or you're afraid of?'

Asher stiffened, unwilling to discuss the depth of her feelings even with Mylla, her horror of being nothing more than a counter in a game of chance. 'It doesn't matter,' she said quickly. 'Anyway, it's for Essa and Carob to decide what must be done. If they say we're to look for this girl, I'll try to find the funds for it.'

'Ash.' Mylla sounded concerned, but evidently Asher's expression was sufficient to deter her from further questions. 'All right, I'll talk to Essa in a day or so.'

'Will you come back with me tonight? There's a spare room in the hostel if you want it.'

Mylura shook her head. 'No, I'll go to my cousin's. Jan keeps space for me when I want, and it's a lot closer. I don't want to walk so far on this knee.' She patted that portion of her anatomy affectionately.

'Don't you ever resent that he has it all – the house and the rest?' Asher found the relationship between Mylura and her family fascinating. Brought up by an elderly aunt, she had grown up first on a smallholding near the Saff border, then more latterly in the old quarter of Venture, where her aunt had built up a useful business dealing with the distribution of stolen goods. When she died, she had intended her niece to inherit both house and occupation, but the courts had ruled in favour of a claim from a nephew, Jan, her brother's son. Mylla had simply shrugged, refused what she saw then as a token proposal of marriage from her cousin, then offered her services to Essa, whom she knew by reputation, and was welcomed by the women's group with open arms.

Now, she shrugged again. 'Why should I? This life suits me, I would hate to be tied down. And Jan has his uses.' There was an odd smile on her face as she made the remark, distinctly startling to Asher whose mind began to work furiously. 'Now, let's get some more ale, I'm thirsty.'

Asher signalled to Cass who responded at once, coming across to refill Mylura's tankard. 'It's good to have you back,' she commented with a smile, wiping a few spilled drops from the table.

'It's a lot warmer here than up north, believe me!' Mylura drank deeply, then excused herself to go and talk to Carob. Silently, Asher agreed with Cass's observation; the younger woman's boundless energy and optimism always acted as a spur, pushing her friends on to greater efforts. It was as if Mylla's high spirits acted as a restorative to her own, and Asher wondered if her own troubles were really so very pressing.

'Let me tell you a story I picked up in Saffra,' Mylura began cheerfully as she returned and sat down again, chuckling as though the memory still amused her. 'There was a Saff and a man from Chance . . . '

Asher listened with only half her attention, the remainder considering the news Mylura had brought and its implications. Essa would insist they find a way to discover whether the girl in the camp was Vallis. Asher knew the place, for it was only a half-day's walk from the farm where she had grown up. Was this just a coincidence or was it more than that? With her knowledge of the area, she was the obvious choice to pay a visit to the camp to spy out the land.

The thought was an unhappy one, taking her back once more to the past, to Mallory, and Callith, and the rest. She could not go back.

I won't worry about it. There's no point. She closed the door to memory with a mental slam as Mylura produced the punchline of her story. Asher smiled dutifully, without the least idea of what she was talking about.

'You look tired, Ash. I am, too. Why don't you go home?'

'Sorry, Mylla.' She yawned. 'That's a good idea. I will, if you don't mind.'

'Not at all.' She waited while Asher placed a few coppers on the table, then picked up her cloak, ready to leave.

Fifteen coppers, that was all that girl needed. The thought came from nowhere. As she followed Mylla's awkward progress towards the door, Asher found herself again a prey to doubt, questioning how much their organization really accomplished, despite their efforts.

'Tell Essa I'll be over in a day or so. Carob agrees we should at least think about this girl in the camp.' Asher gave her friend a helping hand down the steps beyond the inn, then Mylla waved a farewell and turned and limped off down a dark narrow lane. Asher looked up at the stars; Aspire was still invisible, but Abate showed against the sky in a thin and sickly crescent.

A bad omen. Asher yawned again. It was not really late, but she was very sleepy. Let's hope the Fates are kind, for once. It did not occur to her to find it strange to request a wish from something in which she did not believe.

Chapter Three

The following night, Mallory sat waiting for Honora to conclude her meal. Oramen had chosen to dine in her rooms, and the ill-matched pair were alone in the small parlour Kelham had always used on purely family occasions. It had an uncomfortably intimate air, and Mallory was surprised his sister-in-law had not found some excuse to avoid his company; certainly she had thus far displayed no great liking for him. For his part, he would have much preferred to dine with Pars, the clerk, or even Ish, who had been his cabin boy and was now his personal groom, but convention decreed otherwise.

She was, he thought, looking rather better; she wore a flattering but expensive gown in a dark blue colour which was proper for mourning as to modesty and length and neckline, and her hair had been arranged high on her head in a manner that became her. It was a pleasure to see so handsome a woman at table, and she was on her best behaviour, making every effort to sound and seem agreeable, but Mallory now heartily wished she would go; he had a great deal of work to do, and for some reason – which could only, he feared, be ominous to his peace – she seemed determined to delay him.

'And have you completed the unloading of the fleet?' Honora asked brightly, with what he thought was a polite, social smile.

'This afternoon.' Mallory watched her toy with the fruit on her plate; she did not appear to be eating it, only cutting it into smaller and smaller segments.

'It was unfortunate the Chief Councillor's ships arrived so close to your own; it will depress prices. Have you considered how much of the cloth you mean to send downriver for sale? Or are prices higher in the coastal towns? I have not seen the latest figures.'

Mallory smiled. 'It is good of you to concern yourself, Honora, but rest assured that I shall do my best to maximize our profit.' He was amused by her ploy, wondering if she really thought him incapable of marketing their goods effectively. The reversal in their positions made him smile more warmly, but she seemed to find nothing entertaining in the exchange.

'I apologize if you think it not my place to ask such questions, Mallory,' she said stiffly. 'But Kelham and I were accustomed to discuss such matters. Perhaps you forget that I, too, am the daughter of a merchant house, and was brought up to this trade.'

He saw she meant it, and thought more highly of her, approving her efforts to share in her husband's interests. 'Then perhaps we can do the same, in time,' he offered, quite willing to make the offer if it led to more cordial relations between them.

She regarded him more coolly than he thought his response warranted. 'Only if you think I can be of some use to you. But I would not waste your time with my unwanted opinions.' At last, she put down her knife and stood up. He rose politely. 'Good night, then, brother.'

He stared after her, puzzled by the sudden change of mood. How had he offended her? It had not been his intention. He sighed, not for the first time. It was years since he had lived in close confines with a woman, and, while he enjoyed female company, he preferred it to be on less formal terms, finding the code of manners required to accommodate respectable members of the fairer sex a waste of time. He glanced down at his formal suit of silver-grey cloth with no small amount of dislike; it was expensive, and rather tighter than when he had last worn it, but it was the only suitable garment he possessed until the rest of his things were brought up from Kepesake. It represented yet another of the hazards of his new position.

Did Honora enjoy his company as little as he hers? It was a thought which had not previously occurred to him and he frowned, not liking the answer he gave himself. If she were like Callith . . . But his sister was different; even the birth of two active sons had done nothing to dampen her spirits.

Unexpectedly, he found himself remembering another girl who had been a friend, even when he was a tiresome lunk of eighteen and in love with a pretty face for the first time in his life. He thought he had discovered all the meaning in life for at least a month, until the woman who had entranced his adolescent heart sent him away with his tail between his legs. Asher had not laughed at him, even then, although he had deserved it, treating her and Callith during that month as though they were too insignificant for his notice. It had been the summer of the invasion, he thought, the last time they had run free together, before the girls were increasingly confined by long skirts and hemmed about by rules of behaviour. What had happened to Asher? Would he ever know? He shook his head, still experiencing a small pang at the thought he would never see her again.

He deserted the parlour and went downstairs to the office where he had left the records of the cargo from the last run. What Honora had said was true: it was unfortunate Avorian's ships had arrived on the heels of his own; while spices could be stored in the warehouse until prices rose, cloth was a different matter. Mallory searched the pile of papers on the desk and found the latest letter from the clan's agent in Fate, comparing the price per bale of undyed cloth to what he could hope to achieve in Venture, then nodded. It would be better to sell at the inland markets, even after adding in the cost of transport. He smiled to himself, thinking how pleased his sister-in-law would have been to find herself in the right.

He worked until late, trying to get the ledgers into some sort of order, for a certain laxity had entered the system since Kelham's death, now three months past. He did not enjoy the work, which was tedious and time-consuming, and it was with little satisfaction that he finally laid down his pen and sat back, looking around the room at the many shelves of ledgers, at the piles of letters littering his desk, at the records of the last council meeting; and tried to stifle the wish simply to walk out of the house and never come back.

How long, Kelham? he asked the empty air in some bitterness. How long must I take your place? It would be fifteen years, at least, before his nephew Kirin could be expected to take his turn and Mallory could hand over his own tasks to Perron, his younger brother; by that time he himself would be over forty, and would have long lost the old personal contacts with agents overseas. He toyed briefly with the idea of deserting Kelham's family, not seriously, but to satisfy himself there was no hope; he knew he would not do it. He had a responsibility to the clan, for Honora and her children, for Kelham's children, to the city. The clan's fortune was founded in and on Venture.

Perhaps things will change. Perhaps when Lykon dies, Vallis will come back, and the country will rise up against Amrist. No more tribute; and no more need of me here, in the city. If we were free, any half-capable clerk could do most of this work.

He blew out the candle and stood up; he could ask Oramen where his probable future lay, but he did not really want to know, preferring hope to any unwelcome certainty.

He climbed the two flights of stairs to his room and stood looking out through the window at the few points of light still visible down by the harbour and in the old quarter; the second curfew bell had tolled, and the streets would be empty. It occurred to him that part of the cause of his depression was that he was lonely. He had now no wife, no children of his own. For companionship, there had been his officers and crew, but they were lost to him now he was a shoreman and tied, willy-nilly, to the service of his clan. But there was nothing to stop him pursuing interests of his own, as long as they did not interfere with his duty. He thought again of the only chance that would free him to go to sea once more, to live as he chose on his own terms, and his spirits lifted a little.

Why not? Why not me?

He had discussed the political situation of the country at some length with Avorian, who possessed excellent contacts in the capital. Lykon was apparently steadfastly refusing to nominate another heir in place of Vallis, swearing his daughter would be found in time. Here was a task well-suited to his talents. The girl's disappearance had been a mystery, one which appealed both to his intellect and to his curiosity. Mallory made up his mind, and felt instantly better. When a suitable moment came, he would request permission from Hortist, the present Kamiri governor of Venture, and consult the Oracle on behalf of Vallis, not the least deterred by the certainty that many had trodden that same path over the years. He trusted in his own inborn good fortune to be more successful than all those who had tried, and failed.

Asher was dreaming.

She was walking along a narrow track of beaten earth; to either side of her path lay open fields, their extent marked out by tall trees that still bore their burden of leaves, so she supposed it must be spring or summer. In the darkness of the night, the moons shadowed by weaving branches overhead, she could not see exactly where she was, but the path was familiar. Abate was full, Aspire in her final waning segment, and the evil auspices that portended seemed in accord with her own mood. Unhappiness was a heavy weight on her chest, bearing her down; she was aware of a loss as yet only dimly understood, of a pain which could be neither shared nor assuaged.

Dead, she thought suddenly. They are both dead. That was the source of the pain. Her mother and father had died of the fever.

In her sleep, she cried out in protest and misery, but did not wake.

Shapes, large and irregular, loomed up ahead in the darkness, at the end of the path between the trees. She stumbled towards them, knowing them, even in her dream, for her journey's end; no sanctuary, perhaps, but at least inside the house there would be warmth, and light, and life.

Why, then, did she hesitate? Why did her steps falter and slow?

Lights were visible from a downstairs room. She stopped, wondering why the sight frightened her. Summoning the reserves of her strength, she forced herself into motion again, then found she could not bring herself to approach the house. Some instinct held her still. Where the gleam of light should have held out the hope of welcome, instead she saw it as a beacon summoning her to her own destruction.

He's there, he's waiting for me, she thought. She could not remember who he was, but she knew she feared him.

She twisted and turned on her bed, entangling herself in the blankets until, in her dream, it seemed as though she were being squeezed, constrained by supernatural forces in which, at other times, she placed no credence.

I have been here before; I have stood here, in this place and time, before.

The certainty disturbed her, for she could not remember why it was so important. Why had she come back? Was it to change the past? She knew a sudden, chill understanding that if she went on, into the house, she would be conforming to a pattern she had followed before, that from that moment her life would pursue the same unalterable course. For that reason alone she drew back, wary and resisting, fighting a shadowy, insubstantial inevitability. Something – some fate – awaited her in the lighted room. She was sure of it.

A small voice spoke in her mind. You cannot change the past, it hissed. This is done; this is what you did then. You cannot alter what has been, only what will be.

I can, I can change it!

Asher thought she spoke the protest aloud, but in her dream there was no sound, and already her treacherous feet were taking her closer to the house, closer to whoever or whatever waited for her there. She found she had no power to resist the forces that drew her on.

Rounding the side of the main building, she made for the back door, moving silently across the dry mud of the yard into the shadow of the outbuildings. The rear of the house was in darkness, and around her she could hear only the familiar noises of the night, the rustling of leaves, the creaking of laden branches, and the hooting of night owls in the barn.

I must go in. I must find him and tell him what has happened. But she knew, in her dream, that it was from a sense of obligation, not from affection, that she had come; that what was a bitter sorrow to her would bring him what he most desired.

The door was unlocked. She lifted the latch and went inside the house, closing the door behind her. Still moving soundlessly, she carried on through the kitchen and into the passage beyond. There were voices coming from the parlour, and she stopped to listen, puzzled; one of them was unfamiliar, with an accent she could not identify. She wondered what a stranger could be doing in the house at such an hour, and at such a time.

Then she knew.

Memory returned in full, and all at once she was backing away, but she must have made some sound, for as she reached the haven of the kitchen she could hear footsteps coming towards her, moving rapidly, and she began to run. Fear drove her on, out of the house and across the yard, into the night. Fingers brushed her shoulder . . .

She woke suddenly, making the transition from sleep to waking without interval, clutching confusedly at the blankets – to find herself staring up into the eyes of a human face.

'Keep quiet. I've not come to harm you.'

Before she could scream, a hand came down over her mouth. It was the same hand she had sensed in her dream, except it belonged not to *him* but to Stern, and even the shock of finding him in her room, sitting on her bed, was preferable to her imaginings. She blinked, realizing a candle was burning somewhere, for she could see Stern's face quite clearly.

'If I take my hand away, do you swear you won't call out?' he whispered.

The hand was heavy, making it hard to breathe. She nodded awkwardly, and it was withdrawn.

'You should be glad I woke you. It didn't look like a pleasant dream.' Stern sat back, still speaking softly.

'It wasn't.' Asher sat up, as much puzzled as frightened. 'What're you doing here? What do you want?'

'A favour. For me and a few friends.'

'What favour? How did you get in here?' She was fully awake now, and beginning to be angry as her initial fright dissipated. She

64

feared the man in the dream, but she was not afraid of Stern.

He flashed her an unpleasant smile, which held a disturbing familiarity hitherto absent from their relationship. 'I followed you the other night, to see where you lived. I was in the alley at the back when you opened your shutters, so I knew which your room was. It was simple enough.'

'Why?' There was something strange about his appearance; he seemed to have covered his face with some dark substance. He looked quite different from the man she saw in the Treasury each day.

'I told you, I need you to do me a favour.' He looked round the room, his gaze settling on her clothes, lying folded on a chair. He picked them up and threw them on the bed. 'Get dressed. We're going out.'

'Out?' She was mystified. 'Where? What time is it?'

'Late enough. After midnight. Now, get dressed.' The smile became a leer. 'I won't look.'

Sure now his intentions were neither robbery nor rape, Asher wondered whether she was still dreaming. 'Why should I? Why shouldn't I simply scream and call my friends?'

The hand flashed down to her throat, bony fingers circling her neck. 'I wouldn't do that. You'll do as I say, or I tell the Treasurer to go through your books.' The hand tightened. 'Is that what you want? You and your *friends*?' Asher shook her head, unable to speak. Stern released his hold. 'Good. Then get dressed.'

'All right.' Asher rubbed her throat, thinking rapidly. Evidently he had guessed about her fraud. She could, of course, call to Essa, but he had mentioned his *friends*. It seemed wisest to go along with his directions, at least for the moment. She pulled the clothes under the blankets and began to dress.

As soon as she was ready, Stern blew out the candle. 'Now, I'll explain what you're going to do.' He had moved across to the window, where the shutters stood open.

'*If* I agree.'

He cut off her objection. 'You'll agree. I've been watching you. I know all about the money.' Asher felt herself grow cold. This was about her carelessness today, breaking the glass. No other explanation made sense. Stern evidently read her thoughts in her face, for he went on: 'I thought there was something different about you, but you're careful most of the time. It was that girl dying that put you off-balance. I was almost sure before as it's bad luck to take tribute money. But when you broke that glass, I *knew*. I watched, and you weren't worried at all, were you?'

65

'I don't know what you're talking about.'

'Oh yes you do. And you'll help me. If you don't, I inform the Treasurer you've been stealing, and you'll get the brand on your face. Which is it to be?'

There was plainly no point in arguing. 'What do you want me to do?'

'You'll find out. Now, are you coming?'

She had to make up her mind quickly. If she refused, there might be no time to get out of the city before they came to arrest her; if she agreed to what he wanted, whatever it was, he might let her be. 'I'll come.'

'I thought you'd see sense. Over here. We get out this way.'

She joined him by the window and saw how he had been able to gain access to her room. The window overlooked the erstwhile stableyard, but was close enough to the wall circling the inn and stables to be reached by means of a long wooden ladder balanced on wall and window-ledge. Peering out, she could make out a dark figure straddling the wall holding the ladder in place at the far end, perhaps twenty feet away.

'You go first. Hurry. There's not much time left.' His hand was at her back. Reluctantly, she climbed on to the ledge as Stern steadied the ladder, then began to crawl, the ladder shifting beneath her weight. As she reached the wall a hand was extended to her, drawing her on to sit beside the dark figure.

'Jump down. It's not far, and they'll catch you.' The voice sounded younger and more friendly than Stern's. Asher could make out two intensely blue eyes and a snub nose above crooked teeth. One of the eyes closed in a wink.

She braced herself, then let herself drop to the ground, feeling her left ankle give on impact; but at once there was a hand at her elbow, and she was standing undamaged.

'He's just coming,' the man on the wall hissed down.

'About time, too! The watch'll be round in a minute.' The man who spoke was large, with a grumpy voice; his smaller companion merely grunted. The big man did not, however, release his grip on Asher, the hand that had supported her creeping to her waist and attempting to move further up. She slapped it away irritably.

'Stop that!'

'No harm in it, is there, missy?' the big man whispered amiably. His features were obscured in the same way as the others, but nothing could disguise his thick neck and bulging stomach. The hand returned to its search with an insistence that was painful.

'Oh, let her be, Bull.' the younger man jumped down from his perch to join them as the small man accepted the ladder from Stern. 'This isn't a social event!'

'Quiet, all of you. Let's get moving.' Stern appeared beside Asher, and the Bull's hand dropped, much to her relief. 'That way.' He pointed east, down a narrow, winding alley.

'Where are we going?' Asher whispered to the young man.

'Down to the sea, and the Almaine Dock. Come on.'

Stern led the way, keeping Asher at the centre of the line, making it impossible for her to break away. She was unpleasantly aware of the big man and his companion at her back, and found herself half-hoping they would meet the guard as they followed Stern in a circuitous route down unfamiliar streets lying deserted in the hours of curfew; but they encountered no one, and she gathered from her companions' whispered conversation that they had some knowledge of the regularly patrolled routes, and were deliberately avoiding them.

They came to the shipbuilding yards; she saw masts, and smelled the familiar scents of wood-shavings and tar, but they did not stop. Instead, Stern led them north and east, to the sea and the tall warehouse buildings surrounding the Almaine Dock on all sides, leaving only a narrow sea channel at the centre that led east out into the harbour.

'Here.' Stern looked quickly left and right, then gestured to the young man. 'You – Hare. Get going.'

'What are you going to do?' Asher whispered urgently.

Stern was still watching the street, but he grinned. 'We're going to make our Chief Councillor a little poorer.' He spat. 'Not that he'd notice.'

'Avorian?' she said involuntarily. 'You're going to break into his warehouse?' She looked up at the apparently impenetrable building, a rectangle three storeys high and some three hundred feet long. The façade was dark and shuttered, windows and loading bays firmly closed, doors locked and barred. Even the gates, carefully spaced, which guarded the passages leading through the building to the dock behind, were locked. Hare was standing in front of one of them, beckoning to her.

'Put this in the lock.' He held out something that looked like an outsize sewing needle. Seeing she hesitated, he added anxiously: 'You are what Stern says? The hex-wards won't hurt you?'

Everything abruptly fell into place. The warehouses owned by wealthy merchants would be heavily guarded, especially now when they were filled with the cargoes of ships recently arrived in port. Hare was a pick-lock but even he could not break in to the warehouses with impunity, because, unlike herself, he was vulnerable to the deadly effects of wards like the one that had killed the girl in the Treasury.

'No, they won't hurt me.' She took the needle and inserted it confidently into the lock. When she was a child, Callith and Mallory had dared her to break into a hex-warded jewel case belonging to their mother, just to see if it was true no harm would come to her, although the ward was only set to sting, not to kill. She remembered the slight prickling sensation against her skin. There had been trouble about that; she could recall it all too vividly.

Back in the present, she still felt nothing, no stirring of force; evidently, the gates were not regarded as major points of security.

'Quickly, Hare, and you, Club. Get ready,' Stern urged impatiently. There was a click, and the gate opened. Hare passed through, followed by the small man. Stern shepherded Asher and Bull inside the first, waiting as Hare unlocked the gate at the far end of the passage, through which Asher could make out moonlight shining on the water in the dock, where two men were patrolling the sides. The second gate opened, and Club disappeared noiselessly through it. Hare returned.

'The door next?'

Stern nodded. 'And hurry. The guard'll be round soon.'

'I hope Club is as good as he says. I don't want one of the guards ringing the alarm bell.' Hare flicked a glance at the empty street, then beckoned to Asher again. 'Would you be so kind? I don't trust our revered councillors not to ward *these* locks.'

'All right.' Again, Asher took the pick from him and followed him back to the street to a wide wooden door reinforced with brass studs. She wondered why she was putting up no protest. Was it because the whole affair seemed like the continuation of a dream? It seemed impossible that she could, physically, be here in this place, about to take part in a theft from Avorian's warehouses. She both liked and respected the Chief Councillor.

But what choice do I have? Either this, or take the risk Stern meant what he said and be arrested for stealing from the Treasury. For a moment, she hesitated, knowing the honourable thing to do would be to call out and summon the guard, or alert the watchmen by the dock. Yet if she did, at best she might find herself enslaved for embezzlement, and at worst in the Kamiri Games arena, fighting for her life against impossible odds for their amusement. Avorian was rich; petty pilfering would not impoverish him. And no matter how much she might like to tell herself otherwise, her own record was hardly spotless; over the past six months she had taken at least twenty gold pieces from the Treasury purse, even if the money was for what *she* would call good causes.

Put like that, the choice was more easily made; she inserted the pick in the lock.

Instantly, a violent spark leaped on to her hand, and she experienced a stinging sensation all over her body as more followed it, flowing up her fingers and over her hand. They were not precisely painful, but felt as if blunt needles were trying, unsuccessfully, to pierce her skin, bouncing harmlessly over the unbroken surface. Energies flowed around but could not touch her, seeking entry and finding none, the bright sparks extinguished on contact. Somewhere in the lock a ward had been set, made from green schist or carnelian, like the Treasury wards, designed to activate as any unauthorized object was placed in the warehouse lock. The only question was how long would be the duration of its activity.

As the last spark died, with a mocking bow Hare took her place at the door and Asher saw his sensitive fingers probe and juggle the pick.

'There. Now – after you. Just in case.' He stood back and gestured her to lead the way.

This is my last chance to draw back.

Asher was never sure what her decision would have been, but when she took a step back she found Bull standing behind her; evidently Stern had anticipated a refusal, and taken action to ensure her compliance. Reluctantly, she pulled at the heavy door; it opened easily, the hinges well-oiled. A shove from Bull sent her through the doorway into a vast space piled high with dark shapes.

'Is it safe?' Stern whispered.

'There's nothing here.' Asher could feel no other wards. 'You can come in now.'

Hare was the first to follow, not without encouragement from Bull. It was dark inside the warehouse, and Asher could not see his face, but his breathing came fast.

'Lock and bar the door, quickly.' Stern lit an oil lantern as he spoke. 'Then come upstairs. We want the uppermost floor. Asher – lead the way.'

'*Move!*' Bull's hand was at her neck. She swallowed, glancing about at the goods displayed in the light from the lantern, seeing piled hides, furs, and barrels of wine and ale stored round the walls. The stairway was in the centre of the space.

As she reached the top of the first flight, she thought she heard a faint growling noise. From behind, someone whispered uneasily: '*Stop!*'

The sound came again, followed by irregular clicking sounds. Someone – Stern, she thought – lifted the lantern, and Asher suddenly saw what was making the noises; only paces in front of her, head lowered, hindquarters slightly flattened in preparation for the spring, waited the largest cat she had ever seen. Red eyes stared at her unblinkingly, huge in the lanternlight; the fur was unrelieved black, the cat's paws the size of her own hands.

'Hold still.' She recognized the voice as Bull's. She felt movement behind her, and sweat began to trickle down her back; if the cat should leap, she was its primary target. The beast was beautiful, its fur glistening, tail swishing, but it was a deadly and deceiving beauty; the mouth was half-open in a snarl, jaws ready to close about her throat.

She was pulled to the ground as the cat launched itself into the air and Bull threw something towards it, a net of heavy mesh weighted with pieces of metal attached to the edges. The cat snarled as the force of its own leap caused it to become deeply entangled in the net, and instead of landing on top of Asher it fell short and crashed heavily to the floor, thrashing about frantically at the unfamiliar restraint. Claws flashed out, tearing at the mesh, and the long teeth ground and champed, but, to Asher's intense relief, the net held.

'Go on. I'll deal with this.' Bull stepped warily toward the cat, whose red eyes glowed with a fierce hatred. Asher moved on, shaking, keeping her distance, and climbed the second flight.

'Fates, that was close!' Hare mopped his brow as he joined her. 'What was it?'

'An Asiri watch-cat.' His hands, too, were shaking. 'No one told us there was one here.'

'Bull seemed to know.'

Hare gave her a look. 'He did, didn't he?' There was a pause. Stern, who had waited halfway up the stairs, climbed the remaining steps, still carrying the lantern.

'Bull's dealt with it,' he said sharply. 'Get those loading doors open. No – not the ones facing the street, fools! The ones looking out on the dock.'

Hare and Asher crossed to the wooden panels built into the far wall, which were bolted and barred shut. 'Help me, will you?'

Hare asked shakily. Asher nodded, lifting one end of the heavy bar. Together they dealt with the bolts, and pushed at the panels. They swung out, to reveal a square platform looking over the dock.

'Now get out of the way. This is Bull's job.' Stern gestured with his head.

Asher sneezed as her feet disturbed dust on the floor. 'What's in all those sacks?' she asked Hare, who had slumped down into a crouch.

'Spices. Pepper, mostly, but saffron, cumin, and salt too. All from eastern Petormin; nothing but the best for our Chief Councillor.'

'All of them?' Asher stared. The floor was piled high with sacks, too many to count. Now she knew what they contained, she could smell the dryness in the air; the warehouse was rich with it, tickling her nose. She wondered how much it was all worth. Pepper was the most valuable and most profitable of all trade items, light and easy to transport, and it could be stored for years.

'It's what we came for. We're only taking a dozen or so – the boat won't hold much more,' Hare said, sounding more natural. 'Enough for my share, at any rate.'

'Why *did* you come?' Asher found it hard, remembering his anxiety on her behalf at the gate, to think of Hare as a hardened thief.

'Six younger brothers and sisters, and low wages.' He was silent for a moment. 'We're going to buy a smallholding and live on it. We'll net almost enough from tonight's work; a sack's worth sixty gold pieces – ten librium weight in each.'

Asher made some quick mental calculations. A dozen sacks of pepper – seven hundred and twenty gold pieces, divided by four. That made one hundred and eighty for Hare. Not quite enough for his purpose.

'This is only the second time we've been out together,' he observed, guessing the track of her thoughts. 'But the other wasn't as profitable as this. And there's the four watchmen to take into account.'

'I saw only two.'

'There're four, one for the warning bell at each corner, but two of them are in with us. Club looked after the other pair. He's a dirty fighter.'

'I see.' She watched Bull heft a heavy sack, lifting it easily over to the loading platform and attaching it to the pulley used to raise and lower the merchandise. Presumably a boat was waiting in the dock below.

For the first time, it occurred to her to worry about what would happen to her when Stern and his friends had finished their looting.

'Club deals with the watchmen. I pick the locks. Bull does the heavy stuff, and Stern found you – and knows how to get rid of the goods.' Hare was looking at Asher. 'You watch yourself. Club's a bad man, and not fond of women. And Bull – he likes them too much, if you understand me.'

'Thanks.' She tried not to sound ironic. As Bull lowered the seventh sack, she found herself wishing she had thought of a way to prevent the theft, feeling that by her compliance she had betrayed not only Avorian but herself. What *was* she doing here?

There are worse things than theft. It was true, but no consolation to her conscience. She looked up and caught Bull's eye on her, and realized that even if she'd tried to escape, she would never have reached the stairs.

She counted thirteen sacks being lowered before Stern beckoned to her and Hare.

'We're leaving now. Down the rope – you first, Hare.' The young man nodded and stepped on to the platform, his shabby trousers now covered with dust, leaving Asher alone with Bull and Stern, who gestured her to follow. 'You come too. We'll need you again.'

'No.' The refusal was instinctive. 'Never, Stern.'

'You'll get a share.'

'No,' she repeated. 'I don't want one. Just don't ask me again.' Despite the good use to which she knew she could put the money, she shied away in revulsion from the prospect. What if this was Mallory's warehouse? her uncomfortable conscience demanded. Would you have done the same, just to save yourself? Her skin prickled with shame.

'Get down the rope into the boat, there's no time to argue. The tide's on the turn.'

Asher peered down, barely able to make out the shape of the long rowboat below, bobbing up and down in the water in the rectangle of the dock. Carefully, she grasped the rope in her hands and lowered herself, gritting her teeth against the roughness on her palms, rubbing the skin raw. It was only fifty feet or less, but felt much further, and she was terrified of slipping and falling, upsetting the boat.

'Careful!' A hand steadied her, then drew her to one end of the boat. It was Club, and when she sat down in the bow she saw he held a knife in his right hand, pointed at her midriff. 'No sound until we're well away from here. Understand?' She nodded mutely.

The other two joined them, Bull sitting in the centre, taking both oars in his beefy hands. Stern released the rope and the boat began to move away from the mooring with steady swiftness as Bull drew long, efficient strokes, barely breaking the water. The dock was in the shadow of the surrounding buildings, and Asher could make out no movement anywhere; no bell tolled to summon the guard. The boat slipped out into the narrow channel, then past the customs house at the mouth of the inlet and out into the harbour proper.

To the south, the harbour was protected by a natural promontory stretching out several hundred feet and curving round until it reached the deeper water towards the centre. Bull followed its line, keeping his distance, the boat now too far out to be seen easily from the shore for the night was overcast. Only a light breeze stirred the water, but the weight of the sacks had lowered the level of the boat, and sea-water began to slop in until Asher's feet were awash. Obedient to Club's knife, she remained still and silent.

They were heading north, towards Fishermen's Quay, as Asher had expected; the old quarter was awash with goods that were stolen or had paid no duty. She looked up at the town, her gaze rising, irresistibly, to the hill behind, up to the peak, to the high walls of the citadel of the Oracle, where a bright light still burned.

Was it possible that the Oracle could know what she had done? Could it have foreseen it? For a moment she felt as if the Fates in which she did not believe were watching her, laughing at her discomfiture. Asher quashed the thought, furious with herself for even considering such nonsense. What about a more real hazard, Avorian's diviner? Asher had never really understood how divination worked, could not quite believe it, but from what she had heard she gathered such people could *see* patterns in matters relating to good or ill fortune, such as health, or gold, or the weather. Avorian's man was rumoured to be remarkable, capable of *seeing* anything that might affect the prosperity or other fortunes of his master. Had she and the others left an imprint in the warehouse for him to find? But there was no one she could ask, and she let her eyes fall to the ships at anchor in the cauldron of deep water.

They passed the pier dividing Cloth Quay from Spice Quay, and were making for shallower waters; she shifted, rocking the boat, and instantly felt Club's knife at her side.

'Stay still. We overturn and I'll spit you. Understand?' he hissed.

'Yes.' She wondered what had happened to the two watchmen who were not in on the robbery. Had he killed them?

They were drawing near the long pier that marked the beginning of shallower water, the depth only a dozen feet at low tide. Already she could smell the powerful stench of fish, for the fish market lay on ground just behind the quay.

'Get ready. You're getting out here.' Stern leaned forward and was speaking in a low voice which carried less than a whisper.

'Here? But – '

'If the guard catches you, just remember: one word from me and it'll be worse than a two-day in the cells.' He let the warning sink in. 'You say where you've been tonight, and you're dead.' As if it were necessary, Club brandished the knife.

'All right.' She had no choice. 'But I'll not do this again. Just leave me alone in future!'

'Keep your voice down!'

They drew alongside the pier; Bull shipped his oars, and Hare hung on to a rope looped round the end, keeping the boat steady. Asher got up cautiously and made her way forward, clinging on to the edge of the wooden structure. Bull grinned as she reached for a foothold, his hand snaking out and grasping her ankle.

'I know where you live, pretty lady. I'll see you again.'

'Not by my choice.' Asher kicked out, wrenching her ankle free as she pulled herself up and on to the pier. The boat rocked from the force of her movement, and she heard Bull cursing as he tried to settle it. As she lay flat on her stomach, she hissed down: 'Never again. Do you hear me, Stern?'

He only stared and shook his head. Hare let go the rope, and the boat was already drifting away. It would be too dangerous to call after them.

Where do I go from here?

She judged it to be an hour or so after midnight; far too late for any excuse she could invent to pass muster if she were caught by the guard, and the hostel was too far away to reach without passing at least one patrol. She lay flat, staring inland, the open fish market with the public weigh-beam at its centre offering no hiding place; to the right lay the stews of the old quarter. It would be neither safe nor practical to hope for shelter there. With so many ships in port, they would be doing good business, but she had no desire to offer her services; her brief marriage had

74

bequeathed her a poor opinion of the act of sex. There was Carob's, but it was some distance away, and it might be hard to rouse Carob or Cass so late.

Mylla – her cousin's house is near here . . .

That was more promising. The cousin's doubtful profession should mean he was amenable to receiving visitors, no matter how late the hour. Cautiously, she peered in each direction, watching for the guard; they patrolled the old quarter less rigorously than the centre, but it would not do to be careless. But there was no one in sight, although she could hear voices and music coming from her right, where the shabby, close-set houses of the stews were still lit up.

She rose to a crouch, then made her way to the quay, pausing again; the smell of fish was overpowering, although the market had been sluiced down with salt water, and her feet slipped on cobbles covered with fish-scales and the occasional tail. She crossed safely to the far side and stood in the shadow of a doorway, listening; no one called out to her.

The old quarter was a maze of winding alleys and stepped lanes, impenetrable to those not born to the city. Using the river as her guide, Asher kept south, taking the nearest passage pointing inland, and began to climb as the ground rose steeply ahead. She was lost almost instantly, but carried on, moving by instinct, keeping to the shadows from habit, although they were no safer than the open streets. Once, she heard the clicking of paws on one of the rare cobbled passages and froze, backing against a wall; but although the hound and its grey masters passed within sight of her, it did not scent her presence. For once, she blessed the overpowering stench of the clogged gutters and moved on as soon as it was safe again.

Just when she was ready to despair, she turned into an alley that looked familiar. Surely the house with the square shutters was Mylla's? The cluster of thin houses was dark, but the skies had cleared and Asher thought she could make out other familiar details.

Try or die, they said. A dog began to bark as she crossed the muddy street, and her heart leaped; but the noise was coming from inside one of the houses, and she relaxed again.

Tentatively, she knocked on the front door. The house was narrow and looked dilapidated from the outside, paint peeling off in strips and the shutters hanging crookedly from the windows of the upper floor. It seemed deserted, devoid of life, and Asher was startled to hear footsteps in response to her feeble knock.

A small panel in the door opened, and an eye peered out.

'Who's there?'

Asher stepped back so as to be visible. 'I'm a friend of Mylla's. I need shelter,' she whispered softly.

'What's your name?' The voice sounded understandably suspicious.

'Asher.'

The eye disappeared and the panel was closed. Shortly after came the sounds of bolts being drawn back, and the door opened to admit her.

'I thought I recognized you.' The young man who let her in stood aside for her to pass. He was a male version of Mylura, tall and thin, with the same heavy eyebrows and arrangement of features.

'Is she here? I'm sorry to disturb you,' Asher said incoherently.

'It's no trouble. I was waiting for a friend.' Jan winked. 'She's upstairs. First door on your right. Go on up.'

Taking this as a hint to get out of the way, Asher complied, climbing the stairs on legs grown suddenly leaden. Before she had reached the top, a door opened, and Mylla herself appeared on the landing, holding a candle in her hand.

'Asher?' She took a step forwards. 'What are you doing here?' Her voice was not unfriendly, only puzzled.

'It's a long story.'

'Come in.' As if she sensed her friend's weariness, Mylura asked no more questions. She pulled Asher into her room and shut the door. 'Jan's got a customer coming, and he won't want them to know there's a stranger in the house,' she explained. 'A small matter of some scent, he tells me.'

Asher collapsed on to the bed, the only piece of furniture in the room not covered with either clothes or some other object. The room was chaotic in the extreme, as if Mylura never bothered to put anything away. Quantities of small gilded boxes vied with scarves of all colours. A pier-glass festooned with silver chains hung on one wall, and several bolts of bright-patterned cloth leaned against another.

'Jan uses this as a store-room when I'm not here,' Mylura observed. 'Now, sit there and tell me what's been happening, and what you're doing out here in the middle of the night.'

Gathering her wits, Asher complied; Mylura listened wide-eyed as she described the robbery, interrupting only twice for further information.

'At least you got here without being caught,' she said practically, when Asher had finished. 'But how you can stop it happening again, I don't know!'

Asher yawned wearily. 'I don't know either. Perhaps I should leave Venture and start again somewhere else.'

'It wouldn't be easy, especially to get papers.' There was an awkward pause. 'And we need you here.'

'Do you know,' Asher said shakily, surprising herself with the vehemence of her sentiments, 'I don't think I can bear this! I came here to get away from – ' She caught herself up just in time, drawing in a shuddering breath; now she was safe, she realized how sure she had been that Club and Bull would kill her. 'Why can't people leave me alone? All I want is to help Essa and Carob in return for their being so good to me.'

'But other people aren't like you, Asher.' Mylla's response was unexpectedly sad. 'You want a solitary existence, without ties, owing nothing to anyone. I don't mean,' she added hastily, 'that you've no friends, or anything like that. Only that you isolate yourself for some reason you don't talk about. You never ask for help, almost as if you feel you don't deserve to be treated like anyone else. I sometimes think that though you do care about the work we do in Venture, and the slave runs, you do more than your share because you think you ought to, not because you want to.'

It was too close to the truth for comfort. 'And what about you?' Asher retorted, flushing. 'What about the risks you take?'

Mylura shook her head. 'It's not the same; that's just in my nature, but not in yours. And I'm bound to Jan, as well as to you, and Essa, and Margit, and the others. I chose to live this way, but if I change my mind and want to settle down and marry in due course, I will.' She blushed. 'But you – I don't know how to explain it, but you shut us all out; you only *live* in the city, a temporary base from necessity, but it's my *home*. I don't know about the past – you never talk about it, and I won't ask – but you might remember we're your friends. You can deal with your demons your own way, but you might let us help sometimes.'

This appeal, coming from the carefree Mylura, was almost too much for Asher. She trembled, struggling for composure, feeling brittle and hopeless. 'I thought here, in Venture, at least my life would be *mine*, under my control,' she said dully. 'But where's my freedom if a man like Stern can tell me what to do, if *everything* I do is dictated or constrained by other people?' She thought again of Mallory, of the difference his presence made to her, of the malignity of the Fates in which she did not believe. 'Isn't it possible to be free?' she asked despairingly.

'Asher.' Mylura came to sit beside her, putting a tentative hand on her shoulder. 'I'm sorry, I didn't mean to upset you. Come on, it's late, and you should get some sleep. We'll talk more in the morning.'

'All right.' She was too tired to think clearly. 'And thanks, Mylla.'

'No trouble.' Mylura searched through a pile of garments and unearthed a night-gown. 'Here. Take this. The bed's wide enough for three, so get in and go to sleep. I'm just going to have a word with Jan.' She slipped from the room, leaving Asher to undress in privacy.

Why was everything happening now? Her hard-won peace was shattered; neither past nor present offered any hope of consolation. She felt as if she no longer belonged to herself, that she was being pulled in too many directions, none of them of her own choosing. Someone or something would not let her be, would not let her forget the past nor what and who she was.

No. Not again. Never again. Determination surged up in a last rush of energy; she *would* shape her own life, no matter what the odds.

Asher lay down and pulled up the blanket, shutting her eyes against the light and clutter of the room, too tired for further thought.

In an instant, she was asleep; and this time it was without dreams.

Chapter Four

'But I should be first – I'm the eldest!' The words were more weary protest than complaint.

'You're only a girl!'

'Perhaps,' Oramen broke in, shooting Mallory a distinctly malicious glance, 'your uncle should be the one to decide.'

Three pairs of eyes swivelled towards him in appeal: grey, vivid blue, and hazel; Mallory just managed not to laugh. Crisa, his ten-year-old niece, her father in miniature, looked anxious; eight-year-old Kirin, broad-faced, said to resemble Mallory himself, entirely confident of his claim; Lake, who was only five and already very like his mother, worried. Honora cast up her eyes, and the old nurse shook her head at Crisa, who refused to notice.

'Of course it should be Crisa,' he said decidedly. A memory of Callith and Perron in just such a situation assailed him; the injustice had struck him then as it did now. 'There has to be some advantage in age!' He smiled at Crisa, and saw that instead of looking smug she seemed pleased, and even a little startled at his championship.

'Come then, child.' Oramen patted the chair beside her own. Crisa sat down obediently. 'Now make your marks then we shall look up your fortune in the Book of Fate.' The girl took up the quill and began to scratch crosses on a blank sheet of paper.

'Thank you, brother,' Honora said softly, giving him a quick smile. 'It is the same every fair day, but Kirin is a little spoiled and *very* determined.'

This was one of the few times Mallory had ventured into the nursery, and the first by official invitation from his niece and nephews. He had almost forgotten city tradition, whereby on the day of the Foundation Fair everyone consulted a fortune-teller to see what lay in store during the year ahead. Oramen, by her own admission, was not particularly gifted in that direction, her talents being orientated more towards forecasting the fortunes of the weather and the tides, which was why she used an Oraculum for divination.

'See, Crisa,' Oramen's voice was saying. 'Here it is. *You will have more luck than you expect.*'

The girl's narrow face lit up with pleasure. 'Thank you, Oramen, thank you very much.'

The seeress laughed. 'All right, Kirin, your turn next.'

The boy, who had barely succeeded in containing his impatience, was already standing behind his sister, bouncing up and down on the balls of his feet. 'Get off, Crisa. You've had your turn,' he complained crossly. The girl slipped from the chair and went across to her mother, who placed a hand on her head.

That too is in her favour, that she doesn't leave the children entirely to the care of their nurses. Mallory wondered if some prejudice had led him to misread her, and, catching her eyes upon himself, saw she too was thinking the same.

'This is yours, Kirin: *Make yourself contented with your present fortune.* And no, you may not try again. It's Lake's turn.'

'But he won't mind, Oramen. Please?'

The seeress gave him a gentle push. 'Be off with you. Come, Lake.'

Scowling, Kirin kicked the leg of the table as his small brother took his place at Oramen's side. 'It's not fair,' he muttered to his uncle. 'If I'd gone first, I'd have been lucky too.'

'Don't sulk, my son, it suggests a weak nature. Think what the Oraculum said, and remember it,' Honora advised, sounding sterner than she looked.

Kirin made a face at Crisa, then perked up. 'What about my uncle? Won't he consult Oramen too?'

'Of course he will!'

Mallory, recognizing the inevitable, bowed in her direction with heavy irony. Lake slipped from the chair, beaming contentedly.

'Well, Councillor?' the seeress challenged, inclining her head, her eyebrows highly arched. 'Will you take your turn?'

'How could I refuse?' He grinned and sat down, making the required four lines of crosses at random. Oramen counted the marks, then consulted the tables for a match, flipping through the pages of the Oraculum with a practised hand.

'What is it?' Mallory asked, for the seeress was frowning slightly, looking puzzled. 'Is the news bad?'

'No.' She closed the book, pulling herself together. '*You may recover what was stolen.* A useful prophecy, I think.'

'Indeed.' He pondered the words a moment, pleased they should be so appropriate to his mood; he had woken that morning to a sense of perfectly irrational optimism which the day had so far fostered. 'Thank you, Oramen.'

'Do you intend to go into the town this morning, brother?' Honora asked as he stood up.

'I thought I might. Is there something I can get for you?'

She made a signal to the nurse, who gathered the children and took them away to wash their hands, still sticky with honey from the morning meal. When they were gone, she went on softly: 'It is only on this day, Kelham used to bring them fairings, just small gifts. I thought – if you would – '

'Of course I will, Honora.' He was touched, both by the admission and by her trust. 'I should be glad to.'

She smiled sadly. 'You may think he was an over-indulgent father, but he said he had been so happy when he was young, at Kepesake, he wanted his own children to have the same glad memories.'

'He would have been proud of you, sister, for what you are doing.' For a moment they were united in understanding, before a movement from Oramen broke the accord.

'Have a pleasant fair, brother.' Her cheeks rather flushed, Honora gave him a smile and quitted the nursery.

'And you, Oramen? Will you visit the town?' Mallory asked politely. The seeress shook her head.

'I have more work to do; the tides are always capricious, as you know, with two moons to pull them this way and that, and my calculations are not complete. But I think you will have an interesting morning.'

'Is that, too, a prophecy?' He meant it as a joke and was surprised when Oramen hesitated, then nodded her head with slow deliberation.

The streets were already crowded, and it took Asher and Mylura longer to reach the hostel than they had expected. Essa and Margit were seated at one of the long tables as they entered the common room; most of the other women were also sitting about, enjoying the laziness of a rare holiday and the chance to wear their smartest finery.

'And where were you?' Essa demanded as Asher came to join them. 'I knocked on your door this morning, but there was no answer.'

'I woke up early and went to visit Mylla.' It was the lie they had agreed on.

'Do you want some windflower tea, both of you?' Margit inquired, getting up. 'And – don't tell me – some food!' She grinned at Mylla and disappeared in the direction of the kitchens.

'I wanted to talk to you, Essa,' Mylura murmured. 'Ah, thanks, Margit.' She accepted a mug of tea and a plate of honey-cakes with equal pleasure.

'Selma's between posts at the moment, and she made this for everyone; this is our share.' Selma, a cook by profession, had lived in the hostel for two years and was a regular customer of Essa's employment agency, although not involved in her other interests.

Mylura took a cake and began to nibble contentedly. 'Delicious!' She stretched out a hand for a second.

Essa withdrew the plate. 'Not until you tell me what you came for!'

'I told Asher the other night.' She lowered her voice. 'It's something I learned while I was in Saffra. I met a woman who may have given us a clue as to where Vallis is hidden.' She repeated the story she had told Asher in Carob's.

'An internment camp? That could explain why no one has found a trace of her.' Essa frowned as she considered the point. 'It may be so, Mylla. Well done.'

'But how do we find out if we're right?' Margit asked anxiously. 'We can hardly just pay a visit.'

'Of course not! But there must be a way. Asher, that's your part of the country. Do you know this place near Chance?'

'A little,' she said reluctantly.

'Could it be done? I mean, would it be possible to go and look the camp over?'

Asher stared into her tea, feeling a band tightening about her chest. Even so small a reminder was painful. 'I don't know. It might be.'

'You don't sound very enthusiastic,' Margit observed critically. 'I would have thought – '

'Leave her alone, Margit,' Mylla interrupted in haste as Asher flushed a dark pink. 'This needs careful planning, if we're to do anything at all. We can't afford to rush heedlessly in.'

Margit looked annoyed. 'Coming from you that's rich!'

'But sensible for once,' Essa interposed peaceably. 'The camps are heavily guarded. We'll need a great deal of local information if we're to do anything, even take a look. Mylla's right.'

'But we have to do something, surely!' Margit demanded in agitation. 'This news Mylla's brought must be *meant*, we can't ignore it.'

'No, indeed, but we need not act today.' Essa offered Margit a cake, which she took with a sharp gesture. 'We mustn't allow enthusiasm to carry us beyond sense. This is the Foundation Fair; let's allow ourselves to enjoy the day. There's time enough to consider what we should do later.'

Her thoughts diverted, Margit nodded more agreeably. 'I thought I would visit the Treasury baby in her new home, to see all's well.'

'That reminds me, I have some spare cloth for her foster-mother. Mylla, your legs are younger than mine, would you run up to my room and fetch it? It's on the chest.' Mylura rose, neatly appropriating a cake as she did so. 'Really, Mylla! The amount you eat!'

'Do you want to come with me?' Margit asked Asher. 'It's only down by the harbour.'

'I'd like that.' It sounded a harmless enough mission, and Asher thought it would be a relief to do something useful. Unlike Margit, she had no particular fondness for babies, but she felt a certain responsibility to the child.

'I shall stay here,' stated Essa decidedly. 'Devis is coming to read our fortunes later this morning, and I don't want to miss her.'

'In any case, you're not strong enough to walk so far yet,' Margit said, standing up as Mylura returned with a bundle of material. 'Thanks, Mylla. Do you want to come too?'

She shook her head. 'My knee's still a little sore, I'll stay with Essa.'

'We'll see you later, then. Ready, Ash?'

'If you are.'

The streets were not only crowded but extremely noisy. Almost every corner seemed to have sprouted some form of entertainment, whether dancers, singers, magicians, or puppeteers; children ran about everywhere, mostly underfoot despite the best efforts of mothers and elder sisters, and their cries added to the general tumult until the sound level was deafening.

It was a fine day, and the air was warm for the northern spring. Street-pedlars were doing an active trade, for it was considered lucky to buy small gifts on fair-day, and most of the women and older girls sported a new ribbon or other trifle in their hair.

'Wait a minute – I want to buy the baby a present,' Margit said loudly in Asher's ear as she moved to inspect a tray of cheap-looking trinkets, and Asher stepped aside to let others pass. The first drunks were making an early appearance, the taverns and inns having been open since the end of curfew, but for the moment they seemed cheerful enough, beaming ale-inspired goodwill at their fellow citizens.

A crowd of medical students from the college near the slave market swaggered past, arms linked, their scarlet tunics identifying them among the crowds. One stopped and spoke a few words to Margit, who gave an angry but inaudible reply.

'Really!' she said, rejoining Asher. 'You would think they'd know better. I must be nearly old enough to be his mother!'

'I expect he imagines you'd be flattered,' Asher suggested. In fact Margit, flushed with indignation, looked very pretty and much younger than her years.

'I sometimes wonder if young men are actually capable of rational thought.' She sighed. 'And girls, too, at times. Fair-days always bring out the worst in them.'

Asher made no reply, sensing the uncomfortable direction of Margit's thoughts. They walked on down the hill in silence towards the harbour, the sun bright on the still sea. There was hardly a breath of wind, and the air was filled with the cries of circling sea-birds, and the rich smells of roasting meat from street stalls set up to profit from visitors to the fair.

They reached the covered cloth market, crowded with expensively dressed merchants and traders bidding for the cottons and silks brought in from the east of the Dominion. Asher paused, wondering if Mallory were somewhere in the crowd, but she could not see him.

'Buy my sweet scents! Come buy my sweet scents! Brought all the way from Baram just for your delight.'

A pedlar thrust a small bottle of coloured water from a tray into Asher's face, rolling his eyes in feigned admiration.

'Only a silver apiece.' He looked at Margit and winked. 'Far-fetched and dear-bought is good for ladies, they say. I'm *giving* it away.'

Asher shook her head good-humouredly, wondering if the scent had travelled further than a few streets; it smelled powerfully of violets. The pedlar shrugged, turning to seek out more likely customers.

'Did you hear that, Ash?' Margit was tugging at her sleeve. 'They say one of the warehouses down by the Almaine Dock was broken into last night.'

Asher felt her face grow stiff. 'Whose?'

'The Chief Councillor's. The watchmen were all knocked out, and one of them's still unconscious. I heard those people,' and she pointed to two elderly men, 'talking about it.'

So they were not dead? An instant upsurge of relief told her she had feared the worst. 'Did the thieves get away?'

Margit nodded. 'No one knows who they were. Oh, and look – over there.' She pointed east to the end of the street, where the warehouses loomed up in front of the dock. 'There's the Chief Councillor himself.'

Asher looked away, feeling suddenly queasy; despite her resolve the previous night, she still had no idea what to do. 'Come on, it's too crowded to stop here.'

They turned right, heading in the direction of the quays. There were a larger number of women down by the docks, their bright dresses and the bells worn on ribbons round their necks marking them as prostitutes. Asher greeted one or two by name, for the women's group had helped several of them over the years, but they were too busy to stop and chat; fair-days were good for business.

'Look! No, in front of you!' Margit was pointing excitedly in the direction of a small square ahead. 'Do you see him?'

Asher peered as directed. 'See who?'

'That man,' Margit said impatiently. '*There*!'

Asher saw him then, a thin man standing stock still in the middle of a small square of shabby whitewashed buildings. He was dressed in a long white robe, and his hair, too, was white, although his expression was curiously absent. 'What about him?'

'It's one of the priests of the Oracle.'

Unenlightened, Asher only nodded, her attention distracted by another, more familiar figure in the square.

Bull. It's Bull! The shape was unmistakable. The big man was busy serving tankards of ale to customers taking advantage of the fine weather to sit at tables placed on the cobbles outside the tavern; Bull was presumably the tavern's landlord, which explained his generous figure.

He mustn't see me. Self-preservation dictated a speedy retreat, but Asher realized immediately that such a course of action would involve her in unwanted explanations. She bit her lip.

'Is something wrong?'

With an effort, she managed to smile. 'No. Nothing. Let's go and look at the ships in harbour before we pay our visit.'

Margit looked surprised, but agreed. Her attention was

continually drawn back to the white-robed figure in the square, although the man himself seemed indifferent to both surroundings and company, staring blankly ahead into the teeming crowds. Bull disappeared inside the tavern, and Asher breathed again.

They turned down toward the sea, pausing to watch a ship being loaded with barrels of ale. A huge tread-wheel was in operation, eight men inside it trudging at a steady pace as they held the ropes winching the cargo to deck-height; they stamped out a rhythm, singing along in time to the tread. The barrels swayed in an ominous fashion, but reached their destination safely, giving the wheel-men a well-deserved pause.

'He's coming here,' Margit breathed, looking not at the wheel but inland, her eyes suddenly bright.

'Who?' Asher whirled round, expecting Bull, but it was only the white-robed priest. She wondered if he were blind, for his eyes were oddly out of focus, although he did not stumble on the cobbled street and carried no stick. He was making straight for them and Margit's mouth opened, her face lighting up with joy; then, as quickly, the smile was extinguished, as she understood it was not she who was the target of the man's attentions.

The priest paused beside them, and for a moment Asher thought he did see her after all, for his eyes came to rest briefly on her face, and he reached out a hand to her. She pulled away, but not before he had thrust something at her, something soft, and she took it, not knowing what else to do.

'What do you want?' she asked sharply.

'Asher,' Margit began, but the priest seemed to have lost interest in them. The distracted look reappeared and he wandered away inland.

'What was that about?' She looked at the token the priest had placed in her hand; it was shaped like a laurel leaf, oval and pointed, but silver rather than green, smooth to the touch and with scarlet-traced veins. She had never seen anything like it before.

'Don't you know what it is?' Margit was staring at it hungrily, her voice holding a note akin to envy. 'It's a token from the Oracle.'

'Do you want it?' Asher held it out to her.

She swallowed, but did not take the leaf. 'He gave it to you, not to me. I can't take it. The Oracle wishes to speak to you, not me.'

'I don't understand.'

'I forget, you've only been here six years, and you say you don't

86

believe in the Oracle anyway!' She sounded unexpectedly bitter. 'On this fair-day, the Oracle summons eight men and women of Venture, to prophesy for them. This means you've been chosen.'

'But I don't want to go,' Asher protested. 'You go.'

Margit's eyes glittered angrily. 'I can't, she snapped. 'It chose you. You *must* go.'

'How come it chose me?' She realized, too late, that she had touched a raw nerve, for it was obvious Margit wished that she had been the one to receive the token, and resented the fact it had been bestowed on the one person in the city who had neither desire nor use for it.

'The priest's entranced. He surrenders himself to the Oracle so that the Fates may see through his eyes and choose the eight they wish to summon. You have to go today, before nightfall. Show the leaf to the guards on the upper gates, and they'll let you through.'

The explanation sounded nonsensical to Asher, but she had the tact not to say so. 'But I won't go, Margit. You know my feelings. Take it, and use it.'

'Don't you understand? I *can't*! The Oracle has nothing to say to me, only to you!' She was genuinely furious. 'You have to go. You *can't* refuse!'

'Why not?' Asher was stung. 'You know how I feel . . . '

Margit rounded on her. '*Don't be selfish*! How can you even *think* of refusing? Don't you know how lucky you are to be chosen?'

'No, I don't,' Asher retorted firmly.

'Even if you don't care about what it has to say to you, you must go!' Margit paused to draw breath, eyes flashing angrily. 'Why don't you ask the Oracle something useful about Vallis? This is the only chance any of us is likely to be given for months. I said Mylla's news was meant!'

'Then do it yourself!' Asher felt her resolve stiffening in the face of the demand.

'I would have thought this was the least you could do, after all we've done for you!' Margit said bitterly. There was an unpleasant silence.

'I'm sorry.' Asher felt as if Margit had slapped her. Was that how they all thought of her, as *them* not *us*? After six years of friendship and working together, in the Treasury and with Essa and Carob? She turned her hot face away, seeing she was being given no choice. If she did not go, Margit would never forgive her, that was painfully obvious. She remembered all Margit had done for her since she came to Venture, and found it was almost enough. 'If that's how you feel, I'll go,' she said stiffly.

'You'll ask about Vallis? And tell us what the Oracle says?' Margit demanded, pouncing on the concession before it could be retracted.

'Yes.'

'Then go. Go now. I know you don't really understand and I'm sorry for what I said. But go.' A gulf had opened up between them. Asher saw it was unimportant to Margit that to do as she demanded was to compromise Asher's own deeply held convictions; her supposed friend was too filled with self-righteous indignation and jealousy for compromise. Only Asher's submission could mend the tie between them that was very nearly severed.

'Take care, Margit.' Asher turned abruptly away, more upset than she wanted to acknowledge. *She wins her peace of mind at the expense of mine, like Stern and the rest.* Again, she had a sense of being used, against her will, but this time it felt worse, for the exaction of friendship, not blackmail, was being turned against her.

Her reluctance stemmed from far more than lack of belief in the Oracle's powers; to herself, Asher could acknowledge that what she feared most was the loss of that unbelief, to be forced to accept that her control over her own destiny was at best an illusion.

What a coward I am. If I were really sure, I wouldn't be afraid to go! Numbly, she began to retrace her steps, away from the harbour and west, inland toward the highest point of the city. She climbed the steep main street with a heavy heart, feeling an outsider among the mass of people thronging the paved road as she moved against the trend. She was aware of her surroundings only peripherally, automatically noticing the landmarks that told her how far she had come. Her way took her past the wealthy quarter, where the councillors and other merchant clans had their houses, where there were open spaces and walled gardens rather than the narrow streets lower down; her senses registered the decline in noise and numbers of people, but without interest.

In front of her, rising behind the high city walls, the hill of the Oracle soared up, steep and forbidding, topped by the white-walled citadel that housed the Oracle. Asher could just make out a figure about halfway up the slopes, and wondered briefly whether it belonged to another of the chosen, and whether he or she went more willingly than herself.

Why should anyone want to know a future they could not

alter, even if such a thing *were* possible? Asher, remembering certain events in her own life, shuddered; if the Fates had dictated those for her, she had no wish to become acquainted with them.

She reached the Nevergate and presented her leaf-token to the watchful Kamiri duty-guards, only a little surprised when they allowed her to pass through unimpeded; it had been too much to hope for a reprieve. The grey men held the Oracle in a respect bordering on idolatry, which was why they permitted so little access to the common people of the city over which it cast its sway.

As the gates shut behind her, she experienced the sense that instead of letting her out, the city was rejecting her, that she was no longer welcome within its confines. She shook herself, ordering her thoughts.

She began to climb the path leading to the citadel, wide and deeply rutted from centuries of use. Until the invasion, permission to visit the Oracle had lain in the hands of the city council, and the men and women of Venture had made the journey often to consult on their marriages and children, on illness, on where they should build their houses or send their ships; now, it was a privilege the Kamiri governor rarely granted. Amrist sent messengers several times a year, and important visitors to the city were allowed to make the trek, but the old, close connection between city and Oracle had been severed, at severe financial loss to Venture. Many of the inns and shops that had served the Oracle's suppliants no longer existed, their owners now numbered among the poor.

Why me?

Asher found herself wondering whether the gremlins of malicious Fate had heard her long-ago promise to herself, and this was how they mocked her, in forcing her towards the very thing she feared.

Feared? I am afraid of this Oracle? It shocked her to realize it might be true.

To either side of her path the slopes were lightly wooded with pine and laurel which grew more closely as they rose toward the peak. Outcroppings of rock showed the land to be poor, and there were no huts nor arable plots around the walls as there were to north and south of the city. Only the gleaming white stone of the citadel a thousand feet above disturbed the natural contours of the hill.

Halfway up, breathing hard, Asher turned to stare down the way she had come. The city looked unnaturally peaceful from a distance, the layout far more orderly than in reality. The major thoroughfares bisected the city at improbably perfect angles, the square of civic offices neatly centred. The River Sair wove a dissolute line from north-west to east, carving out a drunken route through the old quarter, which looked less maze-like and more inviting from above. None of the tumult of sound inside the walls reached her. Out to sea, a fleet of small fishing boats was making its way to shallow waters, looking like the tiny models boys played with in the harbour. The whole was alien, unfamiliar. Sighing, she turned back and resumed her upward trudge.

Why me?

The cynical part of her mind suggested it was a matter of irrelevance who was chosen; the glamour remained, no matter who was selected. But it was difficult not to speculate on what the Oracle might have to say to her. It was a reluctant admission to curiosity, but an admission nonetheless.

It was foolish to fight the inevitable.

It grew darker as she neared the top, trees blocking out some of the light. Birds sang, their shrill voices oddly muffled as if there were something about the place that prohibited too much sound. Asher was hot after the climb, but in the shade of the trees the air was cool, with a powerful scent of pine resin.

The last section was the steepest; she emerged from the trees on to a wide rock plateau panting for breath. Here, at least, a sharp breeze blew, plastering her skirts against her legs and ruffling her hair. The crest of the hill was flat, barren pale grey rock with only a dusting of scrub, and to the west the land fell away to a precipitous drop that made her giddy as she looked out and down to the inland valley. Behind her were the city and the sea; ahead lay the citadel, tall gates standing wide, high white walls glistening in the sunlight.

How beautiful. As her skin cooled in the wind, the sun high overhead, Asher's eyes watered as she continued to stare at the plain walls. There was no one there to greet her or tell her how to proceed.

I suppose I just walk in.

The narrow archway was three times her own height. She walked under it and found herself in a short covered passage which was unexpectedly cold, emerging at the far end on to a vast courtyard open to the sun, paved in the same glistening white stone as the walls. Instantly confronting her, dwarfing smaller structures to either side, stood a large, unornamented, rectangular building which made her catch her breath. There was no sound at all, and no one about except for a white cat with red eyes that hissed at her approach, then darted away, tail lashing furiously.

'Welcome.'

She blinked as a white-robed priest appeared from a blank face of stone to her left, against which he had been standing, chameleon fashion. Feeling an intruder, she proffered the silver leaf, which he took.

'Do you carry arms?' She shook her head. 'If you wear any charms or amulets, you must remove them. I will keep them for you safely.'

'I have none.'

The priest looked surprised, but acknowledged her answer with a stately inclination of his angular head.

'Then you may enter.' He pointed to the rectangular structure. 'No gifts may be proffered by those whom the Oracle has summoned. May your fortune prove auspicious.' With which words he hurried off, a sprightly figure, his sandals flicking up puffs of dust.

Asher regarded the House of the Oracle with a sense of deep foreboding; its very plainness impressed her against her will, as if the power it was said to contain had no need for false adornment. The structure was long – at least a hundred and fifty feet, by forty wide – the roof slightly arched; narrow slits high along the sides served in the place of windows, and the whole had a dark and forbidding appearance despite the brightness of the stone.

What if it's true? What if the future exists, fixed and unalterable?

She felt a chill hand clutch her heart. Inside lay the Oracle. Was it possible she had been wrong all her life? She took a few steps towards the entrance, then stopped at the sight of two trees, one to either side, each bearing silver, scarlet-veined leaves. This, then, was her token's origin.

There were no doors, only a wide portico open to allcomers. Telling herself fiercely she had nothing to fear, Asher moved on, but there was a new ambivalence to her feelings now that she had come so close. It was one thing to be sure, another to *know*; if she had believed wrongly for fourteen years, she was unwilling to discover it.

You gave your word.

A promise suddenly seemed a small thing to break. Would Margit have been so insistent if she had made her own feelings plain? But it was too late to find out now. Lifting her head and straightening her spine, Asher entered the building.

She was instantly enveloped in a chill darkness, breathing in icy air that felt damp and smelled of stone and an unidentified spice. She wondered why it was so cold.

Faint streaks of light entered the hall, but it was too dark to see, so Asher waited, chilled, for vision to return as her eyes grew slowly accustomed to the dim interior. She thought she could hear the low murmur of voices far away, but the sounds were too low-pitched to carry to where she stood.

Where . . .

An immense figure stood at the far end of the hall, so tall it would have dwarfed even a Kamir; it was the first thing she could make out, and a few seconds passed before Asher realized it was only a statue, a stone representation of Lady Fortune, the Fate said to prophesy in the citadel. Her scales were held out at shoulder height, weighing for everyman the Fates of Chance and Destiny, for health and wealth and fortune.

Her second discovery was that she was not alone; two men were before her, standing with their backs to her, intent on something that lay between themselves and the statue. One wore a priest's robe, she could make out its shape and colour even in the shadows, but the second, a much taller man, she guessed to be a suppliant like herself. She walked towards them, glad not to be alone, for there was something about the House of the Oracle that disturbed her profoundly. Her skin crawled as she drew closer to the statue, and her ankle turned on an uneven slab of stone in the dark; she let out a muffled cry of pain.

Instantly, the priest turned and saw her, uttering a horrified exclamation.' Who are you? What are you doing here?'

Asher flushed, grateful for the concealment of the darkness. 'A suppliant. I was directed here.'

'You should have waited outside until our audience was concluded; consultation is a private matter between Oracle and petitioner.' He sounded both outraged and dismayed, as if Asher might have overheard some dangerous treason. His companion, too, turned to see the cause of the interruption. Asher could make out the angle of his head, and was suddenly conscious of a new sensation, like ice-water trickling down the bones of her spine.

'It was obviously a simple accident.' The second man gave her a quick, dismissive glance. Asher returned the inspection, the advantage on her side, for his face was lit from above by a narrow strip of light where hers was in shadow. She could make out a scar to the right of a well-shaped jaw, a jagged line of awkwardly puckered skin, and wondered how he had come by it. His skin had a leathery consistency, and his hair was a reddish-brown above strong, broad-boned features; not a handsome man, but his face was made remarkable by reason of a pair of eyes of an astonishingly vivid blue, which gave depth and intelligence to his countenance.

'I thought there was no one here.' Her own voice sounded unfamiliar in the gloom. 'I'll go.'

The priest seemed mollified by the offer, but before he could accept another voice issued from further back in the hall, the command seeming to emanate from deep underground.

'*Draw near, Fortune's child.*'

There was nothing even remotely human about the voice. In her mind, Asher knew it came from one of the Mouths of the Oracle, the women who dedicated their lives to channelling the words of the Fates, mere instruments to their power; but in her heart she did not believe the sound could come from a woman's throat. In one instant of unwanted revelation, and against all her beliefs, it made plain to her both that it knew her, and that it was speaking to *her*, knowing what as well as who she was. The priest shot her a questioning glance, then gestured her urgently forward.

'Stand there and listen,' he hissed. 'No! Closer.'

Numbed by cold and shock, Asher stood and faced the statue. In front of her, built into the floor by her feet, she could make out a flight of steps leading down to a deep pit partially obscured by rolling white smoke, but even as she looked more clouds billowed up, so she could not see even the outline of the woman who lay hidden there. Tendrils of curling smoke crawled across the stone floor, low-lying and reptilian in motion; there was a sharp, metallic smell in the air, and it was icy cold.

At last, the voice came again, and it was not hard to believe the unseen presence was there, watching her through the obscuring mists.

'*You, whom Chance has gifted with*
A double share of Fate;
Stand forth.'

The priest pushed her gently nearer the pit, from which more smoke rose, concealing her feet in an icy shroud. She stood stock still, terrified of moving, of falling into the depths.

It was only a brief moment before the voice went on:

'*Fortune's child.*'

A second pause. Then:

'Within your compass
Lies the means to pierce the veil,
The mask of grey enshrouding
What is sought from those who search.'
Another hesitation.
'See the shifting shadowlines;
Mark what may from what must be;
In what was lies what will be;
Look, with eyes that choose to see.'
Again, a pause long enough to be registered as deliberate:
'Look – or lose, Fortune's child.'

The volume diminished, the voice fading into silence with a sigh. Asher could not move. She felt herself utterly remote from the situation, as if the whole experience were happening to someone else, to another Asher who was nearly, but not quite, herself. She knew, with a frozen clarity and without hope of contradiction, whatever the meaning of the Oracle's words, that she could no longer hold to her distant promise.

It was not possible that the priest who had given her the token could have known the circumstances of her birth; in Venture she was only Asher, born to that city, not Asher of Harrows, sole survivor of identical twins: a Fortune's child, as they were termed. And if the priest had not known, then how could the Oracle identify her, unless the Fates had marked her out? And if that were so – and she shot a hasty glance at the tall man standing with the priest – and the rest, then even her natural stubbornness must give way. She was not a fool; or not any more.

It must all be true. The future was there, already written and unalterable. She had deceived herself for fourteen years, and the blow was all the more bitter for the small part of her that still held out against conviction, wishing for the truth to be a lie.

'So you are a twin. How unusual and how favoured.' The priest scuttled to her side, peering into her face with pleased eagerness. 'Small wonder the Oracle summoned you here today. Now, tell me: does this augury have meaning for you, or do you require my help?'

'Help?' she repeated stupidly.

'It seemed to me one of the more – shall we say *dense* – Oracular prophecies.' Bright eyes regarded her searchingly. 'I'm afraid that some are plainer than others, and most more than this. If you were to ask me, I should say this means you may find something lost, something deliberately concealed from you, but that in order to do so you must look at the matter from a – different –

perception. Or that is my interpretation.'

She was shaking with cold, or reaction, or both. What joy can there be in knowing the future? It means living without hope, without happiness, she thought drearily. The priest's words passed over her head; she had lost the protection of her unbelief. She could feel the stirrings of a deep unhappiness that would draw her down into despair. No hope, she thought dully.

There was a stirring from the pit, as if the smoke itself, by its motion, was giving warning of further revelations. The voice, however, when it came again, was less startling to Asher than on the first occasion.

'Stand forth, O seeker. Come to me;
Your fortune waits.'

The tall man obeyed the summons with greater alacrity than Asher had displayed; as he moved further up, she moved back, away from the pit and the light, hardly aware of what she was doing.

'The leopard hunts for hunger,
Not for greed; he satisfies
His appetite and is replete.'

A studied pause.

'In the Shadow, chained and bound,
The Bear sleeps; the leopard stalks
His prey, the flightless hatchling
Who alone can rouse the Bear.'

A pause, as if the Oracle wished to impress the listener to pay closer attention.

'In vain his hunt, his seeking,
Save she whom Fortune favours
Drinks with him from that same cup:
Then the mask is stripped away.
The Bear wakes; the Shadow fades.'

The eerie voice faded slowly on the final sibilant hiss. Asher ducked her head as the man to whom the words had been addressed turned first to the priest, then to her, his expression hidden in shadow.

'This is unheard of!' The old priest, in his agitation, allowed his voice to rise. 'This search, then, concerns you both – be sure of it! *"Drinks with him from that same cup."* And what a purpose.' His tone softened as he took in the meaning of the second prophecy. *"The flightless hatchling – the Bear."* You are looking for Vallis, our young heiress, both of you!'

'I am.'

Asher did not respond, it did not seem necessary, nor did the man seem to expect it.

The priest's voice sharpened. 'You are aware that many have come here seeking her, and all have gone away unanswered over these fourteen years?'

'It seemed likely.' The tall man's voice held a quiet confidence, as though the news did not cause him undue anxiety.

'Well, you may ask the question, if it pleases you to do so. The Oracle has summoned you, and spoken for you.' The priest was looking at Asher in invitation, but she only shook her head, and he turned his attention back to the tall man. 'Then speak, if that is your wish; it is your right to ask the Oracle a question on this day.'

'They say nothing happens here that is not foreseen.' The suppliant cleared his throat and moved a pace nearer the pit, turning away from Asher. 'Very well, then.' He raised his voice. 'Mouth of Lady Fortune, who summoned me here, I wish to ask where I shall find Vallis, third child of Dominus Lykon of Darrian.'

The priest shook his head gently. Asher, however, was not surprised when the cold voice came again; matters had gone far beyond coincidence, beyond any random chance.

'The Hawk will fly no more;
Pinion'd, he lies in shadow.
The land will bear him down.'

There was a new, icier chill in the tone, a dismissal, as if the fate of Lykon, the Hawk, held no interest for the Oracle.

'Unseeing and unseen,
Her wings bound and flightless,
Layered in forgetfulness,
She lies. She waits the day
Of self-revelation.
Come that day of memory,
She casts aside the Shadow,
And, when Hawk may breathe no more,
Flies upwards, soaring free.
She calls, and she is answered:
At her cries, the cold ice cracks;
The sleeping Bear awakes.'

The silence following the pronouncement of the ultimate word was prolonged. Asher groped for the meaning of the prophecy, understanding the beginning – that Lykon was to die – but mystified as to the rest. Did it mean Vallis was a prisoner? And, if so, where? The hawk analogy was plain enough, that if she were free she would take her father's place, but the remainder seemed a mere repetition of the old prophecy – that her luck would deliver Darrian from the grey men.

'Yours the knowledge, his the search.' The priest was surveying her with renewed interest. '"*Drinks with him from that same cup.*" Your lives are in some fashion bound together, I believe. I know I should not say so, but this is a great day, a great day. I am Venture born and bred.' He shook his head. 'But I do not understand it all – even I, who have interpreted a thousand such utterances for the Oracle – this is not for me, but for you.'

Her fellow suppliant was also watching Asher; his inspection was noticeably less impersonal, although equally curious. 'It seems, mistress, that our paths must lie together for a time,' he said coolly. 'We have a great deal to discuss.'

Asher hesitated briefly, then nodded. 'But not here.'

The priest gestured broadly towards the entrance. 'There is a rest-house where we would be honoured if you would take refreshment,' he suggested. 'Unless you have a question for the Oracle? That is your right, mistress, for you have made no request.'

'There's nothing I wish to ask.' Asher, thinking of her promise to Margit, took a last look back at the weaving mists, at the towering statue, and shivered again. The words of the Oracle seemed engraved on her heart; she knew she would never forget them.

'You're cold – come out, into the sun.' The priest hovered at her arm, ushering her towards the light. She stepped out into the courtyard, blinded by the sudden glare, the sun warm on her skin.

'The rest-house is this way.' The priest indicated a square structure to Asher's right, and she turned to it. 'If you will follow me.'

The tall man stepped neatly in her way. 'We will not trouble you, priest,' he said firmly, taking her arm. 'I think I would prefer our conversation to go unheard. Given the subject matter.'

The priest paused uncertainly, then his face cleared. Asher saw he was as old as the other robed men she had seen, and wondered if advanced age were a prerequisite for such office. 'That might be more sensible,' he agreed, looking quickly about the courtyard. It was as deserted as before, although the same white cat crouched before a tiny circular pool, lapping the water urgently.

'Thank you for your assistance.' The man turned to Asher. 'Will you come with me, mistress?'

She looked into his face, unable to read his intent in voice or expression. Only his eyes, blazing down into her own, suggested any force of emotion. The priest, sensing a new puzzle, took a quick step toward them, but Asher put up a hand to ward him away.

'Very well.' Asher permitted her arm to rest lightly on her companion's as he led the way through the chill of the dark passage and out of the citadel.

Too much had happened in too short a space of time for Asher to make sense of any of it; she would not have been very surprised if the ground had opened at her feet and swallowed her. The power of coincidence was one with which she was familiar, but there was no equal to this, to the here and now of her present.

Was it all like this? All my life? So nothing I did, or will do, means anything at all? So it was all destined, that I should live as I did, as I do, and come here, at this time, and no will of mine would have altered my fate one iota? She felt on fire with a range of emotions; it was as if a succession of events had been set in motion which she had no power to divert or delay.

The wind on the plateau had risen, although it had not been noticeable inside the citadel. Asher let herself be drawn down by her companion away from the open and from prying eyes, into the cover of the trees. Only then did he draw to a halt and swing her round to face him.

'I thought you were dead.'

His fingers held her arms tightly, and for a short moment Asher believed herself protected, cherished, all the feelings she had thought never to need from anyone ever again. She looked up, trying to smile.

He had not altered greatly; the thick brown hair with its reddish tint waving across his forehead hid a faint retreat. He was heavier, more solidly built, but it was muscle rather than fat, and it suited his build. And the eyes were the same. Asher felt herself flush beneath his scrutiny, for there was nothing in his face which told her whether he was pleased to see her or simply surprised. He shook her lightly, as though he had to touch her to believe she was real.

'Mallory.'

'I thought at first I was dreaming; that it was just a chance resemblance. Until I heard your voice.' His own sharpened. 'Asher, what are you *doing* here? Why did you never let me know you were alive?'

It was the *me* that shook her, a betrayal she thought he had not intended. It had come, as she knew it must. She had tried to run from her past, but the Oracle had brought her back full-circle. Nothing we do can change our lives; it's all there, all written. Without choice, no hope. She stiffened.

'No one knew.'

For an instant, she read anger in his eyes. 'No one?' he asked softly.

She did not understand him, and shook her head. 'When I ran away, it was better no one knew where I went. It wasn't safe.'

Doubt flickered across his familiar face. He pulled off the heavy blue cloak he had flung round his shoulders and laid it on the ground, which was damp in the shelter of the trees, and soft, covered with cushioning pine needles. 'Sit,' he ordered, as if she were a dog. 'And tell me.' He made the first move, patting the thick material beside him.

She hesitated, but not for long. It was plain there was some deep misunderstanding to be dealt with, but she sat down, pulling her knees up to her chin and hugging them with her arms. 'What do you want to know?' she asked after a time.

Mallory stretched out his long legs, leaning back on his hands, studiously avoiding looking at her. He seemed embarrassed, if such a thing were possible for hm.

'Who was the man?' he asked abruptly; then, as Asher stared, having no idea what he was talking about, he elucidated: 'I mean, the man you ran away with.'

Chapter Five

The air under the trees felt heavy, the sounds of birdsong far distant, as if the world held its breath as he waited for her to speak. Then Asher's head snapped back, and for a moment, before he realized his mistake, Mallory thought she was going to laugh. Yet the gesture was at once familiar to him, and despite her altered appearance he knew he would have known her anywhere from that one movement alone.

'Is that what he told you?'

He caught a flash of irritation in her eyes and found himself confused by the range of emotions the sight of her stirred in him: of pain, and a strong sense of disappointment.

'He told me you'd run off with another man, yes. I didn't believe him,' Mallory said stiffly. 'Obviously I was wrong.'

She flushed, dark colour staining her pale cheeks. 'Oh? Are you quite sure of that?'

'Yes.' He said it to wound, a small repayment for the betrayal of his friendship. 'You never bothered to contact me or Callith, what else should I think?'

He saw he had misread her again; she was not embarrassed but angry. 'And you'd take his word over mine?'

'Why not?' His normally calm temper stirred. 'You left him without a word. You told no one where you were going, and I find you here, six years later, in a city far from home, looking prosperous enough.' His gaze took in her clothes, her general appearance. He did not like the changes he perceived in her, the dyed hair – unbecoming to her fair colouring – the self-assurance so different from the open-hearted girl he had known. The Asher who was so vivid in his memory was young and pretty, with an innocence of mind which had nothing to do with ignorance; now she was older, thinner, *harder* in some indefinable fashion, and he regretted the alteration.

'I see.' He saw pain flicker in her eyes, and felt a stab of remorse;

his welcome had been hardly generous. 'I'm sorry to disappoint you by being alive.'

'Not in that.' He was concerned at the bitter note in her voice. 'Asher, I'm very happy I've found you. Callith and I were desperately worried when we learned you'd disappeared.' He forced a smile. 'I thought Lewes had killed you.'

She relaxed a little. 'Did you? I wondered whether you might.'

'Aren't you going to tell me what happened?' He could not understand her silence. 'If I've made a mistake, then I'm sorry, but what am I supposed to believe?'

She turned her head away, and he saw the glint of tears in her eyes. 'Me, perhaps.'

For a second time his conscience smote him; Callith had told him often enough he was careless of other people's feelings and overly concerned with his own, an accusation of selfishness he did not care for overmuch. 'Try me,' he suggested.

'It isn't easy, Mallory,' she said, making an effort. 'Although I knew you were here, in Venture, and that it was likely we'd meet again. It must be a shock for you.'

'Under the circumstances, for you too.' He smiled. 'Oramen told me I'd have an interesting morning – our seeress,' he added, seeing her puzzlement. 'She forecasts the tides and winds for us, and she has the *sight*, a little.'

Asher brushed the explanation aside, asking bluntly: 'Did you grant Lewes the farm?'

'No, although he petitions for it every year since you left.' The reminder reduced his level of sympathy. 'I said he must wait the full eight years to assume your death. You should have sent me word, Ash. You had no right to walk out, and none to keep his inheritance from him.'

'*His* inheritance?' Her eyes blazed. 'Mine, rather.'

'His,' Mallory said firmly. 'You knew when you married him it would become his one day. That is his right under the law.'

'And I have none?'

It had not occurred to him before to see the question from her perspective, and it gave him pause. 'No,' he admitted. 'Your children would have an interest but not you, unless Lewes put you aside.'

She shook her head. 'He would never have done that; not if it meant loss to him.'

'Then *why*? Why did you leave him?'

She turned to face him, her expression strained. 'It's difficult, Mallory. I will tell you because I must, I know that. Give me your word you won't tell Lewes where I am?'

'He could have you brought back, that is his legal right.'

'But you won't help him. I'm not a piece of land or a horse. Promise me?'

He could not refuse, although as city councillor he was now responsible for upholding the law. 'Very well,' he agreed shortly, wondering what her husband could have done to frighten her so badly; her fear softened his mood.

'Thank you.' Relief was evident in her voice. 'And for not giving in to him for all those years.'

'Where did you go? Where have you been all this time?'

'To my mother's cousin – Varah. Do you remember her? She lived a day's journey from Venture, and she sent me here, to friends who helped me find work and somewhere to live. I didn't go away with another man, Mallory. I came here alone, and have lived alone for all six years.'

He had always been able to tell when she was lying, and she spoke the truth now. He relaxed. 'Then why did you go?' he asked, for still her flight made no sense to him. 'Did Lewes mistreat you?'

'When he felt like it. But that wasn't the reason I left.' He saw her hands clench into fists at the memory, and felt an impulse of murderous rage towards the husband who had dared abuse her. Her friendship with his family should have been sufficient protection for her, if common decency was not enough: until he remembered her stiff-necked pride, and knew she would never have complained, not even to Callith.

'You should have told us.'

She looked suddenly remote, diminishing his self-importance. 'Why? What could you have done? I was his wife, his *property*. And you were away, and Callith newly married.'

He could not explain the strong, protective urge that made him angry, but with himself, not her, for having had no power to defend her. 'Even so,' he said irritably. 'You should have come to us.'

'As I said, *that* was not the reason I left,' she continued, disregarding his comment. 'It was the night Mother and Father died, that night – ' She broke off, lips still parted, as if the pain of those hours were still vivid in her mind.

'Then was it that? The shock?' He softened his voice; to lose both parents the same night was enough to daunt the bravest woman, and she had been only twenty or so at the time, married barely a year. And to a man who gave her no comfort, so it seemed.

'You still don't understand!' She sounded as if he were trying her endurance, and it offended him. She put a hand to her head, as if it ached, then continued more calmly: 'It's true, that was a great shock. I went to the farm when they first came down with the fever, but it was very quick. Only a day. Mother died first, then Father. I was with them at the end. I did everything that had to be done, made all the arrangements for the burning. That was bad, yes. But that wasn't why I ran away. It was something else that happened that night.'

Mallory listened in silence; he would have understood if loneliness and misery had been the cause of her flight, for Lewes was not a man to give sympathy when her loss meant his gain. But that did not explain Asher's reluctance to give her side of the story, and he wondered what more there could be, what she could be hiding from him.

'There are things worse than loss.' She must have seen his confusion, for she went on: 'I had to go home to him, to Carling's, once everything was ready. To Lewes. To tell him.' There was remembered unhappiness in her eyes. 'I married him because Father wanted me to; because he and Mother were growing old, and wanted to see me settled, with a partner who could help me run the farm. I was young, and silly, and thought he would do as well as another, and he was a hard worker; I even thought we could be happy. He behaved well – before we were married.'

Mallory had a sudden image of her on her wedding day, a memory of himself dancing with her and teasing her about the night to come; Melanna, his wife, and Callith had been there too, for the wedding was lavish by village standards. Asher had looked happy, as a bride should, and beautiful, in a pale blue dress cut low at the neck, and he remembered feeling a stirring of desire for her, and rejecting it angrily. It was her wedding day, and his wife was present. 'I wish – ' he began hesitantly, not sure what he wanted to say.

'It was only afterwards, on our wedding night, that he told me the truth.' She made the statement without inflexion, but Mallory thought it more revealing than anything else she had said. 'He wanted to be sure I was under no illusions he loved me, or even liked me; he wanted the land, and I was an only child, so it would all come to me. He had decided to marry me long ago, and wanted me to know he didn't care how I felt. I was not a person to him, but a possession, a means to gain his ends. I think he hated me at times; as I learned to hate him.'

She was shaking, although she tried to hide it; Mallory saw Lewes had succeeded in hurting her badly. He wished there were some comfort he could offer, but it was too late. 'Go on,' he urged. 'What happened that night?'

'I walked back to Carling's in the dark; it was very late, but there were still lights on in the front of the house, so I knew he was there and not asleep; waiting, gloating. I didn't want to go in.'

'But you did?'

She nodded, compressing her lips. 'I had to. I went in through the kitchen and heard voices. I wondered who would have come so late, and at such a time, for the whole village knew about my family. One of the voices was *his*, but it was the other – '

'The other – what?' They had reached the point she had been trying to hide; Mallory was sure of it, and felt himself tense, expecting some dread revelation.

She was so pale he thought she would faint; with obvious effort, she went on: 'The accent was strange. That was what puzzled me first, so I waited outside the parlour door, listening. They were talking about Tyrrel – you remember him? He farmed land north of the village. The grey men took him to the camps for speaking out against the new taxes; he was always hot-tempered, always complaining. He had bought a strip of land Lewes wanted, and Lewes was furious.' Unconsciously, she rubbed a hand along her arm, as though some part of his anger had touched her also. 'Lewes was a collaborator, Mallory. He was informing against our friends and neighbours, just for money. The man he was talking to was a Kamir; in our own home, Lewes was betraying us. *That* was what I married.'

She looked so serious, so bitter, that he almost laughed in his relief, and was hard put to convert the sound into a cough. Her story explained the lack of communication, the apparent betrayal of his friendship he had found hardest to forgive. No wonder she had run away if that was what she believed. Yet he found it hard to credit Lewes was a traitor; they had never been friends, but they had been drinking companions often enough.

'Asher, could you have been mistaken? I mean,' he went on hurriedly, 'you had just lost both your parents. It would be natural enough if you'd overheard a few words and assumed the worst.'

She sat so still she might have been carved from stone.

'Asher?' He spoke her name twice more, still getting no response. He put a hand on her shoulder, alarmed at the extreme rigidity of her body.

She flung his hand away with a violence that surprised them both; brown eyes blazed into his.

'I *know*. I heard them. Don't tell me what I did or didn't hear. I was married to Lewes for a year, and I knew him. What do you know about him and his secrets, about the nights he went out after dark and came home with the dawn? What do you know about where he went and what he did and who his friends were?' She made a violent, dismissive gesture with her right hand. 'Don't try to patronize me, or tell me I was in shock. *I was there, and I know what I heard!*'

He had never seen her like this; she had always been quick-tempered, but the old Asher would never have spoken with such uncontrolled vehemence. 'Calm down!' he said sharply. 'I didn't say I didn't believe you. All I said was you might have made a mistake. Remember, I knew Lewes too, if not as well as you, and it's hard to believe he was a traitor.'

'Why? Because he could take his ale and display other such *manly* virtues?' Mallory had never heard the word spoken so contemptuously. 'You're talking to me, Asher! A person. My hearing is as good as yours, my intelligence just as capable of understanding *what* I hear!' She breathed fast, and again put a hand to the back of her head. 'I didn't run away because Lewes was a bad husband, or because we quarrelled, as you seem to want to think. I ran away because he would have killed me if he'd caught me. He came after me that night, heard me in the passage. I was lucky. I managed to get into the yard and hid among the trees, and before he could set the dogs on me I'd caught the pony and was too far away for him to find me. But don't say again I might have been *mistaken!*'

Mallory found he almost believed her; it was not that he doubted her veracity, but rather that she had convinced herself her story was true in order to justify escape from a violent marriage.

'All right, I accept what you say.' He saw the fury fade from her eyes. 'What do you want me to do about it?'

'You?' She looked at him in blank astonishment. 'Why should you do anything?'

'Because you're my responsibility, here even more than at Kepesake. Did you think I'd not care because of something Lewes did?' He paused, waiting for a reaction, but none came. 'I don't know how you live, Asher, but there's no need for you to work. Callith would never forgive me if I didn't help you. You could even go and live with her, in Fate; she'd be very happy to have you as a companion.' The prospect appealed to him greatly, and he smiled at the thought of the two of them together again. Motherhood had failed to dim his young sister's spirits. 'Or something else could be arranged, if you'd prefer.' He faltered, sensing in her neither gratitude nor acceptance.

'I don't want your help, Mallory. I don't need it and never did.' She was still very pale. 'I don't want anything at all from you. I thought you were a friend, or I wouldn't have told you so much. But you're not my father, nor my keeper.'

The sound of footsteps coming down the trail diverted his attention; they were sitting quite close to the track, and he had no desire for Asher, nor himself, to be seen in such an apparently compromising situation. Their close conversation would look at best amorous, at the worst conspiratorial.

'Get up,' he whispered. 'There's someone coming. We should go further into the trees.'

She did not argue, moving with a swiftness that spoke an equal determination to keep out of sight. Gathering his cloak, Mallory followed her deeper into the pines until they were far enough from the track to be safely hidden. Neither of them spoke as they watched a thin young man pass down and out of sight, whistling cheerfully as he went.

It was some time after the footsteps faded from hearing that Mallory laid down his cloak again. Asher looked much more herself, the interval of silence between them evidently having produced a soothing effect.

'Now, can we begin again?' Mallory smiled down at her, for she was a good eight inches shorter than himself, though taller than Honora; for the first time he noticed the sadness in her face, and wondered how the years since she came to Venture had dealt with her. 'What are we going to do with you?'

Asher was strongly tempted to sweep out and leave him sitting there. The disappointment of discovering him no different from any of the other men with whom she had dealings was a blow, for she had always believed him possessed of a natural sense of justice. She had trusted him to know her well enough to see her as a person, not someone automatically less capable than himself by reason of her sex. The inequity of his attitude filled her with a rage as vain as it was impossible to express, and for a moment she hated him for not understanding her anger, nor its cause. She wanted to shock him, to revenge herself on him for the injustices which had forced her to leave home and friends, to hide herself in a strange city which had, at first, proved both frightening and incomprehensible. Yet she did not. She put a hand to the back of her head, which felt tight, a warning of pain, and tried to massage the taut muscles in her neck.

'Mallory, I have friends, a home, and work here in Venture. There's no need for you to worry about me, I assure you,' she said, striving for patience. 'In two years Lewes can presume me dead and marry again, or whatever he chooses. Let it be.'

'What work do you do?' She saw him looking at her hands, as though he expected to see them red and rough from domestic service, and smiled to herself.

'I'm a chief clerk at the Treasury.'

The silence with which he greeted the information made up for a great deal. That the news was unwelcome as well as a surprise was immediately apparent, for Mallory frowned irritably.

'It sounds very unsuitable.'

Asher was amused. 'You've a lot to learn, Mallory. As you'll discover, about half the city is run by women, thanks to your brother. He found us cheap and effective; the cost of running Venture fell by a third during his time on Council, because you pay us much less than men.'

'Perhaps I should congratulate you. I always knew you were intelligent.'

She could see he hated being made to feel in the wrong, and rejoiced. 'So you see,' she said quietly, 'there's no need for you to feel responsible for me.'

She could see he dismissed her words without a second thought, although she thought his shoulders sagged a little, as if her own weight had been added to whatever heavy burdens he already carried. 'Don't talk such nonsense,' he said sharply. 'Matters can't be left like this. What if you want to marry again?'

The question had never occurred to her, but her answer came at once. 'No.'

'I can understand that.'

She stared at him, surprised by the bitter note in his voice. 'Is something wrong with Melanna?'

'She died – no, don't be sorry. She died in childbed – but the child wasn't mine, I'd been away too long for that. Who knows how many lovers she had while I was gone!'

Asher felt her initial sympathy fade. *He was unfaithful to her; Callith told me. He made no secret of it.* She knew a desire to defend Melanna in her death, for she had liked her, and known how lonely she had been running the Kepesake estate during Mallory's long absences. 'She paid a heavy price.'

He turned on her angrily. 'She was my *wife*! She had no *right* to bed another man, much less to bear his child.'

'Perhaps not. But you went with other women, and you're still alive and here. What gives you the right to judge her so harshly?'

'You – you would sympathize with her! And how many lovers have *you* had?' An angry glare accused her of complicity with the dead Melanna. 'Is that why you defend her?'

'My actions are no concern of yours,' she retorted. 'You think you can do whatever you want, and not worry about the consequences because you don't bear children. Did you never think about Melanna? Did you never think she might have feelings of her own? Or do you believe that only what *you* feel is real?'

'How can any man trust a woman to bear his sons, and be sure they're *his*, unless he makes her faithful?' Mallory was looking at her as if he hated her, and her head began to pound, uncomfortably, from the strain of so much emotion.

'Is that how you see us? As nothing more than vehicles for bearing *your* children, not even leaving us our own?' His attitude saddened her, and she said wistfully: 'Don't you think women might want more than to be wives and mothers? We have our dreams, too, just as you do. When I was a little girl, I wanted to run away to sea, and visit all the lands of the Dominion.'

The admission forced a smile from him. 'Did you?'

'For years. I think I would still like to travel the seas. I was going to be a cabin boy.' She read in his expression the dawning of reluctant recognition of her frustrated ambitions. Feeling better, she went on: 'And I bet you don't know what Callith wanted to do!'

'What was that?'

'She was going to be a doctor.' Mallory let out a shout of laughter, as she had meant him to. 'She was going to come to the medical school here.'

'Oh, that's priceless!' He had to mop his eyes.

'Do you remember the time I fell out of that apple tree, and hurt my leg? Callith bound it up so tightly it went numb, and I thought I'd be crippled for life!'

'Oh, I do.' He was caught up in the sudden mood of reminiscence. 'And when I had the fever one summer, and she tried to bathe my forehead with some concoction she'd invented – the one that smelled of bad eggs! I wished I could die.'

'Think what the world has missed.' Asher laughed. Mallory shuddered theatrically, suddenly the man she knew, no longer the enemy. The pounding in her head diminished as she relaxed.

'A narrow escape.' He sobered quickly. 'Let's not argue, Ash.'

'I don't want to.' She sat back, looking out through the trees; all she could see was more of the tall pines, and, further out, the sea, the sun glinting on its seemingly unruffled surface. Venture, below, was barely visible through the greenery and the branches. 'Will you miss the sea?'

'Yes.' That he said no more told her she had touched a raw nerve. 'Ash, I'm not trying to change the subject, but we should be talking about the Oracle.'

'I know.' She had almost forgotten it in the course of their discussion, and did not relish the reminder.

'Don't look like that!' He hesitated. 'I know you always said you didn't believe in divination or the Oracle, but this is different. You're not a child now, to refuse to believe whatever you don't like. Even you must admit it to be more than coincidence that you and I should meet again, here, in front of the Oracle, and that it should have summoned us both.'

'Perhaps.' But it was what she herself thought.

'It's strange that we should be so fated, that we should both be searching for Vallis.'

'So is half of Darrian,' Asher observed tartly.

'Why are you looking for her?'

She looked at him sharply, but there was only curiosity in his expression. 'For the same reason as you, I imagine. I and some friends want to find her.'

'Friends? What friends?' He was frowning again 'Are you mixed up in some resistance group?'

'Not exactly.' She paused, uncertain how much she ought to tell him. 'Just some women friends.'

'Are you trying to tell me you're part of a political group?' He was still smiling, but there was an edge to his voice.

'Not really, although *you* might say we were political. It's just a group of us who try to help others in trouble.' His expression irritated her. 'The Council of Venture has always put women to one side, as if our problems were in some way separate from the real world – a man's real world. So we women act for ourselves.'

'Doing what, precisely?'

'We offer help – financial, legal or practical – to women; even slave-women. You'll see how much hardship there is in Venture, especially for mothers of small children with no one to turn to. The Council makes no provision for them because their financial contribution to the city is small – or that's the excuse,' she added coolly. 'We even offer a refuge to people like myself, whom the law would force back to fathers or husbands, or even mothers, who can represent a greater danger to our safety than a walk in even the worst part of the city.'

'Breaking the law is foolish for someone in your position,' he said stiffly. 'I hardly think these seem suitable friends for you.'

'I have a responsibility to them, Mallory. These people helped me when I needed them, when Varah sent me here to them. If I can repay them in any way, I must. You should be able to see that.'

'And how does this lead you here, to a search for Vallis?'

'If it comforts you, I didn't want to come to the Oracle at all.' Remembering Margit's coercion still stung. 'But I gave my word I would, and ask about the missing girl.'

'But why? You haven't explained.'

She looked at him. 'Nor have you. If I tell you, it's as a friend, not as city councillor. Agreed?'

'Certainly.'

'It's in our interest, even more than yours, for Vallis to be found, for the financial hardship of the tribute falls most heavily on us; slave labour keeps wages very low for menial or domestic work.' Mallory nodded. 'But all we knew until now is what everyone else knows, that someone came and took Vallis away from the palace in Fate when she was only a child, a tall, fair man who was not a Kamir.'

He was not impressed. 'But why consult the Oracle now?'

'Because we had a new lead recently. Listen, this mustn't go further.' She was worried about the ethics of her proposed disclosure, for while he might accept a women's small self-help group, he might be more agitated about some of their other activities.

'It won't.'

He had never given her cause to doubt his word. Reluctantly, she made up her mind. 'One of our group has just come back from Saffra, and she brought news from a woman who escaped from the internment camp near Chance.'

'Saffra?' Mallory interrupted. 'What was your friend doing there?'

Asher cleared her throat. 'Escorting two escaped slaves; it's something we all agreed we must do, when possible. We've an underground network between there and here to hide them on the journey, all tried and trusted.'

'You must be mad!' He was staring at her in disbelief. 'What if you're caught?'

'We've access to travel passes and other papers. How do you think I got mine? I could hardly use my real ones, since they give me out as married and living near Chance. Mine're very good forgeries, describing me as a native of Venture.' Seeing him about to interrupt again, she hurried on, 'We're very careful, I assure you. It's a difficult trip, but the Saff welcome all the slaves who dare make the journey. You know how deeply they abominate slavery. My friend brought back news of a girl in the internment camp, a girl who was obviously important in some way, and we decided we should find out if it could be Vallis.'

'You can't do this!' Mallory was not to be distracted from his primary goal. 'It's simply too dangerous. I won't let you – '

'Mallory,' Asher interrupted him, 'how many times do I have to say this? *What I do is none of your business.* I'm only telling you all this because of the Oracle, and because I think it's relevant.'

He caught her wrist. 'You are not to go on, is that clear? You are my responsibility, just as much as Callith, or Kelham's widow and children!' He was, she saw, perfectly serious. 'I can't stand back and see you risk your life, not even for a good cause. If I have to knock you on the head and send you down to Kepesake, I'll do it, if you don't see sense and give me your word to do as I say!'

It was the final straw. Asher snatched her hand away, too angry to consider what she was doing or saying, wanting only to force him to understand. In her mind, Mallory's demands and her fear that the Oracle was real merged together, both forces trying to destroy her control over her own life, reducing her to nothing.

'Listen to me! Just this once,' she said tightly. 'I am a grown woman, perfectly capable of making my own decisions. I have made a life here for myself that I consider worth the having, and where I can be useful, and where I have my own responsibilities which are nothing to do with you. I know the risks of what I do and am willing to take them. I *know* you are only trying to *save me from myself,*' she delivered the phrase with the utmost contempt, 'but you're going to have to accept that these are choices I make for myself. What would you say if I told you your life was not your own responsibility, not yours to risk? No one has the right to tell me what to do! And if you won't accept that, then I'll leave, now, and never see you again.'

'Asher – '

She did not hear whatever he said, increasingly conscious of an intense pressure building inside her head; she felt dizzy and sick, as if she were going to faint. She put a hand to her forehead, trying to ease the ache between her temples.

'What is it? What's wrong?' Mallory was hovering over her, only concern registering in his voice.

'I feel very strange.' But the roaring was relaxing its hold a little, and her vision began to clear. 'No. It's all right. I feel better now.'

'I should take you back to the city.'

She shook her head, then regretted it. 'No. Let's finish what we were talking about.'

'All right, you do look better.' He surveyed her critically. 'As to what you were saying: I won't accept I have no responsibility for you. However,' he went on, before she could protest, 'I agree with some of what you said. My reaction came from concern for your safety; but you're right, in that the choice must be yours – though that doesn't mean I won't try to persuade you to change your mind. Is that fair?'

Asher felt a rush of exhilaration. 'Yes, more than fair.' It was more than any other man in his position would have conceded. 'You always were a tyrant!'

'Only when necessary.' He shrugged, the subject apparently closed. 'So, you think this girl in the camp might be Vallis. What was it the Oracle said – "*wings bound and flightless*"? That would fit with some sort of imprisonment.'

'But I didn't understand the rest. It sounded as if she didn't know who she was: "*layered in forgetfulness*".'

'It's possible. She was only five when she disappeared.' Mallory considered the question. 'Yes, it's quite possible.'

'But who would have put her in the camp?'

'I've no idea. The person might be dead by now. It would be a safe hiding place, of course.' His expression lightened. 'Don't you see, Asher? The Oracle said you could discover where Vallis was held, and you have. "*Within your compass lies the means to pierce the veil.*" And you were to tell me. That's what the Oracle meant, that I wouldn't find her unless you helped me.'

'That doesn't explain it all.' His instant assumption of the major role in the search grated on her. 'I'm sure you'd like to believe that, but what about the rest: "*Mark what may from what must be, in what was lies what will be*"?'

'I don't know.' He was not taking her quite seriously. 'I intended to go down to Kepesake in a week or so, in any case. I'll find a way to take a look at this girl while I'm there.'

'I'm coming with you.'

His reaction was automatic. 'It's too dangerous.'

'I can disguise myself from Lewes but the Oracle said this search involved us both,' she reminded him. 'If you go alone, you might not succeed.'

'It's impossible!'

'You can't stop me.'

He smiled unpleasantly. 'I can try!'

'Think about it, Mallory. You want to believe all I had to do was tell you of this girl's existence, but what if you're wrong? If I come with you, it can't harm her. But if I don't, something may happen to prevent your finding her. *That's* the risk, and I don't think it's yours to take.'

'You always had to be right.' He let out a long breath. 'Very well, Ash. You can come.'

'Generous of you!' But she had won.

'How soon can you get away? We shall need more than ten days, there and back and some time at Kepesake.'

She produced her trump card. 'I think I can arrange an official leave.' She told him of Avorian's offer to make up the tribute shortfall, and was surprised he already knew of it. 'It's my job to make up the totals, and it may be I shall have to visit some of the southern districts to check the accounts. I've done such trips before, normally with one of the Treasury clerks. I could ask her and another friend to come and do my work while you and I go on to Kepesake.'

'That would be helpful.' He displayed none of his earlier incredulity at the responsibilities of her position. 'Let me know if you can arrange it, and I'll travel at the same time.'

It was clear he saw her as an encumbrance interfering in *his* business, but Asher let it rest for the moment. 'I'll know in a week.'

'Tell me, is there anything else you think I should know about your activities here?' He was smiling faintly. 'I mean, what do *you* actually do with your group of women?'

'I organize our funding.'

'I'd forgotten you were good with accounts.' He leaned back on his elbows, making himself more comfortable, apparently in no hurry to return to the city. 'How do you manage for money?'

'It's our greatest problem, as you can imagine. We all give what we can but it's appallingly little, and there are so many in need.' Prudently, she did not tell him of her other, more lucrative, source of funds. 'Perhaps you could help us, as a councillor.'

'I think there're more urgent problems to deal with first.'

'But that's the point.' She rounded on him. 'They say there's always something more urgent, or more important, than the

needs of women and children! It's a question of values. We're half
– no, more than half – the city's population, but our needs are
invariably put last – which is to say ignored. Can you really say
that's fair or reasonable?'

'No,' he said slowly. 'Not put like that.'

'I'd forgotten how easy you were to talk to.' She was not sure,
later, why she said it. 'Even at your most annoying; like when
you fell in love for the first time, and discovered girls were
different from boys.' She paused, remembering. 'You were a
dreadful prig then, suddenly telling us girls didn't climb trees,
when only the year before you were helping us to the top of the
tallest.'

'Asher!' He sat up, outraged.

'Don't look so shocked! I know when we were young Callith
and I would hang on your every word, but that was different. And
you were five years older, anyway.'

'I'd have boxed your ears then!'

'Do you know, I haven't asked you what you've done in the last
six years.' The omission struck her forcibly; shamingly, she had
been too engrossed in her own problems to consider his.

'You and Callith always used to ask what I'd brought you
instead of whether I'd had a good journey.' He smiled at the
memory. 'There's nothing to tell. Ships and ports and markets, as
ever.'

'It must be strange to stay in one place now, with a sister-in-law
and nephews and nieces – or are you sending them down to
Kepesake?'

'Not if Kelham's widow can help it!' Asher saw the unknown
woman evidently possessed, from Mallory's long-suffering tone,
a mind of her own. 'I suppose I'll get used to it, in time; living in
Venture, I mean.'

'It's not so bad. So Perron takes your place?' Asher mused,
remembering him only as a sickly boy, younger than herself and
unable to join in their games. She said: 'Poor Mallory.' And meant
it.

'Perhaps I should employ *you* as my clerk.'

She scowled at him. 'Not a hope!'

'But I should enjoy it.' He grinned. 'In some ways, you haven't
changed a bit!'

Asher felt herself relax, sensing that at some point during the
past hours – how long was it? – they had progressed from
argument to dissonance, and back to something approaching
their old friendship; except that in the past he had always been

114

the leader, she the dutiful follower. That was a mistake she would never make again. Yet, despite their present differences, there was an ease, an acceptance that came from having known one another all their lives, that made it easier to talk to him than to anyone else, except perhaps Mylura.

'I suppose we should get back. It's getting late.' She looked up at the sky, astonished to find it well on in the afternoon.

'True.' But he did not move. 'It's good to see you again, Ash. We all missed you.'

She guessed he, too, felt at ease. 'Tell me, Mallory,' she asked hesitantly, 'what was it that changed you? That year, I mean – the invasion year? Before that you were different, a real friend, but afterwards it was never quite the same, as if you couldn't look at me or Callith without thinking *"that's a girl"*, as if we'd changed fundamentally while you were at sea.'

'How odd you should ask that; I was thinking about it myself the other night. And it wasn't you, but me.' Mallory rolled on to his side, leaning on his left elbow, frowning. 'Since you don't seem easily shocked, you might as well know why.' He paused, then went on: 'That was the fourth year I'd been to sea, but it was the first the men on board ship treated me as a man, not a boy, and took me with them when they went to the stews in Refuge.' He glanced up at her, but she was not really surprised. 'When I came home, you and Callith looked different. You were growing up and letting down your skirts, and I knew as well that all the men would have laughed at me for spending my days playing with two little girls. Not a *manly* activity,' he added with a half-grin.

'Strange, isn't it, that *manly* is supposed to encompass all sorts of positive virtues, but *womanly*, if you say it about a man, is a dreadful insult,' Asher mused. '*Womanly* always seems to mean being weak, or soft, or having babies.'

'But those are the qualities men like in women.'

'Are they?' Asher gave an unwomanly snort. 'Only if you believe the Fates created us just for your amusement.' But saying even this, now that she acknowledged they must exist in some form or other, was suddenly terrifying to her; she wondered if it could possibly be true that there was no greater meaning to her existence than that. A feeling of sick familiarity grew in her stomach as she recalled some of Lewes' more picturesque taunts about her own lack of worth.

'What's troubling you?' Mallory was watching her with concern.

'Nothing.' She was not ready to talk about these feelings, not to anyone. 'How do we keep in contact from now on? I can hardly come openly to your house.'

'No.' He considered the problem for a moment. 'By messenger, I think. Mark any note for my private attention. And where do I find you?'

'At an old inn in Scribbers.' She gave him the address.

'It's one of the things I dislike most about cities; all this formality, I mean. At Kepesake it would be much easier.'

Asher nodded idly. 'You're an important person now. I shall have to bob my head and show you a proper respect when you come to the Treasury.'

'Not before time!' But he was joking. 'I wish you hadn't dyed your hair.'

'Why? It was only a precaution, in case Lewes came looking for me.'

'It doesn't suit you.'

'Yours is receding, but I didn't mention it – until now.'

He laughed. 'Message received.' Asher warmed to him, liking him the more for his sense of humour, and even, against her better judgment, for his sense of duty. He, at least, was a man who knew his responsibilities, and would not shirk them.

I wonder, has anything I said today made a difference to his life, or mine, or anyone's, or was everything we said and did predestined? Have we any choice at all in our actions?

The idea terrified her, for it meant that everything she wanted to believe in was a lie, her fears the only truths. The certainty she had known when the Oracle spoke to her was gone, but she had opened her mind to doubt and the fear that accompanied it. What sickness could there be in the minds of the Fates, if they existed, to give her a life destined for pain, to make her suffer in being a woman and thus subject and held in contempt, even deep dislike, by the men who controlled her world? What reason could they have for such cruelty?

'It was only – Lewes was always making comments about how I looked, because he knew it hurt me.' She made the apology so he should not misunderstand her. 'My friends here, they taught me I could value myself, and not rely on his opinion.'

'He's a fool.'

She glanced at him, and saw he meant it; he was far too honest a person to use such weapons against an opponent. 'I have to get back. My friends will be wondering where I am.'

'And I have to buy fairings for my young niece and nephews.'

He got to his feet and reached out a hand to her. 'May I buy one for you, too?'

'No, thank you.' She realized, with a sinking heart, that he still saw her as the Asher he had known, a childhood playmate.

But I'm not. She's no longer a part of me, not any more. Asher of Venture was a very different person, one who had put aside the past and learned to live apart from the shame of her marriage; *she* had a useful existence, one which allowed her to respect herself as the old Asher had not.

They rejoined the track, walking in silence; a soft breeze blew, and the scent of the pines was stronger as they descended. Asher felt quite well again, the headache that had troubled her completely gone.

As they emerged from the belt of trees, the city came into view below, and she heard Mallory sigh. For a while, it had seemed they existed outside time and place, and she found she, too, was unwilling to plunge back into the maelstrom inside the walls. She stifled the feeling, not wanting to admit to herself any dissatisfaction with her present existence.

'You go first through the gate. I'll wait here and follow later,' Mallory said quietly as they drew near the walls.

'It would be better.' She stopped, feeling awkward and not knowing what to say. 'I'll send word, when I've seen Avorian.'

'Be careful of yourself. Come to me if you need anything.'

'Thank you.' She would not, but the offer was well-meant. They stood together, neither of them speaking, unwilling to part now the moment had come.

'Welcome home, Ash!' Mallory did not touch her, but, with a surge of happiness, Asher could feel the warmth of his gladness at seeing her again, at finding her alive. She, who had no family now, still had a home in his affection, roots in their shared history, and it surprised her to discover quite how much difference it made to her to know it. She turned away, unwilling to expose her vulnerability through her expression.

'I must go.'

She left him, walking rapidly, descending the hillside with exaggerated care, acutely conscious of his eyes following her; but she knew that for the moment he saw her as a friend, only second as a woman, and was glad of it. He was not like Lewes.

How much would her life, and Mallory's, change as a result of their meeting, of that one day? Asher sensed that in the future she would look back and say events came 'before' or 'after' her reunion with Mallory, itself a crucial point in her life.

Was it sensible to continue to hope everything, her meeting Mallory before the Oracle, was only coincidence? What if she had not agreed to visit the Oracle, had fought against Margit's coercion? Would that have been possible, or would the Fates have found some other way to bring her to the citadel at precisely the right time? Was everything pre-ordained? What if I hadn't run away from Lewes that night? Then I'd be dead. But had she made the choice to run, or had the Fates made it for her, that she should survive and come to Venture, and befriend Margit, and thus come to the citadel at precisely this time on this day? The thought made her dizzy, for she understood the full implications of such a belief.

She could not accept there were no choices in her power to make. The prophecy of the Oracle had been vague, after all. And what had it said: *'Look, with eyes that choose to see. Look, or lose.'* That suggested she had a choice.

As she reached the Nevergate, she saw there was only one solution to her difficulty. One way or another, the next few weeks should prove the point. If the girl in the internment camp was Vallis, then she would *know* that her belief in her own control over her life was an illusion; everything in life was predestined.

And if not – what then?

It was a question to which there was no answer; or none, at least, that she could discover for the present. But at least if the girl were not Vallis, she herself would still have the hope of freedom.

Chapter Six

The seven days that had elapsed since her meeting with Mallory had been peaceful for Asher. She had received only one un-expected communication: a small crystal flask of scent she supposed to be the fairing he had offered to buy her.

The morning sun was warm after days of cold, gusting winds that had battered the harbour, sending up massive waves of spray across the quays and keeping even the most daring fisherman ashore. Only that morning, rumour had it that another of Councillor Hamon's ships had been caught in the storm and sunk with all hands, unlucky news that spread a pall of gloom throughout the city as a harbinger of worse to come. Asher, however, was more concerned about her own errand; she shifted the heavy ledgers to rest on her hip and began to climb the hill that would take her to Avorian's mansion, experiencing an unaccustomed fit of nerves, borne partly from an awareness of guilt and partly from simple apprehension.

'Make way, make way!'

She stepped to one side to allow a troop of grey men to pass, heading for the Kamiri governor's compound further up and to her left. In their midst stumbled five men and a woman, chained together, all bearing the slave-brand.

They must be for the spring Games . . . Asher shuddered inwardly, knowing it was impossible to help the six; they must have either been caught attempting escape, or taken for some other imagined crime against their owners. The grey men held their Games twice a year, an abomination they had brought with them from their homeland. Games? Slaughter, they should call them. Convicted slaves were forced to take part in a series of games of chance where the stakes were always life or death; many survived one, or even two of the trials, but it was rare indeed for even one to survive them all.

The troop disappeared inside the spiked walls of the compound, and Asher resumed her upward trudge. If Avorian should discover her part in the theft, the Games could be her own fate; although there was some comfort in the thought that the Oracle had suggested no such ending.

Or was there? Her mind still scurried between doubt and certainty, refusing to accept belief or the reverse.

She had entered the north-west corner of the city, dotted with the large houses and walled gardens of the merchant clans. The unfortunate Councillor Hamon's house showed signs of disrepair, in keeping with his increasingly impoverished status. Mallory's, however, which stood higher, displayed every evidence of continued prosperity. Two small boys were visible in the terraced gardens, playing some game or other, watched by a girl a little older; Asher guessed them to be Mallory's niece and nephews. The angle of incline gave her a clear view of them briefly before she climbed higher and they were hidden from sight by high walls.

Avorian's mansion stood highest of all, an immense structure fronted by ornately patterned railings and backed by a brick wall that hid the gardens; his status as the richest and luckiest man in Venture was made abundantly plain to allcomers. Although the gates stood open, two watchmen kept a close eye on her as she approached, ignoring the painfully thin man in tattered rags who sat beside the railings, an empty pewter plate and mug beside him suggesting it was his usual pitch. He was presumably another of Avorian's luck-charms, a minor expense for a wealthy man.

The house was bulky, a three-storey rectangle of pale grey stone with a mass of windows looking down on the city. Avorian's clan symbol had been carved on the cornice over the main entrance, a huge wolf's head that stared down at her, piercing carved eyes reminding her uncomfortably of Stern and her own guilt. Several armed men stood about the foreground, all in Avorian's grey livery with wolf's head badges at their shoulders.

She stated her errand and the gatekeeper waved her through. The forecourt had been paved, but immense formal flower-beds gave colour to what might otherwise have been a dark, if massive, façade, for all that it faced east and the sea. Asher followed the path to the main doors, which were open, and went in, only to be instantly accosted by yet another of Avorian's servants.

'What is your business?'

An elderly man rose from his desk to the right of the doors, regarding her with a look of deep suspicion. Ink-stained fingers held out his quill like a weapon, pointed at her; he was bald, with a beak of a nose, and ears that stuck out at sharp angles to his skull.

'The Chief Councillor asked me to attend him this morning,' Asher answered politely, indicating her ledgers.

'On what business?'

'From the Treasury.'

Dark eyes snapped irritably. 'What is Darrian coming to, that we must have *women* clerks?' He gave her a disgusted look. 'Wasting our time!' Asher remained prudently silent. The old man kept her waiting, enjoying his brief moment of power, and she shifted the heavy ledgers to her other hip; at last, however, he relented, perhaps recalling his duty to his master.

'Very well.' He pointed to a bench set against the wall in the far corner of an immense hall. 'Go and sit there. I'll ask the councillor if he wishes to see you. Stay there, and don't *touch* anything!' With which parting shot he turned his back and hobbled towards a door in the left-hand wall, glancing round every few paces to see if Asher had complied. She moved to the indicated bench and sat down, favouring the clerk with a sweet smile.

Now that she had leisure to observe it, Asher saw the hall was almost as large as the Treasury, but furnished in so lavish a manner that she could only stare, open-mouthed, at the riches on display. Overhead, the ceiling was fan-vaulted, adding to the impression of height, but her eyes were drawn down to the walls and floor, everywhere displaying evidence of the success of Avorian's trading empire. Rich carpets from Petormin were spread in profusion over a costly polished-wood floor; tapestries from Asir and Baram festooned the walls, against which stood ornately carved dressers, their shelves covered with gold plate. The wolf's head insignia was much in evidence, marking wood and gold alike, and Asher was startled to see a full-size marble statue of a wolf confronting her from the far side of the hall.

The overall effect should have been garish in the extreme, but the sheer scale of the hall made the display impressive rather than vulgar, an effective showroom for Avorian's business, which was what it was. Asher wondered whether he ever thought of the disparity between this and the confined spaces of the old quarter where so many of the poorest women lived.

The old man reappeared, beckoning.

'The Chief Councillor will see you now. Make sure you don't take up much of his time, he's a busy man,' he said testily. 'In there.' Unnecessarily, he pointed to the only open door in the

121

hall. Asher picked up her ledgers and walked past him without comment.

'Mistress Asher?' Avorian stood as she entered, an unexpected courtesy; two other figures stood by the hearth. 'I hope Oban did not keep you waiting long.'

Surmising he referred to the old clerk, Asher merely inclined her head in polite confirmation. Compared to the lavishness of the hall, Avorian's private office was plain, the shelved walls only painted, the floor bare. A large desk covered with papers dominated the room, which contained little else.

'Please, be seated.' Avorian gestured to a chair opposite the desk. 'Thank you for your promptness. Do you have the figures I asked for?' He sat down and leaned forward expectantly.

'Certainly, Councillor.' She placed the ledgers before him; but, instead of opening them, he gestured to his companions.

'Mistress, do you know Lassar, my diviner?' Asher bobbed her head, her earlier fears reviving in the presence of the toad-like figure who surveyed her with an unblinking stare. He was dressed from head to foot in black, emphasizing a round, squat figure. 'And my daughter, Menna?'

'A pleasure to meet you, Mistress Asher.' The girl stepped forward gracefully, her ease of manner suggesting she was accustomed to act as mistress of the household. Asher, returning the greeting, remembered Avorian was a widower and had no sons. The girl was not very like him in appearance; wide brown eyes were set deep in an oval face framed by a mantle of hair a shade darker which she wore in a flat cap covering her ears, braided neatly at the nape of the neck into a plait reaching her waist. Her gown was a rich, dark red, cut square at the neck, about which she wore a simple choker of opals that matched the single gemstone set in a thin gold circlet about her forehead. She was not beautiful, but Asher thought there was strength of character and intelligence in the firm mouth and expressive face.

Menna returned her frank inspection with a smile, then looked enquiringly at Avorian. 'Do you wish me to stay, sir? I should be interested to hear Mistress Asher's report, if you have no objection?'

'Perhaps – ' But whatever he was about to say was lost in the sound of a loud crash as a small boy, burdened by a heavy yoke slung across his shoulders, stumbled against the door and fell into the room. He froze at finding it occupied and his load slipped from his shoulders, discharging logs of applewood all over the floor. He stared at them helplessly as they rolled noisily in every direction.

'I – I'm sorry, master,' he stammered, looking frightened. With his face turned to Avorian, it was possible to see the slave-brand on his cheek; he was very young – no more than ten or eleven – and his skin, a pale golden brown, told Asher he was an Asiri.

'Pick up this mess!' Avorian did not raise his voice, but the boy flinched.

'Come, Koris. I'll help you.' Menna put a hand on the boy's shoulder, then bent to pick up two of the nearest logs. Encouraged, Koris knelt and began to gather his load, shooting furtive glances at his master from time to time. Asher caught sight of dark bruises on his face and arms.

In Avorian's house? The fact unsettled her, not according with her initial, favourable impression of the man. She, too, stooped to retrieve some of the wood, handing the logs to Koris.

'Leave it, Menna! Let the boy do it!'

The girl deposited her load in a pile by the hearth and stood up. 'If you wish, sir,' she said pleasantly, dusting her hands on her dress. 'But the load was far too heavy for him. One of the men-servants should have brought it.'

Avorian frowned. The boy scurried about collecting the few remaining errant logs, and, when he had finished, Menna helped him replace the heavy yoke across his shoulders, then led him to the door.

'Now, Koris,' she said firmly, 'another time, come to me if they try to give you tasks beyond your strength.' The boy ducked his head and Menna sighed. 'And what has happened to your new clothes?' She plucked at a torn sleeve. 'These are only fit for the rag pile!'

The boy mumbled what was to Asher an inaudible reply, and Menna shook her head sadly. 'Very well, I will send others. Off with you to the housekeeper. Tell her I sent you, and you're to do only light work today.'

'Yes, mistress.' It was a mere whisper; it was plain he wanted to escape further notice, and Menna let him go.

'Menna!'

She turned back enquiringly, apparently surprised at the tone in which Avorian addressed her. 'Yes, sir?'

'I have told you before: you do the boy no kindness in singling him out for attention. The other servants already resent him, and you only make the situation worse!'

'I am sorry to have displeased you, sir.' Asher could not, however, discover any visible sign of regret. 'But Koris is very young and I don't like to see him bullied. His lot is hard enough,

123

poor boy.'

'The Fates have dictated his place in life; they have decreed his slavery as much as our own wealth. There is only so much luck in the world, and it is not shared out in equal measures; his state is predestined, and nothing you or I can do will change the natural order of the world.'

'So you have told me, sir,' Menna replied demurely.

'Then remember it!' Avorian must have noticed a lack of conviction in her response, for he continued: 'If it were not so, then no one could read the future as Lassar here has the power to do; there would be no Oracle. Our lot is fixed, unalterable. Poverty and slavery exist because they must, because the Fates will it. If it were not so, there would be no slaves, no poor.'

Menna bowed her head obediently, but Asher thought the stubborn set to her mouth suggested only filial duty kept her from arguing the point. He's wrong, he must be, Asher thought, suddenly angry. The poor and slaves are unlucky, yes, but it's men who make slaves, who keep wages so low that the poor have no hope of altering their condition. And am I unlucky, too, in being born a woman, as the saying is? But she, too, remained silent; it was not her place to express her views to the Chief Councillor. She caught Menna looking at her quizzically, and hastily forced a smile.

'Ah, mistress,' the girl said lightly. 'The problem is the servants – they know the presence of slaves in our cities keeps their own wages low, so they mistreat poor Koris, as if that would change anything. My father was given him in place of a debt, and there has been trouble ever since.'

Avorian tapped his fingers on the wooden surface of his desk as if impatient at the conversation. 'The figures?' he inquired mildly.

'Here, Councillor.' Hastily, Asher stood and opened the ledgers at the relevant pages; there were five in all, representing the organizational districts of the city and its environs. Lassar, who had remained by the hearth during the whole of the incident, came to join Avorian, his bulging eyes and lack of neck making him look more like a toad than ever. He touched each of the ledgers with caressing, oddly sensitive, fingers.

'As I thought.' Avorian frowned at the totals at the bottom of the pages. 'There has been a considerable decline in tribute contributions this year. Do you have a final estimate of the shortfall?'

Asher subtracted a loose piece of paper from one of the ledgers and handed it to him. 'I estimate twenty thousand gold pieces,

Councillor.'

'So much?' He seemed momentarily disconcerted, which was not surprising; it was a massive sum. 'Lassar?'

The diviner licked his full lips. 'I will ascertain, Councillor.' He walked round the desk and returned to his former place by the hearth, reaching inside his jacket for something.

Avorian turned back to Asher. 'Let me assure you, mistress,' he said smoothly, 'I mean you no discourtesy. I always verify significant calculations with Lassar. Your figures are, after all, reliant on the accuracy of the information you are given which is so often – shall we say – *distorted*?' His look invited her to agree.

'Certainly.' He was right, of course; fraud was commonplace, no matter how hard they tried to guard against it. She wondered what exactly Lassar was going to do as Menna retreated to sit in the window embrasure behind Avorian, watching the diviner with detached interest, as though his actions were, to her, a familiar sight.

'Lassar is never mistaken, he's worth more than his weight in gold,' Avorian observed conversationally. 'No ship of mine leaves the harbour without his accord. I buy nothing, bet on nothing he has not approved. Some diviners have the *sight* in regard to health, or the tides and the winds, or general good fortune, or for far-seeing, but my diviner has more than most. He is a man of many talents, although he has a special affinity with gold.' Seeing Asher's interest, he went on: 'Did you know that though gold itself is lifeless, there are fortunes and emotions which attach themselves to its flow: greed, envy, desire? Lassar has the power to concentrate his will on these, to see them as points of a compass. As you will discover.'

The diviner had subtracted a small leather pouch from a pocket of his coat. Drawing a stool towards him, he sat down and sprinkled the contents of the pouch on the fire, breathing in the blue-grey smoke that instantly rose up from the burning wood. There was suddenly a metallic smell in the room, and Asher's eyes began to water as the smoke reached her. The diviner continued to inhale deeply.

At last he spoke, in a voice sounding distant and deeper than his normal tones.

'*Ask your questions, Councillor.*'

Asher's sight began to blur as smoke from the fire thickened and spread out towards her seat; she blinked several times, trying to clear her eyes.

'Is the figure Mistress Asher has given me correct? And, if it is not, is this through falsification, miscalculation, or misinformation?'

Asher was less concerned with the questions – for she knew her calculations to be accurate, as far as such a thing was possible – than with the diviner. Was it possible he could, by some arcane means, discover the answers Avorian sought? Was this also a means of looking into the future, that Lassar could somehow *see* where the gold might be? But if that were true, then did his *sight* somehow alter events? For if the gold were, in the future, to be in the Treasury vaults, why need it be sought at all? None of it seemed likely to Asher's confused mind. The room was now hot and stuffy, and a wave of dizziness struck her; more blue smoke drifted from the fireplace, and she tried to breathe in shallow inhalations.

'Awry, yet true. I see falsehood in all, but most strongly to the south and to the west.'

Avorian nodded, listening intently. 'Inside the city, or without?'

Again, Lassar leaned forward, inhaling the choking smoke. It reminded Asher of the pit of the Oracle.

'Not here. Towards the boundaries with Chance.'

'How much may be recovered?'

'Much. Perhaps five thousand gold, in all. The emanations are strongest at a point south-south-west.'

The diviner had begun to sway, an unpleasantly hypnotic motion. Asher found herself unconsciously mimicking the movement; her head swam as she breathed in more of the metallic scent.

I shall fall asleep in a moment! She felt her eyelids begin to close, unable to resist the pressure. They were heavy, and she let them fall.

'Is there more?'

Asher could hear Avorian's voice, but only from a great distance. Her chin dropped to her chest, her mind whirling as shadow-images confronted her from behind her closed eyelids. They appeared as a series of coloured lines, like the kaleidoscope she remembered Callith owning as a child, but these stretched out and away from her, along a straight pathway. The strings did not stay still but seemed in constant movement, shifting, reaching out, curving to touch one another before moving away again. Some of the lines were much thicker than others, as if drawn by a pen with a heavy nib, but others were mere scratchings, barely visible.

126

They look like snakes, Asher thought dreamily. She tried to open her eyes, but it was too great an effort. The lines continued their writhing motion, repeating their previous patterns; their ceaseless action was urgent and disturbing, as if their movements held a meaning beyond her present ability to understand. Irritated, Asher tried to blank them out, wondering what would happen if she followed them; it almost seemed as if they were inviting her to do so.

'I have no more questions. My thanks, Lassar, as ever.' His voice broke through Asher's dream, and she stirred, shaking herself awake. The metallic smell lessened, and she could open her eyes again as the smoke turned white, then brownish-grey as the diviner poured a new substance on to the fire.

'You see?'

It was a moment before Asher realized Avorian was speaking to her. 'Yes,' she murmured, still dizzy. An unwelcome thought occurred to her: if Lassar were capable of detecting such distant fraud, surely it would be possible for him to uncover her part in the theft from Avorian's warehouse? But almost at once she berated herself for her gullibility; there was no proof that he was correct in his accusations.

Avorian coughed. 'And have you any suggestions as to how the monies can be recovered, mistress? We have only some seven weeks before the tribute must be sent. Obviously I shall dispatch a new warden to the district, but we shall need new assessments, and we cannot trust our local representatives. Fraud on such a scale suggests a wide circle of complicity.'

Asher forced herself to concentrate. 'I – yes.' She had almost missed the opportunity she had been looking for. 'This is not the first time accounts from the south-west have been falsified. I would be willing to travel there and perform any necessary calculations and checks. I've done so before.'

Avorian did not reply at once. Lassar turned and was now watching her intently.

'I hesitate,' Avorian asserted at last, 'because I do not approve of young women travelling unaccompanied. And in particular attractive young women,' he added, as if he meant it as a compliment. 'You would need at least one female companion, and an armed escort. The road south through the Forest of Marl is not safe.'

Asher strove to keep irritation out of her voice. 'There's a cashier in the Treasury I'm sure would be willing to come with me; she's done so before. And I have a friend with family near

Chance who might be willing to travel with us.'

'Have I offended you?' He gave her a warm, unnerving smile, but she did not care for the accuracy of his reading of her thoughts. 'Then I apologize, but not for my concern for your well-being, mistress. I should be pleased if you would undertake this task, for you are, I think, a lucky person, or you would not have risen to your present post. But you must be protected from those who would see you only as a woman alone and thus vulnerable. If these two women will accompany you, then I agree to your suggestion. In fact, if the timing suits, my nephew, Kerrick, is to visit our clan's estates near Chance in a week or so. You could travel in his party for much of the way, which would be added protection.'

'That is very thoughtful of you, Councillor.'

'Then I will make the necessary arrangements – travel passes, horses, and so on, and I shall speak to the Treasurer. You shall have my own authority for your searches, and I shall, of course, fund the journey for you and your companions, since it is for my benefit.'

Is this happening because of what the Oracle said, or could it be just another coincidence? But it all seemed too neat, too easy. Despite a lingering queasiness, Asher spared a thought for Mallory's discomfiture when he heard the news; he would *not* be pleased. Kerrick's reputation with women was not of the best; a fact which appeared to have escaped his uncle's awareness.

'You are very good,' she said formally.

'Ah, but it is *you* who are to save me several thousand in gold!' Asher thought there was mischief in his eyes, as if he found her entertaining in a fashion she did not quite like.

'Sir, we have offered Mistress Asher no refreshment, and I'm sure she has given up many of her leisure hours to do this work for us.' Menna had risen from the embrasure. 'If you have finished with your business, let me remedy this lack.'

'Of course.' Avorian looked to his daughter with approval. 'What should I do without you, child?' There was deep affection in his voice, and Asher listened to the exchange with interest. Perhaps, having no sons, he was willing to allow a greater freedom to his daughter than was the norm, for although very young – perhaps the same age as Mylura – Menna had an air of confidence rare for a woman from the secluded upbringing usual among her caste.

'Will you come with me?' Menna asked Asher in her clear voice.

'Thank you.' She made to stand up, but another powerful wave of dizziness struck her; her legs buckled, and she felt herself falling, the ground opening at her feet.

When she next opened her eyes, Avorian's arm was round her waist, supporting her in imitation of an embrace.

'Mistress?'

She tried to free herself, uncomfortable at his proximity, but he did not release her. 'I – forgive me. I felt faint.'

'Wait a moment. It's my fault, I forgot that the smoke affects some people, and you were much closer to it than I. Please – '

She managed to stand upright. 'If I may, I think some air would help.' Idly, she noticed Avorian had a mole on his chin, a mark that was held to foreshadow that he would be gifted with riches and held in high esteem. She was suddenly eager to get away, from the house and from him.

'Let me help you.' Menna appeared at her elbow, and Avorian at last let her go. 'Lean on me, Mistress Asher, and you will be better shortly.' Her eyes met Asher's.

'You're very kind.'

She allowed herself to be assisted across the huge hall to the main entrance, where she stood breathing in fresh-scented air that smelled only faintly of the sea and rather more of blossom and grass.

'I saw you were uneasy, mistress. Let me assure you, the Councillor meant no disrespect. He was only afraid you would fall and hurt yourself.' Menna said quietly.

'I'm sorry my feelings were so obvious.'

'Only to me.' She smiled sadly, and Asher saw she was not so innocent as she had believed. 'Please, come back inside and let me have wine sent to you. I would stay myself but I have a music lesson.' She grimaced. 'Poor man – my tutor, I mean. I have no ear, and no talent for the lute.'

Asher shook her head. 'I feel quite well, and must be back at the Treasury by noon.'

The intelligent eyes registered polite disbelief, but Menna only inclined her head. 'Then let me have the carriage brought.'

'No.' Asher saw she had been too abrupt and softened the refusal. 'Truly, the walk will do me good.'

'If you wish. Then perhaps we shall meet again, mistress. I should enjoy doing so.' She bowed slightly then re-entered the house, an upright, dignified figure. Asher waited until she was out of sight before walking away towards the gates, but had gone only a few paces when she was brought up by a shout. Turning, she saw Lassar hurrying after her, his arms filled with her ledgers.

'For you, mistress.' He held them out to her. 'The Chief Councillor sends his gratitude, and will speak to you again before you leave the city.' She acknowledged the message with as much courtesy as she could muster, wishing him far away; his continued watchfulness made her uneasy. He bowed, half-mockingly, or so she thought. 'Until we meet again, mistress.' He made it sound like a prophecy.

She could feel his eyes pursuing her all the way back to the road.

'Do you believe now, Ash?' Margit said triumphantly. 'This is all providential. Of course I'll come and do the work, and I'm sure Mylla will, too. The girl in the camp *must* be Vallis.'

Asher crumbled a piece of bread on her plate, still unsure, but whether from desire or genuine doubt she had no idea; it was still an hour before curfew, and she was restless. The common room of the hostel was crowded, for it was a cold night and rain had been falling since late-afternoon. 'And you?' she asked Mylura, who had joined them at supper. 'How do you feel about a trip south, and a few days spent scrutinizing falsified accounts?'

She grinned. 'You know me – I hate staying in one place too long. And who better to sniff out thievery than me?' She winked at Asher. 'Don't worry, I'll take your place while you go gallivanting with your councillor. Margit and I're quite capable of doing your job.'

'Mallory is *not* my councillor!' The note she had received from him in response to her news had been less than enthusiastic, the only high point of the affair to date.

'Are you sure this is sensible, Asher?' Essa asked, doubtfully. 'What if your husband should see you and try to get you back? I think your friend is right, and you should let one of us go.'

'I told you what the Oracle said – it has to be me.' Yet despite her words, her feelings about the prophecy were still as unsettled as ever. She wavered constantly between acceptance and rejection, resenting the ease with which the journey south had seemed to fall into place, implying again that her own wishes and choices meant nothing. Afterwards, I'll know afterwards, she repeated to herself, as if it were true.

'Perhaps.' Essa frowned uneasily. 'I know we must find her, but not at your expense, Asher. And I'm glad the Chief Councillor suggested you take a chaperon or two. Kerrick is not a man to trust.'

'No.'

'And I like your descriptions of Avorian and his daughter.' Essa smiled. 'I've sent them maids from time to time, but they never have anything to report. Our Chief Councillor seems to lead a busy but blameless life.'

'Yes.' Asher wondered if she had been mistaken about Avorian's intentions; Menna could have been right, and he had only held her to stop her falling. She was glad she had kept the incident to herself.

'It's a disgrace there should be so much fraud,' Margit remarked indignantly. 'Don't these people know that for every copper they hold back, the more it costs the rest – and the councillors most of all?'

A loud crash interrupted her speech; a dark head appeared round the rear door.

'Sorry. I just dropped a few things.'

'It sounded more like the roof caving in!' Mylura observed quietly. Essa, however, half-rose, looking worried.

'I wonder – '

Asher stared moodily at the occupants of the other tables, wishing it were late enough to retire to the solitude of her room; she did not feel like talking at the moment. Everything seemed to be conspiring to upset her fragile self-possession, which was far more delicate than she wanted to believe.

'What was that?' Essa sprang to her feet, muttering distractedly: 'Then it was knives she dropped!'

All conversation died as a high-pitched scream, followed by sounds of a second crash, filled the room. The cry was cut off, then came sounds of low voices and heavy footsteps coming along the passage. The door to the common room burst open.

'Not again!'

Essa was already retreating to the rear of the room, shoving tables into a defensive position with help from Margit and Mylura. Other women followed her example, hastily grabbing any implement that would pass for a weapon. Most of the hostel's inhabitants had experienced such raids before, and they reacted quickly and efficiently, forming two lines behind a barricade of tables. Asher stood beside Mylura, Margit next to Essa.

A crowd of shabbily dressed men surged into the room, mostly young, a few rather older, pushing aside the obstructing benches and streaming forwards in an undisciplined rush.

'Keep together,' Essa said in a clear whisper. 'Work in pairs, as we planned.'

Asher gripped the fork she had elected as her own weapon; this was the fourth time the hostel had been invaded since she had moved in, and she knew what to do. Quickly, she counted heads on both sides, relieved to see there were only twenty men for the full complement of the hostel; two to one were good odds.

'Well, Sim?' Essa called out wearily to a man who stood at the centre of the line, who checked at the sound of his name; the whole group came to an abrupt, staggering halt.

He came forward alone, an unappealing figure. Despite powerful arms and shoulders, he had the appearance of a man whose appetites had been too often indulged; his grey hair was sparse and oily-looking, and several chins bounced above a tunic stained with grease. His belt strained against the bulge of his belly, and when he spoke Asher caught a strong smell of ale on his breath.

At least he was unarmed. A quick glance showed her none of the others carried weapons, and she breathed more easily.

'Me and my friends here,' Sim began, slurring the words slightly, 'thought we'd pay you a little visit.' He belched loudly, and his companions let out a cheer at this eloquence. 'We thought you ladies'd be glad of some company on such a wet night.'

'We did not invite you or your friends,' Essa replied icily. 'And we would be glad if you would leave – at once.'

'*Leave*?' He managed a look that succeeded in being both incredulous and lascivious. 'You surely don't mean that?' He turned to indicate his companions. 'Look at these fine and thirsty lads. Why don't you bring us all some ale, so we can get down to enjoying ourselves!'

'This is neither an inn nor a brothel, as we have told you before,' Essa observed carefully, speaking slowly.

'*Isn't* it?' Sim opened bloodshot eyes in feigned surprise. Raucous laughter erupted from his followers. 'Ladies, forgive us.' He swept them a low, mocking bow. 'Fetch out the master of this house, and we'll willingly make him our apologies.'

Any minute now. Asher had enough experience to judge the mood of the mob; the scene altered little from raid to raid. Why do they do this? They drink too much, then all together decide to show us how big and brave they are; do all men think with their groins? Why does valuing themselves so highly mean they have to devalue us? She tensed, and felt Mylura ready herself.

'Get on with it!' urged a thin voice from the rear. Asher recognized him as a youth who worked alongside Sim in the tannery several streets away. Other voices took the cry up into a chant.

'Enough.' Essa raised her own voice to be heard above the hubbub. 'You should be ashamed of yourselves. What would your mothers, or sisters, or wives say if they could see you now?'

Sim's face flushed an angry red. 'Shut your mouth, bitch!'

Is this what the Fates dictate? Asher wondered bitterly. That men should hate us just for not being like them? Although there were times when Asher resented the restrictions of being born a woman, she could not conceive of wanting to be male. For a moment, she would have liked to kill Sim and all his kind, for their stupidity and their drunken viciousness, for the way in which together they ceased to be human and became only a pack, before reason returned. Not all men are like this, not Mallory.

'What're we waiting for?' called a tall youth on the left. He came forward, shoving aside a table, which fell with a loud crash; his friends followed.

'Shall we call the guard?' asked a frightened voice from somewhere behind Asher.

'No!' she said sharply. If they could not fight their own battles, they had no hope; and in any case it seemed a kind of collaboration, at least in her own mind.

'Now!'

Sim lunged for Essa, who deftly evaded him. Total chaos ensued. There was no time to think as the wave of men surged forwards, pressing the women back towards the far wall, relying for victory on their greater strength. Asher found, as before, that she was too angry to be afraid. At a signal from Mylura, she dropped promptly to all fours, and a moment later a man crashed over her and fell heavily to the floor. Mylura promptly sat on him, taking and holding Asher's fork to his neck.

'One down! Go and help Margit.'

Asher turned to see her friend in the grip of a tall man whose hands were busy at her bodice; seizing a mug from a nearby table, Asher brought it crashing down on his head, wishing it were heavier. He released Margit, putting his hands to the back of his skull; instantly, Margit kicked him between his legs, and he bent forwards in agony, groaning lustily.

'Thanks,' Margit panted. Asher made an ironic bow, then looked round to see who else was in difficulties. The battle was raging along its accustomed lines; each man faced not one but two women, negating his physical advantage. Several had joined Mylura's victim and lay prone, but Sim and some of the others had seen their error and now stood defensively back to back, lunging forwards in formation. She could not see Essa anywhere, but spotted a young man rush and grasp one of the smallest women, picking her up and running towards the exit. His progress was hampered by her weight and her struggles. Asher had time to snatch a brand from the fire; she made for him at a run, applying the burning brand to the seat of his trousers. With a shout, he dropped the girl, who scrambled away and hid under one of the tables. It was the woman who had suggested calling the guard, and Asher guessed she had little heart for the battle.

'*Stop*!'

It was surprising that any voice could make itself heard above the tumult. Asher looked up to see Essa standing on top of one of the few remaining upright tables, surrounded by a protective circle of women.

'That is enough!'

Sim hesitated, then signed his companions to pause as he counted the number of men still standing; there were nine, apart from himself. Nine more lay flat on the floor, pinned down by an equal number of women; the one Asher had burned had made a hasty exit, beating frantically at the smouldering material of his trousers.

'There are ten of you to forty of us,' Essa continued in her most carrying voice. 'No doubt you think your strength vastly superior to ours, but look – and see. We did not invite you here; we do not exist for your entertainment. If you will do so peaceably, we will let you go.'

'There'll be a settlement for this!' Sim shook off several restraining hands and came forward, his face flushed scarlet. 'I swear it. You may be lucky this time, but there'll be another!' he said hoarsely. 'You may think yourselves high and mighty, answering to no man, sharing your filthy favours with each other. Unnatural bitches!' He spat, aiming at Margit who was closest. She stood her ground wiping off the spittle fastidiously with a scrap of cloth.

'I wonder why bitches are always so maligned?' Mylla murmured softly to Asher. 'You'd think Sim and his lot hated all females in the animal kingdom!'

'How many times do I have to tell you?' Essa asked wearily. 'We want nothing from you; we take nothing from you. All we desire is to be left in peace.'

'Is that what you call it? What use are you, any of you?' There was deep loathing in his voice. 'The Fates say nothing's more unlucky than a houseful of women. You bring down ill-fortune on our city, on all of us!'

134

'You do that well enough yourself,' Mylura observed from her seat on one of the downed figures. Essa frowned at her, but Sim glared, openly malevolent. Asher listened, depressed.

'"What can you expect from a pig but a grunt?"' Sim quoted coarsely. 'All right. We'll go. But don't think you've won.' He turned on his heel and stalked away; disconcerted, his youthful followers moved after him as Essa signalled to release the fallen.

'Bar the door after them,' she called out to Mylura. 'Is everyone in safely?'

Asher did a rapid head count. 'Yes – no. Wait. Where's Sara?'

'And who let them in?' Mylura demanded at the same moment; their eyes met and they headed jointly for the door.

A slight figure lay in the passage by the main door, head buried under one arm.

'Sara?'

The woman stirred. Asher could see at once that her right arm was broken; the angle was all wrong. There were also bloodstains on her head and hand.

'Don't move,' she said quickly. 'Mylla, fetch Margit. She's the best at broken bones. And some wine, too.' There was a dark bruise over Sara's left eye, and another on her forehead. Asher swore quietly; Sara was a seamstress and would be unable to work for weeks – a financial burden to the others.

'It hurts.' There were tears in Sara's thin voice.

'What happened?'

The woman tried to move, then groaned. 'I – there was something blocking the eyehole in the door, and I couldn't see so I opened it, Then – '

'Don't worry about it.' Asher moved aside to make room for Margit, and, after a brief inspection, two of the women were detailed to carry Sara to her room; Margit followed, looking grim.

'We shall have to increase our precautions,' Essa was saying to Mylura when Asher rejoined them. 'Next time Sim might bring rather more of his friends, and they might come armed.'

'Surely not?' Mylura frowned. 'We can bring the law down on them if they do real damage.'

'As they did to Sara? Do you really believe that?' Essa sounded sceptical. 'And how much value do you imagine a judge would assign a few women, without male relatives to appease? If any of us is attacked or raped, whose rights would Sim and his friends have stolen? Only ours, which is to say very little in the eyes of the law. And how would any of us prove we were virgin or not? The law has a value system which rates men more highly if they aren't innocents, and women more if they are. A curious state of affairs, but there it is.'

Gloomily, Mylura nodded. 'I know.'

'You'd better stay tonight, Mylla. Share with me.'

'Thanks. I don't want to meet the one with prong marks on his neck again in a hurry!' She grinned at Asher, then frowned. 'What's happened to your badge? I just noticed. I saw it earlier today, I'm sure.'

Asher looked down at her lapel in surprise. 'You're right.' The seven-pointed star was no longer there. 'It must have come off in the fight. It'll be in here somewhere.'

'I'll help you look for it.'

'I've another, just in case. But thanks.'

'Well, my dears, I'm too old for all this.' Essa rose to her feet. 'I shall go to bed and meditate on our defences. Are you coming, Mylla?'

'In a moment.' She was already on her knees, hunting around on the floor, holding up a candle in one hand and feeling the surface with the other. At last, she gave up.

'Don't worry, Mylla, I'll find it in the morning.'

'All right.' She yawned, then replaced the candle in its sconce and blew it out. Order had been restored in the hall, and there was remarkably little damage; only one bench had been broken. Asher continued to search, but only desultorily. 'I'm for bed!'

Asher followed her up the stairs, realizing at last how tired she was. She said goodnight to Mylura and went into her own room, performing the routine search with less than her usual assiduousness, but nothing had been disturbed.

She sat down wearily on the bed, wondering again why Sim should hate them so much; in what way did their existence offend his pride?

Because we don't need him, or his friends, or want them; we act and believe that we have a right to live as we choose, not as they decide. She checked the thought, knowing where it would lead; she would not lump all men together with Sim and his kind, or she was as guilty of blind prejudice as they.

A trip to the country began to seem distinctly attractive. She began to unbutton her shirt –

– and froze. She could feel eyes boring into her back. She whirled round, but there was no one there. She stood up, looking under the bed, in the chest, then opened the shutters and peered out. There was no one visible, no ladder perched on the wall by the alley, yet she remained convinced that someone, somewhere, was watching her. She was quite certain of it.

She tried to think rationally: If I can't see anyone, there's no one there. It's just my imagination. But no amount of argument could persuade her that was all it was. She could not stay in her room; it no longer offered peace and privacy. She ran downstairs, retreating to the comfort of the fire in the empty common room; but even there, in the eerie darkness, lit only by the sinking embers in the hearth, the feeling of being observed did not diminish. She huddled by the wall, waiting for her eyes to grow accustomed to the night, for all the candles had been extinguished and she was alone in the room; but even when she could see clearly again, there was still nothing and no one there.

She shivered.

She had come to Venture believing it a haven of safety in her flight from Lewes, but now it seemed to hold nothing but menace and violence, a place where others used and manipulated her against her wishes. She wanted to blame the Oracle, the Fates, for the whole, but that sounded too ridiculous. With ears attuned to the slightest movement, eyes constantly starting at shadows, Asher sat with her back to the wall for what felt like half the night, waiting; nothing happened.

At last, the feeling subsided, and her terror began to abate and she summoned sufficient courage to leave the comparative safety of the hearth. Whoever she had sensed seemed to have gone. Silently, she returned to her room, opening the door nervously; but it was empty, and she felt no resumption of her earlier panic.

Swiftly, she undressed and got into bed. There were no sounds from any of the nearby rooms, not even Sara's, where she knew Margit would be keeping a nightlong vigil. She reminded herself that Essa and Mylura were only next door, a shout away.

What are you? she jeered silently. A small child afraid of the dark? She was disgusted with herself. I told Mallory I could cope, and needed no one's help. Now look at me! She huddled further under the blankets.

What had happened to her? The Asher she had become over the past six years, the new Asher, strong and self-sufficient, seemed to her at that moment little changed from the Asher of the past with all her fears and vulnerabilities. Perhaps, she thought bitterly, her fate had always been to be weak, vulnerable. She tried to tell herself she was not afraid, only tired, but she could still feel unseen eyes watching her, still smell the metallic smoke of Lassar's incense; and, when she closed her eyes, she saw again the writhing lines, like dark-coloured serpents, stretching away into the distance.

Home. I want to go home. The longing she had suppressed for so many years surged up as she lay in the dark, the blind instinct of the wounded. She knew it for foolishness, for her family was dead, and there was no one left to run to except Mallory, and to him she would not; but the desire, once acknowledged, refused to go away. Home.

She felt herself relax as the word hummed in her mind. In only a few days she would, indeed, be going home.

PART TWO
Fixed Fate

Chapter Seven

The trail wound round and down, rising again in the distance about a hill burned almost bare by firestorm. Where once shrubs and other greenery had covered the slopes, there was now only grey rock and scree; but, as the party drew closer, it could be seen that some growth had, after all, managed to survive the inferno. Here and there, tall poker-shaped flowers on white stalks stood out against the rock, and among the bare, fire-blackened stones and stems were odd patches of brown, even red, of living plants. The flames seemed to have followed a path of their own making, sparing growth above and below an allotted line with an arbitrary wilfulness.

'Had enough already?' Mallory enquired.

Asher scowled. 'Of Kerrick, yes!'

'You should be honoured he considers you sufficiently worthy to receive his pearls of wisdom.' His expression was innocuous, but Asher knew Mallory too well to be deceived.

'He wouldn't, if he knew what I was thinking,' she muttered darkly.

They had set out at day-break, and Asher's spirits, never at their height at such an hour, sank lower as she surveyed the ill-assorted party. Kerrick, like his uncle Avorian, was a good-looking man, though darker of hair and eye, but there the resemblance ceased; he had made it plain at the outset that he considered most of his unwanted travelling companions beneath his notice, speaking only to Mallory and Asher with any degree of civility. Val and Tarm, the hired guards, he either ignored or spoke to in such offensive tones that Asher wondered how long it would be before they rebelled.

As she had feared, it began to rain; the skies were the heavy grey that promised a prolonged downfall. Asher huddled in her riding cloak and tried to remember she had been looking forward to the journey.

The party spread out along the trail, Val in the lead, his brother bringing up the rear. Horton, Kerrick's clerk, rode behind Val; a man of about fifty, with a fussy manner, he seemed to share his master's prejudices with regard to his companions. Pars, who came next, had already tried conversing with Horton but been treated to a stare of such haughtiness that he quickly retreated inside his sensitive shell. At only twenty, he was uncomfortably plump; Asher thought he looked like a puppy longing for a bone but expecting a curse, and hoped Mallory was kind to him. Kerrick, Asher, Mallory and Margit followed, then Ish, Mallory's fifteen-year-old groom, who had accompanied his master on one long sea-voyage and behaved as if a journey of only five days were beneath his contempt.

Behind Ish, Ancil, Kerrick's Petormene slave, sat slumped in his saddle, a picture of misery; he was only eighteen or so and had no cape, so that his thin shirt and breeches were already soaked. Mylura rode alongside him, speaking to him in low tones.

The rain thickened until it was difficult to see the trail at all; Val urged them on, despite Kerrick's protests. There was no shelter to be had until they reached the Forest of Marl, and the prospect of a night spent on the open hills was less than enticing.

'How far to the forest?' she asked him, peering through the curtain of rain.

'Down there.' He pointed to a large patch of darkness some way below.

She sighed. 'I feel as if we've been riding in circles all day.'

'We have!'

Val halted and indicated they should dismount and lead the horses; Asher, having already felt her mount stumble twice on the track of slippery mud, complied willingly. The rain had eased up, but a quick look at the sky convinced her the respite was only temporary; gloomily, she wondered if it would rain the entire length of the journey.

'We'll make camp inside the forest,' Val called back. 'There've been reports of a robber band further south, and there's no point in taking chances.'

'Just get on with it!' Kerrick sounded irritable.

The forest began at the base of the slope; once it had stretched from the edge of the hills south to Eagle Lake, only a day's journey from Chance, but over the centuries the southern section had been slowly eaten away as timber was needed for export, for building and for fuel. Now it was only a wide belt of trees, less than a day's ride from north to south, a visible witness to the slow but steady drain on Darrian's resources made by an increasing population and the heavy burden of the tribute. In the twilight, however, the dark shadows of the trees gave a promise of shelter, holding out hope of dry warmth and rest.

As Asher plodded on, she turned back to exchange a word with Mylura; her feet slipped and she slid then fell, measuring her length in the mud. She made an exclamation of disgust, and Mallory looked round.

'Any damage?' He extended a helping hand.

'No.' Her own hand, slimy with mud, slipped from his and she fell again, splattering him as well as herself, unable to stop herself laughing at his obvious distaste. 'I might as well slide down – I'm so wet now it wouldn't make any difference.'

'Just *try* to stay vertical!'

She glared back, but he was already moving on. She was aware of being wet through and extremely uncomfortable, unhappy in the knowledge that she would have to wear the same, mud-soaked clothes the next day; she thought longingly of a stream of clear water. Then laughed again as the skies opened and rain streamed down, and her cloak began to drip in muddy rivulets. She lifted her face and tried to wash her hands in the downpour.

They made camp in a small grove of trees, interlaced branches overhead providing a measure of shelter. Val, with an expertise Asher could only envy, built a fire, using kindling carried in his packs, and the whole party gathered eagerly round it.

'What are you doing there?' The sight of Ancil kneeling on the sodden ground, hands held out towards the flames, apparently enraged his master. Kerrick kicked out at him, catching him on the ribs. 'Go and do something about supper!'

Ancil retreated at once, walking dejectedly towards the pack-horses where Mylura joined him.

'Where does he sleep tonight?' she murmured to Mallory.

'In the open, unless I'm much mistaken. Don't worry, he can share with Ish if Pars comes in with me.' He beckoned to his groom, who listened to the proposal then nodded his head vigorously. 'Does that satisfy you, Ash?'

'Thanks.' Then, finding Kerrick eyeing them curiously, she moved away to help Margit erect their tent. It was not part of their plans for him to discover they already knew one another well; nor, given the circumstances, could they easily explain their long acquaintance.

After the meal, Margit claimed most of the party for a few rounds of cards; Asher, who did not enjoy games of chance, was

143

content to watch until drawn away by a summons from Kerrick, who was talking to Mallory on the far side of the fire.

'Mistress Asher, my uncle has asked me to take great care of you, given the errand on which you have come.' She smiled doubtfully, wondering where the speech was leading. 'You must forgive my surprise at finding a woman so capable to be also young and attractive!'

Asher sighed inwardly, less at the laboured compliment than at the gleam in Kerrick's eye; it was plain his reputation was not exaggerated. 'You're very kind,' she replied, careful not to look at Mallory.

'You look tired, mistress,' he intervened promptly. 'Perhaps you should retire. We've an early start in the morning. I'm sure our host would excuse you.'

'How thoughtful of you.' Her bland expression was fully the equal of his own. 'I think I shall. Good night, Master Kerrick; Councillor.' She caught the look Kerrick shot Mallory and felt *that* satisfaction well worth his easy victory. Then Asher scowled. It was unwise to allow Mallory even so slight a degree of control over her actions. It came to her that her strong dislike of being given orders was perhaps at the heart of her desire to believe the Oracle false. She shook her head; this journey was the test of the truth, and it had barely begun.

She walked to the tent she was to share with her friends and arranged her bedroll, and was already half-asleep by the time the others came in. She listened to them with only part of her attention, the rest centred on the sounds of the night. She could hear the horses shifting restlessly, the branches stirring overhead; there were calls of night-birds hunting, and odd rustlings in the distance that spoke of other predators. Feeling drowsy and comfortable, she realized it was the first whole day she had been free from the sensation of being watched since the night of the raid on the hostel. She had come to recognize the warning signs, the uneasiness which was the precursor to what she tried to convince herself were mere attacks of nerves, and mentioned to no one.

The smell of wood-smoke from the fire and the scents of damp earth and leaves reminded her of her childhood. I'm going home, she thought sleepily. Mallory deserved some gratitude from her for making it possible.

Mallory thought even Ancil looked happier the next day as they rode along the straightest trail through the forest. Rain continued to fall, but not so heavily, and it was warmer in the shelter of the trees. The slave-boy was now wearing an old cloak of his own, and Mallory wondered idly where Ish had found it; he did not object to its bestowal, which would please Asher, for the Petormene boy obviously felt the cold severely. He sneezed from time to time, and wiped his nose on his sleeve when he thought no one was looking.

Tarm, leading, held up a hand and the procession ground to a halt while he dismounted and bent to inspect some blackened marks on the trail.

'A few days' old,' he said, speaking to Kerrick loud enough for the others to hear. 'We'd better be alert for trouble; keep together, and be ready to ride for it if I give the word.'

'How many men?' Mallory called out.

'Hard to say. A dozen, perhaps?'

They rode on. Mallory found himself continually scanning the deep shadows to either side for signs of movement, but he felt no sense of menace in the quiet of the forest. There was only the constant patter of rain on leaves, and the flight of wings as birds fled at their own noisy approach.

'Look!'

It was Margit who cried out. Following her pointing hand, Mallory turned and saw a lone black crow perched high on a branch to the left of the track. Instead of flying off, as they intruded on to its territory, it seemed to be waiting for them to draw closer. As Tarm passed, it opened its beak and cawed, not once but three times.

'Three times for death,' Horton murmured audibly. Kerrick glared at him. The crow lifted its wings and flapped away, deeper into the forest; after a frozen moment, Tarm kicked his heels into his horse's sides and set off again. The rest followed, subdued. Mallory noticed Asher looking impatient, as if she thought it all so much nonsense, and only wished he could share her indifference.

It was well past midday when he first noticed the smell, a sickly, penetrating odour that grew stronger as they approached a section of forest where thick undergrowth reduced visibility to either side of the trail. One area looked well-trampled, as though it had been used in the not so distant past by more than one person, and it was there Tarm called another halt.

'There must be something dead in the bushes,' Mallory muttered to Asher. She nodded, fumbling in her skirts for a cloth to cover her nose. Tarm dismounted and headed off into the thicket, and before Mallory could say a word, Asher had followed suit.

His eyes met Mylura's to his right; she shrugged, grinning. 'Asher,' he called after her, then cursed himself for his carelessness as Kerrick turned to stare at him in astonishment. Asher had already disappeared in Tarm's wake, and their progress could only be heard, not seen, as they made their way through the concealing undergrowth.

Has she no sense at all? he thought wrathfully, dismounting in turn and hurrying in pursuit. Val, in the rear, strained his eyes, alert for signs of the robber band, but it seemed unlikely they would hide themselves so close to such a penetratingly unpleasant smell. Mallory pushed aside trailing greenery and brambles, speeding his pace at the sound of a distant exclamation of disgust. He heard footsteps, then Tarm appeared, breathing fast through his mouth.

'What's the matter?' Mallory asked urgently.

Tarm spat, as though to rid his mouth of an evil taste. 'Through there!' he said curtly, indicating a faint trail. 'We'll have no more trouble with robbers.'

Mallory let him go, moving on along the path. The stench of decay was overwhelming, and he wondered why Asher had not come back.

He found himself in a wide clearing, man-made – and stopped.

Asher was on her knees, her head in her hands. As he looked up he saw something brown and furred disappear among the trees, although his arrival did not disturb the crows, who, having found something edible in the clearing, were too intent on their meal to take fright. It was the content of that meal that had so affected Tarm.

A dozen trees formed a circle around the cleared space of ground, which had once evidently served as a camp-site; there were thick deposits of ash and pieces of charred wood strewn all around. The source of the smell, however, came from the trees, where remnants of what had once been men had been dismembered and fixed to the trunks with long nails, in no particular order; only the heads were missing. These, of which there were ten, had been rammed on top of pointed poles and stuck into the earth in a neat line.

Mallory swore. Seeing Asher still incapable of movement, he picked her up and carried her back along the path, shoving aside the trailing undergrowth until the unspeakable grove was no longer in sight. Once far enough away, he put her back on her feet.

'Thanks.' She was very white. 'I couldn't move.' Further explanation seemed to be beyond her.

'Why don't you sometimes *think* before rushing into things?' Mallory demanded furiously. 'There was no need for you to have seen that!'

For once, she seemed too shocked to resent his tone. 'No. Who did it?'

'The Kamiri. I've seen something like this before, in a village in Asir.' The memory was still vivid, an image of wailing brown women and weeping children, and the smell of death and blood; the place had been a den of robbers. It was one of the few memories that came back at times to haunt his dreams, for in his travels he had seen a great many unpleasant sights, most of them the handiwork of Amrist's men. 'They've left the bodies here as a warning.' He tried not to think about the crows, bile rising in his throat. 'Can you walk? Because I think we should leave at once.' She nodded.

They found the remainder of the party waiting but impatient; Mallory wasted no time in helping Asher to mount, meeting Kerrick's interested gaze with a stare that gave nothing away.

The group moved on, subdued and eager to get out of range of the smell. Mallory found himself watching Asher with increasing concern as she rode between himself and Mylura, for the track was wide enough for three abreast. He was struck by an alteration in her, not simply a change in character which could have happened during her years in Venture, but a new element that puzzled him, as if she were trying to prove to him – or to herself? – that she was equal to anything, no task beyond her ability. He had noticed it that morning, watching her try to lift a pack as heavy as herself, refusing to ask for help, even from one of the other women. That she was reckless he had always known but now he could almost believe she was fighting an internal battle with herself. He wished, for the thousandth time, that he had not agreed to her coming.

Although how he could have stopped her was a moot point.

They left the forest as dusk was fading into night, the landscape ahead changing from a seemingly endless vista of trees to one of flat, arable lands stretching away as far as the eye could see, broken only by low walls and hedgerows. The Assart Plains were good farming country, irrigated by two major rivers and a great many tributaries which led west-east towards the coast, and to Mallory it was a relief to return to open ground; a life spent at sea inclined him to prefer wide skies to the darkness of the forest.

'There should be a smallholding not far off,' Kerrick observed importantly. 'My uncle sent word ahead we should want accommodation, the place belongs to him.'

'I know the one.' Tarm, still leading, did not look back, obviously finding the reminder unnecessary. 'It's only a short ride from here.' He pointed to a light not far distant. 'That's it.'

'Asher, you'll keep with the other women tonight?' Mallory asked warily. 'Don't let Kerrick get you alone.'

'Don't worry, I won't.' Her expression satisfied him and he said no more. The rain had ceased, and both moons lit up the sky, Aspire dominant, though waxing; Mallory hoped it was a good omen for the remainder of the journey.

As they rode along a narrow track he began to be able to make out a cluster of buildings grouped together, obviously the promised smallholding. The farmhouse was larger than he expected, a square, cheerful building with lights showing downstairs; the front door swung open as they approached and a woman came out to meet him, obviously alerted to their arrival by the sounds of the horses.

'Is that Master Kerrick?' she asked, rather anxiously, at the sight of the long tail of horses and people.

'You've rooms ready for us? And a meal,' he demanded, nodding curtly.

The woman screwed up her eyes and counted, using the fingers of both hands. She was very thin, with mousy hair thickly speckled with grey; her back was bowed, by weakness or disease, but Mallory, when he saw her face, realized with a shock she was little older than himself.

'If the ladies would be willing to share, there's my son's room, and my daughter's as well as two more. The rest could sleep in the barn – it's clean, and warm.'

Kerrick's nostrils twitched, and Horton gave a snort of disgust, but there was no choice to be had. 'Then the Councillor and I will take two of the rooms, the women another, and my clerk here can share with the Councillor's man,' he decreed haughtily. 'My slave will sleep with the horses.'

'Come in then, sirs.' She gestured towards the door. 'I've a parlour you can use, then I'll see about your suppers.'

Neither Horton nor Pars seemed delighted by the arrangement, but the party dismounted, Ish and Ancil joining the guards in taking the horses round to the rear, the remainder entering the house.

'How long have you lived here, mistress?' Asher enquired, as the woman led them to a barely furnished room at the front of the house and knelt to light the fire.

'Since I was married, eighteen years since.' She blew on the sparks and got to her feet, hauling herself upright with difficulty. 'My man died before my son was born, but we've only fifty acres and help from a hired man so we manage; my daughter, bless her, is a hard worker. Now, if you'll excuse me, I'll send Liss with ale for you and get on with your dinners.' She hobbled out.

'I suppose this is better than a night in the open,' Kerrick observed doubtfully; the room was spotlessly clean, but there was no rug on the floor, and the chairs and table, though highly polished, were poor-looking and had known long use.

'Better than more rain.' Mallory walked over to the fire and re-lit it, for it had gone out. Kerrick sat down at the table and began to drum his fingers on it impatiently. Asher and the two women joined him, waiting for the fire to take the chill from the room, which felt damp and unused.

A knock at the door heralded the arrival of a girl bearing a heavy tray carrying the promised refreshment. Mallory judged her age to be about sixteen. She was a little plump, fair-haired and very pretty, and he saw Kerrick's sour expression alter to one of positive geniality as he watched her pour the ale.

'Supper won't be long,' she said softly; it was a pleasant voice, low and lightly accented. 'Is there anything more you'll be wanting?'

'Not for the moment.' Kerrick actually smiled at her. Mallory thought he could guess what service Kerrick would be requiring from her later.

'If you will excuse us?' Margit and Asher had risen. Kerrick nodded a curt dismissal; he drained his tankard, then refilled it, losing interest in his companions. Mylura, Mallory noticed, was keeping an eye on Kerrick, and he wondered why. He liked Mylura, finding her easy good nature appealing in contrast to Margit's more sober temperament, although the older woman was physically the more attractive. He did not, however, approve of Mylura's indifference to convention, which extended to her wearing men's trousers for riding, unlike the other two who contented themselves with more modest divided skirts. The women of Darrian had considerably more freedom than most in the Dominion; in Petormin in the east, a country where decent women did not appear in public, Mylura would have been stoned for such a display of long, thin leg.

It was Liss who served their meal, when it was ready, and Kerrick watched her as she did so, his gaze greedily following the curves of her breasts in a tight-fitting grey dress which was a little too small for its wearer. It was plain he believed his uncle's ownership of the property extended to its tenants, and Mallory was amused to find himself silently warned off, although there was no need. He had never been attracted to girls half his age.

'I hope you enjoyed it?' the girl asked shyly when she came to clear the table, surveying the host of empty plates. 'My mother's generally accounted a good cook.'

'Excellent,' Kerrick said agreeably, sitting back in his chair. Asher and Mylura offered their own compliments as Liss moved round the table, gathering up the debris and piling it on a tray. As she bent to take Kerrick's plate, she started, then blushed; Mallory felt suddenly uneasy as Asher and Margit exchanged glances.

Kerrick followed Liss from the room, and Mallory seized the moment. The other members of the party were being entertained in the kitchen, and he was alone with the three women.

'Why do I get the feeling you're planning something?'

Margit opened her mouth to answer him, but someone must have kicked her under the table for a look of pain crossed her face and she remained silent. Instead Asher said hurriedly: 'Why do you ask?'

She assumed a look of innocence which filled him with deep suspicion; when she was younger, it was a look that had always meant she was intent on some mischief or other. He sighed. 'Just natural foreboding.'

'We were talking about our hostess,' Mylura said easily. 'She has two children – Liss, who's sixteen, and a son, Garris, who's fourteen. Liss is betrothed to a local farmer, but they can't wed until Garris is old enough to take over the farm in a year or so; Hanna says Liss does most of the work, because Garris is not too clever.'

'I see.' The information did not relieve his mind. 'Quite a paragon, in fact.'

'Yes, she is.' Margit looked defiant. He was surprised at her speaking, for she rarely addressed him. He had the impression she did not care much for men, which was a pity for she was very good-looking even now, when she must be close to his own age. Asher had told him Margit was to do her own work while she travelled to Kepesake with him, since Avorian had not allowed enough time for her to do both journeys; he had been surprised and not a little shocked, but Asher had only said the job was not so difficult. Anyone could add up a few numbers.

'I'm tired, I think I'll go to bed.' Asher yawned ostentatiously. 'Are you coming, you two?'

'I think so.'

Mallory watched the trio depart, his suspicions unallayed.

150

Kerrick returned, carrying another brimming tankard; he made no secret of the fact that he would prefer his companion's absence to his presence, staring moodily into the flames of the fire and ignoring Mallory. Assuming him to be waiting for Liss, Mallory decided to leave him to it and seek out his own chamber, although it offered scant comfort; it was, however, as clean as the rest of the house, and Ish had obviously been busy setting his things in order.

He was not especially tired since travel in all its forms had been his life for many years, and even this short journey he found preferable to sitting in the Council Chamber in Venture. He sat down on the hard bed and listened, trying to hear what the female voices coming from the neighbouring room were saying, but he could not distinguish the words. Not sure why, he did not undress, and was glad a short time later when he heard the door next to his own open and close softly.

Now what?

Someone was going downstairs; he could hear the boards creak. Carefully, he opened his own door and looked out, to have a rear view of Asher disappearing down the passage on the ground floor. Without a second thought, he followed her.

By the time he had descended the stairs, Mallory knew there was only one place she could have gone: the parlour. In that instant, it occurred to him it might be for Asher, not the girl Liss, that Kerrick was waiting. A surge of fierce rage ran through him before common sense reasserted itself, reminding him Asher had shown nothing but dislike for the Chief Councillor's nephew; whatever she wanted with him must be something quite different from his fears.

He trod softly down the passage and stopped outside the door of the parlour, which was ajar, and listened to Kerrick, who was speaking and sounding less than pleased about his visitor.

'– do you want?'

'To talk to you.' Asher's voice was clear and confident.

'What about? Can't it wait till morning?'

'I don't think so.'

'Oh, very well then.' The acceptance was bad-tempered.

There was a pause. Mallory felt a touch on his shoulder and turned to find Mylura behind him, a finger to her lips. He nodded, no longer angry but frankly curious to know what was going on.

'Master Kerrick, I've come to say something you won't want to hear,' they heard Asher say. 'But it must be said. I know your plans for tonight; I heard you talking to Hanna. All I want to say is, you must forget them.'

'*What?*' Kerrick sounded as incredulous as Mallory felt at that moment. He found he could almost feel sorry for the other man; Mallory knew what Asher was like in this mood.

'The girl Liss is not included in the assets of the property, Master Kerrick. She's a decent girl, and soon to be married; it's not right for you to threaten her family with the loss of their tenancy unless she beds you. They have farmed here for six generations, and they're well respected and pay their rent. Leave her alone.'

'How *dare* you!' Mallory tensed, sure Kerrick would lose his temper and strike Asher, but a touch from Mylura held him still; she shook her head.

'What business is it of yours what I do? And,' Kerrick added more firmly, 'just how do you propose to stop me?'

Mallory, still stunned by Asher's outrageous demand, listened harder.

'You forget, I travel with authority both from your uncle and from the city,' Asher was saying calmly. 'A councillor of Venture is also staying in this house, and he would have to back me in this. I'm aware it was not the reason I was given such authority, but I'll use it. If you force me to.'

'*You* . . .' A series of expletives followed. Mallory saw Mylura put a hand to her mouth, trying not to laugh. He, however, had no desire to smile; he was furious with Asher. Even though they were to be under this roof for only one night, she could not resist interfering in matters which did not concern her.

'Come away. It'll be all right now,' Mylura whispered. 'I only came to offer my support, if needed.'

Mallory followed her grimly down the passage, drawing her aside when she would have gone up the stairs.

'Whose idea was *that*?'

'Asher's.' Mylura grinned, obviously expecting him to share her satisfaction at the outcome of the affair; Mallory breathed out heavily through his nose.

'Where's the girl?'

'In our room. We thought it might not be safe to trust Kerrick, even after this. She'll spend the night with us, don't worry.'

'It's not her I'm worried about. Do you know what you've done? What happens when Councillor Avorian gets to hear of this?'

'Oh, I don't think he will, do you?' Mylura was quite composed. 'It hardly reflects well on Kerrick. Hanna and her family are good tenants. And I hear the Chief Councillor is an excellent landlord.'

Loud footsteps came noisily along the stone passage, and Kerrick appeared, passing Mallory and Mylura with an angry glare before he began to climb the stairs with a heavy, wrathful tread.

'I want a word with your friend!' Mallory took Mylura's arm and pulled her back toward the parlour. Inside, he let her go, and she walked across to join Asher at her place beside the fire, which had gone out. There was a brief, hostile, silence.

'What's the matter?' Asher asked.

'Don't ask such a silly question! What do you think you're up to?' Mallory snapped. 'And why didn't you tell me what you were going to do?'

'You know the answer to the first, and I don't think I need explain my reasons for the second,' Asher answered calmly. 'Would you have helped us if I had?'

'Why should I?' He could not understand why she felt so strongly about a farm-girl she had only just met. 'No doubt Kerrick would have paid her for her favours, and they could certainly use some coins here.' He glanced about the bare room.

'And you think being paid is enough recompense?' There was a new, cold, light in her eyes. 'I see. Her feelings aren't important?'

'She would have come to no harm,' Mallory responded dismissively.

'How nice you can be so sure of that!' She spoke to him as if he were a stranger. 'And I thought you believed in responsibility, Mallory, owing a duty to those weaker than yourself.'

'But not to the whole world, and not when I have a greater concern,' he snapped back. 'Or had you forgotten our reasons for coming here?'

'No.' She stared down into the cold grate, at the grey ash. 'And I wouldn't use that as an excuse to stand back and let a young girl be abused by a bully. But I forget, her problems aren't real to you.'

'Why do you say that?' As his ill-temper waned, Mallory tried to comprehend some of Asher's concern. 'Of course they're real!'

'No, it would be real to you if Liss were your daughter, or your sister, or even a member of your own caste, but it isn't real now.' The flat tone of voice made the words a chill rebuke. 'Your experience is on the reverse side, isn't it? If a man wants a woman, he can always find one, isn't that how you see it? Custom gives you the *right* always to please yourself, where we have none. No doubt whenever your ships made port you visited the brothels, or your men did?'

Mallory was silent, shocked at her frankness but also struck by the weariness in her face, wondering what experiences could have made her so bitter. Was it only the memory of Lewes, or had there been others? 'I've never taken an unwilling woman,' he said stiffly.

'I didn't accuse you. I simply said you don't understand, or care, why we did what we did. You're only interested in how our actions might affect *you*.'

'What if it had been Asher?' Mylura asked coolly, after another uncomfortable silence. 'If Kerrick had a hold over her or her family? How would you feel then?'

Remembering the rage he had experienced at the thought of Asher with Kerrick, there was only one truthful response Mallory could have given. 'Would you really have used the authority Avorian gave you?' he asked her.

'If I had to.' There was a pause. 'He never even asked her name.'

He sighed, disgusted with the absent Kerrick and a little with himself. 'I wish you'd told me, I would have dealt with it.' It was the closest he was willing to go, at that moment, to an apology.

'Would you?' She sounded openly disbelieving.

'I'm not quite lost to decency!'

'No.' She looked away. 'Then I'm sorry.'

'With men like Kerrick in the world, I shouldn't be surprised you don't trust me.' Yet he could not help himself remembering his dead wife at that moment, Melanna who had been unfaithful, and found it hard to be accused of a lack of sympathetic understanding by reason of his sex when he knew that women, as much as men, were capable of deceit and cruelty.

'I think we see the question of duty differently, Mallory.' Asher's voice was still remote. 'To me, all of us have a duty to those weaker and more vulnerable than ourselves, but you seem to see the responsibility as being *for*, not to. If Liss were your tenant, you'd not have let Kerrick near her, but as she was not, you let the matter pass. You'd have helped her if he'd held a knife at her throat, but you can't see that that's exactly what he was doing.'

Mallory caught a glimpse of the difference she was trying to explain, but all his instincts were against agreement; he frowned, saying nothing.

It was Mylura who tried to make peace, holding out her hand. 'If we need your help in the future, we'll ask for it, Councillor. A bargain?'

'Asher?'

She hesitated, then said reluctantly, 'A bargain.'

But, looking at her, Mallory found it hard to believe she meant it.

*

In the morning, Kerrick was nursing both a grudge and a hangover. Asher observed his behaviour with disgust, surprised Avorian should entrust the man with any position of responsibility, nephew or not. Her intense dislike for Kerrick deepened when she caught sight of their hostess, who was sporting a livid black eye; she had no doubt who was responsible.

'I must apologize,' Mallory murmured. 'You were right: no woman deserves Kerrick.' Asher wondered how he felt, if he was disappointed with himself and wishing he had displayed a greater concern for the girl the previous night. She felt weary, tired of arguing, not even in the mood to take Mallory further to task.

The entrance of Val with news that Ancil had disappeared, taking with him Horton's horse and unspecified supplies, enraged Kerrick further. He shouted abuse at everyone in turn, heaping censure and insults on Hanna, Horton, and finally the hired guards.

'We were paid to protect your party from thieves, not to watch your slave,' Val answered stolidly. 'In any case, it's most likely he'll be caught; it's a long way to the border.'

'*I want him caught and sent to the Games arena!*' Kerrick rounded on Mallory. 'Bear witness, Councillor! He stole my horse, and who knows what else!'

'Mistress Hanna,' Mallory said politely, looking at the bemused woman, 'you must tell us what has been taken from you, and we will make up your loss.'

'I'm not paying a copper coin!' Kerrick snapped.

'The boy was your slave, and you bear a responsibility for what he took.' Mallory surveyed the other man coldly. 'In law.'

Neither Asher nor Mallory was prepared for Kerrick's response; the man glared at them malevolently, his gaze flicking from one to the other. 'I'm sure my uncle will be interested in your views, Councillor. And in many other things as well. I can see now why you asked to come on this journey.' Having delivered the threat to his apparent satisfaction, he glowered at Hanna. 'What did he take?'

'Only a little food, and a few coppers.'

'Here.' Kerrick flipped a silver coin in her general direction, which she caught with unexpected dexterity. 'Take note, Councillor, that I have paid my dues.'

There was a general stir as the party prepared for the day's travel.

'Do you think he meant it? That he'll say something to Avorian?' Asher asked anxiously.

Mallory gathered up his cloak. 'We'll just have to take more care. There're only two more days of travel in Kerrick's company in any event.' But, Asher thought resentfully, it was easier for him to say than for her to take comfort in the brevity of the time remaining, for even if Kerrick made good his threat, the Chief Councillor would think no worse of Mallory for womanizing; but he would certainly imagine the worst of her, and might even lose her the Treasury post.

The events of the previous night continued to cast a gloom over her thoughts. While there was some satisfaction in Liss's escape, Asher felt a dull pain as she remembered Mallory's reaction, recalling what he had said and how little he had understood. Was his view of the world the right one, or only a pragmatic statement because he did not care or want to change old customs and attitudes of mind?

It was an ill fortune to be born a woman, but was that because of the Fates, or only because people believed it to be true and thus it was so? Was it custom or a gendered imbalance of luck that restricted the lives of women throughout the Dominion, born to wealth or to poverty?

I don't know. I don't suppose I ever shall. But none of it makes any sense, or not to me. She was shocked to find herself close to tears, she who never cried.

At last the party got underway, Horton riding Ancil's mount, more soured than ever by the exchange. The rain, which had held off overnight, began to fall again in earnest, soaking them all within minutes. The trail was heavily muddied, and the plains across which they travelled were dotted with dips and hollows filled to the brim with flood-water, offering new and undesirable hazards. Some of the lower-lying fields, too, were flooded, and Asher's spirits fell further as they progressed through the sodden landscape; it seemed doubtful the sun would ever shine again.

In the late-morning they encountered a Kamiri troop on patrol who forced them to wait for what felt like hours while their papers and travel passes were inspected, and every piece of luggage was unpacked and the contents scrutinized. Asher and Mylura handed over their papers, on Asher's part with some trepidation, and she saw Mallory watching her; but there was no outcry, no accusation. The only thing to catch the captain's interest was Kerrick's demand for the recapture of Ancil, which brought a gleam to his grey eyes.

'You say he had a horse. Which way did he go?'

'North,' Kerrick said sulkily. 'Or that's where the tracks led.'

'We shall find him, and inform you. He will take his place in the arena.' The captain placed Ancil's papers, which Kerrick had given him, inside his thick jacket. 'You may continue on your way. Everything is in order.'

'Do you think he could manage to get as far as Saffra?' Asher asked Mallory in a low voice, although she was better qualified than he to know how unlikely it was.

He shook his head. 'It's too far, and the brand on the boy's face would give him away wherever he fled. I wish it weren't so, I abominate slavery.'

Slavery in the Kamir sense, yes, because it degrades men as well as women and children, owner as well as owned, Asher found herself thinking, with renewed despair. If he were capable of sympathy for those who suffered the misfortune of being branded slave, why could he not see that there was another form of slavery, equally degrading? Lewes could divorce her, but she could not leave him, or not in law. In any court, his word would weigh three times more heavily than hers, although he was a liar born. That many women found happiness in marriage did not alter the essential imbalance of justice, the inequality of value one half of the human race placed upon the other. But perhaps that, like Ancil's slavery, had been predestined.

'He'll not get away from *them* so easily,' Kerrick observed in vicious satisfaction, glaring at Val's rigid back. No one answered. Mylura's expression showed her inner rage, although she was silent for once.

They rode on. The rain thinned, and they were making better progress; Asher had travelled the route before on rare visits to her cousin Varah and could pick out a few familiar landmarks. At the front of the column, however, Val raised a hand, calling for a halt.

'We're coming to the river, and it's high,' he called back. 'We may have to swim for it. I'll go ahead and try to get a rope across.'

'How deep is it?' Kerrick asked irritably.

'Can't say until I try. The water's too muddy to see bottom.' Val waited until the others caught up with him, and the cause of his concern became instantly visible; the water was very high indeed, struggling to burst its banks, and the current was strong, especially towards the centre, swelled by recent heavy rains.

Val struggled to persuade his nervous mount into the water. 'Pay the rope out slowly,' he called back to Tarm. His horse condescended to take a few steps, but the level was already up to Val's knees; soon the pair would be swimming. The river was only some fifty or so feet wide, but there was not only the current to contend with; amid the swirling waters lay unseen hazards, branches and other debris washed downstream at a rapid pace. Despite all this, however, Val emerged on the far side, drenched but safe, and proceeded to attach a line of rope to a convenient tree while his brother did the same on the near side. He then beckoned Ish forwards, looking to Mallory for permission.

'You're on the light side, boy. Hold to this as your horse swims.' He put Ish's hand on the rope. 'Can you swim? No? Typical sailor's lad! Then hang on tight; we'll get you across safe and sound, never fear.'

Ish, following the instructions to the letter, reached the far side without incident, although there was a certain rigidity in his posture that bespoke his nervousness. Tarm looked to Horton to go next; Mallory edged his mount sideways to make room for him to ride forward as Asher watched. Horton made heavy work of the crossing, clinging with one hand to the saddle and the other to the rope for dear life.

Are the Fates watching us at this moment? Have they already decreed which of us will cross over safely?

Asher shivered as an odd excitement grew in her, issuing from her earlier despair. She had no need passively to wait for the Oracle to prove itself to her. The cautious part of her mind told her such thoughts were foolish, but her old, impulsive self no longer had the patience to wait and wonder. It would be better to know. The impulse frightened her, but her fear served only to urge her on, to seize the moment before it was gone.

She saw Tarm gesture to Margit, the tallest and heaviest of the three women, but before she could answer the summons Asher suddenly dug in her heels and urged her horse forward.

No one was close enough to stop her. She was a fair swimmer, for Mallory had taught her and Callith to swim one summer long in the past, and her horse had less fear of the rushing water than Horton's bony mount. She was not close enough to take hold of the steadying rope stretched over the river, but urged her horse on towards the centre of the current. Asher felt quite alone. The water sped past her thighs, soaking her long skirts, and on a further impulse she took her feet in their heavy boots out of the stirrups, letting herself sit only loosely in the saddle, trying to entrust herself entirely to the will of the Fates.

'Look out – upstream!' Val shouted, waving his arms. Asher gave a rapid glance in the direction he was pointing, her heart beating rather faster, but simply sat in her saddle, turning her head to the front once more so she should not see the thick branch being driven towards her in midstream.

It had occurred to her before that she might die, but suddenly, against her will, her resolve faltered; the concept now seemed real, immense and terrifying in its finality. Asher knew she did not want to die. She clutched frantically at the pommel of the saddle with both hands, realizing she had been stupid, tried to get her feet back into the stirrups. But it was too late.

Travelling at high speed, the branch swept down and caught her an agonizing blow high on her right thigh. For a moment, poised between balance and descent, Asher hung in the saddle, then slid sideways, half-stunned, into the rushing water, and was swept instantly away. She no longer had any control over what was happening to her as her head sank under the surface and her mouth and nose filled with water, suffocating her. In panic, Asher tried to raise her head and gulp in air, knowing there was no more time to reflect on what she had done, or why. The only choice left was to struggle to live, and perhaps fail, or to let herself go with the current and certainly drown.

In her frantic attempts to gain the surface, the thought flashed through her mind that perhaps the Fates had already made that decision for her.

Her horse swam placidly on until Val could grasp its bridle and pull it out on to the far bank, but Mallory could only watch, shocked into immobility. Asher's head disappeared beneath the water, resurfacing only briefly moments later.

The near river bank was barely passable, with high grasses and intervals where willow trees overhung the river, but Mallory urged his mount to a trot, then an injudicious canter as he followed the course of the river, desperately trying to discover any sign of Asher, alive or dead. He did not want to contemplate how low were her chances of survival, not unless the river widened or met some natural obstacle downstream, but he refused to despair. There was a frozen place in his chest which would not acknowledge the possibilty of Asher's loss, that he would be alone again with only the prospect of a dozen years of duty ahead for companionship.

She can't die. The Oracle said . . . But there was no time for thought, or for anything else in Mallory's headlong plunge as he fought to control his mount, to keep him from breaking a leg in one of the many potholes that marred the surface of the bank. 'Asher!' he shouted, without any hope of being heard. 'Asher — keep your head up! Swim!'

Chapter Eight

The shock of the icy water sent Asher down beneath the surface. She struggled, trying to force her way back to air, her lungs feeling as if they might burst from the pressure. Her head came above the surface momentarily, but she barely had time to draw in a breath before the strength of the current pulled her under again. She was aware of pain in her right thigh, and a thundering in her head which might have been the sound of the river, or simply panic.

Again, she forced her head up, spitting out mouthfuls of muddy water; she panted for breath, using her arms to keep herself afloat. The impulse that had caused her descent into the river was obliterated in a more powerful desire to live; if she was to have any chance of surviving she would have, somehow, to get herself away from the mainstream current.

Her knee-length riding-boots acted as heavy weights, bearing her down, but there was no way to rid herself of them. Asher tried to remember all she had been taught, how to float *with* the current rather than struggle against it, positioning herself sideways to avoid water filling her mouth every time she opened it to breathe. There was no possibility of resistance – the force of the current was too strong for that – only of keeping her head above water.

From a corner of an eye, she sighted more debris in mid-stream, a branch caught up in another course of the current, and, as it drew closer, reached out to grab it, hoping it would give her more buoyancy. It eluded her grasp. At the same time she felt herself drawn under again, unbalanced, and held her breath. She came back to the surface spluttering desperately, beginning to feel unpleasantly weak, her arms too feeble to bear her up much longer. She could hear nothing but the rushing of the river and a high-pitched ringing in her ears.

There was a moment of terrified certainty when she was sure she was going to drown, completely powerless, her body at the mercy of the current.

There must be a way.

Some impediment below water level struck her legs as she was swept along; it could have been anything – a tree trunk, a boulder. The pain was agonizing. Asher wondered if she had broken her right leg, which had for a second time taken the main force of the impact, because when she tried to move it pain screamed at her; but when she tried a second time she found it would bend. Roaring sounds in her head disoriented her, sending dark messages to her vision, and she swallowed several more mouthfuls of filthy water as she tried to clear her eyes.

The river widened out, that much she could see from her present position. The current was no less strong but Asher gathered her remaining strength, knowing she could not afford to wait any longer. Wearily, she tried to swim a few strokes sideways, not against the current but with it; her arms felt desperately heavy, her sodden clothes and boots making every movement an extraordinary, impossible effort. She kicked out, ignoring stabs of pain from her right leg, and thought she had gained a very little; she continued her efforts, trying to move out of the main current towards the weaker flows at the side. Yet still her body was flung onward, downriver, out of her control, and a brief lucid thought shouted: Fool, fool, fool!

At last she gave up, no longer having any command over her limbs, which were too heavy to obey her ebbing will. The banks seemed as far away as ever. This time, as she felt herself slipping underwater, she made only token efforts at resistance. Her mouth and nostrils filled with water, and it seemed to her it would be no great difficulty to breathe it in, that water would do as well as air.

The Oracle was wrong. But that no longer mattered.

She let the current take her.

She grew gradually aware of being still in the land of the living. It took time for bodily sensations to penetrate her mind, as though the pace of time had slowed in response to her own sluggish reactions. First, she discovered she was lying on something hard, for her back hurt; second, she ached all over, as if she were covered from head to foot with bruises; and third, she felt extremely, and imminently, sick.

'She's coming to.'

There was an arm at her back, lifting her up. She coughed up a mouthful of water and spat it out; the effort hurt her chest horribly.

'Asher?'

It was Mylura's voice, but it was beyond her abilities to respond.

'Leave her be.' That was Mallory. 'She's swallowed half the river; we'll have to get rid of it for her.'

The next few minutes were painful and exhausting. At the end, Asher was shaking with cold and weakness. She let them do whatever they wanted, unable to resist or care, and, when they had finished, lay back, totally spent.

'We can't leave you here, Asher.' Mallory again. 'I'll put you up in front of me. Can you stand?' She managed to nod; it would be too great an effort to speak. 'Mylla – help me with her.'

They leaned her against the flank of Mallory's horse, clinging to the bridle, while he mounted; then she felt herself being lifted into the saddle, an awkward process. She clung to the pommel to avoid slipping off, for her clothes were soaked and the saddle felt like glass; but she did not fall, and an arm came round to grasp her waist, making her feel more secure.

'We've to rejoin the others.' He sounded perfectly calm. 'Just hold on.'

She closed her eyes. She was cold, and tired, and she ached; that it was her own fault did nothing to mitigate the sensations. Her mind, however, was clear enough to recognize that the fact that she was still alive weighed heavily in the balance against her tenuous hope of free fate.

Mallory left questioning her until the following morning, when she looked almost her old self again. A night spent in a large and comfortable farmhouse had done much to restore her strength, and, while Kerrick had complained endlessly at the delay, even he seemed relieved at her recovery; the miraculous nature of her survival had affected even his sense of importance.

'Why?' Mallory asked eventually. They were riding in pairs, for the track was broader along the flat farmlands; Kerrick, some way ahead, was busy admonishing Horton and out of earshot.

Asher did not look at him. 'Why? Because I wanted to *know*, I suppose.'

He was puzzled. 'Know what?'

'About the Oracle.'

He was none the wiser. 'I don't understand.'

She shrugged her shoulders impatiently. 'If it was true; that it can see the future, and it's all there.'

Suddenly, he grasped her meaning. The outrageousness of her

conduct appalled him so much he wanted to shake her. 'Asher,' he began, 'are you trying to tell me you risked your life just to get *proof* of this peculiar belief?'

She looked at him with defiance. 'Yes.'

'Then you're out of your mind! Listen to me, just this once?' Her expression, however, was not receptive. Sighing, he continued: 'Just because the Oracle prophesied you *might* be involved in the rescue of Vallis doesn't mean your life is charmed.'

'Doesn't it?'

He saw from the stubborn set of her mouth that she was not convinced. 'I always thought you had *some* intelligence,' he said angrily. 'Can't you see? The prophecy only said *might*. If you succeed in killing yourself – and you will, if you go on behaving like a fool – then perhaps you put Vallis, everything, in jeopardy. Who knows? But nothing – *nothing* – is going to save you from your own stupidity!'

She turned on him, eyes blazing. 'Is that so, Mallory? How do you know?' But her anger drained away almost at once, and she slumped despairingly in the saddle. 'If everything we do is predestined, then it doesn't matter what we do. If I'd been meant to drown, I would have drowned. I *should* have drowned. Nothing I decide makes any difference at all.'

He heard defeat in her voice, and was troubled. 'Ash,' he said, more gently, 'it isn't like that. Of course it makes a difference. Think rationally. If you'd stayed behind the night you heard Lewes and the Kamir talking, you might be dead. But you didn't. You're alive, and you're here.'

'Perhaps.' It was obvious she did not believe him, and he could see she was in no mood for further discussion. Reluctantly, he let her be, increasingly uneasy about her. Remembering the girl he had known, he could not reconcile her with the Asher who rode beside him. Or was it only that he had never really *known* her at all? Had he only understood her within the bounds of his own expectations, so that he had seen her as young, pretty and vivacious – attractive – and approved of her as a friend for his sister and as a follower for himself, without really thinking about the sort of person she was? Her marriage to Lewes, despite any reservations about the character of her future husband, had seemed, at the time, a sensible union; yet, with the benefit of hindsight, how would he have felt if he had been given in marriage to someone who had wanted only his lands, and had no obligations to treat him with even common courtesy. From whom he could not free himself.

What of Melanna? Why did she agree to marry me? He could never think of his wife without remembering her betrayal. It was that, not grief at her death, which had blotted out the memories of the years they had shared; but it was true she had been alone much of the time, for he had been away at sea, often for months on end, and his own family were scattered by then and hers far distant in the port of Refuge. During their days together, if he was honest, she had been a pleasant companion, always solicitous to his wants and needs. He had expected it; that was the way in marriage. But – and he wondered why he had never thought of it before – he had never considered what she might want from their union, from life. She had said she wished he were not so often absent, but he had thought her wishes mere form; he *had* to leave her. It was his duty to go to sea, hers to stay behind and administer the clan estates – his estates – entrusted to her.

How could it work any other way? Men were strong, women weak and submissive. But the thought lacked conviction, not only because in Asher's presence it was so plainly untrue, but also sounding horribly as if he were viewing Melanna the way the Kamiri invaders viewed his own people, as weak and subordinate by virtue of their physique and lower aggression. The Darrianites had always been traders, priding themselves on their skill and daring rather than on martial dominance, sailing further and faster than ships of other nations. But what was the good of that, when faced with the overwhelming military might of Amrist and his armies, to whom force was the only reality?

Is that how we control our women? With force? He thought of the girl on the smallholding, how Kerrick would have taken her, whether she wanted to bed him or not, and the memory shamed him. He had not considered her feelings important, nor the possible consequences to her from a night spent enduring Kerrick's lust. She was an ephemeral moment in Mallory's life, a girl he would never meet again, and he had worries enough of his own; but Asher and the others had seen what might happen, and taken steps to prevent it. True, it was easier for them; they were women, and the consequences were more at the forefront of their minds. But he *should* have considered them. He had always thought himself a fair captain and an honourable man. There was no honour in the rape of a young girl, innocent or not.

Asher, lost in her own broodings, paid scant attention to Mallory. Her thoughts oppressed her; she, who had always prided herself

164

on being in control of her life, was nothing. Her achievements – or what she thought of as her achievements – were nothing. From the moment she was born, her life had been mapped out. She could find no moment of remembered joy as she considered the full implications of the Oracle's powers. What was the sense in fighting injustice, if matters would either right themselves or not, as the Fates dictated? Her twin brother, conceived at the same time as herself, had been destined to die at birth. What was the meaning in that? Had he only been created to give her, Asher, his share of good fortune, to free her from the casual intrusions of chance so that she might help men like Stern to steal? Had he not been designed to exist for any other purpose? The arrogance of the idea horrified her.

She was glad when the day ended and she could retreat to the room she shared with Mylura; the farmhouse was large and prosperous, and there was space for them all. The following day they would reach Eagle Lake and their paths would diverge, hers in the direction of the internment camp and, perhaps, Vallis; in her present mood she no longer cared. Only the prospect of parting from Kerrick temporarily lifted her spirits.

Low-lying mist obscured the plains the next morning, allowing the party only sufficient visibility to keep to the track, but by afternoon it began to lift, and Asher could see the glint of sunlight on water not far ahead.

Eagle Lake, at last.

She drew the scarf that covered her hair lower, so that it hid her face. The lake was a landmark she knew well; once past it, she would be on home ground. The city of Chance lay a day's trek to the south-east; Kerrick's clan holding lay due west. Her own path was south, and as she looked out at the familiar landscape her depression lightened.

The moment of parting came earlier than expected, prompted by Kerrick's insistence on halting at a prosperous-looking inn further along the road, the first they had come to that day. He dismounted and signalled Horton and the others to do likewise; only Mallory and the three women did not follow his example.

'Join me,' he suggested to Mallory with a broad wink, his conviviality somewhat restored by the prospect of drink and willing female companionship. 'The ale's good here, and the company.'

'Thank you, but I think not.' Mallory was barely able to suppress his impatience. 'This journey has already taken longer

165

than I planned.'

'And you, Mistress Asher?' He managed to make the invitation sound unpleasantly suggestive. 'And your friends, of course,' Kerrick added hastily, seeing her look.

'You're very kind, but we too must be on our way on the Chief Councillor's business.' Asher bowed stiffly from the saddle. 'Please accept our thanks for your escort, and my apologies for the delay I caused you.'

The smile on Kerrick's face faded; too late, Asher realized the reference to Avorian had been unfortunate. 'Of course,' he sneered. 'The Councillor here will give you escort at least part of your way. I'm sure he's more than capable of – *escorting* – you all.'

Asher wondered how it was possible to imbue a simple word with such vulgarity; tightlipped, she directed herself to Val and Tarm and thanked them for their protection. Finally, she turned back to Kerrick.

'I'm sure you'll find plenty of women here who'll be glad of your own – escort, for a price,' she advised calmly.

He took a step towards her. '*You stupid sow!*'

'Ah,' Mylura interjected brightly. 'Another one who dislikes the females of the animal kingdom. I told you there were plenty, Asher.'

Kerrick's hand went to his sword, then dropped, but the three women had already turned their horses back down the road to join Pars, Ish and Mallory, leaving Kerrick and his party staring after them.

'I wonder how our Chief Councillor gets on with him?' Mylura commented to Asher, once out of earshot.

'He probably never sees him in this mood.'

'No.' Mylura expelled a long breath. 'Thank the Fates we're free of him now! Even the air smells fresher.'

The six rode on, Ish leading, Mallory at the rear. It was only a short distance to their own separation.

When they reached the parting of the ways, the three women drew apart.

'I wish I could have come with you,' Asher said, sighing. 'And I'm sorry, Margit, to wish all the work on you.'

'You'd better take these now, before we forget.' Mylla drew a packet of papers from inside her jacket and handed them to Asher. 'Remember, if the guard stops you, you're visiting a sick relative in your village.'

'Thanks.' Asher scrutinized the new identity papers, but could find no fault with them. 'Am I really called Imagene?'

Mylla grinned. 'You left the choice to me.'

'This is Avorian's authorization.' In turn, Asher handed Mylla her own papers. 'And this is from the city. If you're in any doubt what to do, ask Margit; she knows all the tricks. And thanks for what you're doing, I'm very grateful. Take care of yourselves.'

Mylura grinned happily. 'Not at all, and don't worry. I'll do everything Margit tells me!'

'Don't forget,' Margit chimed in. 'We meet at the village of Bounden's Fen in seven days.'

'I shan't forget.' Asher suddenly wanted to go with them, not go home at all. It would feel strange to be in the company of Ish, Pars and Mallory, without another woman present.

'Good Fortune, Ash. I hope with all my heart this girl is the one we're looking for.' Margit gave her a quick smile.

'I also.'

'Go carefully. And don't worry about me in the hands of this maniac here!' Margit waved at Mylura's tall figure; Asher grinned.

'Good luck.'

Mallory was waiting at the place where the second trail forked west, taking Margit and Mylura to the start of their tour of inspection. The cottages of the first village were already visible only a short distance along the track.

'The Chief Councillor has arranged an escort for you in each village, and accommodation and so on,' Asher reminded both women. 'It's only a matter of going through the ledgers and looking for the old tricks – you know them all, Margit.' They embraced briefly. 'Thank you both again.'

'In seven days,' Mylura repeated.

'Good Fortune!'

Asher waved a final farewell, then turned her horse south.

'Regretting it already?' Mallory asked, as he rode at her side. 'You could change your mind and go with them.'

'Perhaps a little.' Asher sighed. 'I'm not sure how I feel, but no.'

'Try not to worry too much.' Considerately, he left her alone, dropping back to ride with Pars. She was glad to follow Ish's rigid back in silent company with her own thoughts, listening to the steady plodding of hooves along the muddy track. To be going home was so momentous an event, reopening the way to the past and to a host of feelings she had believed long forgotten, that Asher wondered how her decision to come had been taken with so much ease.

They made camp that night south of the lake, and Asher woke

to the sight of the eagles that had given it its name. She watched them for a time, enjoying their easy, soaring flight, the way they hovered and swooped, and wished it were warm enough to swim. Despite her experience at the river, she had no real fear of water, and the lake, though very cold so early in the spring, was still and clear. The sun had risen to cloudless skies for the first time in days, and Asher's spirits rose with it.

She rode the whole day with the hood of her riding cloak pulled well forward, covering her face and hair, but still felt conspicuous as well as constrained as they passed through country where every hedgerow brought with it a rush of memories from the past. The afternoon sun was bright and the day unseasonably warm. Spring had arrived with a vengeance after the rains; field-flowers which, only the day before, had slumped low amid the mud, now blossomed forth into rich seas of red and gold. Fruit trees burgeoned into sprays of strong-scented blossom, and birds sang out lustily. Even the few labouring men and women they encountered smiled as they rode by, calling out cheerful greetings. Some were known to Mallory as well as to herself; they were now very close to her village. Asher wanted to fling back her cloak and drink in the familiar sights, to surprise old friends and neighbours, but the knowledge that if she did so Lewes would be among the first to know she was back deterred her.

She was hungry for home, but strangled by her enforced anonymity. Her feelings of frustration and discomfort intensified, and it was only belatedly Asher knew them for what they were; this was the first time since leaving Venture she had been visited by the sensation of being watched. She shivered and sank lower in the saddle.

'Is anything wrong?' Pars was looking at her, his soft, round eyes filled with an habitual anxiety.

'No, not really.' His reaction made Asher regret even so mild an admission. 'Just an attack of nerves.'

He hesitated, gathering his courage. 'Are you sure, mistress?' he ventured at last. 'You l-look as if you were being pursued by all the Fates at once.'

Asher bit her lip, wishing his guess had not been so accurate; despite his friendly presence, the eerie feeling did not diminish.

'What's the matter?' Mallory had moved up to join them; he looked questioningly at Pars.

'Something disturbs the lady, sir,' the clerk answered nervously.

Mallory gestured him back, taking his place at Asher's side. 'Has

168

someone recognized you?' he asked urgently.

'No.'

'Then what?'

The concern in his voice weakened her resolve to keep silence. Asher realized she wanted to tell him, even if he only dismissed her fears as nonsensical. 'It's just a feeling.' She struggled to find the right words to express her meaning. 'As if someone was watching me, someone I can't see; but they can see *me*.'

'Is this the first time you've felt like this?'

The sensation was now very strong. 'No – a few times in Venture. It's nothing, Mallory, just my imagination.'

'Tell me, have you lost anything lately? Some item you always wear or use? A comb or some such thing?'

She frowned. 'No, I don't think so . . . No, wait. I lost a brooch about twelve days ago – like this one.' She pointed to the seven-sided star she used to pin her cloak.

'Where?'

'In the hostel, I think.' She thought back. 'It was the night . . .' She stopped herself; she had never mentioned to Mallory the attempted invasion of the hostel by Sim and his friends.

'What night?'

She tilted her head sideways until she could see his face. 'About a week before we left Venture,' she offered.

He shook his head. 'Not good enough. Try again,' he suggested. 'What is it?'

Unwillingly, she related the events of the evening, seeing no help for it. Mallory frowned, more in thought than anger.

'How often do these men break into your building?'

'Once a year, more or less,' she admitted unwillingly.

'Do you report the incursions to the city guard, or take legal action against these people?' Asher shook her head. 'And why not, since you know who they are?'

'What would they do?' Incautiously, she flung her head back, and had to lift a hand to pull her hood down again. 'Fine them a few coppers? They might not even bother to do that!'

'I see.' But instead of pressing the topic, as she had expected, he reverted to their earlier conversation. She was aware of disappointment, expecting him to display a greater concern, then shook her head at her own inconsistency: she wanted no interference from him in her private affairs. 'Would any of these men have a reason for wanting to spy on you?'

'None.' She saw at last what he was getting at. 'You think someone is *overlooking* me? But why? And how?'

'I don't know.' He frowned. 'But your brooch would be a good talisman.'

She wondered if Stern could have taken her brooch; he seemed a more likely candidate than Sim or his friends, and had a real motive for wanting to know where she went. But if she mentioned him she would have to tell Mallory the rest, and her courage shrank from *that* confession.

Mallory broke into her thoughts. 'Omond is still at Kepesake. We'll consult him when we get there.'

'He's alive, then?' Asher asked unthinkingly; Omond, the clan's diviner, had been an old man when she left.

'And well. Asher, I'm not trying to order you what to do, but you *must* tell him about this. What if it has something to do with our mission? It comes so pat.'

She considered a moment, the old resistance resurfacing, but the sensation was too uncomfortable to ignore; finally, she agreed. 'All right.'

He looked relieved, and pleased, and she suspected he had bargained on more argument from her. 'Thank you.'

A distant figure drew her attention away from him; there was something very familiar about the walk, the stoop of the narrow shoulders, that took her instantly back to her childhood. Mallory, too, recognized the man.

'He can't see you, just keep your hood over your face,' he advised calmly.

It was not so easy for her to comply; Kerr had been her father's right-hand man on the farm as far back as she could remember, and she had known him all her life. Not to be able to talk to him, to let him see her, amounted almost to torment.

Now, every field they passed was familiar. To her left lay the pasture belonging to – what was his name? Helm? – where she had been given her first kiss, when she was only fifteen. She had not enjoyed it much, and been glad when her father came looking for her after the harvest-festival supper. The young man – not Lewes – had shown himself eager to progress beyond a few kisses, and he had frightened her.

Ahead lay Harrows, the home of her childhood, a large cluster of buildings standing a little way outside the village. A glance relieved her of the worst of her fears, for Mallory's steward was doing his job well; the fences and stone walls were in good repair, and the huge Oak Field was planted with wheat. But it was hard to picture the farmhouse standing empty, without her parents, without the familiar trail of wood-smoke rising from the chimneys. No one lived there now; Mallory had told her a caretaker kept watch over it.

Home. There was a lump in her throat.

'My steward deals with everything; all taxes and so on are up to date,' Mallory observed. 'He tells me yields have been fair.'

'It looks almost the same.'

She turned away, seeing Carling's across the fields, the farm where she had lived with Lewes during their brief marriage; it was too far away to see if there had been changes, but the sight brought with it far less welcome memories. Her stomach contracted in self-disgust and hatred, remembering the days and nights with him, and the last night, the shame of knowing him a traitor. And he continued to do harm, for it was because of him she was in disguise, because of him she must steal through these old loved places like a thief. But she refused to allow resentment to destroy her moment of pleasure, and she looked back again at Harrows in the distance.

'It's good to be back,' she said softly.

Mallory smiled, but made no answer. They had reached the point where the main trail diverged, a narrow track leading west to the village proper, a small cluster of cottages centred round the inn, and another heading south to Kepesake, the wall surrounding the great house now visible. Gates at the centre of each section of wall gave access to stables, the farm office, the house and the gardens, for the partition was intended only to demarcate the private portion of the estate from the farmlands.

They passed through the gate in the north wall, facing the house. Asher swallowed; little had changed. The oak trees to either side of the avenue still stood, and the great house itself, perhaps smaller than she remembered, had the same welcoming appearance – perhaps by design, for two matching circular windows on the eastern and western extremes could easily be mistaken for a pair of friendly eyes. Built by the founder of the clan, the original Kelham, over one hundred and fifty years before with the spoils of his first successful trading voyage to Petormin, the long, three-storey stone building glowed pale gold in the late afternoon sun. Double doors stood wide, as always, in open invitation, above which the leopard that was the clan's symbol was incised, a regal figure. As primary landlords in the district, the estate office of Kepesake was the hub of the village in all matters regarding land disputes, taxes and other legal matters.

To the right, hidden from the house by a high wall, lay the stables; to the left, the formal gardens reserved for the ladies of the house. Asher caught her breath, remembering; she and Callith had spent many happy hours there, lying on their stomachs in the grass trying to catch the small pink fish that swam along the muddy bottom of the ornamental pool. It had been a matter of pride between them to be able to stay perfectly still and silent, waiting for the moment to pounce; they had always thrown the fish back, but the challenge lay in the catching.

Their arrival seemed to have come at an awkward moment; instead of any sign of welcome, there was a commotion by the stable wall, and people were running towards a boy hanging on to the bridle of a horse that resisted restraint strongly, rearing high, the boy too light to hold his head. On the ground Asher caught sight of the prone figure of a man, and as they drew closer she could see his leg was bent at an awkward angle. Several men stood by, watching rather than helping; a black-gowned woman hurried forward.

'What an intriguing scene.' Mallory looked amused but Ish scowled, as if at a deliberate slight to his master.

The woman knelt by the prone figure, but looked up at the approach of Mallory and his party; Asher hastily lowered her head.

'What's happened here?'

'Master Mallory! I'm that sorry you should have such a welcome!' She rose clumsily to her feet, smiling her pleasure. She was plump and grey-haired, and there was a jangling sound as she moved, the heavy bunch of keys hanging from her belt swinging against her long skirts. Tilda had been housekeeper at Kepesake in Asher's own childhood, but although she seemed to have shrunk in stature, in every other way she looked exactly the same.

Mallory signed one of the men to help the boy with the horse. 'Has there been an accident?'

Tilda shook her head. 'It's Griffin here.' She pointed to the stricken man. 'The horse kicked him, and looks to have broken his leg in two places.' Her voice was filled with disapproval, but it was aimed at the man, not the horse. 'Not that it doesn't serve him right; he's no business to go courting another man's wife, and no cause for complaint if he's ill-wished! But it's downright inconvenient, and that's a fact!'

Mallory dismounted, handing his reins to Ish. 'Have you summoned the healer?'

'Oh, yes, Master Mallory. But he's away at a confinement.' She shot a contemptuous glare at the prone Griffin, then turned her

172

ire on the boy holding the horse. 'Take that great beast away before he does worse!' she snapped impatiently.

'I'm *trying* to.' The boy glared back.

Mallory knelt to see to Griffin, who was groaning loudly. 'Keep still,' he advised. 'I can set this, but not if you keep thrashing around.' He looked up. 'One of you men, fetch wood for a splint and some long pieces of rag. I can bind this and relieve the pain until the healer arrives.'

A fair young man peeled off and disappeared in the direction of the stables. Asher continued to sit her horse, feeling terribly in the way. Mallory, however, had not forgotten her.

'Tilda,' he said, looking up and indicating Asher, 'this lady will be staying here for a few days, as my guest. Will you show her to her room, and see she has everything she needs?'

'Very well, sir.' The housekeeper drew herself up stiffly, looking less than pleased; she gave Asher a frigid smile. 'If you will come with me?'

It was plain Tilda assumed her to be Mallory's mistress. Amused at her old friend's distaste, Asher dismounted, keeping the hood of her cloak low; it seemed everyone in the house had come to see Griffin's broken leg.

Tilda led her into the house by the main entrance. They passed through into a large half-panelled room, the walls covered with portraits of members of the clan, living and deceased, the furnishings covered with dust-sheets. She did not look back to see whether Asher followed. 'This is the hall,' she said coldly. She opened a door to her left and went through. 'This is the library.' Shelf on shelf of books made the explanation unnecessary; Asher was hard pressed not to laugh at the sight of Tilda's affronted back. Glancing to her left at the layers of thick leather-bound volumes, she found herself remembering the time she had climbed up to the top shelf in response to a dare from Callith. She had managed it, but been unable to get down again. Callith, only eleven then, had screamed, thinking she was going to fall, and Mallory had come in. Asher had fallen, on top of him, knocking the breath from them both, and she could still see the resigned look on Tilda's face as she rushed in to find them lying in a heap on the floor, Callith shrieking that they were both dead.

It had been Tilda who had sewn up the long rent in her skirts, too, though Asher's keen-eyed mother had seen it at once and inquired at the necessity. Yet another speech on the virtues of common sense had been the result, if she remembered correctly.

They emerged into a dark, stone-floored passage and climbed

the main stairway. The house was uncomfortably empty and silent; Asher, remembering it filled with the noisy games of Mallory's siblings and other kindred, felt the emptiness keenly as a physical loss. The place felt dead, or in mourning. She climbed meekly in Tilda's footsteps and followed her across the landing and down a long passage to a door at the far end.

'I hope this will suit you,' the housekeeper said, her tone suggesting the reverse. Asher knew herself to be in the guest quarters, as remote as possible from the rooms of members of the family; clearly, Tilda meant to make the supposed liaison as difficult as possible. 'I will send a maid with hot water for you.'

'That would be most kind.' Asher brushed past her and went in, finding herself in a south-facing room of pleasant proportions. She went across to the window and stared out over the fields. Home. I can see my home, she thought, with a rush of happiness, as she looked at the distant but familiar shapes of the house and outbuildings. She threw back the hood of her cloak, eyes blurring with unshed tears.

'Is there anything else you require, madam?'

Asher turned back to the housekeeper. 'No, I don't think so.'

The sight of her face gave the older woman pause, for she had been about to leave the room. She frowned, peering at Asher; the blue eyes that had been hard grew suddenly soft.

'Why, it's young Asher!' A beaming smile lit up her face and she came forwards, arms held wide. Asher accepted the embrace gladly, returning it, her eyes burning again; someone, at least, was glad to see her. Tilda stood back, demanding forthrightly: 'And what are you doing back here, I'd like to know!'

'Not what you were thinking, Tilda,' Asher said wickedly. The housekeeper shook her head at such foolishness. 'It's good to see you again.' It was always Tilda who had slipped forbidden cakes to herself and Callith and Mallory, who could be relied on to bandage knees and mend holes, and even sometimes make excuses for Asher to her mother, when she went home yet again with muddy skirts.

'Have you come home, then? Did Master Mallory find you and bring you back to that no-good husband of yours?' Tilda did not wait for an answer, going on: 'Because he's taken up with another girl – that Dora, from Penger's Farm.'

'Really?' For a moment, Asher was disconcerted, then she shrugged. 'She always liked him. But no, I've not come back to him, Tilda. In fact, please ask the servants not to mention I'm here to *anyone* outside the house.'

'Of course, what do you take me for?' Asher realized it would be impossible to keep her identity secret within Kepesake itself during her visit; too many of the servants had known her, and would recognize her. She was intensely grateful Tilda's long-held dislike of Lewes was still at full force.

'You look well.' The housekeeper surveyed her critically. 'A bit too thin, mind, but well. So tell me, what happened to the man you ran off with?'

'There was no man.' Asher took off her cloak and threw it over a stool. 'I'll tell you the story another time, Tilda. But have you seen Callith and her children? How are they?'

She could not have chosen a better change of subject. 'She comes here every summer,' the housekeeper said importantly, picking up Asher's cloak and folding it neatly. Callith had always been her favourite. 'She brings her boys with her; fine young lads, the pair of them, one four years old, the other only two. The little one's the spit of Master Mallory!'

'I'm glad.'

'You've no children, I suppose?'

Asher smiled. 'No.'

This was received with a sniff of approval. 'And so I should hope.' The blue eyes looked carefully at her face and sharpened. 'And what are you going to do with yourself, if you've not come back to your lawful husband? You know he's looked for you?'

'I know.'

Tilda's expression softened. 'Don't fret yourself,' she said gently. 'I'd not tell him you were here, and nor will the others; he's a bad man, and that's the truth. You're well out of it.' Asher found herself close to tears again at the warmth of her welcome but the housekeeper's next words rallied her and put her firmly in her place. 'And now, young woman,' Tilda said wrathfully. 'Just *what* have you done to your hair?'

Chapter Nine

Late-afternoon sunlight streamed in through tall windows in the long attic, which was furnished in somewhat haphazard fashion. Floor-to-ceiling shelves housed assorted books, a mass of specimen jars, vials of powders and odd-coloured liquids, as well as a variety of incomprehensible devices whose purposes it was impossible to define with any accuracy.

'Wait one moment.'

The old man waved a hand, but did not turn round; all his visitor could see of him was a purple-robed back and a mass of silver-white hair. His hands returned to their occupation, busy with a glass vial into which a steaming substance emitting sinister clouds of smoke was being poured; when it was done, the old man stoppered the vial and placed it in a wooden rack, only then turning to greet the newcomer.

'Young Mallory, a surprise and a pleasure!' Sharp eyes flickered to the visitor's face. 'I am glad you have spared the time to visit Kepesake. We have not seen you since last summer, unless I mistake.'

'Omond.' Mallory inclined his head, laughing. 'No, your memory is as keen as ever: I have been neglectful. But I find you well occupied.'

'This?' The diviner looked vaguely at the well-filled shelves. 'Perhaps, perhaps.' He was old, with the frailty of advanced years; a thick white beard and moustaches covered the lower half of his face, hiding a lower lip that sometimes shook, but watery eyes, deep-sunken hazel flecked with green, were still bright with a formidable intelligence. 'Is this a casual visit or have you some specific purpose in mind in coming here?'

'Both.' Mallory glanced back to the doorway, but there was no one there; he lowered his voice. 'I need your help, Omond. Do you remember a girl named Asher, Erward's daughter? She was here often as a child. I believe someone is using the sight against her.'

'Where is she?'

'In this house; she came with me from Venture. I sent for her to come here to you, but I wanted a word before she arrives. I should explain – she has always scorned the use of charms and protections, and would refuse your help, if she could. But it's not only the *sight*, there's more . . .'

Omond held up a hand restrainingly. 'Slowly, slowly, young Mallory, if you please. Of course I remember the child. She was the one whose twin brother died at their birth – hardly surprising; female children are far stronger than their male counterparts in the early years. Tell me why, first, you believe her to be *overlooked* by one of my calling.'

Mallory described Asher's sensations as accurately as he could at second hand, and Omond nodded.

'Then your guess may be correct. Have you any notion why it should be so?'

'No.' Mallory sounded frustrated. 'Unless it has something to do with our reason for coming to Kepesake.'

'Which is?'

He hesitated. 'We are searching for Vallis; having summoned us, the Oracle of Venture suggested we may both have some share in discovering her whereabouts, and there is a girl who just might be Vallis in the internment camp in the Vale. Asher and I met before the Oracle itself, Omond. It must be more than a coincidence, after six years.'

'Interesting, and certainly it must be more.' He turned the idea round in his mind. '*Fate*. It is possible you were brought together for this purpose, and this may indeed be the reason for your concern. But *who* is keeping the girl under observation?'

'I've no idea.'

'That is not very helpful,' Omond observed dryly. 'No matter. Your second request, if you please? It sounded as if you were disturbed for the child's safety for more than one reason?'

'I am.' Mallory sighed. 'She was married here, seven years ago, to a man named Lewes – from Carling's Farm, you might know it? – but ran away after only a year. It's not safe for her to have returned.'

'Of course I know it, and him – a most unsavoury character,' the diviner said crisply; it annoyed him that his advanced age seemed to give others licence to imagine him forgetful.

'While she's at Kepesake I want some watch kept over her, in case he learns she's here. I don't trust him, and I don't trust her to have enough sense to keep out of his way.'

'I see.' Omond considered the request. 'This is a difficult question from the ethical viewpoint. You wish me to place some watch over her without her knowledge – in effect, to spy on her yourself!'

'Yes,' Mallory admitted bluntly. 'There's no other way.'

'I cannot like it.' Omond frowned. 'It is, of course, perfectly possible, although my range is limited in these days. But I cannot agree until I have seen the girl for myself; it may be she has no need of this protection.'

'That's all I ask. But I warn you, Omond, she's not very amenable to your craft.' Mallory sighed. 'In fact, I think she resents it.'

But the diviner was looking beyond him towards the open door, and Mallory turned to find Asher coming towards them, fortunately displaying no sign of having overheard their discussion.

'Ah, I should have known you anywhere!' It was not entirely true, for this girl with the drawn face and air of taut nervousness did not greatly resemble the child he remembered. Omond had lively memories of that girl, always up to some mischief or other with young Callith; but surely her hair had been fair, not dark? He was about to make the observation, then decided it safer to vouchsafe no remark, in case he had it wrong.

'Master Omond.' Asher bobbed her head.

'Well, child, it is a pleasure to see you again. Mallory here tells me you are having some trouble with one of my fraternity,' Omond essayed, noting with dismay the antagonism in her expression.

'I'm hardly a child, Master Omond.'

'To *me*, anyone under the age of seventy is a mere infant!' he said grandly, and saw her smile, reluctantly, and knew he had hit the right note. 'Mallory,' he went on imperiously, 'you may leave us. We shall do better alone.'

The tone of his command seemed to please the girl, and Omond found his curiosity aroused. Why should there be such antagonism between the two? He corrected himself: from the girl to Mallory. Yet he could have sworn Mallory was not only concerned for her, but with her. Intrigued, he moved to seat himself in a high-backed, high-armed chair drawn up to the long table where he conducted most of his experiments. 'Come, child,' he instructed. 'Sit beside me, and tell me about the last occasion on which you felt yourself subject to the *sight*.'

She took the proffered seat, sitting on the edge of the chair, as if she wanted to be free to jump up at any moment. 'A little time ago, as we rode through the village.'

'Excellent.' Omond reached for her hands. 'Permit me to hold these a while; sometimes there is a lingering residue of the mind of the observer, which may be traced back or sensed by another of the same kind. In this instance,' and he bowed ironically, 'myself!'

Her hands were slender, with short, thin fingers which felt cold in his own, and had ragged, bitten nails; there was a tension in her which communicated itself in every nerve, and again he wondered at the cause. There was something very wrong. He shook himself mentally and set to concentrating on the purpose in hand, seeking to discover what kind of man kept her under his watchful eye.

Strong, very strong. And distant, too. He did not speak his thoughts aloud, permitting his will free rein as he felt at once the bond that linked the girl to her unseen observer, concentrating on his sixth sense.

At last, he let her go, sunk deep in thought. The mind he sensed caused him concern for it was far more powerful than his own, plainly younger and more focused — but then it possessed a talisman which led him directly to the girl, wherever she was; in addition, it was a mind which guarded itself from intrusion.

'Well?' Asher was regarding him with some suspicion, and he loosed her hands.

'You are thinking this is all a dreadful waste of time,' Omond observed pleasantly. 'Perhaps you are correct but it can do no harm to try, I think?'

She flushed. 'I'm sorry.'

'Ah, all you see here is mere paraphernalia, which has nothing to do with my craft. These jars and vials I see you looking at are my hobby, to see how various substances act on one another; but the powers of divination are very different, as is the *sight*.'

'Aren't they the same thing?'

'Indeed, no.' Omond was pleased she possessed sufficient curiosity to ask the question. 'Although divination is an inner eye, a form of sight, as you seem to know, the gift whereby those of my kind perceive the ebbs and flows of future fortunes. Rather as a water-diviner seeks the tug of water. No, the *sight* I would describe as a roving eye, one that can be bound to a single person rather than limited in place; it is another sense that sees with the will, not the eyes.'

The girl looked confused, which was not entirely surprising.

Omond knew he had not explained himself very clearly. 'Then how does divination work?' she asked, frowning. 'Is it an active or a passive thing? Can you stop it, if you want to?'

'The powers lie in the mind and the will of those who possess the gift. And now I shall demonstrate to you the *sight*, and I intend to make use of one of those substances I mentioned earlier. Will you fetch me that copper bowl from the lowest shelf?'

She did so, handing it to him. 'What are you going to do?'

'There are many ways of *seeing*,' he explained. 'Some diviners make use of the smoke, some the cards or even lots to increase their power of focus; some have no need of more than their will alone. Your observer has a talisman belonging to you, once worn by you and thus connected to you, and I wish to discover if I can find it – or him. Help me rise.' She gave him her arm, and he struggled upright. 'Thank you. I find the process of standing most awkward. Once on my feet I experience no difficulties.' He moved to the shelves and selected a vial of dark blue liquid from a rack. 'Would you be so good as to pour water from that pitcher on the floor into the bowl for me? It saves me having to bend.'

He returned to the table to find all ready for him and unstoppered the vial, pouring the viscous liquid into the bowl of water, stirring it with a thin metal rod until the substance was dispersed; it was not soluble, and floated on the surface, forming circular patterns which revolved around the bowl.

'Now stand behind me, and be still.' Asher obeyed. 'Stay there until I say you may move.'

Omond stared into the bowl, submerging himself in the forms that met his eyes; this, he had discovered, was the most effective method of increasing his own powers of focus. The blue oil revolved, the patterns reflected in the shining sides and bottom of the copper bowl, forming and reforming images which, as he stared more intently still, opened in his mind his other eye, blotting out what he saw with his eyes and showing him – *a chain, a chain which led from the girl behind him north, north, towards Venture. The mind to which it was attached was cool, strong; a man, definitely, by the feel* . . .

'Why did you move?' he asked sharply, for something knocked his chair and his inward eye had closed, so that now he saw only the images in the bowl.

'I felt dizzy.' Asher swayed, a hand on the back of his chair.

'Sit down.' She complied. 'Now, tell me, what made you dizzy?'

She frowned. 'I was looking into the bowl. I think it was the way the oil moved.'

'What did you see?'

'Just movement. But when I shut my eyes I kept seeing patterns coming together and separating, and a thick strand that seemed to go against the rest.' She stopped, blinking, pressing a hand to her forehead.

'Have you seen such things before?'

'Once when I was in the same room as a diviner using the smoke, I think he called it.'

Omond gave her a sly smile. 'Has it never occurred to you, child, that you may have, in small part, a gift for divination?'

'*No!*' From her expression, he might have been accusing her of some heinous crime. 'Never.'

'You sound very sure,' Omond said mildly. 'I find it curious you should reject my suggestion so strongly. Have you reasons for your dislike of my profession?'

'It's only that I never believed in such things, not since I was a child,' she said stiffly.

He frowned, uneasy, for what she said was nonsense. 'But it is not a question of belief, child; that is like saying you do not believe in the wind. I am aware you are the survivor of identical twins, which for some reason we do not fully understand grants you immunity from common acts of Fate, so what to the rest of us are causes and effects are mere superstitions to you. But you are not immune to the Fates. How could you be so? You have your own place in the balance of good and evil in our world. And you have not explained your antipathy to my craft.' Omond tilted his head, bright eyes meeting hers. 'Explain to me your reasons, if you will?'

He thought she was going to refuse, but something stirred to life in her as he watched, perhaps anger, perhaps resentment.

'I never believed there was a way to divine the future,' she burst out. 'All my life I told myself it was a lie, all clever guesswork, or even less than that. Until I went to the Oracle in Venture.' She stopped to draw in a shaky breath. 'Then I wasn't so sure. It knew me. That's what frightened me most, that it knew what I was; and then Mallory was there, and that seemed impossible, too, so the Oracle had to be real and I'd been wrong all my life.' There was pain in her voice. 'What's the point of *anything* if our lives are planned for us from the moment of our birth? Why should we bother to strive, to work, to care, if nothing makes any difference to the lines of our lives? If there are no real choices? Why should we want to know what will come when such knowledge means nothing – if you tell me I'm going to die in a year, or a month, why should I want to know? What good does knowing do me if I can't avoid it?'

'I think . . .' But she had not finished.

'I hate it. It's as if whatever I was used to thinking of as *myself* was just self-deception. How can men and women be so important in the grand design of the Fates that they should write each one of us into their master-plan? What is it they want? What do they gain? I don't – *won't* – believe it!'

Omond coughed. 'I think you misunderstand the precise nature of divination, child. That is *not* what can be *seen*; the gift is to discover what is most probable, not what must be. Of course there is a choice – '

She did not hear him out. 'Is there? When men can say they thank the Fates they were not born women, and at the same time circumscribe *our* lives because we are, and justify doing so because that is *our* fate? If that's so, then the Fates must hate women, so we are unlucky from the very beginning, and any good fortune they permit us is only a mitigation, not really luck at all.'

'You mistake custom for – '

Asher did not hear his interruption. 'When people are sure the Fates dictate who is fortunate and who is not, who rich and who poor, who live and who die? It seems to me an obscene game played at our expense by those who would pull our strings for their own amusement, and laugh at our misery and happiness, knowing whether it will last or be destroyed at a stroke. Where, then, is the *choice* you speak of?'

'Yet,' Omond said calmly, 'from what you say, you *do* believe. And wrongly.'

'No!'

'The Fates are not gremlins to blame when matters go awry; fate, chance, fortune – they are all these things, and they exist as in a sea, where the tides may go with us or against us. Our lives are influenced by them and their vagaries, since our health, wealth and happiness are all matters for good or ill fortune, from which foot we use when first we set out upon a journey, to whether we are born to be men or women – yes, that is true, but to be either is neither good nor bad; it is the society we have made which makes the one more highly valued than the other. Be grateful you were born here and not in Javarin or Petormin where they have far less use for those of your sex.' Omond fixed Asher with a stern eye, but she only shook her head. 'Nor have the Fates written a future for you that cannot be altered. Only one where their influence

182

may affect the outcome of the choices which are freely yours to make – '

'No.' She turned away from him, her face set.

He could see it was no use arguing with her; she was still too agitated for detailed explanations. Instead, he rose to his feet and fetched from the shelves a mechanical device, a scale model of Tenebran, both moons transfixed by thin metal wires to attach them, one end of each depending from one of two grooved metallic circles ringing the world approximating to the moons' rotations. Those in turn were themselves secured to the frame built round the model by solid pieces of wire from top to frame, in order not to impede movement.

'Take a look at this apparatus. I am quite proud of it for I made it myself a few years back,' he observed to Asher. 'See how I have tried to make it accurate by separating the rotations of our moons, so that Aspire is further away than Abate, and larger, so that it takes longer to go round our world. It resembles an orrery, but uses Tenebran as its focus.' He took a small handle from his pocket. 'This is not only a model, but a working model. Come and look closer.' He inserted the handle into a slot in the base and began to turn it; as he did so, all three globes began to rotate at different speeds, at first slowly, then faster. It was possible to make out the individual lands of the Dominion marked on the main globe, shaded grey to differentiate them from Saffra, marked in white, and the seas in deep blue. There were other landmasses marked far away to the west of Darrian.

'What are those?' Asher asked, pointing.

'Just a notion of my own.' Omond was pleased his ploy was proving effective. 'I have postulated the existence of other lands, beyond the reach of our present knowledge, so I incorporated them into this design. I may be wrong, but westward migrations are commonest. Look at the moons. Just as they affect the tides of the seas, so, too, they affect the tides of our fortunes, for good or ill, Aspire in our favour when waxing, Abate working against us when waning. This is why their positions on the night of your birth are so important.'

The moons had been marked in divisions, so it was possible to see, if they moved slowly enough, which sections would be visible on any one night throughout the year. Asher was fascinated, especially when the globes began to move faster, moons and world rotating on their separate axes so precisely that the same face of both moons was always presented to the world.

'Watch the globes carefully,' Omond said softly, glad of her absorption. 'See how the moons move round the world, and at the same time rotate on their axes; that is known as a *captured* rotation. Abate moves faster than Aspire. Watch, and see how they turn, faster and faster, until they blur before your eyes.' Prudently, he looked away, for it was impossible to follow the speed of the spinning globes.

Asher seemed bemused, unable to turn her head away as she listened to Omond's soft voice.

'See the oceans, how wide they seem compared with the Dominion; see how small and insignificant Javarin appears,' he went on, in the same, quiet tones. 'Strange, to think of our world ruled by that one small piece of ground, that so much of the world's good fortune should for this time attach itself to that land. Can you make it out? Try. See if you can.'

Asher strove to comply, but she seemed suddenly too weary to stand; there was a chair immediately behind her and she sank on to it.

'Look,' Omond's voice went on. 'Look, and tell me what you see.'

Asher's head fell forwards, and her eyes closed, as if it were too great an effort to keep them open. He put a hand to her shoulder and it felt relaxed, almost boneless, as if she had drifted into sleep.

Quickly, Omond took a gold chain from one of his pockets and placed it over her head, settling it about her neck. 'This is yours, your chain; it has always been yours. You wear it even in sleep. It was a gift from your mother who is dead, who gave it to you believing that the eight-petalled flower which hangs from it would keep you safe. You know this and no matter that you do not believe it, you would never loose the chain, nor the charm.' He paused, and Asher's left hand came up to touch the chain, then the gilded flower, only briefly, as if she wanted to be sure they were still in place. Satisfied, he continued: 'This chain, this charm, bind your life to me; if danger threatens, be sure I will know of it. Through my will, I attune it to you, to you at this place and this time when you are safe from all harm. If the pattern changes, then I shall know of it through my sight. Keep this safe; keep it always with you.'

He felt the subtle pressure on his own mind, a small part of his sixth sense attuned to her present self, the chain a link between them, and knew he had done all he could. He stepped back and touched a hand to the model, slowing the whirling of the globes until they revolved at a more sedate pace, but when he was about to speak the words to awaken Asher, he hesitated. Might it not be wiser to look and *see* if there were danger threatening her? Awake she would refuse, but entranced, it was possible. He had complied with Mallory's request because of his own concern for the girl, but he felt a twinge of conscience at taking advantage of his gift in a way which she would undoubtedly reject, if he gave her a choice.

He took her hands again, noticing the difference in tension. With her conscious mind relaxed, the link between them should be sufficient for him to *see* a short way into the maze of future possibilities. He concentrated his will towards her, seeking the tides of fortune flowing round her, and *saw*:

Death. Around, ahead, and at her side. Everywhere I look, there is death. Omond shuddered, the sense of horror reaching out to embrace him as his inner eye watched the patterns merge together. *So many choices, and so many deaths. But how – how may this be avoided?* Make the right choice – but which was it? He could not *see* clearly, possibilities merging with probabilities so that there was no clear path through the maze. It frightened him, for he had never *seen* anything like it in his life; he let go her hands, wondering what to do.

Perhaps the girl is right. What does it profit me to see this, but to be helpless to save her or those close to her? He felt, suddenly, old and frail and powerless. He would tell Mallory; that was all he could do to help the girl. But first he must rouse her.

'Wake now, and as you do so, remember only the globes.'

Asher stirred, then blinked, sitting up with a yawn. 'I'm sorry,' she apologized, shaking her head to clear it. 'Your model seems to have made me sleepy.'

'You have had a long journey. But I have finished my tests now, and you may rest.' Omond was shocked to see his hands were shaking, and hid them in the long sleeves of his robe.

'Is there someone, then? Watching me?' She looked wary, as if she were not sure she wanted an answer to her question.

'There is. A diviner of great strength who observes from a distance, from Venture. I fear that is all I can tell you.'

'What does he *see*? When he looks at me, I mean? Can he *see* in the dark?' Her left hand strayed towards her neck, touching the chain he had placed there. For a moment she seemed puzzled, then smiled and let the hand drop back to her side.

'The extent,' he said hurriedly, 'depends on the magnitude of his gift and his will. He *sees* you, of course, and to a limited extent what is physically close to you. He cannot know what you say, unless he can read lips, a skill learned by few, but he can *see* in the dark, like a cat.'

'So he might have *seen* Mallory on our way here?'

Omond nodded. 'Very probably.'

She looked disturbed. 'Do you think this has anything to do with our reason for being here?' she asked abruptly. 'Mallory told you?'

'He did, and I regret I cannot say. But it is possible – even likely.' Omond cleared his throat. 'I will give you this protection, although I fear it may not be enough; the fortune that protects you from hex-harm may hinder this in its effectiveness. There are so few identical twins born, and even fewer where only one twin survives, that I have paid less heed to a study of the effects than perhaps I ought.' He fished in his pockets again, and this time withdrew a ring, large enough for her middle finger, set with an octagon-shaped blue stone. 'Take it. It is charmed, and may at least obscure your watcher's vision.'

She looked at it doubtfully. 'Is it necessary?' Once more he could hear in her voice the antagonism to his craft.

'Wear it, child,' he insisted. 'To placate my anxieties, if no more.' He smiled. 'And now, if you will forgive me, I have other tasks awaiting me; less urgent, but belated. Would you be so good as to wait until the globes cease to turn, then replace my model on that shelf? Thank you.' He estimated it would take enough of her time to allow him a private word with Mallory. Stiffly, he walked to the door, feeling every one of his eighty years.

'Thank you,' Asher called, as an afterthought; Omond waved a hand in response. He was weary, for it was many years since he had been asked to expend so much of his energies.

He only hoped his strength would prove sufficient for the task.

It was more than a few minutes before Asher went in search of Mallory and found him in the library. She delayed, needing time to reflect on what Omond had said, wanting to be alone to walk through the parts of the great house that held most memories for her. Yet she found no peace in the old nurseries where she and Callith had spent the rainy days of their childhood; shrouded in dust-sheets, the rooms felt empty of life and the laughter she remembered.

As she descended the main stairs to the ground floor, she passed a woman a little older than herself, one of the maids from the apron covering the print of her dress; they exchanged meaningless smiles, and it was only afterwards Asher realized she knew the woman, although she could not recall her name. Had she, too, been recognized? she wondered. She had come back, but as a stranger, her hunger for home strangled by the need to evade Lewes.

'Asher, come and join me.' Mallory rose to his feet as she entered, gesturing to a deep-seated chair on the far side of the hearth, where a welcoming fire burned. 'What've you been doing?'

'Just walking about, thinking of the past.' She joined him, sinking down gratefully into the comfort of the cushions, holding out her hands to the blaze, suddenly realizing she was cold. 'I hope you don't mind?'

'My house is always yours, you should know that.'

She gave him a quick smile. 'Everything changes. Nothing stays the same, does it?'

He glanced round the room, nodding. 'Do you remember when you fell on top of me from that shelf?' He pointed up to the ceiling. 'I was thinking about that when you came in.'

'You weren't a very comfortable cushion, if I remember right, and it was your own fault. I wouldn't have fallen if you hadn't shouted at me to come down.'

He refused to rise. 'Probably not.'

'Have you found out anything? About the camp in Storm Valley?' She wanted to widen the distance between them, wary of a sudden atmosphere of intimacy. There was a look in Mallory's eye that made her nervous, as if he would like to become a friend of a more intimate nature than she would allow, although in her present loneliness she might almost have welcomed such comfort. A physical companionship might be better than the cold of her self-imposed isolation.

'I've been with Carne, the estate steward, most of the day.' If he noticed her withdrawal, he gave no sign of it. 'There's a lot of work to do here, and only myself to do it at the moment, but he was able to give me some useful information. Apparently, most days the common prisoners are taken out of the camp and down the hill to work a stone quarry – carefully guarded, of course. But that gives us a chance to take a look at them, although Carne did say that after the recent escape of one of the women prisoners the Kamiri keep a close watch on everything that goes on in the valley.'

'I don't know the place well. Do you?'

He nodded. 'I went there once, to look at the old bandits' hideout which is now the camp; there're one or two good vantage places on the opposite hill, although it's a bad spot for firestorms, so there may not be much ground cover.'

'It's the season for them, I suppose,' Asher agreed. 'Perhaps we should take along a sheep or two, to give us an excuse if the Kamiri see us there.'

'Good suggestion.' He paused, looking down at his lap. 'You don't have to come, Asher.'

'Yes, I do,' she replied, angry at the attempt to exclude her. 'You can't leave me here.'

'It's your decision.' Mallory shrugged. 'Lewes came today.'

'What?' Her tone was sharp. 'What did he want? Does he know I'm here?'

'Not so far as I could tell. He came to ask about Harrows again. As you know, it's held in fee from the Kepesake estate, and even after all due debts have been paid there's still a surplus from the farm. He argued that he should receive that at least, and he's petitioning the Governor of Chance over my head to have Harrows transferred to his ownership.' He hesitated, as if he had not wanted to say as much. 'I thought you should know.'

'Thank you.' Asher suppressed a shiver, glad she had not known he was in the same house. She looked down at her lap, at the shabby dark material of her divided skirts, at her thin fingers and their ragged nails, and felt herself grow scarlet at her own earlier imagining that Mallory might want to become her lover, to caress the body Lewes had so often stigmatized as ugly and unarousing. Six years of friendship with Essa were not enough to eradicate the damage Lewes had inflicted on her self-esteem; although Asher knew, intellectually, that she was neither ugly nor malformed, she could place no value on her physical appearance.

'Asher? Did I say something wrong?'

'No,' she said quickly, shutting off the past. 'No, I was just thinking.'

'Omond told me he wasn't able to *see* your watcher very far.'

She was grateful for the change of subject. 'No, but does it really matter so much? It's probably not important.'

'The fact that someone attaches sufficient importance to you to have you watched worries me, at least, Asher.' Mallory looked away. 'Omond also mentioned he thought you might have a touch of his gift.'

'That's nonsense!' Her temper flared. 'Going to see him was a waste of time!'

'Anything that isn't your own idea seems to be, at least to you.' There was an answering spark of anger in Mallory's retort.

'Just because *you* think something's worthwhile doesn't mean I have to agree with you,' Asher flashed back irritably. 'I'm quite capable of making my own decisions.'

'I never said you weren't!' Mallory exhaled angrily. 'Asher, I'm trying hard not to argue with you, but you make it very difficult sometimes.'

'*I* make it difficult!' The accusation added fire to the flame, though Asher was not sure why she was angry; but she was glad of the mood, revelling in it as a defence against her thoughts, her doubts. 'What you mean is that you're so used to laying down the law that even the slightest dissent from your opinion on my part seems like mutiny.'

She knew she was wrong, but would not take back the words, pride stiffening her resistance. She wanted to lash out at someone, anyone, because she was lonely and frightened, and could admit to neither feeling, and Mallory was *there*. He said nothing.

An uneasy silence ensued. Asher fidgeted with the arm of her chair. Mallory sat staring broodingly into the flames of the fire in the hearth, not looking at her.

'Is there something wrong?' she asked eventually, half-wanting to apologize.

He sounded remote when he answered. 'You have, of course, a right to your opinions. But you seem to allow yourself a freedom to express your views while denying others a similar opportunity.'

The accusation stung. 'That's not true!'

'You hear only what you want to hear, isn't *that* true?' he countered. 'You think I discount much of what you say because you're a woman, but I *know* you discount most of what I tell you because it goes against what you want to think. You seem to have lost all sense of proportion, forgetting what's important – '

'That's the trick, isn't it? Belittle me because there's something *more important* to do? More important than my wishes, at any rate.'

'I didn't say that,' Mallory said evenly.

'You don't have to.' She struck back in bitterness, because like Lewes he was a man, and because at that moment she hated him for being an enemy, because the Fates had made him so. 'There's no need, is there? I should know it without being told.'

'There is such a thing as priority,' Mallory said coolly. 'And ours is to find Vallis. You see everything in terms of black or white. Have you no sense at all?'

The question gave her pause. 'What do you mean?' she asked warily.

'What are you trying to prove to yourself? Why is it always "Asher knows best"? There's nothing wrong with asking for help.'

'No? And have you say I shouldn't have come?' she challenged, hurt.

'That's your justification? *Your* pride?' He flung up his hands. 'And what about other people's feelings, not just your own? Don't you see, the risks you've been taking damage your friends as well as yourself. Try to imagine how I felt when I saw you fall into the river and thought you were going to drown? Don't I have the right to share your thoughts, since we're together in our search for Vallis, since the Oracle brought us together? Or don't you trust me or any of your friends, and think yourself superior to us all?'

'Of course not!' But her face flamed, remembering how often Essa had said much the same thing.

'Then why do you never listen, but simply rush in where any sane man or woman would hesitate, and trust to luck to carry you through? A luck you say you don't believe in? What was the lunacy you uttered – that you thought the Oracle wouldn't let any harm come to you? You're lucky to be alive!' His voice was filled with real feeling. 'What happens when that luck deserts you, Asher?'

She felt she was being backed into a corner and struck back. 'If I were a man, would you be saying this?'

'Yes.'

The plain answer gave her pause, for it was obvious he meant it. Asher felt suddenly confused. *Had* she been trying to prove to him she was capable of standing alone, without his help? To show she was his equal, or superior, in every way? Where was the need? Mallory was a friend, not her lover or a member of her family. And where was her much-vaunted independence, if she must prove it at every turn? Had Mylla been right and she was trying to shut him out, with all the rest, to make him leave her alone?

'Asher.' His voice came less harshly. 'If our positions were reversed, would you stand by and let me rush towards self-destruction without trying to stop me?'

'I'm sorry.' But the words came out stiffly, lacking in conviction. Mallory had proven himself a friend, yes, but on his terms not her own. The anger she continued to repress pulsed in her mind; if it were not for Lewes, for Stern, and for other men like them, who had shattered her life and peace, she would be free. To Mylla, to Essa, she was a person they liked and trusted to make her own decisions. She broke off the train of thought, remembering some of what Mylla had said that night in the old quarter, which bore an unpleasantly close resemblance to Mallory's accusations.

'There's one more thing.'

She looked at him suspiciously. 'What?'

'I want your word you won't leave these grounds alone. Please, Asher. I know you must want to see Harrows again; in your place, so would I. But it isn't safe.'

The appeal was so unexpected that the promise hovered on her lips. He had made no attempt to command her compliance, only to ask for her pledge, but she could not bring herself to speak words which would bind her quite as strongly as any physical restraint.

'I can't.' She sensed his instant withdrawal. 'Not now.' In the moment she said it, she had a sudden vision of the shifting patterns she had seen in Omond's copper bowl, of the echoes in her own mind, and knew, before she had time to analyse why, that they represented a warning to herself, that the decision she took now was important. No lies, no false promises; not to Mallory.

'Why not?'

He sounded cold and remote, leaving no room for compromise. His way or not at all, Asher thought bitterly and without justice, sensing the rift between them grow from crack to chasm; yet he was still too much a friend to let him go without some attempt at explanation, and she tried.

'Because I won't make a promise I might not be able to keep.' He remained silent. 'Mallory, at the moment, I could give you my word. Yes, of course I want to go to Harrows, but I can wait a little longer, after so many years – '

'– but you want the choice to be yours, and yours alone, as in everything else,' he concluded for her. 'I see what the Oracle meant now. "*Look with eyes that choose to see; look – or lose.*" You've already made your choice, Asher.'

'Mallory . . .' She reached out to him in a rare gesture but he drew back, turning away to stare once more into the fire. His withdrawal was so complete she was at a loss to know what to do, experiencing a deep unhappiness that she might well have gone too far to draw back.

'I'll see you tomorrow morning, Asher. We should visit the

camp as soon as possible, while the weather holds.' His voice held a remoteness that suggested he had distanced her in mind, as in looking away he refused to acknowledge her physical presence.

She waited, hoping for a sign he would relent, but there was none. Her head began to ache, so badly she wondered if she were going to be ill, but she found it impossible to find anything to say that would bring him back, beyond the past hour. At last, she shrugged.

'Until tomorrow then,' she said softly. He did not acknowledge her words; she might as well have been alone in the room. Without anger to sustain her, there was only a deep and unbearable sadness, and a feeling of having lost something precious which could never be recovered.

She got to her feet and walked towards the door, feeling an intruder in the quiet room. As she let herself out, she was careful not to look back.

She lay on the bed, her mind whirling with unacceptable thoughts. It was only early-evening, but she had no appetite and could not face the prospect of having to sit at dinner, trying to make conversation with Omond and being ignored by Mallory. Hunger and thirst were better than rejection. Lewes had taught her all about rejection.

At last she fell asleep, dozing in uneasy fits and starts until she woke in the early hours of the morning and knew, with absolute certainty, that there was no point in trying to stay in bed. Wide awake, she got up and padded across to the window and looked out; the skies were a clear, velvet black, dotted with stars, Abate barely visible and Aspire in her last waning quarter.

Her thoughts tormented her. It was impossible to forget what Mallory had said, nor her own contribution to what had been a peculiarly bitter quarrel. Bitter, because it concerned a principle on which they could not agree, because he would not accept that she had the right to risk her life if she so chose. But bitter also because she had abused his friendship, punishing him for what another man had done to her. She wished, desperately, that she had admitted how much she knew she had been in the wrong. On their journey, it had been as much Mallory as the Oracle she had been testing, as if he had to *prove* his goodwill to her at every step.

It was acting a lie, and worse, because I was and am afraid. Of coming back here, of showing Mallory what a coward I was and still am. I thought the old Asher was dead, but she's here – she's me. I didn't care what the risks I took cost him or Mylla, and it was only luck or the Oracle that saved me, not my skill or good judgment.

With a constriction in her heart, she wondered if she had destroyed forever a friendship she had barely begun to value at its real worth, understanding only now, in the darkest hours, how much it meant to her. She did not love Mallory – or not in the physical sense, or as a lover should – but he was a person with whom she felt at ease, who would accept her as she was, not as she tried to present herself. Her sense of independence railed against his dictatorial habits of manner, but she trusted him and knew he would never let her down. With him, she was no longer lonely, but at home. And she – no matter how hard she tried to justify herself – had shown herself arrogant and thoughtless, caring not a jot for his feelings as long as he did not tread on her own.

I would never have treated Mylla like that. Because he's a man, I acted as if he had no feelings, or no right to have feelings. As if he were first a man and only second a friend.

A deep depression settled on her, partly because of the lateness of the hour, but largely from an awareness that the misunderstanding between them was of her own making. Mallory had shown himself willing to meet her halfway, and she had flung the offer aside as if only he, not she, must make the effort, as though *he* must atone for all the wrongs all women had suffered at the hands of men.

What can I do?

The answer was obvious; she could give him the promise he wanted, and did not understand why she still hesitated. Was it simply stubbornness, resisting the sensible solution for no apparent reason other than the salvation of her pride? If so, then she would give her word. Or lose him, and the loneliness would return, and this time there would be no end to it.

She stared up at the moons, her vision blurring as she watched, as if clouds had been blown across their faces, and Asher thought she saw in the skies a comet's trail divided into three distinct tails, one solid, the two to either side thin and wavering.

I treated Mallory as badly as some men treat women, the way Sim and his friends behaved to us; as if his views and feelings didn't matter. Is this the only way for women to be independent, by behaving with the same disregard men show us? Could they not be friends, companions, instead of enemies? It shamed her deeply that Mallory had shown himself capable of such a relationship where she had not. His concern for her was evidence it was so, his continued attempts to overcome a disposition which had been trained to habits of authority; which was only the way of the world, and no fault of his.

As the comet trail faded, she wondered drearily whether she should make a wish, for it was said to be lucky; but she did not feel as if anything would ever be lucky for her again, as if she had wasted her share of good fortune with a profligacy that appalled her.

When we've been to the camp. When we've seen if this girl is Vallis, then I'll tell him I'm sorry, and hope he's generous enough to forgive me. If he did not, she would have to accept her loss and remember the fault was her own. It was all she could do.

She sat by the window until dawn came up, revealing red skies as a promise of heavy rain; the visit to the camp would have to wait for another day, for the prisoners would hardly work in such weather.

Unthinkingly, her left hand slipped up to the chain round her neck, fingering the charm. For a moment it puzzled her, her mother's gift feeling briefly like an unwelcome constriction, and she was tempted to tear it off, but she did not. She had removed the ring Omond had given her, and went over to the bed and recovered it from its hiding place under her pillow. That, at least, she would wear, in token of her better resolution. She got back into bed and slipped it on; that was one promise to Mallory she could make, and keep.

Chapter Ten

'I suppose these blasted things are doing it deliberately?' Mallory inquired irritably, as yet another of the goats slipped past him and headed back downhill towards the slow-flowing River Esperance.

'Perhaps we should pretend to be going the other way – then they'd climb up,' Asher suggested.

'I thought Loder said these creatures were *used* to being driven!' Exasperated, he swung his stick towards the rump of the billy-goat nearest to him, which responded by trying to eat the tip.

'At least you're wearing your own boots. Ish's are big enough for a giant.'

Mallory looked down at the cause of her complaint and found himself sympathizing; the hill was steep and slippery enough without trying to clamber about in footwear that threatened to slip off at every step. Asher, dressed in Ish's clothes as well as his boots, made quite a reasonable boy at a distance; close to, however, her features were too obviously female to pass muster. He hoped no one would come sufficiently near to notice.

'Come *on*, you brutes!' He began to climb again, and, with the perversity of their kind, the goats decided up was more interesting than down and followed – or, rather, led, leaping with effortless ease up the steepest possible path. The watchfulness of the Kamiri guards at the camp had persuaded Mallory some form of disguise was a necessity, and Loder, the owner of the goats, whose smallholding lay near the base of the hill, had been willing to loan them – for a price. Mallory was beginning to wonder if even a copper coin was too much.

'Is that a cave?' Asher asked, pointing to a shadowed depression just below the false crown of Gaunt Hill.

'I think so.' One of the goats disappeared inside the recess, bell tinkling distantly, only to reappear almost at once, chewing contemplatively. 'It's not far now.'

'Good!'

They had set off before dawn after two wasted days when rain had fallen in sheets, making the venture pointless since, even if the prisoners were taken out to work in the quarry, their faces would be invisible through the downpour. They had left the horses some way from the base of the hill, unsure whether two riders might not be regarded with suspicion by the guard, for the camp occupied the highest piece of ground for miles around and strangers could be spotted all too easily, the original reason the old fort had been built on Gaunt Hill by a robber band a hundred years before. The Kamiri had seen its advantages and made use of it; the camp could only be approached from one direction – the west – since from all others the sides were too vertiginous for even a goat to scale.

They crested the first peak and found themselves staring across at the second; to reach it, they had to descend to a narrow gully, then climb again up a mostly barren slope, the upper reaches deliberately denuded of vegetation, to a height several hundred feet above their present position. The high walls of the old fort had been strengthened and reinforced, and two watchtowers added for security. Mallory could just make out the tiny figures of guards in each.

'Where should we watch from?'

He peered down towards the gully at the sparsely wooded slope and pointed to a jumble of rocks halfway. 'There, I think. There should be enough cover, and we'll get a good view of the quarry.'

Asher nodded. 'I agree.'

It was obvious that at some time in the fairly recent past a firestorm had passed directly over the hill, for much of the undergrowth had been burned away, leaving blackened scars; however, much of the serious deforestation was evidently the work of local farmers, and of the Kamiri themselves, for there were more neat stumps than standing trees dotting the hillside.

'I wish it weren't so open.' Mallory frowned. 'Oh, well. Let's go.'

The herd had already split up and spread out over the slope, bells tinkling in every direction; one stood perched precariously on a narrow ledge overhanging a perilous drop. Mallory was glad Loder had offered to gather them himself, and equally thankful he did not have to make his living escorting such uncooperative beasts; although, glancing at Asher, he thought he recognized a similar recalcitrance in his companion.

'Isn't it horrible?' She was staring up at the grey walls of the camp, rearing up towards the skies, apparently impregnable.

Even so early in the day, guards manned each corner of the forbidding structure. Mallory wondered how many prisoners were inside. Would it even be possible to rescue one of them, if the girl they had come to find proved to be Vallis? It looked a hopeless endeavour.

The jumble of rocks proved better suited to their concealment than he had expected; two large boulders, a crack between them, hid them from sight to the fore, and another, overhead, leaned forward, providing shelter from above. It was rather like being inside a cairn, and Mallory and Asher slipped inside and sat down to wait, Mallory unwrapping a small portable telescope from inside his jacket. The quarry was almost directly opposite their hiding place, a deep pit dug into the further hillside, perhaps two hundred feet or more in diameter; he could make out wooden-runged ladders leaning against the walls and some sort of pulley mechanism on the rim nearest to them, presumably used to lift cut stone from the pit.

'How soon, do you think?' Asher asked softly.

'Anytime now.' She looked tired, dark rings under her eyes suggesting she had not slept well for days; the high, narrow cheekbones were more prominent than a week ago, and in her boy's clothes she looked smaller and slighter than her normal self. That she was obviously unhappy softened him towards her; since their argument at Kepesake they had spoken little, but he had had time to reflect on the points of conflict and to try to understand a little the reasons for her rashness. Whom, after all, had she been able to trust in all the years since her disappearance? Why should she place reliance even on himself when he had not been *there* when she needed him? His feelings for her at that moment were a mixture of frustration and admiration; frustration for her cussedness, and admiration for her courage and strength of will.

'Do you think she'll be there?'

Mallory started, temporarily forgetful of his surroundings. 'How should I know? We can only hope.'

She turned back to the crack in the boulders, watching the gates of the camp. He shared some of her tension; if this girl should not be Vallis, where else could she be?

'How do we recognize her?' she asked suddenly.

'When she was small, they say she looked very like her father; she was dark, like him. But I think if we see her, we'll know. Otherwise why have we come?'

The hills were very still; around them hummed the buzz of insects, the chirps of birds, and the chiming bells of the goats. The suddenness of the grating sound from the camp shattered the stillness and made them both jump.

'They're coming.' Asher did not make the mistake of pointing, but Mallory, looking toward the camp, saw gates being opened. Asher stroked the ring on her middle finger in a nervous gesture.

A long line of people began to stream from the camp in single file. Mallory counted at least forty prisoners and more than a dozen guards, with even larger numbers of scent-hounds.

'They're taking no chances,' he whispered. No prisoner could hope to escape alone in such open terrain against these odds.

'No.'

The group was still too far away for Mallory to identify individuals, all dressed identically in brown tunics and trousers; only their shapes and movement told him there were several women as well as men in the party. Compared with their guards, the prisoners looked short, none approaching the height of the Kamiri, and Mallory felt renewed loathing for the invaders who herded their prisoners – his own people – like so many sheep, depriving them of their dignity as well as their freedom. *This girl must be Vallis; she must.*

'They're too close together; I can't see,' Asher said impatiently.

'They'll spread out when they get down to work.' Even as he spoke, several of the brown-clad figures were already descending into the pit via the ladders, their guards arranging themselves about the edge, some of the hounds now loosed but most on long leashes held in the hands of the grey men. Shouted orders could be heard in the distance, and in a short time only two brown figures were still on the rim, standing by the pulley; unfortunately, a guard obscured his view, and Mallory could see neither prisoner clearly.

'Get out of the way,' he muttered.

The wind, which had been only a gentle breeze, was growing stronger, coming now from the north-west; against the sky ominous orange-grey clouds were forming still some distance away. Mallory noticed the change and crossed his fingers, hoping they would come no closer, although there was a breathless feel to the air that came as a warning.

'Where's the glass – I can't see *that* one,' Asher whispered.

'Which one?' Holding up the telescope, Mallory looked towards the quarry.

'The one wheeling the barrow.'

The guards had moved away and he now had a clear view, briefly, of all the prisoners. A quick glance assured him there were only half a dozen women, most of them in their thirties or forties.

He sought out one who looked younger, but saw at once it could not be Vallis; not only was she too old, but fair-haired, where the young Vallis was dark, like both her parents.

He turned the telescope on the two women working the pulley, one of whom was certainly young, from her demeanour. She was very tall for a woman, with long, narrow bones, and for a moment his heart leaped; but then she turned, and he saw that what he had imagined was dark hair was only a trick of the light. The girl was about the right age, but her hair was almost white, her appearance subtly alien, separating her from her companions; this was no Darrianite. Although he could not see her eyes, he knew they would be a deep greyish-brown, the brows and lashes as pale as her hair.

'But that's a Saff girl,' Asher protested. 'What's she doing here?'

'I can't imagine.' Feverishly, he fixed on each prisoner in turn, unwilling to accept that the worst had transpired: the girl was not in the quarry. And probably not in the camp at all. Mallory tried to tell himself her absence was due to accident, or some other excuse – that she was ill or injured – but he could not help himself believing she was simply not there.

'She's not there, is she?' Asher's despairing whisper echoed his fear.

'I don't think so,' he answered shortly, filled with a consuming disappointment. If the girl was in the camp, they had no means of discovering her unless she came out with the work party; if she was not, they would have to begin all over again, and he had no idea where to start.

'It's my fault. We wouldn't have come if I hadn't suggested it.'

'Don't be silly. How could you have known?' He felt constrained to try to lift some of the burden of failure from her. He had, after all, been as anxious as she to believe this the solution to Vallis' disappearance.

'That woman – the one who escaped to Saffra – this must be what she wanted to say, that one of their people was here.' Asher sounded utterly defeated.

'I wonder how she got here?' It was rare for the Saff to venture outside their own lands, and he had never met one as young as this girl, who could be no more than twenty. Even Amrist received their roving ambassadors with an overt respect for members of a race he neither understood nor had any power to dominate; in any case, their status as neutrals in any dispute, offering only refuge but not assistance, meant they presented no threat to his military authority.

'What do we do now?'

'Don't give up, Ash.' He put a hand on her arm, taken aback as she flinched from his touch. 'This is only the first try. We'll find her, you'll see, even if we have to look somewhere else.' He wondered bitterly if he would ever be able to offer her more than a friendly hand, or whether the scars of her marriage went too deep to heal, and knew a flare of impatience with himself, and, unfairly, with her, for his frustration.

'But I don't *know* where else to look. I don't know what the Oracle meant, if this was wrong. Unless the Oracle is false.'

'Yes, you do know. You *can* find her,' Mallory contradicted. 'If the Oracle said so, it was true. Think.'

'But I don't know where to begin.' She turned away in despair.

'Don't!' He had not expected her to take it so hard. 'This isn't like you, Ash, you don't give up.'

'Perhaps I should learn how.'

He thought at first she was joking, then realized she was in earnest. There was anguish in her expression, as if she had lost everything she held dear, and Mallory was silenced by feelings of inadequacy not entirely free from exasperation.

'Do you want to go back now?' she asked, after a short period of silence.

'There's no hurry.'

Mallory watched the prisoners morosely, wishing it were possible to stage a mass exodus; it was intolerable to have to leave them in this place. At a distance, it was possible to be pragmatic about their collective existence, but close to he could not ignore the stooped backs and weary faces; the women disturbed him most, working alongside the men, taking their share of the heaviest tasks. It seemed unnatural, and he was shocked that none of the men thought to help as two struggled to hoist a weighty block of stone on to a wooden cart.

Each of them has a family, a home. It was Amrist and his Kamiri, in their quest for ever more lands to rule and gold to swell their coffers, who had condemned his people to this existence. There were those who admired Amrist's achievement, his conquest of the known lands, as if his dream of an empire should be assessed of greater value than the aspirations of all those whose lives he destroyed, whether soldiers, or farmers, or merchants, or their wives and children; Mallory was not among them.

Perhaps this is how Asher feels, for the women she tries to help. He had not grasped before how easy it was to overlook the plight of people who did not impinge directly on his own life. Sympathy there was, but a distant sympathy, tinged with impatience for those who must in some way have contributed to their plight. His thoughts wandered to some of the things Asher had told him of the poverty and ill-treatment of the women of Venture, and he was struck by his own automatic dismissal of much of what she had said; he had always believed that while men had a wider remit, it was somehow natural for women to spend their lives bearing and rearing children and caring for their husbands, as if in being born female this was what they wanted in life, not that they were sentenced to this form of life imprisonment by their menfolk.

Now, he could see it was not so great an exaggeration as he had imagined; bound by the necessity to care for their children, by the constrictions placed upon them by custom, they were almost as much prisoners as those in the quarry. Yet their function had a financial value and was vital to the economy of the cities of Darrian; without children, there was no purpose in building trading empires or cities. They might as well let it all rot and live on what they had. In giving birth to and bringing up the next generation, women were a significant force in the economy; unpaid and unregarded, their labours – in every sense – were quite as essential as those of their men.

His thoughts were uncomfortable; just as many ignored the plight of those in the internment camps – unseen, and thus out of mind – so they ignored this, too. Not nature, but the value placed on a woman's labours, set her low in the scale. Why were Amrist's soldiers, with their power of destruction, rated more highly than those who gave and nurtured life? Was it only that it was easier to reward aggression than generosity?

He was glad to be disturbed in his musings by a commotion from the pit. Peering across, Mallory realized he could no longer see clearly. While he had been absorbed in his private abstractions, it had grown dark as the orange-grey clouds he had seen earlier were blown directly overhead, their colour now more copper than orange; the air crackled with heat-energy. The wind had changed direction and brought the storm straight to them.

'Asher!' he said urgently. 'Get back under cover. Quickly.'

She looked at him blankly. He gestured upward.

'Firestorm!' The colour drained from her face. In Venture, on the coast, such storms were rare and she had forgotten the ferocity of what had once been a familiar fear.

'Stay under the leaning rock, it's our only chance. It's too late to make a run for it.' He was pulling her back as he spoke, the first cracklings overhead warning of the imminence of the storm. The rock at their back was broad enough to shelter them both, at least partially; there was nowhere else to go.

The prisoners in the quarry were beginning to scurry up the ladders, urged on by the guards, but they had left it too late and the first sparks began to descend to the sparse undergrowth, rapidly extinguished as they fell on damp scrub. Wisps of smoke appeared as more and more sparks rained down, catching prisoners on exposed faces and hands. Some of the hounds began to yelp their own protests.

The first bright sparks fell randomly, most extinguished as they met only dust on landing; but as the fall thickened, the odds on survival improved as droplets of burning gas – heavier than air – met dead twigs, last year's leaves, and even green shoots and moss. The air thickened, dotted with scarlet, blown on the wind, the sparks drifting remorselessly down to find skin, hair, clothing – nothing was immune. The grey men stood their ground, alert to their duty, but they wore gloves and had scarves drawn across their faces, unlike their prisoners. Mallory heard a woman scream.

'What was that?' Asher asked, trying to peer through the scorching rain.

Mallory shook his head, using the telescope to watch events round the quarry. The last man had exited the pit and the party began the ascent towards the prison; scent-hounds were barking furiously, driven wild by sparks falling on their fur. The descent grew thicker, and the first real flames showed through the deluge as trees caught fire and scrub ignited; smoke billowed up until it was hard to see anything at all.

'Look!' Asher was pointing wildly to a running figure heading not for the camp but downhill, toward their hiding place.

It was plain from her height it was the Saff girl, making use of the unexpected storm in her bid for escape. The guards had not yet seen her; there was no outcry, no pursuit, as the drifting smoke covered her traces. He wished her well, but saw at once the danger to themselves. Her escape would soon be noticed, and her scent would lead the guard straight to them. He scanned uphill for any possibility of retreat, but the storm was now directly overhead and there was no interval in the rain of falling fire; their only safety lay in remaining where they were.

'What are you doing?' he asked Asher, seeing her struggling to remove her boots.

'I'm going to give them to the Saff girl. It should confuse her scent for the hounds,' she said flatly.

His first reaction was to tell her not to be a fool; with bare feet, she could hardly hope to walk across the burning ground. His second was a more reluctant admiration that she had so quickly seen what was needed; with not one but three separate scents to follow, the hounds would be befuddled, not knowing which one was their quarry.

'We can't stay here much longer,' he advised, beginning to cough as smoke from scrub burning nearby reached his lungs.

'She's coming.'

It was true; the Saff girl had already reached the gully and was starting the climb to their hiding place. Mallory risked a look at the work-party, and saw there was still no pursuit; presumably that would come when the guard counted their prisoners back inside the walls of the camp.

'Oh!'

He turned to find himself staring into the face of the Saff girl, and it was difficult to say which of the two was the more astonished. Asher, however, beckoned the girl to join them in their makeshift shelter, holding out the boots.

'Put these on.' She did not bother with introductions, taking a quick look at the other girl's feet. 'They should fit.'

'Thank you.' The Saff took the boots and sat to pull them on; as Asher had surmised, they were a good fit, for she had much larger feet than herself. 'My name is Rhia.'

There was still no sign of pursuit. Rhia peered at the fall of fire, evidently bracing herself to make her run.

'Have you been in the camp long?' Mallory asked.

'Since the riots in Chance – four years, I think.' A pulse beat at her left temple, the only visible sign of emotion in her pale face; the Saff girl's expression was otherwise calm. 'What are you doing here?' She looked at Asher.

'We came looking for someone who might be inside the camp: a girl, your own age, but dark, a Darrianite?'

Rhia shook her head, frowning. 'I know no one like that. Most of the women inside are much older than I, although there are a few children, perhaps eleven or twelve.'

'You're sure?' Mallory asked urgently.

'Oh, yes, I'm sure.' The Saff girl's expression hardened. 'Ensor, the cousin of your Dominus, and his friends, have an interest in all the young girls in the camp, and boys, too.'

Mallory could think of nothing to say; Asher, too, was mute. All three turned to watch the progress of the storm, for such attacks, though fierce, were normally of short duration.

'This place must attract fire,' Rhia observed more naturally.

'Each spring I have been here there have been four or five such storms.'

Asher looked down at her feet, now clad in drab woollen socks. 'Do you know where you're going from here?'

Rhia nodded. 'I know the way home.'

'When you reach a village called Coverdon, about two days' south of the border, you'll see a cottage on the outskirts with green shutters. The people there will help you.' Rhia nodded her understanding. 'And if you need to ask your way at any point, ask the old – they're less likely to give you away, although I think most people would hide you.'

'Do you?' Rhia had both boots on and was breathing more easily. There were burn marks on her face and hands, and her tunic was scorched, but her long, pale face looked almost relaxed as she readied herself. 'But you have my thanks, friend.' She looked into Asher's face, apparently troubled by what she saw. 'If you should need to, come north to us. There would be a place for you among us. And now I must go.' She moved to a crouching position, peering at the gully below. 'You also, they will come soon. Go safely.'

With that she was gone, out into the rain of fire. Mallory, who had listened to the exchange in some bewilderment, was not sure whether to be relieved or disappointed. He felt curiously and uncomfortably excluded, an eavesdropper in some affair that was none of his concern.

'They're coming, Mallory.' Asher pointed towards the quarry.

He pulled himself together. 'Come on, then. How many?'

'Two. And two hounds.'

'Then we'd better run for it.'

The wind was getting up, blowing the clouds away toward the west; unfortunately, it also had the effect of spreading the fire more rapidly than Asher had hoped.

'What about the goats?' she asked suddenly.

Mallory cast up his eyes. 'They can run a lot faster than we can! Now, *move*!' He slipped out of their shelter, pulling her after him.

She had no way of guessing how long it would be before the guards lit on their hiding place, nor which trail they would follow. With their longer legs, the advantages were all with the Kamiri, especially since she no longer had any boots. The ground was hard and uneven, loose pebbles bruising the soles of her feet and burning scrub singeing her socks, but Asher made no complaint; it had been her own decision. Or not a decision, more a reflex action; it surprised her Mallory had made no protest.

Who knows? Our lives touched hers for a brief, perhaps a vital, moment. Perhaps this, too, was foreseen by the Oracle. But it was hardly the place to consider the Saff girl's words as she followed Mallory, disoriented by the drifting smoke billowing in every direction. They had to go up, then down again toward the river, but it was hard to see anything at all.

'Oh!' She gasped as a nearby tree burst suddenly into flames, showering her with a mass of sparks.

'Put something over your face – cover your eyes and mouth,' Mallory shouted over the crackle of flames. 'Don't breathe too deeply.' He coughed, as if to emphasize the point.

She held on to his hand, not daring to let go in case she lost him, for the smoke was as bad as a heavy mist, clear in patches, but in others quite opaque. They reached the crest of the hill and spared a moment to look down in both directions; neither offered any comfort or refuge. Behind them, the Kamiri were approaching the rocks where they had sheltered; ahead, the downward slope, more heavily wooded, was a mass of flame. There was no sight of Rhia, and Asher could only hope she had managed to get away safely.

'What about the cave – do you think we should take shelter there?' Mallory shouted in her ear.

'No.' The word sprang from instinct, not considered thought. She was certain, without any remnant of doubt, that if they went into the cave they would be trapped and taken by the guard; even the prospect of breasting the flames was less terrifying than that.

'Then we have to risk the flames. Hold on tight.'

She had no real hope of outrunning the Kamiri; their best chance was if they managed to reach the river, where they could wade or swim to disguise their scent. If they did not, at best they would be imprisoned, for they could have no conceivable reason for being discovered so close to the camp, especially at the time of an escape. Mallory's position as councillor of Venture would work against, not for, him; it would be assumed he had come to rescue Ensor. Her mind told her the facts as she ran, trying to ignore the agony of her burned feet. For herself . . . but she did not wish to contemplate her own fate.

Mallory stumbled and almost brought her down; the air was hot and thick, choking them. Asher began to cough, almost strangling herself in an effort to stop as she heard the baying of hounds not far behind.

'They're coming closer,' she shouted unnecessarily.

'Come on.'

The Kamiri were gaining with every step. Asher grasped the near-inevitability of capture, her legs feeling weak and boneless. Lewes had once threatened to set his dogs on her, two immense beasts made savage by constant hunger, and for a moment she was back in the past as she listened to the hounds baying on their trail.

'Asher – *hurry!*'

Mallory's voice broke the spell and she jumped as a line of fire ran from behind, passing between her legs and scorching her borrowed clothes as the grasses ignited. For a moment the smoke lifted and they could see ahead quite clearly, the river still too distant for comfort.

'This way.' Mallory drew to an abrupt halt as they were suddenly confronted by a sheet of flame. A thick patch of scrub was ablaze and had set fire to three trees that stood in a row, creating an impenetrable barrier of flame. Exhausted, Mallory tugged Asher sideways, looking for a way through, but this time she held back.

'Mallory, stop!'

'We can't.' He was impatient.

'We haven't time to go round. They're too close.'

'If you don't come, I'll knock you out and carry you!'

'Listen!' she shouted. 'We have to go through. It's our only chance. The fire will kill our scent.'

'And we'll burn to death!'

Indeed, as she looked at the roaring flames, it did look as if she were proposing a bizarre form of suicide; but Asher was sure she was right. She pulled herself free.

'If you won't, I will,' she shouted, nerving herself for the run.

He hesitated only a moment. The hounds were very close; they could not see but could hear them, perhaps only fifty yards away.

'Damn you – then I'll carry you! Cover your face!' he yelled at her, picking her up before she could protest. Taking a deep breath, he ran straight into the thick of the flames.

The wall of fire was the most terrifying sight Asher had ever imagined; the heat was so intense she did not think she could bear it. Her hair began to smoulder at once. She shut her eyes, then opened them again. Their progress seemed to take forever, although in distance it could have been no more than fifteen feet or less. It seemed impossible to survive, but a freak wind divided the flames for a scant instant, and in that instant Mallory had passed through, and they were on the far side, their clothes licked by tiny flames, and Mallory was putting her down and beating them out before seeing to his own. The smell of burning was all around her.

'Get up. We've got to run,' he coughed. 'They may still be able to see us.'

Asher tried to stand, but could not. The pain was excruciating, and when she lifted her feet she understood why; her socks had been burned away, and in the process removed at least one layer of skin.

'I'm sorry, Mallory. I can't walk.' She was surprised her voice sounded so calm. She looked at him, taking in the scorch-marks on his face, the singed brows and hands, and saw he was bracing himself to lift her again. She guessed he, too, was almost at the end of his strength, exhausted by inhaling so much smoke.

'I'll carry you.' He bent to pick her up, and she tried to help, clasping her hands around his back and neck.

He staggered as he walked, each step an effort, and his breathing was laboured; he smelled strongly of sour smoke and burnt cloth and singed hair. Looking back over his shoulder, Asher could see nothing except the wall of fire; there was no sign of the guard, nor the hounds.

'Stop here,' she said, pointing to a patch of bare ground further down the slope where there was no scrub. 'You can't go much further, Mallory.'

He did not reply, but when he reached the spot he laid her down without argument, as if too wearied for speech.

'If it didn't work, it's too late anyway,' she said softly. 'Rest.'

He nodded. Distant yelps could still be heard, but further away than they had been. The wind had changed direction again, blowing the flames back up the hill. It was still appallingly hot, and sweat dripped from Asher's forehead into her eyes.

'We may have thrown them off,' Mallory gasped.

'I can't see them.' Asher looked back again, but there was only fire and smoke.

'What made you want to take the risk?'

She shrugged. 'The fire seemed the only chance we had.' It was a part of the truth.

'I can go on now.' Mallory heaved himself to his feet. 'It's not far to the river.'

Asher had closed her eyes briefly; she opened them in wonderment. 'They've gone,' she said in astonishment.

'How do you know?' Mallory demanded.

She shook her head impatiently. 'I don't know. But they have.'

She could offer no tangible proof, but she was sure she was right. Woman's intuition, perhaps? she asked herself mockingly. Whatever that was. Essa always said it was a defence mechanism, born of an unconscious observance of small details. It sounded good enough as an explanation, but Asher remained sceptical, remembering occasions when her nerves had given her warnings that proved baseless.

'Let's hope you're right!' Mallory heaved her up again and began to walk down the slope, where most of the timber near the baseline had already been removed by local farmers, and the scrub had burned down to smouldering. The worst of the fire had passed on and up.

At the base of the hill, Mallory stumbled the last few paces to the river bank. The Esperance was no swiftly flowing river but a mere tributary, barely a dozen feet across and with a sluggish current, but no less welcome for that. Asher fell into the water, gloriously cool against her hot skin and sore feet, floating on her back, glad to rid herself of the worst of the smell of burning.

'We survived.' Mallory sounded incredulous as he joined her, ducking his head under the water with a sigh of pleasure.

'It is extraordinary, isn't it?' Although they were still too close to the camp for comfort, Asher felt no sense of menace near them; she wondered where the Saff girl was, and whether she, too, was safe. 'I wonder what happened to the goats?'

'They'll be back at Loder's smallholding by now.' He gestured in the general direction of the buildings on the far side of the river, which had escaped the fire. 'Perhaps you're right after all. Perhaps the Oracle does protect us,' Mallory mused. 'I wouldn't have thought this possible.'

Asher stared up at the burning slope, still smoking defiantly, thinking about Mallory's comment. What was it someone had once said to her: fixed fate, free will? She could no longer agree, her feelings altered so that the answer no longer looked as obvious as she had once believed. Was Fate decided by choice, not by an arbitrary hand? If so, how was it possible to divine the future? Both concepts could not be true, for they were contradictory. And why had the Saff girl seemed to invite her, particularly, to go north, to Saffra? What had Rhia seen in her face, that she should have felt so compelled to make such an offer on such brief acquaintance?

'Do you know, Mallory, we could swim some of the way from here,' she said idly, unwilling to speak of her thoughts. 'So you wouldn't have to carry me.'

'*That* is one of your better ideas. But if you don't mind, I'll walk. You can swim. I'll go ahead and fetch the horses.'

'All right.' She was as much startled by his assent as by the suggestion. Not long ago, he would never have agreed to leave her alone in such surroundings. Is he saying he trusts me, and treats me like an equal? It seemed he was. 'Mallory, I'm sorry. That I brought you here.'

He pulled himself out on to the bank, looking quizzically down at her. 'I chose to come, you didn't bring me.'

'Yes, I did,' she contradicted. 'It was my fault, no matter what you say. If we'd been killed, *that* would have been my fault, too.'

'But it was you who found a way out.'

She began to laugh, relief making her light-headed. 'Are we arguing about who's to blame now?'

He grinned. 'If you like.'

'Oh – get going!' Putting her feet down on the muddy bottom of the river, she found walking less painful than she had feared. With a wave, Mallory strode off, dripping, in the direction where they had left the horses, about a mile east.

Half-swimming, half-wading, Asher followed, making slow progress and growing colder by the minute. With Mallory gone, less pleasant thoughts crowded her mind; their whole journey had been misconceived, for whatever reason, and her disappointment in their failure was acute: what she had said was true – she had no idea where to start again.

What was it the Oracle said? '*Within your compass lies the means to pierce the veil.*' That suggested a disguise of some kind surrounding the girl, but what? The possibilities were endless. Could the prophecy mean that perhaps she would stumble on the answer by luck, or did she already know it, but was unaware of what she knew? She lifted a hand and found the talisman at her neck, warm against her skin. She needed help in deciphering the puzzle.

Yet help there had been; whether it had sprung from her own intuition or from some other source more deeply buried, *something* had told her that the flames were their only hope of escape, just as the same inner warning had rejected the false security of the cave.

Asher shivered. There was too much she did not understand, could not understand. '*Look – or lose*', the Oracle had said.

It would be a great deal easier if she knew what to look for.

Chapter Eleven

A night's rest at Kepesake and large quantities of soothing ointment did much to restore Asher's ease of body, but little to appease her mind. She spent most of the morning in her room, keeping out of sight while Mallory received a long line of petitioners in the estate office; watching the many familiar faces of the villagers from her window, she was sure what her next course of action should be, but considerably less certain of its execution.

I don't believe we came back here for no reason; therefore, the answer must lie in the Oracle's prophecy. *'In what was'* — that was the key. But which *was*? In her present surroundings it was easy to immerse herself in the past, to remember back to the time before her marriage to the many happy days she had known at Kepesake. What clue to Vallis's whereabouts could possibly lie hidden in those memories? She racked her brains, increasingly frustrated as the hours passed and she came no nearer a solution.

Eventually, she took her difficulty to Omond in his attic chamber, who greeted her civilly and listened with close attention while she repeated the prophecies of the Oracle, nodding as she detailed her conclusions.

'Interesting,' he commented, when she had finished. 'But somewhat inconclusive. I am not convinced your interpretation is the correct one. If you will forgive me for repeating myself, I think you miss the point. *"See the shifting shadowlines"* — that, of course, is a reference to your latent gift for divination.'

'I *told* you,' Asher said irritably. 'It doesn't exist, and if it did, I wouldn't want it.'

'That is an irrelevance.' He surveyed her with detached interest. 'You will find no solution to your difficulty in denial, as you must already have discovered. And I see you do not wear the ring I gave you.'

Asher wished he had not noticed the omission. 'It didn't work.

Last night, I felt it again – the watching. I had the ring on at the time.'

'I see, although I am not entirely surprised. As I surmised, your own immunity to the magnetism of such warding stones unfortunately works against you in this respect.'

Asher sighed. 'I wish I knew what he wanted, whoever it is.'

'What do you propose to do now?'

'I'm not sure.' She hesitated. 'I've tried, but get nowhere. I've no idea where to *look*, if the solution to the riddle really does lie in the past.' Some of her frustration came into her voice. 'I feel that so far I've done nothing but cause trouble for everyone.'

'Your encounter with the Saff girl near the camp suggests otherwise,' Omond observed. 'Without your assistance, she would unquestionably have been taken; perhaps *that* was your purpose in returning here. Who knows what part she may play in the balance of luck in our lives in the days to come?'

Asher nodded, for that was in accord with her own thoughts. 'I wondered, too. It seemed to me our lives *touched* briefly, for a reason. But that had nothing to do with finding Vallis.'

'And do you believe this search the sole justification for your existence?' Omond inquired caustically. 'In the course of our lives there are many points at which we may be of service to others, intentionally or no, and whether we are aware of it or no. In your pursuit of Vallis you may accidentally touch on many other matters outside your immediate concern, but they are no less important for that.'

'How can you say that? Everything I've done so far is *wrong*.'

'That remains to be seen. I maintain that your chief difficulty lies within yourself. If you could forgive yourself for a very natural mistake – and your assumption the girl in the camp was the one you sought was perfectly understandable – then you will find your answer. No one blames you for the error, except yourself.'

'No?' Asher gave him a wry smile. 'How can I tell? I used to be so sure of everything.'

'Wherein lies your problem,' Omond interrupted her impatiently. 'You have a good mind, child, use it! Learn to *accept* the inevitable, rather than fight against it and waste your energies. What must be, will be, but not everything is of great matter. Preserve your strength for what obstacles *can* be overcome.'

'That sounds like something my mother used to say.' She gave a bitter laugh. 'It goes too much against the grain, Omond. I'm not a fatalist.'

'And you find self-recrimination a more profitable exercise?'

The acerbic question caught her unawares, not least because the implied criticism was just. 'Sometimes!' she said, stung.

Omond peered down his nose. 'You will find what you seek, child, but only if and when you have the courage to admit to yourself what is true and what is false. Do not allow your wishes to lead you astray.'

'How can I tell?'

'Is there nothing you have hidden from yourself? Nothing in your past you should remember, even if it gives you pain?'

She turned away. 'It may be.'

'Then let the memory come; think of what *was*, and what came from it.' There was compassion in his voice, but Asher did not respond to it. After a moment, Omond went on: 'The Oracle said that in this the choice was yours, but I think you must choose at least to look.'

'Perhaps.' Asher struggled against denial. It was as she feared, that there would be no place left to hide from the period of her past she could barely endure to acknowledge existed.

'Child – ' But Asher ignored the appeal in his voice and took a hasty leave of the diviner, retreating with her thoughts to the silence and solitude of the library on the ground floor.

Lewes. Is that what it means, that I must see him again? But what part could he possibly play in all this? She was reluctant to name him even in her thoughts, but allowing herself to remember him gave her no startling moment of revelation. He was a man without conscience, who saw the world solely in terms of status and possession, and who had treated her as if she were less to him than one of his dogs. She wondered what there was in Lewes that made him choose to exercise domination through violence, what inadequacy persuaded him that force should earn him respect. Nor was he unique; there were many like him in Venture.

Asher let out a bitter laugh. Was Amrist the Conqueror so very different? His ambitions might lie along a grander scale, but the impulse seemed to her very much the same.

All I ever wanted was to have control over my own life, not other people's. Is there a flaw in men, that they feel this need for dominion? But that was to fall into the trap of believing them all alike, and Mallory at least had shown himself to be a little different; if bound by custom, his authority stemmed from a sense of responsibility, not the desire for power. Or – was he really different? His motives might be more acceptable to her, but was the intent not the same? Or did the Fates really make us physically the weaker sex for their own amusement, while giving us minds to know ourselves of equal value with men, but not to them; we work as hard, or harder, our intellects are as capable. Is it all a joke, to make us vulnerable, and to make men hate us? For what else but hate could make them behave towards us as they do? Or was the joke the other way around, that the Fates should dictate that men should create a world of their own choosing, then spend their lives squabbling endlessly for possession of it? In Petormin, it was said that girl babies were often killed at birth, so poorly were they valued by custom. Asher wondered what they would do when the imbalance in the population grew so extreme there were few women left to bear children. Would they then value their women more highly, or would they simply become a more prized commodity, gifts to be given out to the winners in some game of power?

'*Within your compass lies the means to pierce the veil.*' That was what the Oracle had said. A veil suggested disguise, something deliberately hidden. But the rest of the lines of the prophecy – did they suggest Asher would fail in her task unless she was willing to tear down those veils she had erected, those behind which lay Lewes, and the year of her marriage, and all the horrors of that time? She believed that was what Omond had meant. Must she remember it? Or was even that not enough, and she must actively confront the past in the person of Lewes himself?

She could not bring herself to believe it. Lewes hated her, perhaps more than she him. He would have greater cause, now, after Mallory's denial of Harrows as his inheritance.

Yet, surely, what she feared most was, by the very nature of the Fates, what they would destine for her? If it was true they were malign more often than generous, this would be their pleasure.

Was she too great a coward to face Lewes? Or should she leave her future entirely to the Fates and make a choice with what she wanted to be free will? The decision felt instantly right, sliding into place in her mind as neatly as if a niche had already been prepared for it.

Tonight. It must be tonight, or I won't be brave enough. The die was cast, she thought; she had thrown down a gauntlet to Fate, to know at last what was real and what only her fears.

The remainder of the day went by too fast and too slowly for Asher. Having made her decision, she found herself more and more unwilling to keep to it, as if the inner sense that had helped her the previous day was warning her against her own folly. After wandering restlessly about the house, she found herself returning to the library after dinner, staring at the embers of the fire; it was still too early to retreat to bed, and she had no inclination to do so, knowing what task awaited her.

'Are you all right, Asher? You seem pensive.'

Mallory had come in without her noticing, and she looked up, startled. 'Yes, thank you.'

He took the chair opposite hers, sinking into it with a weary sigh. 'Fates, I'm tired. I expect you are, too. I'm sorry you've been tied to the house all day, but with all the comings and goings to the estate office it was too risky for you to be about.'

'I didn't mind.'

'There's still tomorrow. What would you like to do? Perhaps we could find a way for you to visit Harrows?'

His thoughtfulness was nearly her undoing. She was powerfully tempted to admit to her confusion and ask his advice, but she did not. She had placed herself in the hands of the Fates, and only they should intervene now. 'I don't know,' she said, affecting a yawn. 'I think I'll go to bed, if you don't mind. I can hardly keep my eyes open.'

'Stay and talk a little longer,' he invited. 'I've hardly seen you all day.'

'I'm too tired to be good company.' She softened her refusal with a smile. 'Good night, Mallory.' She made as if to rise.

'Asher?' he said. She paused. 'You would tell me if you were worried or troubled?'

Something in his expression, perhaps hope, perhaps a wholly unexpected depth of feeling, made her catch her breath. 'Of course,' she said, forcing lightness to her tone. 'There's nothing.'

He looked at her a moment longer, then nodded absently. She left him, wondering if she had fooled him even for a minute; she was hardly a great actress. But it did not matter; he had not pursued the question. She made her way upstairs to her room, wishing she could go back, but at the same time proud she had sufficient strength of will to resist the temptation to take the easier path.

Am I being even stupider than ever before, or is this all predestined by the Fates?

She moved to sit by the window, looking out across the fields and the common to Harrows. No lights shone in the farmhouse. The night air was cold enough to keep sleep at bay and the skies were clear. Images stirred in her mind, of a night six years ago, of shadows weaving across a darkened path which lay out there among the fields. Coward that she was, she had tried to bury the past and failed. Now it arose to haunt her waking as it had haunted her dreams, and she could no longer run from it. If she did, she would spend the remainder of her life running, not only from Lewes but from herself; for what else was her life in Venture if not an escape? It was only now, at a distance, that she could see that truth for herself.

I've been wrong about everything else. What if this, too, is wrong? Her old confidence had deserted her, and she was aware of strong doubt, torn by opposing compulsions which both urged her to pursue the path she had chosen, yet at the same time warned her of danger, perhaps even a threat to her life.

If I don't go, I shall never know.

That would be worst of all, perhaps to regret forever that she had not possessed the courage to confront the ghosts of her past and conquer them. The day after tomorrow they would leave Kepesake, and she could never return; it was now, or never.

The long hours of waiting gave her too much time to think. Asher was grateful when, well after midnight, she was sure everyone in the house was finally asleep and she could leave her room.

At each corner, as she crept along the passage, as she slipped down the stairs, she thought of it as testing Fate. Would someone hear her and come out? Was Mallory still up, listening for her? If a door opened, would that be a sign? But nothing happened, and she reached the ground floor unhindered, glad to be on the move. The big house was eerily silent, and each sound of shifting timbers made her start nervously in the dark as she made her way along the narrow corridor at the rear of the house leading to the estate office.

She had been afraid it would be locked, but luck, or some other Fate, was evidently with her, for the door opened with only a faint creaking at the hinges. The room was as she remembered it, filled with a clutter of papers and ledgers, boxes filled with documents relating to the estate, but she concentrated on the desk, finding her way to it by moonlight, opening the top left-hand drawer where the keys had always been kept. Her heart leaped as she felt inside, and was rewarded with the cold touch of metal.

They must be here.

There were a large number of assorted keys in the drawer, providing her with an embarrassment of choice, but she took a chance selection over to the light of the window and spared a moment to bless the estate-steward: all of them were neatly labelled. Quickly reading the inscriptions, she discarded her first choices and returned for a second bunch; this time she was more fortunate, finding three keys to Harrows. She chose the largest, the one that opened the back door, then replaced the rest in the drawer, shutting it carefully.

She left the office and tried the side door next to it; it was bolted, but the latches were well oiled and the bars drew back easily enough. Opening the door, she stepped outside and into the gardens.

Cold air struck at her, even through her thick dark skirts and tunic, and she was glad of the dark-coloured scarf that covered all. She hesitated, knowing there was still time to draw back, tempted by the prospect of warmth and comfort in contrast with a lonely walk in the chill of the night. Now or never. Would Mallory forgive her if he knew what she was doing? More to the point, could she forgive herself if she did not go? Sighing, she moved away from the house; look or lose, it was all in the hands of the Fates.

To her right lay the orchard, and beyond it the wall surrounding the house and gardens; the gates would be shut and locked, but such barriers had never deterred her in the past and would not now. She remembered the time Callith had dared her to walk at midnight through Death Hollow, where the ghost of a murdered man was supposed to rise when Abate was full. Asher almost laughed at the memory of how she had run all the way to Kepesake once it was over, climbing the wall, tearing her skirts in the process, to throw stones at Callith's window and prove she had kept their bargain. She had encountered no ghosts but her own fears, but had invented a story for her friend, filled with eerie sounds and muffled wailings, which had terrified them both for weeks.

She slipped among the trees and was at once impaled by further stabs of memory; how many times had they stolen into this orchard, climbing the trees and eating the unripe fruit (an activity strongly forbidden, which had added powerfully to its charms), enjoying the suspense of wondering whether they would be found out? These shadows, at least, held no terrors for her, and she felt her courage returning as she reached the wall, moving with remembered ease; her foot reached up automatically for the foothold they had always used, a gap made by a broken brick, and she scrambled up and over without difficulty. This had been their private route, hers and Callith's, as familiar as her own home.

Home. I'm going home. Her eyes filled with sudden, unwanted tears, and she blinked them away.

The path they had worn was overgrown now, from disuse, and Harrows was invisible, shrouded from sight by the shrubs and bushes of the common grazing ground of the village which

216

divided Kepesake from her home. What had once been a well-trodden track was now no more than a faint trail, a lingering memory. Asher felt her excitement rising as she began the walk along the path, experiencing a longing for home so intense it seemed impossible she could have hidden such a hunger from herself for so many years. Just once more to wander about the familiar rooms, to feel the comfort of the house where she had grown up, to know there was a place where she had once belonged, was a lure too strong to resist. In two more years, Mallory would have to cede Harrows formally to Lewes, and she could never enter it again; she would be legally dead. Asher of Harrows would cease to exist, and there would only be Asher of Venture, who had no past and no place that was truly home.

She walked slowly, listening out for any sounds warning her she was no longer alone; small creatures scurried away at her approach – the night-hunting wild-cats, the small corn-mice and predatory owls. But she was not afraid of them; on the contrary, their presence acted as a reassurance that no one else moved in the thickets and shadows around her.

Two-thirds of the way along the path opened out, giving her a view of the farm. She stopped and looked, catching her breath. The years between *then* and *now* dropped away, and she could feel herself as she had been ten or more years ago, going home after one of her escapades, looking forward to warmth, and love, and safety, and all the promises conjured up by *home*.

The trunk of the old oak that marked the edge of the common had been split by lightning at some time since she had seen it last, and its branches now hung low, laden with the weight of years. Asher remembered that she and Callith had once used it as a meeting place, leaving messages in a knot-hole for each other in secret exchanges that had pleased them while they were still young enough for such things. Feeling foolish, she reached in a hand, but the hole was empty, as she should have expected; those days were long gone.

The final section of the path was more exposed, approaching the farm obliquely at the open end of the yard, and she wondered, belatedly, what arrangements had been made for the caretaker. Did he sleep in one of the barns? But the house looked reassuringly empty, the windows dark, the chimneys without their trail of smoke. She wanted to be alone when she revisited the past. '*In what was . . .*' Perhaps the answer lay here.

As she crossed the farmyard, she spared a glance for the old poultry pen; it was empty now, the gate sagging on its hinges, but it reminded her of the day of the invasion, when she had sworn she would never again be tempted to believe in the Fates, in divination or the Oracle, and she almost laughed, thinking how thoroughly she was breaking *that* promise.

The house looked smaller than she remembered, a square building, only two storeys high like most of the nearby farms, but larger and more solid than the rest in accordance with its status, for Harrows had almost twice the acreage of its neighbours. On her left stood the big barn, behind it a second used to store hay and other winter feed; to her right lay the small stable where her own pony had been housed, for her parents had indulged her, an only child, in ways beyond the means of the other local farmers. There were no sounds of movement from any of the buildings, which felt wrong, for in her memories there were always people or animals about in the yard, and even at night she had been able to hear the snorting of the dray-beasts from the barn. Now, there was nothing.

Uneasily, feeling oddly guilty, Asher fitted the key into the lock of the back door and turned it.

The door opened stiffly and she stepped into the kitchen, feeling the dank cold strike through her tunic. No one had used the wide hearth for many a year, and the room, unlike her recollection of it, smelled damp and musty, and of something else less easily identified. The long table which had always gleamed so whitely lay covered with a thick layer of dust; Asher idly traced a design with her forefinger, thinking how shocked her mother would have been to see it in such a state, then sneezed loudly as she disturbed it. The sound was horribly loud and she stayed still, waiting to see if anyone had heard; but no response came from the silence.

She had forgotten to bring a lantern, and the house was very dark. Cursing herself, and without much hope, Asher felt her way across to the larder and groped on the shelf where candles had always been kept, and was surprised to discover two long stubs and a tinderbox. With fingers that trembled, she struck a spark and lit the longer of the stubs, holding up the candle to reveal the worst.

Unused and uncared-for, the kitchen floor was covered with mouse-droppings as well as dust and dirt; on one wall was a large damp patch, and the ceiling and corners were stiff with spiders' webs. It was a very far cry from her memories of warmth and gleaming surfaces, but, surprisingly, it did not hurt. It was only dirt, nothing more.

At last she brought herself to leave the kitchen and wandered along the passage that led to the front of the house, to rooms they had used only rarely, mostly when they had company. The main parlour was much as she remembered, although someone had put away the few items her mother had liked to display – the porcelain Gormese vase Callith had given her; the mirror, framed with a vine-leaf design which had belonged to her own mother; two silver plates – her dowry. Asher wondered where they were, and whether Lewes had taken them. It would be very like him.

She found herself climbing the front stairs with some reluctance; they creaked noisily under her weight, and Asher felt suddenly like a thief in the stillness of the house, stealing through rooms made strange by emptiness and disuse. She paused at the door to her parents' room, hand on the handle, but could not bring herself to go in; she knew an unreasoned fear that if she did she would find them as she had last seen them, both lying dead, laid out ready for their burning, and she passed on hurriedly down the passage and up the three steps that led to her own room, unable to cope with such a vision of horror. Her own door stood partially ajar, almost as if awaiting her return, and she pushed against it and went in.

The bed was still made up. Unthinking, she sat down and sent up a shower of dust that made her cough; but she did not mind. This was *her* place, free from any taint of Lewes; this was where she had lain and dreamed on the long summer nights, of the future, of her hopes, her ambitions, even of the man she would marry – not, in those long past times, Lewes – and the children she would have. This was where she had planned her adventures: how she would run away to sea and visit foreign lands, and find a great treasure which she would bring back to her loving parents; how she would save Callith from drowning, and everyone would be proud of her; how she would be the one to rescue their country from the invaders, by some means as yet undecided – in this room, everything had seemed possible, nothing beyond her reach.

But those were the dreams of a child; there was nothing here for a woman grown except the memory of hope, of a time when she had thought her sex no limitation to her ambitions. Now, whatever she chose, she knew that even dreams were not safe, that even a life of solitude did not offer complete security; there would always be people who would seek to use her for their own ends. The world was not the place she had believed then.

Regretfully, Asher forced herself to get up and retrace her steps,

219

instinct returning her to the kitchen which had once been the centre of life on the farm. In her present aura of nostalgia she could imagine the room filled with people, her parents, the farm-hands, even Callith and Mallory, who had often shared their meals.

The back door stood open.

Asher froze instantly; surely, she remembered closing it, putting the key in the lock on the inside? The hand that held the candle shook as she lifted it high, heart beating fast and noisily, trying to dispel the shadows which had held only emptiness but which now seemed to offer shelter to any demons of the night.

'Who's there?' she called out.

No one answered. There was no sound at all other than her own breathing. The long room was still mostly in darkness, and she could see only within a small radius.

'Is anyone there?' she called again, more sharply.

A shadow detached itself from the far end of the room, separating itself from the wall against which it had leaned unmoving.

'I thought I'd find you here.'

He came towards her with measured steps, finding his way in the dark without difficulty. Asher gripped the candle tightly, terrified of dropping it and finding herself alone with him, without light.

'I'll take that.' He took the candle from her numbed fingers, and its light shone down on his still-blond hair, displaying the handsome features which had altered little with the years. His cheeks had grown puffy, as if he had taken to drinking heavily, but his tall figure was that of a labouring man, still well-muscled, without surplus flesh. The round blue eyes that stared into hers held the same hard, bright colour she remembered all too well, quite lacking Mallory's intrinsic kindness of heart and breadth of vision; they were the eyes of a man who knew nothing of the softer emotions, and cared not a whit for the lack.

'Why did you come here?' Asher asked coolly. 'Were you looking for me?'

She was not surprised to find him at Harrows; it seemed inevitable they should meet, for how could she conquer the ghosts of her past when he, of them all, was the one who haunted her most powerfully? '*In what was . . .*' There was unfinished business between them, and the Fates had decreed it was time to be done with it –

– or die? It was more a suggestion than a thought, and it gave her pause, for it held the same quality of warning she had sensed near the internment camp, an inner, intuitive certainty that could not be denied.

'I could ask the same of you, and with more reason. And, yes, Cousin Elissa told me you were visiting at Kepesake – or had you forgotten she was up at the house? I knew you'd come here one of these nights; all I had to do was watch for a light.' Lewes was still inspecting her face, as if seeking some overt display of fear, for she was, after all, at a strong disadvantage; several inches shorter, considerably weaker, and alone. She met his gaze squarely, but only pride allowed her to maintain a show of calm control, for she had forgotten one thing; she was still, as she had always been, afraid of Lewes.

'I just wanted to see Harrows once more, that's all.'

'Checking up all was well on *your* property?' Asher started at his tone, and was annoyed with herself, for he saw it and pressed his advantage, saying viciously: 'But it's not yours, it's *mine*, and has been all these years!'

'Take it.' She turned away from his scrutiny, loathing the sight of him. 'I won't stop you.'

He reached out his free hand to her chin and pulled her back to face him again. 'You must take me for a fool,' he said with contempt. 'I know why you've come back after all this time. But you won't take it from me. I swear it.'

'Don't touch me!' She slapped his hand away, shaking with the force of her revulsion; surprised, he let her be. 'Think what you like, Lewes, you always have. But I meant what I said. Take it. It's yours. I only wanted to come home one last time.'

'You mean you didn't want to see *me*?' The blue eyes clouded momentarily, as they did when he was in one of his more volatile moods. 'Because you're mine too, *if* I want you!' He raised his arm and slapped her across the cheek with the flat of his hand.

'And is that the mark of your possession?' Asher demanded angrily, careful not to touch her burning face. In this mood, it was all too easy to provoke further violence from him. 'You don't own me, Lewes. You never did,' she went on, more evenly. 'You've got Dora, and you'll have Harrows. Let that satisfy you.'

'Why should I?' He raised his hand again, and to her horror Asher found herself shrink as time flew backwards, and she was once again the old Asher of the year of her marriage, who had known there was no escape from her husband's selfish moodiness; remembered fear crept through her, and she felt sick.

Although she had known the risks she ran in coming to Harrows, she had thought herself sufficiently changed to be able to cope should she encounter Lewes – which had always been probable; she had not forgotten Elissa was a maid at Kepesake, a fact Mallory had overlooked but she had not. In the eyes of the villagers she was still Lewes' wife who had deserted him, whatever the cause. She had not understood that the physical reality of his presence would sap her courage and return her to the past, where she no longer believed the Oracle's prophecy offered any hope of protection. If the Fates intended her to die, she had aided them in the endeavour beyond all reason.

'Lewes, I'm leaving the day after tomorrow.' She took a deep breath. 'I came here because there was something I had to do, and it's over now. You won't see or hear from me again. Let me go.'

It was plain he placed no credence in her assurances. 'Then why did you come back? To betray me?' He paused suspiciously, waiting for a reply, but none came. 'No one would believe you,' he said, but with less confidence. He rallied, working himself up again: 'You've made me look foolish, coming here with another man. I'll not stand for that!'

'Oh, Lewes,' Asher began patiently, 'you know that's nonsense. I – '

There was no warning. One of his fists lashed out, knocking her squarely on the chin before she could fling up a hand to defend herself; she struggled against unconsciousness, fighting back an overwhelming dizziness as she sank to her knees.

'We'll finish this elsewhere,' he whispered. Asher felt him bend over her and tried to push him away, scarcely conscious of doing so. His hands were on her arms, reaching for her, lifting her, and she went limp as her head whirled; kaleidoscopic patterns invaded her mind, writhing in the way she remembered seeing before, but this time they seemed to make some sort of sense, as if they were letters she was just learning to read. *Danger;* they all say *danger, warning.* She wanted to protest, but could not speak.

The last thing her conscious mind registered was the solid sound of a door closing, and the grating of a key in the lock.

Omond woke, sitting up with a cry.

He had grown accustomed, with age, to dozing off at any time, and at first he could not remember what time it was, whether day or night. Had he gone to bed? He blinked, reassured as his posture and coverings told him he had; the lack of light persuaded him it was still night.

He experienced an unexpected surge of anxiety; something

had woken him, something needed him. He took a few moments to calm himself, breathing in and out slowly and carefully, for his heart was racing in a way that caused him some unease; composing his mind, he waited until the cause of his distress should come back to him.

'The girl.'

That was what had roused him. The chain and charm he had given her were keyed to his *sight* as well as to her lifeline; it was an alteration to that lifeline that had triggered this waking. She was in some sort of danger, of the kind he had foreseen.

Stiffly, he climbed out of bed and put on a warm robe against the cold; his joints protested at the abrupt movements, but he ignored them. This was what Mallory had feared and he must be told at once. Forcing his reluctant limbs into movement, he tried to hurry as he made toward the stairs, careful not to stumble and fall in his eagerness; an accident would be disastrous for him and the girl.

He reached Mallory's room on the floor below and entered without knocking first, shaking the sleeping form impatiently, willing the young man to wake. Mallory stirred, then sat up abruptly.

'What is it?'

'Something has happened to the girl. Get up, quickly!' A sense of urgency propelled him to greater effort, and Omond knew an immense gratitude that he had gone against his conscience in watching over the child. '*Hurry!*'

Mallory was already out of bed, groping for his clothes and swordbelt.

'Come, up to my rooms, I will try to *see* her for you.' Omond found himself fretting at even the smallest delay. 'Now!'

'I'm ready.' Mallory buckled his belt.

As he entered the attic and stooped to gather his bowl and pitcher, Omond found himself muttering charms of protection, for himself as well as for the girl, willing himself to find the reserves of power he would need for his search.

The charm, it is a talisman that binds her to my sight.

He wiped rheumy eyes as he poured the liquid into the bowl, stirring the patterns into motion. He sat and concentrated his will, staring at the patterns until his mind was fully engaged and he could open his inner eye.

Show me, show me where she is. He looked deep into the circling patterns in his mind until an image formed, and he saw.

She was lying on a pile of hay with her eyes closed, arms loose. Her head was turned to one side, but as Omond studied her he saw the steady rise and fall of her chest; he had known her to be alive, but whether asleep or unconscious he could not say. All he could tell was that she had suffered no serious harm, or so his mental bond informed him.

Satisfied for the moment, he tried to extend the range of his vision to take in more of her surroundings; the place was dark, but there was a source of light somewhere in the room, and he could make out a wheeled vehicle of some kind – a barrow, he thought – and various tools hanging on a wall; shovels, a spade, and a long implement that could have been a scythe. So – she was in a barn.

'But which one?' Mallory demanded impatiently.

Omond could not tell him. There was someone in the barn with her, a tall man, visible only in outline, but his identity was easily guessed. He described the man to Mallory, who caught his breath.

'Tell me more – anything you can *see*,' he urged. 'A clue as to the location.'

'It is north of Kepesake.'

'But that could be either Carling's or Harrows. *Which*?'

Omond sought for his last reserves of strength, knowing that if he failed this time there were no more chances. He fixed his mind on the talisman round Asher's neck and tried to pin-point its location – nearer or further? His heart began to pound in an uneven fashion, making him breathless, but he did not stay his efforts.

At last he sat back, exhausted.

'Carling's.'

'Thank you.'

Mallory was already on his feet. Omond heard his steps pounding down the stairs, but was too drained to move or do anything at all. He would sit and wait, and perhaps sleep.

If anything happened to the girl, he was not sure he would be able to withstand the shock the severing of the link between them would bring him. His heart, as if in answer to his doubts, began to beat with an uneven rhythm.

Mallory struggled with the girth buckles, cursing fluently; the stallion stood placidly waiting while he tied a bag to the pommel and put his foot in the stirrup. Mallory considered waking Ish, but on balance he preferred to go alone, wanting no witnesses to the night's work.

What had possessed Asher to take such an insane risk? Why had she chosen to confront Lewes alone, in the middle of the night? How had it happened? It seemed to Mallory she was commanded by a demon that spurred her on to greater and greater tests of her own capacity, as if she could not live with herself without such proofs of courage; he had known men of a similar character, who rushed to embrace their own destruction with open arms. Yet in Asher's case it was different, for he sensed her recklessness had its origins in a degree of self-hatred which could only have been engendered by her marriage to Lewes; the man had destroyed her ability to enjoy being a woman, so that she saw only the weaknesses of her sex and none of the strengths or pleasures.

Small wonder, if all he made her feel was ugly and unwanted; a thing to be owned and despised. The day of her wedding came back to him, and he remembered how he had teased her about the night to come, and pain stabbed him in the pit of his stomach; how easily Lewes must have been able to destroy the open spirit of the girl he had married. Her sexual inexperience would have made her an easy target for his cruelty.

It was not the desire to protect her frailty that sent him out into the night, although that was still a part of it, for Asher was strong in will but not in physique; it was his feelings for her as an individual, as *Asher*, whom he valued for her sense of humour, for her transparent integrity. *That* was what was important, not the rest. Some men might see such emotion as weakness, but Mallory had learned how highly to value friendship in his years at sea, and was not afraid or ashamed to admit to affection, even, although he was not quite certain of it, to love, if love could be defined as a form of friendship.

He dared not spur his horse to a a canter; the night was too dark, and there might be any number of potholes along the trail. Abate's malevolent eye stared down at him, pale and chill across the ploughed fields, and Mallory had to check his pace as a hare ran between his horse's legs, making the beast rear and almost unseating him. Sweating, he held on; time was slipping away – too much time.

He intended to kill Lewes. He had thought for some time it was the best and simplest solution to Asher's dilemma but had hesitated to present it to her in case she felt some lingering sense of obligation towards her husband – although he doubted it. The man deserved to die on many counts; not least for what he had done to her. Mallory knew he could easily justify his intent; Lewes was a collaborator, a traitor, condemned by his own deeds. He had broken the moral, if not the written, laws of Darrian. But a hard core of vengeful anger told Mallory that his desire was as much personal as pragmatic, that he would find real satisfaction in killing the man. He should not deceive himself into believing he acted from any elevated motive, unless there was something lofty in wanting to avenge the hurts Asher had endured.

If he came too late, they would never find Vallis. That, too, was a motive, but a lesser consideration.

Carling's was visible now, and he decided to go round and approach the house and barn north, from the rear, for the wind was coming from the south and would otherwise take his scent straight to the dogs; he was glad he had remembered their existence in time. There was no need to alert Lewes to his presence until he was ready.

He left his horse in a wheatfield, draping the reins over a convenient branch and untying his bundle from the saddle; the rear of the barn was only some three hundred paces distant and he made his way on foot towards it, stepping carefully through the grasses and brambles to make as little sound as possible. No lights shone in the house, but he could make out a faint gleam from the yard ahead.

As he reached the barn, a warning growl came from somewhere to his left, and he became aware of a fetid smell; he froze instantly, seeing the head of an immense black mastiff appear round the side, jaws open. He could smell the rankness of the creature's breath. Mallory crouched down, but to his relief the animal came no closer, although even from a distance he could see its prominent ribs; hear the rattle of links of chain. He realized Lewes, as he'd hoped, had set his dogs to guard the front of the farm, not allowing them to roam free. He felt inside his bundle and withdrew three small, spherical objects and a tinderbox; with them in his hands, he edged forward, until he was only feet from the yard, and the mastiff was about to progress from a warning growl to a full-bloodied frenzy of barking. Quickly, he struck three sparks, igniting the paper tails attached to the spheres, then threw all three into the centre of the yard. He knelt down to watch the results.

A flurry of deep baying came from the mastiff, bringing forth an echo from its fellow, which he could not, for the present, see. The first of the spheres began to emit bright sparks and a rose-coloured sulphureous smoke as it jumped about, and a series of small explosions set off a chain reaction, resulting in more sparks and denser smoke. Mallory had bought the spheres on a visit to Baram, which lay east of the Kamiri homeland, where they were used to celebrate the Day of the Dead, the festival the Baramites held once a year to commemorate their ancestors. He had intended them as a gift for Callith's children, for they were harmless and entertaining, but he was sure Lewes, who had no interests beyond land and gold, would never guess they were

226

toys. He was as superstitious as any sailor, certain to read some omen or other into their appearance; more importantly, they would provide an excuse for the dogs to bark while Mallory carried out the second part of his scheme.

He heard the creaking of a door, then a voice shouting over the noise of the spheres.

'What's all that racket?'

The voice belonged to Lewes; Mallory knew it instantly and sent silent thanks to Omond for identifying Carling's accurately. The dogs were barking louder than ever, excited by the leaping sparks and the smoke, and Mallory heard Lewes strike one of them with a link of chain; then he came into view as he moved further out into the yard, keeping a wary distance from the sparks.

'Fates preserve us!' He made a gesture of aversion, and Mallory smiled grimly to himself; he had never thought the man particularly intelligent. Lewes glanced round, obviously trying to decide the meaning of the strange visitation. The dogs continued to howl, but after a quick inspection of the hen run and a look at the house, Lewes turned back and disappeared again inside the barn.

Mallory reached inside his bundle and withdrew a large piece of meat removed from the kitchen stores at Kepesake. Creeping forwards, he threw it towards the mastiff, now at the full extent of its chain. Surprised, it stopped barking and bent to sniff the offering, at first with suspicion, then with real interest; within moments it was lying down, chewing the joint between its forepaws while its eyes roved warily for any danger to its prize. Lewes, like so many of his type, relied on starvation to keep his dogs savage, and its need for sustenance was greater than its desire to guard. Keeping his distance, Mallory walked silently round to the front of the barn. The mastiff's companion, a gangling beast barely out of puppyhood, had scented food and was howling and leaping against the restraint of its chain. Mallory neatly threw his second offering, which landed by the animal's haunches. It emitted a yelp, then set to, without further hesitation, too ravenous to care that its territory was being invaded.

The barn doors were shut, but Mallory inched open the right-hand side with extreme care, peering in through the narrow gap; he drew his sword in his right hand, holding it loose but ready, touching a finger to the needle-sharp point.

The Fates might be the arbiters of which of the three of them should live or die that night, but Mallory had every intention of making their decision an easy one: if he had harmed Asher in any way, Lewes would die.

Chapter Twelve

While Omond sat and waited, and Mallory fought his horse along rutted lanes, Asher lay asleep.

She first became aware of being awake because she could feel rough stalks tickling her cheek and nose, and she wanted to sneeze. She was perfectly comfortable, lying on something soft, breathing in a reassuringly familiar odour compounded of the scents of wet hay, leather and sawdust; the only thing troubling her was that she had no clear idea where she was. She thought about sitting up and opening her eyes to look, but at that moment it seemed too much trouble, and in any case she was not absolutely sure she wanted to know; she had a hazy memory of something bad, some undesirable event, and the recollection kept her still.

Many-coloured patterns played before her closed eyelids in a slow series of random forms darting out in all directions, some shaped like tree trunks, others like narrow branches, all originating from a single point; she tried to blot them out, for they were making her dizzy, but it proved impossible.

I should wake up, she thought dreamily, her head aching and heavy; but somewhere nearby there was movement, as if she were not alone, and the sounds made her nervous.

A chain rattled not far away. It was a familiar noise but it puzzled her, for she had thought she must be in her room at Harrows: but no, that was wrong. Perhaps she was at Carling's – but no, she had left years ago . . .

Memory returned with a rush as she grew conscious of soreness on her face and jaw, and knew their cause. *Lewes – she was with Lewes!* Cautiously, she allowed her eyelids to lift, but only a crack; a rapid glance brought her a glimpse of a section of wall with various tools hanging from hooks in an orderly fashion: a scythe; a drill; a spade. Quickly, she lowered her lids once more, but not before she had recognized the place; this was the barn at

Carling's, too small to be Harrows. Lewes must have brought her here after he had knocked her out, and was now nearby, watching and waiting for her to revive. But in order to do what?

Suddenly time seemed immensely precious, the longer she could lie still the better. She waited, keeping her arms and legs lax while listening intently for sounds of Lewes' approach, and after a while there came the scuffing of booted feet across the wooden floor; she made herself breathe slowly and evenly as they drew closer, then stopped. For a moment, nothing happened, and she wondered if her ploy had succeeded; then a shower of cold water was thrown over her, and she sat up, gasping with shock.

Lewes stood laughing down at her, hands on hips, an empty pitcher dangling from one hand.

'That shook you, I'll bet! You should see yourself – you look like a drowned rat! And that's an improvement.'

She wiped the water from her eyes with a sleeve, then felt for the scarf round her head and pulled it off, using it to tie back her dripping hair in a loose tail; she did these things extremely slowly, as if every second she could gain was important. Lewes watched her impatiently. Beyond him, Asher saw the barn doors stood shut, but at least the dogs were not in sight; presumably they were outside, for which she was grateful. Lewes trained them through a combination of cruelty and hunger, and his animals were always savage. For the second time in two days she tried not to remember the horror of his old threat to set them on her.

'You've no looks left,' he commented casually, as if he were judging the points of a horse he did not intend buying. 'Mind, you were always a plain, scrawny, little thing, even when you were young.'

She gave a non-committal shake of the head, horrified to find the old feelings of inadequacy returning full force; she had never been vain, but in the early days of their marriage she had made an effort to look attractive, hoping it would put him in a better frame of mind. Instead, he had wasted no time making it plain he found her lacking in face and form, pointing to the other village girls and telling her exactly where her own deficiencies lay: she was too thin, too pale; her eyes were too small; her nose was an ugly shape. The list had been endless, and the steady stream of invectives had sapped her self-confidence until she found it easier simply not to care about her appearance.

It doesn't matter, I know it doesn't, and he only does it to hurt. So why do I still mind? She bit her lip.

'Nothing to say?' Her silence seemed to anger him, and he came closer, stretching out a casual foot to kick her; it landed on her thigh, and she suppressed a cry of pain.

'What do you *want* me to say?'

Lewes seemed pleased with her reaction. 'Better. Perhaps you should try telling me you're sorry for all the trouble you've caused, for a start.'

'I would have thought that was a waste of time.' She was glad to hear the steadiness in her voice. 'Even if I meant it.'

'Oh, it would be, but I'd like to hear you say it.' He eyed her speculatively as she sat on the pile of loose hay, her back against neatly stacked bales; the position seemed to offer less of her as a target than if she had been standing.

'Why did you bring me here?' she asked quietly, shifting back until she was out of range of his booted feet.

He stepped forward, unwilling to allow her any margin of safety. 'To kill you, of course. Or were you hoping I wanted to bed you?'

She felt a chill travel down her spine. There was no doubt he meant it. 'Hardly that.'

'I've no use for you in that way. Dora's eight times the woman you were,' he said pleasantly. 'And she'll give me a son before I've done with her. Not like you – worthless slut!' He kicked her again. '*And* I'll have Harrows.'

'It's yours,' she said wearily. 'I've told you – '

'And has been, but for you and your precious friend *Councillor* Mallory, for the past six years.' His eyes blazed a deeper blue in the lanternlight. 'Years you stole from me, the pair of you, keeping from me what was rightfully mine. Do you think I'd have married you otherwise?' He kicked her again with greater viciousness.

Pride kept her face expressionless. 'I took nothing from you, Lewes, and I *want* nothing from you. I have a life of my own, far away from here. Let me go, and you'll never see me again. But if you kill me, Mallory will know.'

Lewes showed no concern at all at the threat. 'You think so?' He chuckled, an unpleasant sound. 'Your *lover* won't be able to prove anything. *Anything.* Dora will swear I was with her all night, and none of the villagers will care. If a man's wife goes straying, it's no surprise if she turns up dead in a ditch!'

'Mallory is not my lover, and never was.' But she stated the fact with little hope of being believed; Lewes was a man who had only one use for a woman. 'And you're wrong. Your reputation is catching up with you, Lewes. Or so I heard at Kepesake.'

'*No!*' He lashed out again, and she knew he would make her pay for the perceived offence; he was a man who not only bore grudges but nurtured them into full-grown grievances. She had learned that, too, during their marriage. 'You expect me to believe you? You were always close with him, and that sister of his; too close. Was it him you ran to, that night? Or was there some other man, one who threw you out when he found out how useless you were, and you went bleating to *Councillor* Mallory for help?'

'Believe what you want,' Asher said coldly. 'You always did.'

'Oh, I will.' His foot caught her on the hip, a moment of agony. 'Do you know, I went looking for you when you left? For a long time. You cost me money!'

'You know why I went.' There was no point in trying to placate him, she thought wearily. 'Not for another man, but to get away from you and what you were. A *traitor!*'

'*Shut your lying mouth!*' He bent and took a handful of hair in his fist, pulling painfully. She struck out, scratching the back of his hand with her ragged nails, and he swore, letting her go.

'Don't touch me!' Anger came to her rescue, as it had so often in the past. 'You always twisted things in your mind so that *you* were right and everyone else wrong, but you can't lie to me. I despise you. You sell friends and neighbours to feed your greed and self-importance because you're a weak man, and always were! And stupid, to believe no one would ever find you out.'

He let her finish, but his face flushed an angry red and she was ready for the onslaught when it came, curling up to shield face and stomach from his hands and feet. It was soon over, and he stood back, breathing hard.

'Sit up!' he ordered. 'I'll not let you tempt me to leave too many marks on your skinny body. Your death is going to be an *accident.*' Although his fury had not subsided, common sense returned some semblance of his self-control. 'Unless people believe your precious lover tired of you, and tried to put the blame on me, the innocent husband, when he killed you!' Asher wondered fleetingly if such a thing were possible. '*No one,*' and he spoke so emphatically that Asher could not doubt him, 'is going to stop me. Least of all *you.*'

Shakily, she sat up, more afraid than ever before in her life. She had placed herself in the hands of the Fates, but at the same time she had hoped – or believed? – that no harm would come to her. Now, stripped of anger, of hope, and of confidence, Asher knew her luck had finally run out. She fingered the chain round her neck, thinking bitterly that she deserved it should be so; she was guilty of the same self-importance of which she had accused Lewes, the same selfish assurance that she, and only she, was right. None of this would have happened if she had listened to Omond and Mallory.

I thought I could manage him. I'd forgotten . . . During her years in Venture, she had grown to believe herself immune to her old terrors – another mistake.

'Worried?' Lewes' voice taunted her; hating him, she shut her eyes.

I tempted the Fates to show me what in the past I had to confront. Is my death their answer?

'What's that chain?'

She looked up, puzzled at the unexpectedness of the question. 'Mother gave it to me. I've always worn it.'

'Liar.' Lewes reached down and snatched at it; the chain broke, and the charm dropped into the pile of hay. With a cry, Asher began to search for it. 'I've never seen it before,' he said angrily. 'What is it? A gift from one of your *lovers*?'

'I told you.' She was still fumbling where she thought the charm had fallen, but an uneasy doubt stirred in her mind. Was what she had said the truth? She remembered she had always worn the chain, but she seemed to have no memory of actually being given it; the distress she felt at its loss seemed to suggest both chain and charm meant a great deal to her, but emotionally not rationally.

Omond.

At once, she saw again in her mind the moving globes of his invention, remembering how the moons had gone round and round, faster and faster until she was dizzy, and now she could recall his soft voice quite clearly: '*This is yours, your chain; it has always been yours.*' The chain had been his gift to her, and must be a form of protection she would never knowingly have accepted, doubtless made at Mallory's instruction. She wondered what had happened when Lewes snapped the chain, warmed by the concern that had prompted the gift; once, only that morning perhaps, she would have been annoyed at such an infringement of her freedom, but now it gave her hope.

Something of her feelings must have shown in her face, for Lewes stood back. 'Well?' he asked sharply. 'What is it?'

Asher shook her head. 'Nothing.'

A low growl came from outside the barn and Lewes stiffened, instantly alert. 'Did you hear something?'

'Only the dogs.' And at that moment one of the mastiffs began to bark, deep yelps of distress, and there came another sound, rather like the crackling, spitting noises of green wood in a fire. Lewes moved swiftly to the wall and took down a heavy spade.

'If you struggle or call out, I'll kill you now.' He held the spade menacingly in both hands. 'I'll crush your skull. But if you're still, I'll let you live a while longer. Which is it to be?'

'I'll be still.' Asher fought to control her terror. Every moment seemed infinitely precious as she watched Lewes replace the spade on its hook.

'This is only a reprieve, mind that,' he warned. He gathered several strips of leather harness, one of which he proceeded to buckle round her neck; forcing her arms behind her back, he placed more straps on each wrist, then linked them with another to the band round her throat, half-choking her. She lay on her back to relieve the pressure on her windpipe, for it was hard to breathe at all and the awkward position of her arms was painful. With a last backward look, Lewes left her as the dogs' barking reached a crescendo.

Asher felt with her fingers for the buckles of the straps, trying desperately to undo them; if she could free herself, she could escape, but trussed as she was she could not walk, let alone run.

She could not bring herself truly to believe she was going to die; it was impossible, too horrible to imagine. It shocked her to discover how very much more frightening death became with imminence. It was not so much the fear of pain, but an almost uncontrollable terror of the unknown, of simply ceasing to exist, that drove Asher on to struggle with the unyielding straps.

Her mind was no longer confused, either by Lewes' blows or her own unresolved doubts and fears; as she fought with the leather, Asher found that these obstructions had been removed, to be replaced by a chill clarity that left her no one to blame for what had happened except herself.

Time played another trick on her, and seemed to cease its motion. Her fingers became still. From nowhere, Asher thought she could hear the voice of the Oracle:

'Mark what may from what must be;
In what was lies what will be;
Look, with eyes that choose to see.'

For how long had she chosen to blind herself, seeing only what she wanted to see in people, men or women, so absorbed by her own concerns that she had spared no real thought for anyone else? Her judgments over the years had been more the result of her own prejudices and willing refusal to *see*, so that she had not understood what was so plainly in front of her.

'*Look, with eyes that choose to see. Look – or lose . . .*' It was only that until now she had not made that choice. Was it too late, now that her resistance had crumbled and she was willing to look? She did possess the key to finding Vallis; it had been *there*, in her mind, all along.

Her fingers slipped on a stiff buckle but closed on the end of one of the straps and she pulled, freeing one of her hands, with an instant relief to her lungs. She struggled with a second, listening out for sounds of Lewes' return, but there were only the same odd crackling noises and the barks of the mastiffs.

'*In what was lies what will be . . .*' Stupidly, she had taken the words to mean that the Oracle intended her to confront her past in the physical sense; now she saw it was acceptance and understanding which were needed, a willingness to open her eyes to *what was*. So she should no longer blind herself with false images of the truth, or what she desired to be the truth. How could she, of all people, have so deluded herself as to take anyone at their own valuation? To judge a man by the way he behaved among equals or in public life was a great stupidity, such occasions giving few clues to his real nature. Probity in business dealings might have its origin in pragmatism rather than innate honesty. What she should have looked for, and could not see until now, was a man whose actions proved him a different person from the man others saw, rather as Lewes had been, for no one but she herself had known the underside of his nature during her marriage. There was only one man among those she knew now to whom the Oracle could have referred.

It seemed to Asher that at that moment of revelation time began to move on again, and she was filled with a new panic, that she would not free herself and Lewes would come back and kill her before she could speak. The responsibility terrified her, now she was sure she held the key to finding Vallis, that she had identified the one person who must know where she was. She must not die, not until she could give his name to someone else.

'*See the shifting shadowlines; mark what may from what must be . . .*' The choices had always been hers to make, not fixed and unalterable; no malign Fate had condemned her to die, here, now. Only her own folly.

There was a yelp and the rattle of a chain; the barn door opened again. Desperately, Asher tore at the constricting leather and freed her other hand, but it was too late to run. Lewes had returned, and he was now carrying a heavy wooden pestle in his right hand, selected from two that had been lying on the floor by the doors.

'Just in time, I see.' He came over and surveyed her loosed hands. 'If you'd run, I'd have sent the dogs after you.'

Outside, in apparent response, one of the dogs gave a low growl then grew silent. Asher, watching the hand that held the pestle, knew with unwelcome clarity that her death was very close, that any move on her part would provoke it. She froze, hardly daring to breathe. Odd flashes of thought came to her; resentment, that she should die at the hands of a man so worthless; anger, that she should die because of her own stupidity, when she was unprepared and unresigned and there was still something vital she must do.

Lewes lifted the pestle behind and above his head; her eyes followed it but her body would not move in response to her commands, her muscles locked rigid. Sweat formed on her brow. She was totally unprepared for the suddenness with which events were moving.

'It'll be quicker than you deserve,' Lewes said darkly, as his body tensed. 'Good riddance, wife. Your luck's done, but mine begins again!'

'*No!*' Barely in time, she kicked out, catching Lewes on the knee as he struck, giving herself time to roll to one side, and the pestle landed heavily on the hay, not her head. Instantly, he reached for her hair to hold her still, readying himself for a second blow; she raised her hands frantically to ward him off, seeing in that moment all the patterns in her mind instantly still, and knew them at last for the lines of her future lives, and they were telling her there was no more time, no second chance –

'Stay still!' Lewes barked as she clawed at him.

'*No!*' She screamed the word out.

'No,' came a second, deeper voice from the doorway.

The shock was so great that Lewes lowered his weapon, although he maintained his grip on Asher's hair. Turning sideways, very slowly, he stared toward the door where Mallory stood, sword unsheathed.

'Let her go, Lewes.'

He looked as if he could not believe what he saw; his mouth gaped open and eyes widened as he took in the presence of his enemy. Mallory advanced a few steps. Feverishly, Lewes tugged at Asher's hair and half-raised the pestle.

'Stay there!'

Mallory took another step. 'No.'

'Move, and she dies.'

'You mean to kill her anyway, so why should I do what you say?' Mallory asked reasonably, advancing a further step.

Lewes hefted his club, and Asher caught her breath.

'Because it'll be sooner rather than later, *Councillor* Mallory, and that'll be your fault,' Lewes said viciously.

Mallory shook his head. 'If you harm her, you die.'

'But she'd still be dead!' Again, he pulled agonizingly at Asher's hair. 'What'll you give me for her? If she's *worth* anything to you.' He managed a coarse laugh.

'Infinitely more than you.' Mallory came on again.

'No nearer!' Lewes was unnerved by his opponent's slow approach; his grip on the pestle tightened until the tendons on the back of his hand stood out against the tanned skin. 'Or I kill her now.'

Mallory took one more step, then stopped. 'If I stay here, Asher dies. You've said so yourself. If I come closer, *you* die. It's your choice, Lewes. Let her go.' His tone was still even, but Asher saw no movement in the shadow patterns in her mind, no hope.

'Mallory,' she gasped, desperate to tell him what she had discovered, willing to believe that death would come more easily if she could fulfil at least that duty. 'I – ' But Lewes had no intention of letting her speak.

'If I let her go, you'd kill me anyway,' he said angrily, pulling at her hair.

'Yes,' Mallory agreed.

'You'd not dare – I've friends who'd not let it pass! Friends not even you can pay to silence. The whole village'd know who did it. You've stolen my wife, you flaunt her in your house as your mistress – the grey men'd come for you before the night was out!'

'Are you sure?' Mallory let the question stand while Lewes' expression shifted from anger to uncertainty. 'You've no friends left, Lewes. You've sold them all.'

'So *she* told you?' His eyes held a glint of calculation, and he kicked Asher hard in the ribs.

'I wouldn't do that again.' Mallory's voice hardened. 'And, yes, Asher told me. How you betray your neighbours for money; how you abuse women because you think that makes you a man, when instead it places you lower on the scale than any beast!' He took another step forward. 'Asher chose to start a new life, with nothing, rather than live with you. You asked me what she was worth: ten thousand of you, and more. Even to kill you will taint my sword. Don't believe your friends will save you, Lewes. You have none.'

Asher could feel Lewes working himself up to act. 'Mallory,' she whispered, trying again. 'I know the answer – '

'Shut up!' Lewes shook her cruelly by her hair; she was kneeling, half-supported by him, when his hand loosed her, slipping to her neck and grasping the strap still buckled round it. She slumped, but his arm held her up, cutting off most of her air supply.

'Make up your mind, Lewes.' But Mallory was looking at her, rather than him, and he seemed to be expecting something from her.

What does he want? she thought desperately, keeping her eyes on his face because it was the only way to hold back her terror. It was difficult to think at all, not least because if she did not watch Mallory she saw only the still patterns in her mind which told her she was going to die. Nothing that had happened since his arrival had altered that. She was glad she was not alone with Lewes, grateful to Mallory for being there, and could not blame him for ignoring Lewes' threats; there was no other way to act, and he would be as trapped as she was.

As I am. The thought stirred her sluggish brain to action; *that* was what Mallory expected. Not for her to lie passively waiting for death, accepting Lewes' assumption she was powerless, but for her to save herself. She had allowed old fears to paralyse her, knowing the violence of which he was capable; but it was only remembered terror that held her still, and she could free herself from that at will. *I will not be afraid*, she told herself fiercely. Fear of Lewes was rational, for he was a man who knew no reason but his own will; but it was also her weakness and gave him power over her, making her complicit with her own murder, which was the worst foolishness of all. *My life is mine, not his!*

And she knew she could move again, shifting her balance from knees to feet in readiness. Mallory was almost within striking range.

'Your last chance, Lewes.'

'Then she *dies!*' He raised the club high and brought it down with tremendous force towards Asher's head.

He was unprepared for her sudden upward leap, and his own grip on the harness round her neck sent him off-balance as her weight surged against him; he struck again awkwardly, where her head had been, but she had moved and it was no longer there. The pestle met only air, and before he had a chance to aim again

Mallory's blade was at his throat, and the club dropped to the hay as the point pierced his skin, then carried on through flesh and vein and muscle. He gave a gargling cry and collapsed, pulling Asher down with him, his fingers still wrapped in her makeshift collar.

She landed on top of him, breathless, and in revulsion tugged at his hand as a narrow stream of blood spurted from the wound in his throat; rolling aside, she undid the buckle and flung the harness away in disgust. Unexpectedly, from outside came a chorus of howls from the two mastiffs, but the sound came only briefly; then there was silence again.

Mallory stooped to wipe his sword on the hay. 'Are you hurt?'

'No.' She was bruised, but Lewes had broken no bones. It had never been his way; there was too much work on the farm for that. She thought it odd how familiar pain could be.

'Are you sorry I killed him?'

'Sorry?' She looked at him in astonishment. 'Mallory, I can only thank you from the bottom of my heart.'

Some of the constraint left his voice. 'I wondered.'

She looked down at the body which had been Lewes; alive, she had hated him with a passion she had never allowed herself to express, but dead he meant less than nothing. Exept that in the moment of his death, her own life *changed*, the patterns in her mind leaping into instant motion and offering so many new opportunities that it seemed impossible one small event – one man's ceasing to breathe – could mean so much.

She stooped and picked up the chain Lewes had broken, handing it to Mallory. 'This is yours, I think,' she said quietly. 'The charm's somewhere in that hay. I owe you a great deal, Mallory. More than I can ever say or repay.'

'I thought you might be angry.' He took the chain and held it in his hand. 'Even Omond was unwilling to give it to you at first, without your permission. He said it was spying on you. But it brought me here tonight.'

She shook her head. 'Once, I would have said it was you trying to control me, but not now.'

'We have to bury Lewes, somewhere he won't be found in a hurry. If there's no body, his grey friends won't come after us.' He looked down, kicking the small amount of hay stained with Lewes' blood. 'We can burn this.'

'Let it be at Harrows. By the ash tree down by the stream. No one ever went there but me.' Asher faltered, remembering when Lewes had come to see her there, on the day of the invasion fourteen years before, and how angry she had made him. Had that day influenced him in his relations with her? Was that the choice she had made that day?

He nodded. 'All right.' He put the chain in his pocket and reached out a hand to touch Asher's face; she winced as he traced an emergent bruise. 'Did he hurt you?'

'He said he wanted my death to look like an accident.' It was almost an answer. 'Mallory, I'm sorry – about everything. You don't need to say this was all my fault, because I know it was. But I'm glad he's dead. He was like a leech, a weight I had to carry wherever I went. Because of him, I treated you as if you were like him; as if there could be *any* resemblance between you and him.'

'You taught me the error of my ways!' But he was smiling, and Asher knew he had accepted her apology.

'So I did. As always Asher knows best.' She sighed. 'Just remind me of that a few hundred times a day.'

He laughed, but it did not sound incongruous, despite their surroundings. 'We'd better get to work. We've a lot to do before morning.'

'You keep saying *we*. It makes me feel like a partner instead of an encumbrance.'

'And so you are.' He hesitated. 'Asher, you're not the only one who made a few mistakes.'

'Truce, then.' She held out her hand, and he took it. 'Mallory, what I said – I know who took Vallis.'

He paused, then shook his head. 'Tell me when we're back at Kepesake. Not here.'

She shivered, looking down at Lewes; there was no reason for her not to speak in his presence, but it would be easier away from Carling's. 'You're right; not here.'

He grinned. 'Now *there* is an admission I never thought to hear you make!'

Mallory replaced the key and shut the drawer of the desk. 'We've only a little time before the maids will be about, Ash. Tell me now.' He, too, was bone-weary, and the estate office was chill.

'Is Lewes the only man you've ever killed?'

'No. Are you regretting it now?'

She shook her head vehemently. 'Never. The world's a better place without him.'

'And all men? Or are you willing to make a few exceptions?'

She frowned, unwilling to let the comment pass. 'You meant that as a joke, and of course not. I know there are other men like

239

you, Mallory, and women who are as bad as Lewes. But perhaps I should explain something, before I tell you what I think about Vallis.'

'What?'

She looked down at her hands. 'Do you know why I married Lewes?' she asked. 'It was because my father wanted me to; he thought he would be a good husband, a hard worker for Harrows. He liked him. But, you see, he didn't know him at all – or, rather, he only knew Lewes as he presented himself to other men, and saw only that side of him. Afterwards, I wondered – but not for long, for I knew he and my mother had a very different relationship, based on trust and affection, and respect; yet my father married me to a man incapable of trusting, or any form of affection. So if I seem to doubt your judgment at times, it's only because what *you* see, and what I see, may be entirely different.'

He nodded. 'Fair enough.'

'It's like the crew on your ship; they may be a fine crew at sea, but when they reach Venture they change. They may have been only common sailors on board ship, but they feel when they come home that everything should be arranged for them – as if their absence gave them a *right* to behave as they please and indulge themselves, as if their wives and children had been in stasis during their time away, without an independent existence.' She shrugged. 'All I'm trying to say is that there are two sides to all of us, and most of us only see one side of another person.'

'Agreed. But what of it?'

'It's just so you'll listen to what I have to say about finding Vallis. Let me tell you what I saw when I was with Lewes.' She bit her lower lip. 'It's all about a willingness to see what really is, not what we expect to see. Now, first, begin with my being *overlooked* – because I find it too great a coincidence to believe it's not in some way connected to our search.' Mallory nodded. 'The man lives in Venture and must be rich; Omond said the diviner was powerful, and his services must be paid for. Agreed?'

'Certainly.'

'Second, he must be ambitious. The Oracle suggested Vallis was a prisoner: "*her wings bound and flightless*". The man who has her must have taken her for some reason of his own, not just to preserve her life.'

Mallory considered the point. 'That seems reasonable.'

'Then, third, he has my brooch, so four, I must know him, or at least have met him; that would explain what the Oracle said to me: "*within your compass lies the means to pierce the veil*".'

240

Mallory sat up straight, looking grim. 'Who are you saying?'

'Avorian.'

'Why?' He made the word an accusation, but she was ready with her answer.

'Because it must be.' She hurried on: 'I'm not like you, Mallory, I know or meet very few rich men. The brooch I lost might have been during the invasion of the hostel by Sim and his friends, but the fight made me forget that earlier the same day I visited Avorian to go through the tribute contributions with him.' She hesitated, deciding to edit the account. 'I fainted in his house; the brooch could easily have been taken then.'

'It's possible.'

'That was what I meant about seeing different sides of the same person. You see, with you I'm sure Avorian is not the same man *I* see,' Asher said flatly, trying to explain. 'How well do you really know him? Not very, I think. I thought I liked him, because he was courteous and he flattered me; but when I thought about it I knew he allowed ill treatment of a slave in his house, for I saw it myself. He believes absolutely in the disposition of the Fates, for I heard him say so to his daughter.'

'That hardly proves him guilty, and the man is famed for his integrity throughout the Dominion,' Mallory observed irritably.

'True. But a reputation for fair-dealing doesn't mean anything more than that he's a clever merchant; it says nothing about the man within. There's more. Consider Kerrick, Avorian's nephew. You saw how he behaved on the journey here – would you entrust such a man with your business?'

'I might,' Mallory answered, and Asher saw that while his opinion of the man was the same as her own, his reactions were quite different. 'After all, Kerrick is a member of Avorian's clan, close kin, and the Chief Councillor has precious few of those.'

'Would you?' Asher sighed, realizing their opinions were far apart, for she would never trust a man like Kerrick with any task, however small. 'Then explain to me why, during the time we were with Kerrick, I felt no *overlooking*. It was only after we parted that the feeling came again.'

He was silent for a time. At last he said unwillingly: 'There may be something in what you say; in fact, there must be. If I sound as if I doubt you, Asher, it's because I simply don't want to believe Avorian could be guilty. He's too important to the future of our city – even the country, given his contributions to the Tribute – for me to accept this charge against him unproven.'

'I'm aware of all that.'

'Then, assuming you're right, how do we go about proving it? And where is the girl? He has a daughter – could she be Vallis?'

'It seems very unlikely, doesn't it? Too many people would have to be involved for Menna to be Vallis, although she's dark and the right age. But as to how, I think that will need a certain amount of cooperation between you and me.'

Mallory frowned. 'In what way?'

'Essa, the woman who owns our hostel, runs an employment agency for domestic staff, and she's found maids for Avorian before.' Asher smiled. 'In fact, providing Kerrick keeps away from Venture, Mylla might go into the house. She's very good at ferreting out information.'

To her surprise, Mallory looked appalled. 'You mean to spy on him in his own house?' he said, in a tight voice.

'What better way is there?'

'No.' He scowled. 'I'm sorry. I didn't mean to sound critical, but it never occurred to me before that any of the maids in my own household could be more interested in what I do than in her wages.'

Asher hid her amusement. 'No, I don't suppose it did.'

He gave a sigh. 'All right. Let's go back to Avorian. We shall need to look at his history and his investments. I'm in the best position to do that; there must be records in the Administration and Records offices.'

Asher nodded. 'I find myself growing more curious about his offer to make up the tribute; fifteen thousand or so in gold is a vast amount of money. Do you still believe his motive is solely generosity?'

'A point. But for the present I can't imagine any other reason.'

'See what you can find out, Mallory. You could even ask him, which is more than I could.'

'The more I think about it, the more unlikely it all seems.'

Asher shivered, seized by a sudden premonition of disaster, unspecific and unhelpful. 'I think he'd make a bad enemy.'

'But why should he have taken Vallis? It makes no sense.' Mallory sounded irritable, too tired to hide it. 'What purpose could he have?'

'I don't know, but nothing that has happened to us so far has been coincidence, not since we met before the Oracle on the same errand. What if Avorian, too, acts in accordance with some prophecy? A man who believes so absolutely in the Fates could justify any action.'

'So you would have said, not so long ago. You've changed,'

Mallory said abruptly. 'I can't tell you how, but there's something –'

She nodded. 'I *saw* my death, in the barn with Lewes. That was why I didn't try to help myself.'

To her surprise, he accepted the explanation without question. 'Omond said you had something of the gift.'

'Gift? Yet it nearly killed me, because I thought there was nothing I could do to alter my fate.' Her feelings towards this new talent were distinctly ambivalent.

'You're a free woman now. Your life is yours, whatever you choose to do with it.'

She was unsure whether she detected envy in his voice, her boundaries widening as his had contracted. 'Yet now I seem to *see* too many choices, and any one may be wrong.'

'I could wish I saw the same. We leave here in two days,' Mallory said, abruptly changing the subject. 'Will you come with me or rejoin your friends? You could give me a message for – Essa, was it? – to get the investigation started.'

'I must meet Margit and go on with her to the last few villages, but Mylla could go back to Venture with you. There's no need for her to stay with us.'

'I liked her. I don't think I've ever met anyone with more energy.' Mallory smiled. 'An unconventional young woman.'

'I shall miss her when she marries her cousin Jan this summer.' Asher sighed. 'Sometimes I feel sorry they found they were suited after all.'

'I thought you women were opposed to marriage?' The question was only half in jest.

'Oh, no. Margit is, of course, and one or two of the others. But Essa is a widow, and most of the others will marry when they meet someone to share their lives.'

'And you?'

There was an uncomfortable moment between them. Does he mean – ? Asher thought in surprise; she had no wish to change their new relationship, had not considered that passion might succeed the comfortable affection of friendship. Yet she could see that Mallory, at heart a conventional man, looked at her in a different way now she was no longer bound to another man, as if he might now be free to speculate on the possibility of their becoming lovers.

For a moment she was curious herself, wondering what a physical relationship might be like with a man who wanted her, rather than one whose use for her had been at best perfunctory.

That there was a physical attraction between herself and Mallory she did not attempt to deny, but it was well within her control. One day she would like to discover what that sort of love was like, yet *that* seemed always an unequal partnership, offering the prospect of deep unhappiness as well as great joy; with love came bonds of obligation, and, for the woman at least, a lessening of freedom. For him, too, perhaps, with a sense of responsibility for the woman. If she gave Mallory her body, she would have committed herself to him. Would he find her ugly, as Lewes had done? And there was the chance of children, of the lifelong chains of duty, effecting a subtle alteration in their relationship and reducing her to dependence.

'Come on. You're half-asleep.' Mallory stood and held out his hands to her, pulling her to her feet; the palms were warm and dry and hard, and she let herself wonder what it would be like to have those same hands caressing her.

No. I will be free – anything is possible now, anything at all! She drew back abruptly. There was the first hint of dawn in the darkness outside; Asher walked to the door, then turned back.

'Thank you, Mallory. Thank you for everything.'

She stumbled up the stairs, barely aware of grey skies and a rising wind as the darkness brightened perceptibly, daylight coming in through the windows along the passage. When she reached her room she sank on to the bed, not bothering to undress; she pulled the blankets over her and shut her eyes.

Before she fell asleep, she knew a moment of rare and perfect happiness, as if she were a child again without the burdens of maturity, and the thought returned to her: Anything is possible now; anything at all!

PART THREE

Free Will

Chapter Thirteen

The twin troop transporters had docked at Cloth Quay at midday, but two hours later the councillors were still waiting for the new governor to disembark. The quay was surrounded by a phalanx of Kamiri guardsmen, who kept back the ordinary citizens of Venture who had little real interest in the new governor but relished more any spectacle that disrupted the working day.

'I rather think,' Avorian murmured softly to Mallory, 'that we are supposed to be impressed by this spectacle, instead of cursing the wretched man for keeping us waiting.'

'I only hope it doesn't start a riot.' There was certainly a restive air to the crowd, but that was natural enough, given the occasion; the arrival of the ships that were to take the tribute money to Javarin was hardly a cause for celebration.

Both warships were immense, built carrack-type but with the addition of castle structures fore and aft for use in keeping watch for sea-raiders during the month-long journey. Painted in blues and greens, each carried three hundred soldiers in addition to its normal crew of four hundred, replacements for those who had already served a full term of duty in Darrian. They were slow-moving, lumbering vessels compared with the smaller caravels favoured by the merchants, but Mallory could not deny they looked impressive, even oppressive, their pennants displaying Amrist's symbolic jackal waving in the breeze from masts which stood higher than any of their fellows. If the new governor's intent was to demonstrate the superiority of his own nation over that of a mere tributary, it was effective.

There was a commotion from somewhere near the top of the gangway; Mallory shifted his weight to his left foot, hoping it heralded movement. He, Avorian, and Councillor Hamon had been delegated the dubious honour of forming the reception party for Haravist, the new governor of Venture, but since this was his first experience of such an occasion he had not known how much time it would consume. Was the man keeping them waiting deliberately, as Avorian suggested? He glanced at his fellow councillor, wondering yet again whether Asher could be correct in her identification of him as their opposition. In the two weeks that had passed since his return to the city, Mallory had encountered Avorian almost every day, and by no sign had the older man given any indication that he regarded Mallory as anything but a potential ally.

'Ah – the musicians are ready,' Avorian remarked with satisfaction. 'Soon now, I think.'

Looking up, Mallory could see that on deck eight drummers and a further eight men, carrying the odd horn-shaped trumpets favoured by the Kamiri, had ranged themselves to either side of the gangway. At some unseen signal, a deep drumroll began; all the grey soldiers on the quay stiffened to attentive response and a tall figure appeared on deck, dressed in grey cap and formal full-length robe. He processed down the gangway with slow-paced deliberation, well aware of the impression he was making in his descent. Midway, he paused, looking up at the city, and higher still to the citadel of the Oracle, and Mallory had the impression that he bowed very slightly in the direction of the latter, a mark of deep respect from a Kamir.

Avorian, as leader of the delegation, advanced to where a sheet of cloth of gold had been spread over the cobbles of the quay in the Kamir's honour.

'Lord Governor.' He inclined his head, not deeply but enough for courtesy. His dress for the occasion was a flamboyant coat of purple, but unlike the Kamir he wore no head-covering; although a tall man, he was still several inches shorter than the new governor, but nonetheless an impressive figure. 'As Chief Councillor of Venture, I welcome you to our city.'

The grey face evinced no pleasure in the greeting, nor did the Kamir return Avorian's courtesy. Cold grey eyes swivelled from left to right, taking in the waiting crowd, over whom an uneasy silence had fallen.

'Why have these people come?' he demanded, speaking in the slow, harsh accents of Javarin.

'A mark of respect, Governor,' Avorian said easily.

'Disperse them. Crowds make for disorder and violence.' Haravist was looking directly over Mallory's head, giving orders to a soldier standing behind him; it was an extraordinary display of arrogance, as if the three councillors were, to him, as insignificant as the cloth beneath his feet. Avorian caught his eye and winked; hastily, Mallory looked away.

'Has the tribute been collected?' Haravist asked Avorian coldly. 'There is no shortfall?'

'None, Governor.' It was hard not to admire the man's ease of manner, unabashed by the Kamir's intentional rudeness.

The new governor did not seem pleased with the response, for he frowned. He possessed neither beard nor moustache, which was unusual among his race, and his skin was a darker grey than most, almost slate in colour; it was difficult to judge his age, but Mallory guessed him to be close to fifty, a battle-hardened soldier too old, now, for active service, who resented this apparent demotion to civil duty.

'My fellow councillors – Councillor Mallory, and Councillor Hamon,' Avorian continued smoothly, indicating each in turn. Mallory imitated Avorian's own inclination of the head, but Hamon, an elderly man of florid complexion and stiff-necked pride, merely blinked. Haravist favoured each with a brief glare.

'The wind is cold. I wish my escort to the residence.' An order was barked out from somewhere to his left, and four men came forward at a run bearing a litter. 'I shall doubtless receive you in due course, once I have communicated my orders to my predecessor. You have two further weeks before he leaves with the tribute.'

'We are quite ready, Governor.' Avorian waited until Haravist had been installed in the litter and removed, at the centre of a heavily armed squadron, before speaking again. 'How useful to know how highly our new governor values us! Although it seemed to me he would prefer our heads to our gold,' he observed dryly to his companions.

'Only temporarily,' Mallory corrected. Their eyes met. 'Why take a leg when with a little effort you can have the whole horse?'

Avorian smiled. 'How well our minds agree, Councillor. Will you walk with me? I have a small matter to discuss with you – concerning this new amendment you propose to the city statutes.'

'Certainly.' Mallory turned to Hamon, who was staring at them, puzzled, not having followed what was being said. 'If you would excuse us?'

Hamon seemed relieved and walked away. Mallory made use of the moment to look at what little remained of the crowd, for Asher had said she was to meet Mylura at the docks during the afternoon, but he could see neither of them, nor recognized any of the faces of those still lingering on the quays.

'I gather Councillor Hamon has already agreed to your proposal,' he found Avorian saying as he turned back. 'Perhaps, if you are willing to explain your reasoning, I, too, shall add my approval, and the amendment may be signed and sealed tonight; although it seems to me an odd detail with which to concern yourself at this time,' he added, with a quizzical smile.

'Certainly.' Mallory was pleased to find the Chief Councillor so amenable; he wondered how Asher would react when she heard what he had planned. He thought by now he knew her well enough to imagine her response: pleasure and irritation combined. It was a view with which he had some sympathy. 'It is a small matter, Chief Councillor, but one I consider justified, taking into account all the costs we save in the process.' He outlined his proposals as they walked inland in the direction of the civic offices, Avorian nodding thoughtfully at several points. When he had finished, the Chief Councillor raised his hands and clasped them together.

'Then do you agree?' Mallory asked.

'Why not?' Avorian looked amused. 'There is no cost to ourselves, and a benefit in goodwill. Councillor, I approve. Let it be done.'

It was, thought Mallory, almost impossible to believe the man a villain; only Asher's warning that in different company Avorian was quite another person gave him pause, for he had seen for himself often enough the changes in a man he thought he knew well, but who became someone quite unfamiliar in other surroundings or company. Together they entered the Administration building, in a mood of perfect amity.

Asher stood at the top of a flight of steps, looking out over the collected heads of the crowd to where Mallory and Avorian stood on the quay. She was early for her meeting, but the day was bright and she had a rare leave of absence from the Treasury in recognition of the tribute monies recovered by herself and Margit; work on the city taxes remained to be done, but that was always a more leisurely affair than the tribute, and there were another two months before the accounts had to be completed.

The sea was in one of its rare benevolent moods, barely a ripple disturbing its glassy surface; the sun was warm, lighting the formal scene on the quay and making the giant transporters look like painted ships on a painted ocean, a backdrop for the playhouse near the cloth market. Asher wondered idly whether the new governor would prove more or less rigid than the present incumbent, but knew it would make little difference; the only issue at stake was for how long Darrian could withstand the burden of the tribute and hold off the inevitable subject status. Which in turn depended on whether Vallis was found; with which thought Asher turned to look for Mylura.

She saw her almost at once, coming from the direction of the old quarter, her usual energetic stride slowed by the black servant's dress, constrained by the heavy flowing skirts. She waved at her and waited while the younger woman ran lightly up the steps.

'Am I late?' Mylura panted. 'I went to see Jan, and I'd forgotten all this nonsense was going on today.'

'No, I was just watching Mallory. See – there he is, in the blue, beside Avorian.' Asher pointed. 'Poor man, he must be bored. They've been there all afternoon.'

'Do you want to stay and watch, or can we go and get something to eat? I'm starving!'

Asher grinned. 'What a surprise. No, let's go. This may go on for the rest of the day. Where?'

'There's a small inn behind the fish market that has good food, if you don't mind the walk?'

'Lead on.'

Shortly afterwards, ensconced in a small, dingy parlour which Asher was not surprised to find empty, Mylura greeted the arrival of a steaming plate of what looked to Asher like fish bones in dirty water with an inordinate amount of enthusiasm.

'Don't you want some?' Mylla asked, surprised.

'I never developed a passion for fish; it's what comes of being brought up inland.'

Mylla shrugged. 'Your loss. What are you grinning at?'

'It's just – you look so demure in that outfit.'

'Never earn your living as a maid; it's downright slavery, let me tell you, and for a pittance at that.' She wiped her brow theatrically. 'This is my first afternoon off in more than a week. And look at my hands!' She held them up; they were, indeed, rough and red from her unaccustomed labours, although the dexterity with which their owner wielded her spoon suggested no serious injury.

'You did volunteer,' Asher said mildly. 'Anyway, eat, and tell me what news you have.'

'Not a great deal. It's a very ordinary, well-run household, if larger than most; they eat, they sleep, they work, and I scrub, wash pots and dust.'

'Are the other servants friendly?'

Mylura thought about the question. 'Reasonably,' she said at last. 'A bit reticent, perhaps, but that's common enough with a stranger, and I've only been there two weeks. It may be a little time before they loosen up.'

Asher was troubled by their lack of progress, sensing a need for urgency. 'And do you see much of the family?'

Mylura shook her head. 'The housekeeper gives us our orders, though I see the girl, Menna, sometimes because I do out her rooms. She's very pleasant and always speaks politely to the servants, even me.'

'And have you ever spoken to Avorian?'

Mylura rubbed a hand over her brow. 'Once, after I'd been there a week. He asked me my name.'

'And was that all?'

'Yes.' Mylura stopped eating, a sufficiently rare event for Asher to urge her to continue. 'Why?'

'I'm just curious, Mylla, in case he's suspicious.'

Mylura's face cleared. 'Oh, I see. Sorry to be so slow, but I'm not used to all this hard work!' She reached for her spoon once more. 'Now, I have various pieces of family gossip which will interest you. First, young Menna is *not* Avorian's daughter by his dead wife, Katriane, but was adopted by them at an early age and is said to be the Chief Councillor's natural daughter by a mistress. It seems to be common knowledge, but happened so long ago nobody talks of it any more.'

'Such things are common enough, but of course it increases the possibility that the girl *is* Vallis.' It was so tempting to accept the obvious that Asher was wary, looking for flaws.

'As you say, but I don't know how we can prove it. Unless you want me to search Avorian's private papers?'

'No!' Asher experienced an instant upsurge of anxiety at the suggestion. 'Don't even think about it; even if he kept such proofs, they're bound to be warded. It's far too dangerous. Is there anyone in the house who's been there long enough to remember Menna when she was a baby, someone you could talk to? An old nurse, perhaps, or even the housekeeper?'

Mylla frowned. 'No, only old Oban, the clerk, and he wouldn't talk to me – he hates women. And I'd have no excuse. But surely somewhere in this city there must be someone who was here at the time? Avorian hasn't always been Chief Councillor, but he's been one of the Twelve for eighteen years, and I can't believe such a piece of gossip would be quite forgotten, even after so long.'

'See what you can find out. We must be able to prove Menna's parentage one way or another.' Asher added with a sigh, 'I know Mallory still doubts Avorian's involvement, and I can hardly blame him. It's very frustrating.'

'I'll talk to the housekeeper again. I told her I've a doting but frail and sickly mother to support, and she's been most sympathetic; she's even given me several strengthening brews to try on her.' Mylla laughed. 'I gave them to Jan, and he said he'd sell them off as love-potions.'

'What does your cousin think of all this?'

Mylla smiled and went pink; it always surprised Asher how easily she was embarrassed by mention of her personal life. 'He's happy enough — you know him. He doesn't mind what I do as long as I come back to him, and we won't take the oath until late-summer.'

It was difficult to envisage Mylla married, although there was, of course, no reason such a union should change her. Asher wondered, suddenly, why her friend felt the need for a formal promise, what insecurity had persuaded her to take such a step.

'And in case you want to know,' Mylla said, looking fiercely down her nose at Asher, as if she could see into her thoughts, 'it's all Jan's idea, not mine. I was quite happy with the way things were!'

Asher held up her hands for peace. 'There's no sign of Kerrick? Because you must leave Avorian's house at once, if there's any risk of his seeing you.'

'No, he's to stay in Chance for the summer — I heard Oban say so.'

'Does Avorian have a mistress? You said his wife's been dead for the past eight years, and I can't believe he'd be without some companion for all that time.'

'I'll try to find out, although I've heard nothing.' Mylla frowned. 'You're right, I hadn't thought about it, but he must be very discreet or unusually restrained. His daughter acts as hostess when they entertain, so there's no woman he cares to place ahead of her.'

'Ask, but do take care.' For no reason she could discern, Asher experienced an acute uneasiness, but the shifting patterns in her mind were still more often a mystery than helpful, and the sudden flare of warning she sensed was imprecise. 'Mylla,' she said on impulse, 'don't go back to the house. We'll find another way to get the information we need.'

Mylura looked at her incredulously. 'Not go back? But why,

Ash? What's the matter?'

'I don't know, I just have a feeling about this.' She wished she could explain, but the day she had spent with Omond at Kepesake had only touched the surface of her ignorance about her unwanted gift. She looked at her friend in the black servant's dress, which bore Avorian's wolf's head on a silver badge sewn on to the right shoulder, and knew she could not dismiss her fears. 'It's not safe,' she tried.

'But it's the best chance we have,' Mylla protested. 'Anyway, I've a charmed life! Nothing will happen, Ash, stop fretting.'

Her brimming confidence helped to dispel a little, but not all, of Asher's alarm. 'But Avorian has Lassar, Mylla, and if he found out what you were up to . . .'

'He won't. And now I must get back. I only had leave for the afternoon.' She stared down at the plate in front of her, as if surprised to find it empty. 'I'll do my best, and I will be careful. You'll hear from me as soon as I've anything useful to tell.' She rose firmly to her feet, plainly opposed to further argument.

'Then take care.' Asher placed a few coppers on the table, then got up and walked with Mylla back out on to the street, where she watched her make her way up the hill with mounting misgivings; it was true Mylla's powers of self-preservation were extraordinary, but Avorian was a different kind of enemy from Kamiri frontier guards.

She found a quiet spot and wrote to Mallory, informing him what Mylura had reported and suggesting a meeting the following evening; sealing it, she selected a small boy from the many playing in the street and sent him on the errand with the promise of a reward from the recipient of the note. The boy ran off happily, tucking her letter into a distinctly ragged shirt.

The new Kamiri governor must at last have decided to disembark, for Asher saw the crowds down by the quay had dispersed. A fresh east wind had got up, as was usual as it grew dark, and she looked out to sea at the spectacle of the sun descending to the horizon, leaving a long red-gold trail on the water, a sight that never failed to satisfy her. There was a hush to the city at sunset, as if there was a real moment of change from day to night, something Asher had never felt inland. Then the lights began to spring up all along the harbour and up the hill, and Venture came alive once more, but to a different, dark existence.

It was time she went back to the hostel; although the days were growing longer as spring advanced, Asher felt less than easy in the twilight and quickened her pace. The streets were busy enough, but she wondered if some of Mallory's often-expressed concern for her safety had begun to infect her, for she no longer felt secure in the city which had once seemed to offer her so safe a refuge. No one approached her, for she was protected by her dress, marking her as a working woman and not a prostitute, but she did not enjoy the old feeling of invisibility among the crowds as she walked, and she passed the Treasury building with a strong sense of relief; the hostel, with its company of forty women, offered powerful protection against an attack of nerves.

Music spilled out from open windows of the more prosperous houses, and in the distance the playhouse was alive with lights; several groups of young men prowled casually along the street in search of some amusement in the warmer evenings. It was all familiar, unchanged from previous years, but Asher was aware of an alteration in herself, a new wariness born of knowledge of her own vulnerability; if Avorian had any notion of her own and Mallory's intent, this was *his* city. Since the public announcement of his contribution to the annual tribute, the Chief Councillor was enjoying a high level of popularity in Venture which made her own suspicions less credible than ever. One thousand five hundred years' wages, she thought wearily. More than fifteen thousand gold pieces. No wonder Avorian was cheered wherever he went.

Popularity: could that be all he wants?

As she passed a noisy inn the doors burst suddenly open, disgorging several men on to the street, impeding her path. She drew back as whatever brawl had been the cause of their eviction was continued, with evident enthusiasm, by the four participants, for it was impossible to step past them. She waited, listening to the grunts and exchange of drunken insults of the quartet, wondering why they should feel brute force was a satisfactory means of deciding an argument. What, after all, was the value of strength if unallied to judgment? If force alone were proof of rightness, then the Kamiri were justified in their domination; they were the most powerful nation in the Dominion, as they had proved many times.

It's all about control; if you're stronger, you can make the weaker ones agree with you. The thought brought with it a resurgence of her old resentment against Sim and his kind, against the sort of men who believed their physical prowess gave them a moral superiority, as if aggression, by itself, without purposeful direction, was a valuable quality. She looked with loathing on the winner – the only man still on his feet – as he turned to survey her with bleary eyes, an invitation in the look. Asher lowered her gaze and began to step over the sprawling bodies, shaking off the hand that touched her arm.

'What's your hurry, pretty thing?' he asked, his breath rolling towards her in a cloud of ale.

Wisely, she did not answer and merely ducked under an outstretched arm.

'Earn yourself a copper or two – with a real man!' he called after her; she lengthened her steps but could not resist making a backward vulgar gesture with her left hand. What, in the name of Fate, was a *real man*? She sighed to herself; her observation suggested *real men* had fewer wits and less humanity than the average.

There was no reason for the incident to have annoyed her so intensely, but it did. Why should she have to put up with such nonsense?

One day . . .

'Watch where you're going!'

She had bumped into a slight figure as she turned down the side street leading to the hostel, but as she stepped back to apologize, she found a hand holding her fast.

'I've been waiting for you.'

She gave Stern an angry look. 'I don't want to talk to you.'

He stood in the shadows at the corner of the street, her own figure hiding him from general view; only Asher could see his sour expression as bony fingers dug into the muscles of her forearm.

'But you will talk, you've no choice.' He pulled her closer into the shadows, and her skin crawled. 'We made a deal, and we need you.'

'I said never again, and I meant it.' She tried again to pull away, but Stern, with greater strength than she would have expected, held her back; she felt panic rise, for a moment forgetting who he was, digging the nails of her free hand into his. He gave a grunt of pain and let her go.

'You don't want to mean that. I warned you what would happen.' He looked quickly to left and right, but there was no one in sight. 'You be outside your hostel, in the alley, in three nights' time, at midnight, or I inform on you to the Treasurer.'

'If you do, I shall tell the Chief Councillor who robbed his warehouse,' Asher countered, as calmly as she could. 'I'd have nothing to lose, would I?'

'Do you think he'd believe you?'

'Yes.'

Stern's eyes grew cold. 'You'd not want me to tell Bull nor Club you said that,' he advised unpleasantly. 'They'd not be happy at being threatened.'

'And nor am I!'

He suddenly swung her round and pushed her against the wall with an unnecessary amount of force, winding her. 'You think yourself safe,' he whispered hoarsely. 'In that house, with all those women round you. But there's not a door in the city Hare can't open, and ten of you wouldn't be a match for Club and Bull. You be there, or they'll come for you.'

'No, I won't do it, Stern.' She had to stop to breathe in. 'Leave me alone.'

'Be there, or you'll be sorry.' He shot her an unfriendly smile. 'I'll let Bull have a turn with you, before I inform.'

She could not disguise the shudder of revulsion that ran through her, but the threat removed any lingering fear. 'Touch me once more and I'll curse you, Stern,' she hissed angrily, raising her left hand and pointing her index and little fingers at him. 'To the end of your life. May your strength fail you and your legs grow crippled, may – '

Her tirade was cut off by his hand across her mouth, but it had produced an effect for Stern paled. 'Keep quiet!' he said shakily. 'No more. I swear, I'll set the Bull on you.'

'I know him – I know who he is. Tell him that, too.' Asher pushed him away, his aggression turned to disquiet. 'Now go, and leave me be! I won't be involved in your games.'

'In three nights, in the alley.' He stepped back, breathing fast. 'Be there or I inform!' Before Asher could refuse yet again, he turned the corner and moved rapidly out of sight.

It was nearly laughable; now he had gone, Asher found it hard to take Stern seriously in the face of events far more pressing. She did her best to dismiss the interview from her mind, but wished she could talk to Mylla, the only other person who knew of her involvement with Stern and his friends. The prospect of displaying yet another unedifying episode in her life to Mallory did not appeal to her pride, nor did she enjoy the sense of vulnerability it suggested. On the face of it her counter-threat should be sufficient to deter Stern from further action, but she was not quite sure of him, and considerably less so of Bull and Club.

She achieved the remaining short distance to the hostel without further incident, and as she entered the common room was glad, for once, to find it crowded, even though the noise-level was deafening. Every woman who lived in the hostel seemed to be present, all talking at once.

'Asher – here!' Essa beckoned, and Asher went to join her at a table in the centre of the room.

'What's all this?' she asked, speaking loudly to make herself heard.

'There's been some trouble. I don't know how it happened, but someone broke into the hostel this afternoon.' Essa was plainly furious. 'When Margit came back this evening she found the door unlocked, and the benches, chairs and cushions in here had been thrown all over the room.'

Asher's heart began to race. 'Was anything stolen?'

Essa shook her head. 'Not as far as we can ascertain. Sara says she heard someone moving about downstairs, but her arm was hurting, poor thing – the bone seems to be knitting far too slowly – and she thought it was one of us. You were the last to leave, weren't you? I think you were here this morning?'

'I was, but I locked the door when I left.'

'I've asked everyone else to check their rooms, and there's nothing missing or disturbed. You'd better do the same. I'd have looked myself, but your door was locked.'

'Thanks.' Asher was already on her feet. 'I'll be back in a moment.'

She took the stairs three at a time, the memory of Stern's threat all too vivid in her mind; she did not doubt Hare's ability to unlock the hostel door, given the ease with which he had breached Avorian's warehouse. Her own door was shut and locked when she tried the handle, but she knew an uneasy moment as she took out her key and turned it, then pushed at the door.

The chaos that met her gaze was beyond description; everything she possessed seemed to have been taken out, looked over and then discarded on the floor in an untidy heap. The mattress had been taken off the bed and now leaned drunkenly against the frame; someone had slit both mattress and pillow, and feathers floated about the room in the draught as she held the door open. For a moment she could only stare helplessly at the confusion, too appalled to come to any decision as to what she should do first.

She shut the door and picked up one of her divided skirts from the top of the pile, holding it up in trembling hands; it was intact, and she folded it neatly and put it back in its cupboard, now quite empty. Automatically, she continued the task, gathering the rest of her clothes and shaking them to get rid of feathers and dust; she hefted the mattress back on to the frame, covering it with a blanket to prevent further deluges of feathers. When that was done, she picked up her few remaining belongings, putting them away until the pile was gone and the floor clear. Only then did she contemplate the other damage.

Knife-marks scarred the floorboards, as if someone had done a thorough search of the room, not caring to conceal his or her efforts. The right-hand corner where Asher had hidden the false travel warrants and her real identity papers had not escaped notice; the loose flooring had been lifted. Asher knelt and put a hand inside her secret cache, and, after a minute, stood up, frozen-faced; everything, including the small store of coins, had gone. Someone had stolen her papers.

Who?

She dismissed Hare almost at once; to begin with, Stern had only just made his threat, and there had been no time for him to have carried it out. Second, there was no reason for Stern or his friends to have suspected the existence of forged papers in her room, whereas the person who had searched here must have had some idea for what they were looking. None of the other rooms, from what Essa said, had been disturbed; only hers.

Could it have been Avorian's doing? That sounded altogether more plausible, for he – and Lassar – had every reason to be aware of her covert activities. She had felt herself to be under observation in her room on several occasions. Her illicit days of travel with Mallory would have told him either he or she had access to forged papers; in addition, any careful scrutiny of the city records would uncover the fact that Asher was not the person described in her identity papers – that such a person did not exist. But why the unnecessary mess?

A warning, so I'd know I wasn't safe, not even here.

A chill crept down her spine; if it was a warning, she could not ignore it. Even forty women were no defence against the Chief Councillor and the power he wielded in Venture. He had all the resources that wealth and authority could bestow at his command, whereas she was a woman living under a false name, lacking legal or other protection. Could this be his way of telling them to stop looking for Vallis? He held a strong hand, stronger now if he knew her real identity.

She left the room, not bothering to relock the door; there was nothing left to hide or steal.

'Asher, what's the matter? What was taken?' Essa demanded urgently, and Asher realized she must look as shocked as she felt.

'Everything. All our spare money, the travel passes, and

everything else.' Asher fell on to the bench and leaned on the table, burying her face briefly in her hands. 'My own papers.'

Margit stared at her blankly. 'But why? And how did they know where to find them?'

'How should I know?' Asher shook her head, suddenly very weary. 'We need to replace everything, as quickly as possible. We might need travel passes at any time.'

'I'll arrange it,' Margit offered.

'But Asher, if someone has your papers, they must know who you are,' Essa said a moment later, plainly very worried. 'What are you going to do?'

'I can't *do* anything. If they're gone, they're gone.' She shrugged irritably, remembering no one but herself and Mallory knew her husband was dead, and that she had no more to fear from him. 'It concerns me more that whoever took those papers must wonder why I had blank travel passes; they might guess what we use them for.'

'This must have something to do with *Vallis*,' Margit said, dropping her voice. 'Though I don't understand how anyone could know to search only your room, Asher.'

'I don't like this at all.' Essa drummed her fingers rhythmically on the table, making Asher grind her teeth. 'Perhaps we should – '

'Please. Enough speculation,' Asher interrupted. For no particular reason, she found her friends getting on her nerves. What was the use in *talking* about something they could not prove? 'Let's concentrate on what we have to do next.' She related Mylura's findings, and Essa nodded.

'I don't entirely understand why you think we may discover something about Vallis from the Chief Councillor's household, since you refuse to explain your reasons, but it was providential he should have needed a servant at just this time. I've known you long enough to trust you.' She smiled. 'It can do no harm, in any event.'

Privately, Asher was doubtful; her sense of disquiet did not diminish, and she wondered if she had been wise to refuse Mallory's offer of financial support. The meagre sum she earned represented a mere fraction of his wealth, and if she were free from the Treasury she could ignore Stern and other demands on her time and concentrate on the search. But their partnership was still too new and fragile for her willingly to weight the scales in his favour by relinquishing her independence, and her pride refused to allow her to be a pensioner of any man, even a friend.

She had begun to question every part of her life. Her work among the women of Venture needed to be done, but not necessarily by herself. There were others equally capable, except in the matter of obtaining funds from the Treasury, but Asher had always known that was a source of limited lifespan. But if she gave up her part among the women, what would she do? What did she want to do with her life? Asher was annoyed with herself for being so discontented with an existence she had once found so fulfilling. She did not want to go back to Harrows, and now it seemed she did not want to stay in Venture either, where she felt constrained by her responsibilities instead of finding satisfaction in her achievements.

She wondered if Mallory felt the same way about his own shrunken world, where once the whole Dominion had been his territory.

'I have news which may please you,' Essa announced suddenly, giving Asher an arch look. 'You'll be glad to know we may have seen the last of Sim and his friends!'

Both Margit and Asher turned to her. 'How?'

'It appears the Council of Twelve has enacted a change in city law – I heard on my way home tonight that it has actually been sealed.' She paused, continuing triumphantly: 'The Council is to raise the level of fines to be levied for assaults on working women to *the same as those on men!* Sim and his boys won't be able to *afford* to raid us now!'

'Is it true?' Margit's eyes shone. 'How did it happen?'

'I learned of it yesterday, from one of my women who works in Councillor Hamon's household; she overheard him discussing the subject with his wife, and even *she* agreed, and she's the most conservative woman in Venture! Tonight, however, our Chief Councillor added his seal to the statute, so it's law. What do you think of *that*?'

Silence greeted her statement, for it was well known that Hamon, almost as stiff-necked as his wife, was the most reactionary of all the Councillors, abominating change in any form.

'But,' Asher asked at last, 'how did it come about? It sounds too good to be true.'

'Your friend Councillor Mallory, my dear. It seems he calculated how much less the administration of the city has cost the Council over the past ten years, since his brother began employing so many of us as clerks, and argued the savings were worth some acknowledgement.' She laughed breathlessly. 'I gather he suggested we might demand higher wages unless they did

261

something to show their appreciation, so naturally they all agreed. After all, this costs them nothing. So now we have value in *our own right!*'

'No more raids!' Margit looked dazed. 'Oh, Essa!'

Asher felt a glow of pleasure, and surprise that Mallory had not mentioned his plans to her. 'I must thank him – I had no idea he intended this.'

'Indeed you must, from all of us.' Essa beamed at her. 'Your friend is a rare man indeed. Just think, he has accomplished more in a few short weeks than we in years!'

'Don't you resent it? To know how little we've achieved?' For Asher, not liking herself very much, did find herself resenting the ease with which Mallory could accomplish such an alteration in their status; their own efforts seemed petty set beside such a grand gesture.

'At my age, you learn to be grateful for any help.' Essa gave her a look. 'Don't be angry, Asher, or begrudge your Mallory the glory of the moment; after all, if we'd not laid the ground by taking on our share of the work, this wouldn't have been possible. That it's done is what matters.'

'I suppose you're right.' She forced a smile, then thought how angry Sim and his friends would be, and had to laugh. 'Now we can tell Sim we're too expensive for him!'

Essa's eyes twinkled. 'But we always were. And now,' she added more sharply, 'if you've no more questions, I want to talk to the duty-women about the state of the kitchens. They were left in a disgraceful state this morning!' She got up, taking Margit with her, and soon a buzz of excited talk filled the room as she passed the good news from table to table.

One of the youngest women, a girl named Jani, came over carrying a folded piece of paper which she handed to Asher, looking rather harassed.

'I do apologize, Asher. This came for you a little while ago, but I didn't see you were here.'

'Thanks.' She took the note, recognizing Mylura's writing. 'Who delivered it?'

'A very small boy. I gave him a copper.'

Asher fished in her pocket and retrieved a coin. 'Here, thanks.'

Jani looked relieved as she put the coin carefully away. 'So long as it's all right – it's been a lean few weeks.'

'No, it was good of you.' She was already unfolding the note, and Jani drifted away.

'What's that?' She looked up to find Margit trying to read over her shoulder.

'It's from Mylla. She wants me to meet her at Carob's tomorrow night. She says it's urgent.'

'Shall I go?' Margit's brow creased. 'You've done so much already, Ash, and with this theft of your papers . . .'

'No.' She said it so sharply the older woman looked offended. 'Truly, Margit. You have to deal with the travel warrants. You're the one with friends in that section.'

To her relief, Margit was appeased. 'Perhaps you're right, but you will take care? I hate all this – when someone can break into our home, nothing seems *safe* any more.'

'I know.' Asher shivered. An awareness crept over her that she had just taken a decision which would have a significant impact on her life, for her mind was suddenly filled with the darting patterns Omond had explained represented future possibilities. That several of the darting lines came to an abrupt end was a warning, but on what choices they depended was impossible to tell. The futility of the gift assailed her, and she was terrified, for there seemed a plethora of choices, any one of which could lead her to disaster; but the next minute she was laughing at herself, for had she not once feared there were no choices at all?

A woman called to Margit and she moved away, leaving Asher to her own thoughts, but these gave her no comfort. *A coming moment of crisis, of choice.*

After a few more ineffectual efforts to identify the source of the warning, Asher gave up; whatever must be would be, and she would have to make her own choices, as she had done all her life. She rejoined Margit and the others, trying to match their pleasure in Essa's news, but unable to feel more than a momentary delight. The loss of her identity papers made her feel curiously insubstantial, as if they had been more real than she was, and without them that part of her ceased to exist, so she must begin again and create a new Asher from the little that remained.

Perhaps tomorrow everything will change. What could Mylla have learned in the short space of time since they parted? Again, *warning* stabbed at her mind, a moment of crisis, of decision; angrily, she wished her gift had remained dormant instead of emerging only to prove so vague and unhelpful. She hesitated, wondering if it might be wise to provide some form of safeguard: she could let Mallory know where she was going, and why.

It surprised her that so small a decision could effect so powerful a change in her spirits.

Chapter Fourteen

Mallory watched as the sails of the blue-painted caravel faded further into the distance, moving slowly before the wind; reaching into his pocket, he drew out a silver coin and threw it into the waters of the harbour.

That should buy him an easterly wind. It was the first time Perron, his younger brother, had sailed in sole charge of the fleet, and Mallory could not suppress a pang of envy; Perron's horizons were widening as his own were contracting.

'One day,' Asher murmured behind him. 'This won't be forever.'

'Is that a prophecy?'

The quay was crowded with mothers and wives and children waving farewell to the sailors, but they began to drift away as the third ship moved beyond the protection of the harbour, too far away for clear sight or sound. 'Do you want to stay here or go somewhere warmer?' Mallory asked.

'I've got to go in a minute – I said I'd meet Mylla in the old quarter, but I wanted to tell you where we'd be.'

'What's wrong?' Absorbed in his own reflections, he had not registered Asher's extreme tension; now, however, he saw, and what he saw alarmed him. 'Has something happened?'

'No.' She was nervous, fidgeting with her fingers. 'I just feel something may go wrong.' She took a quick look round, then turned back. 'It's as if someone's watching me – no, not like at Kepesake. I mean really watching.' She shook her head irritably. 'I'm sorry. I don't know what's the matter with me.'

'Let me come with you.'

She gave him an unhappy smile. 'To Carob's? You'd ruin my reputation, Mallory. No men allowed in our room.'

'Such prejudice!' He said it to make her laugh, but she was infecting him with her own nervousness. 'Is there anything I can do? Keep watch?'

'I wish there were.' The admission, if anything, increased his anxiety. 'You said Avorian hasn't mentioned anything to you, but the hostel theft must have been at his instigation. Nothing else makes sense. And Mylla, too – '

'Tell her not to go back.' Mallory had not liked the implications of Asher's note the previous day. 'I think you were right, it's not safe for her. I've all the details we need on the property Avorian owns here – and it's a long list, believe me, although there are some mortgages out. Tell Mylla she's done well, but we can manage without more risk to her.'

'My feelings. All right, I'll tell her. If she'll listen.'

'Let me know as soon as you can whatever news she has. Any hour, Ash.'

'I will.' She seemed reluctant to go. 'Mallory, be careful. *Something* is going to happen soon.'

'To you, or me?'

'I don't know. I can't *see*.'

'Shall I walk to the inn with you?'

She considered the offer at some length, but finally shook her head. 'I don't think that's a good idea. Just wish me luck, or whatever sailors do.'

The quay was now almost empty, and Mallory knew it was time to separate; they were conspicuous enough as it was, but it was just possible anyone watching them could think her his clerk. Unless they *knew* otherwise. Unwillingly, he let her go, observing the confident pace at which she made for the narrow streets of the old quarter, wishing she had let him accompany her.

Mindful of her request, he looked towards the northern pier and found the oddsman, a thin, elderly man, dressed in piebald colours, who always did a brisk business when merchant ships sailed. Although some thought their function pure superstition, it was a rare sailor who could not find a copper coin to gamble himself a better fortune on his journey. Mallory felt in his pocket and discovered five gold coins, an unusually large sum, and handed them over.

'What d'you want for this?' the oddsman asked, astonished at the scale of this unexpected largess.

'Good fortune, for a friend.'

The man threw the pair of dice he kept in a leather box at his side, surveying the outcome through narrowed slits of eyes; one landed with the four uppermost, the second showing a three.

'Good and bad,' he said at last. 'Maybe the good'll outweigh the other; should do, the price you've paid. Want me to try again?'

'No, thank you.' Mallory nodded, walking away towards the fish market with no particular aim in mind. Halfway across the quay he turned back, deciding to pay a visit to the warehouses, feeling a need to occupy his over-active imagination.

As he did so, he thought he noticed a man at the southern end of the quay begin to move in the same direction; and when he reached his destination he was disconcerted, but no longer surprised, to find the same man still in sight.

The inn was less crowded than usual and Carob nowhere in sight, but Cass smiled a welcome as Asher entered.

'She's over there,' Cass volunteered, pointing to a table in the far corner.

Mylura was sitting in front of an empty plate. Her face lit up when she saw Asher, who hooked a nearby stool for herself and sat down.

'I thought you said they fed you well?'

Mylura grinned. 'Just not often enough.' She was still wearing the black dress, although a cloak covered the wolf's head badge at her shoulder.

Asher leaned forward. 'What's so urgent? I didn't expect to hear from you so soon.'

'Gold, I hope.' Mylla, too, opted for discretion, lowering her clear voice. 'Last night, when I got back to the house, I struck lucky. I've the name and address of the nurse who was maid to Katriane, Avorian's dead wife, and Menna's, too, when she was a child.'

Asher felt a thrill of disquiet. 'How?'

'I was in the housekeeper's room, making up the fire, when a message came.' Her tones sank even lower. 'It was from a woman here in the old quarter, asking for a relief so she could leave her post to visit her sick daughter. Mistress Nan – that's the housekeeper – was annoyed because it was so late, but she left the room to look for another of the maids, forgetting I was still there. I had a look at the note and saw the address was near here, in the Street of Good Hope, and when I'd finished with the fire I went down to the servants' hall and asked one of the other girls who lived here. She told me there's a woman takes care of the old nurse, called Alys, who was Avorian's wife's maid. Ash, it was the purest good luck.' She looked up earnestly. 'I do believe that. The coincidence is too great. It must be *meant*.'

'How did you get away tonight?' she asked sharply. 'Did you ask leave?'

'I pretended my mother was sick and needed me. Mistress Nan was kind and let me go.'

'Mylla . . .' Asher frowned. It was all too pat, too easy. 'Do you think anyone could have followed you here?'

She looked astonished. 'I don't think so. Why do you ask?'

'Just a bad feeling. What do you want to do – try to visit this woman tonight?'

Mylla produced a second wolf's head badge from the pocket of her cloak and slid it across the table. 'If you wear this, we'll say we've come from the house to help. You can be a servant up from the country – my cousin, perhaps, in case this woman knows the members of the household. Ash, this may be our only chance. We have to take it!'

'I know.' As she said it, Asher was sure it was true, but for some reason that knowledge intensified her disquiet; her mind ran through the ramifications of Mylla's discovery. Could this be a trap? It was possible, but, trap or not, they had to try. 'All right. Where is this place?'

'Not far from here. It's down the alley at the back, then two streets on.' Mylura looked up eagerly. 'Now?'

'Better before dark, I suppose.'

'Oh, there's another thing.' Asher looked askance. 'Menna's gone away.'

'What do you mean?' Asher asked sharply. 'Gone where?'

Mylura shrugged. 'Just gone. No one said where, or even that she was leaving. But by the time I went to do her room this morning she wasn't there, and one of the other maids told me she'd gone away for a while.'

'Mylla, don't you think this is wrong? Why should she go now?'

'Coincidence. How could they know we suspected Avorian?' Mylura sounded puzzled.

'Lassar.'

'The diviner? But how could he tell – what could he possibly know?'

'It just feels wrong, especially after last night.' Briefly, Asher told Mylla about the thefts from the hostel. 'But even so, we'll go and talk to this old woman.' Reluctantly, she got to her feet, nodded at Cass and made for the door, Mylura following.

Outside, she glanced to left and right, but there was no one about who looked out of place.

'Down here.' Mylura led the way down the side of the inn to a narrow alley, too dark for Asher's peace of mind. Houses loomed close to either side, overhanging the street, all in poor repair, and the smell coming from the gutters was rank.

At the entrance, Asher hesitated. 'It's not exactly inviting!'

'Nonsense. Don't be so fussy!'

It was still daylight, and Asher tried to still her apprehension as they walked down the shady alley, glad of the noisy presence of children playing some complicated game who did not bother to look up as the women passed. She could detect no pursuing footsteps, but when they emerged into a wider street at the end she let out a long breath.

'Why so nervous tonight?' Mylla gave her a curious look. 'Has something happened?'

'Only what I told you – about meeting Stern, and losing my identity papers.'

Mylura nodded slowly. 'Everything's coming together, don't you think so? It's as if we're near the end.'

It was so much like her own thoughts that Asher nodded. 'I hope so.'

'I felt it in Avorian's house, too.' Mylura made a face as she struggled to find the right words. 'A *waiting* feeling. There's something going on that no one tells you, but it underlies everything else.'

Asher glanced back. 'Let's get on. I don't like it here.'

At the end of the second, wider street, Mylura turned the left corner, scanning the tall houses to either side before coming to a halt in front of a stone doorway bearing a butterfly insignia. 'This is the place, I think. Put on your badge, Ash.'

The street was in marked contrast to most in the quarter; deep gutters ran clear, and the buildings were in good repair. No cracks marred the frontages of the terraces, and the shutters on all four storeys of the house they were looking at had been painted a cheerful shade of yellow, colour of good fortune. The only quality to disturb Asher was the silence. Elsewhere in the old quarter, streets were filled with raised voices and crying babies and slamming doors; here, there was something dead about the place, as if the residents went about their daily business in whispers behind the shuttered windows, walking on silent feet from room to room.

The air felt still and breathless, sounds from beyond the street muted and far away.

'I wonder who else lives here?' Asher said aloud.

Mylura shrugged. 'No idea. It looks prosperous, doesn't it? Mighty generous of Avorian; it must cost him a few gold coins a

268

year.'

'He probably owns the building – or the street.'

Mylla shrugged. 'Are we going in?'

She led the way through the porch, and they found themselves in a cool stone passage with stairs leading up to the left, and an open door to their right.

'Who're you wanting?' called a sharp voice from behind the door.

Mylura lifted her cloak to reveal her badge. 'Mistress Alys.'

An elderly woman shuffled out to the passage and looked closely at them both, then nodded. 'Upstairs, second floor.'

'Even a portress!' Mylura whispered to Asher as they climbed the stairs. 'No expense spared.'

'Or a wardress.' It was too late to wish the woman had not seen their faces.

There was only one door leading from the second-floor landing, and Mylura, signalling Asher to display her badge, knocked on it loudly. A response came in the form of heavy footsteps, then there was the sound of bolts being drawn back. The door opened, perhaps a handspan.

'What do you want?'

Their interrogator was a dark woman with a closed and angry face; she displayed a large hand which rested on the edge of the door as she peered suspiciously at her visitors, although her expression lightened on seeing the wolf badges.

'Mistress Nan sent us,' Mylla said hastily, before she could shut the door again. 'She thought you might need to be spelled tonight, if your daughter's still sick.'

The door opened a trifle wider. 'What's your name? I haven't seen you before, have I?'

'I'm Clara, a new maid up at the house, and this is my cousin Karis. No, we've not met, but I've heard a lot about you.' Mylura was at her most convincing, her plain face void of any hint of duplicity. 'She's come to keep me company, up from the country for a spell.'

'I didn't ask for you!' The suspicion was still there, but reduced in intensity. 'I'd not have it said I didn't earn my wages!'

'No, no. This was Mistress Nan's own idea. She's always so kind,' Mylla said reassuringly. 'And it's no trouble to sit with Mistress Alys.'

'I've given the old lady her supper.' The woman said it grudgingly. 'There's nothing much needs to be done, just to sit with her, because she doesn't like to be left alone. And there's a drop of wine the master sent. She likes a cup after supper.' She seemed torn between duty and desire. 'My daughter's close to her first confinement, and fretting herself near to death!'

'So Mistress Nan said,' Mylura agreed, nodding. 'Just show us where she is, and we'll be happy to sit with the old lady.'

The issue hung in the balance, and Asher was not certain which outcome was to be preferred; but Mylla's innocent expression must have been the decider, for at last the door opened fully, and they were ushered inside.

'Come through to the bedroom. You can wait there. I won't be gone more than an hour.' The woman led them through a large, surprisingly well-furnished apartment with long, light rooms that smelled of polish and rosewater; Asher wondered why Avorian should go to such expense for a mere servant, no matter how highly valued.

'Here, Mistress Alys,' the woman said, raising her voice as she addressed the tiny prone figure lying on the bed, covered by thick blankets. A pair of dark eyes swivelled towards Asher, paused, then moved on to inspect Mylura. 'I've two visitors for you. They'll sit with you while I visit my daughter.' She gestured to a pitcher standing on a table. 'There's wine there. Help yourselves. I'll not be gone long.'

The room faced west, catching the last of the sunlight; a fire burned in the hearth, but the shutters stood open, for it was a warm evening. The room had a musty smell, but sparkled with cleanliness. Asher glanced at the old woman's face, vastly relieved to find it held an expression of sharp interest rather than the vacancy she feared; old she might be, but Alys still had all her wits.

'Would you like wine?' Mylla asked her, going closer to the bed. The old lady blinked in apparent agreement, and, with a last backward look, her guardian departed. Soon, the shutting of the door told Asher the three of them were now alone.

'Here.' Asher put an arm under the old woman's shoulders. 'Let me help you sit up.' Efficiently, she placed a pillow behind her back, raising her so that she could drink.

'And who might you be, young missy?' Dark eyes snapped in the tiny face, and Asher wondered just how old Alys was; her figure was wasted, barely disturbing the blankets. 'Though you seem to know what you're doing!'

'I've a little experience in nursing. I'm Asher, and this is Mylura.' She had forgotten the names Mylla had invented, and in any case there seemed little point in deception. Avorian would know who had come once the truth was out. 'We've come to talk to you.'

'What about?' The same suspicion exhibited by her own nurse showed in Alys' face. 'Is there sickness up at the house? Is the master ill?' She sounded almost hopeful.

'None.' Mylura put the cup of wine to the old woman's lips, and she took a sip. 'We've come to give your nurse a chance to see her daughter, and to visit you. Were you long in the Chief Councillor's service, Mistress Alys?'

'His?' There was an encouraging note of antagonism in her voice. 'What's it to you? But I was never in *his* pay. I came with my mistress, my nursling, Katriane, on her wedding day. All her life, sweet thing that she was, and her promise that got me this.' She made a feeble gesture round the room with a skeletal hand. 'She made him swear to it as she lay dying, I heard her. When he said no, she said she'd curse him if he'd not abide by her wishes, so he did swear.' She sounded as if the promise still gave her immense satisfaction. 'The master knew the powerful ill luck of the curse of the dying, and he had to keep his word or lose his luck.'

'Why shouldn't he do as she asked?' Asher inquired. 'Why did she need to threaten him if you'd been with her all her life? Surely, it was his duty to provide for you?'

'Because – ' She broke off, glaring at Asher with sharp intelligence. 'You're no servant, nor the other. I'd give you no room in any house I ran.'

Asher inclined her head. 'No,' she admitted equably. 'I'm no servant. But I still want to talk to you.'

'No.' Alys tightened her lips. 'I gave *my* word, too.'

'What about?'

The dark eyes snapped at her. 'I'll not be caught like that, young missy, and don't you think it!'

'We need you, Mistress Alys,' Asher said quietly. 'Badly. We think only you can help us.'

'In what way?' But it was obvious that, despite her age, the old woman understood all too well what Asher wanted.

'We want to know about Menna.'

'The master's daughter? What about her?' Her eyes would not meet Asher's, slithering sideways in a sly fashion. 'She's well, isn't she? You said there was no sickness.'

'Certainly,' Mylura intervened, seeing Asher's hesitancy. 'She's well. Was she your charge, too, when she was a babe?'

'What's it to you?'

They were getting nowhere; from the craftiness of the woman's expression, Asher guessed they could ask questions all night without result. There must be a way to reach the old nurse, but how? What was the key to loosen her tongue?

Katriane. The answer sprang to her mind like a revelation.

The woman's love for her nursling was still intense. On impulse, Asher said suddenly: 'They say the Chief Councillor is considering marrying again soon.'

Mylla sent her a puzzled look, but a breathless silence settled over the room. Alys gripped the stem of her wine cup in bony fingers, staring at Asher.

'Married, you say?' she said at last.

Asher nodded. 'Soon.' Again, inspiration struck. 'He wants more children, now Menna is grown and he has no heir for the trade.'

'*Him?*' She spat the word out. 'He'll father none, nor ever did!' Her look dared Asher to refute the statement. 'He blamed my Katriane, and said it was her doing he'd no sons, but it was him – all the time it was *him*!' The words spilled from her in defence of her love. 'And she with seven brothers and sisters, and him with only a sister, and a sickly one at that! No, I knew from the time he was taken ill with the swelling fever there'd be no children in that house.' She shook her head emphatically. 'When that takes a man, it takes his seed, and he may whistle for his sons!'

Mylura was stunned into rare silence, but Asher urged: 'So Menna is *not* his daughter?'

The eyes turned to her. '*His?* How could she be, tell me that, when he'd been married to my girl for six years without even a false alarm? No, he bought the girl to salve his pride! To prove it was my mistress and not he who was barren – that's what I believe, and that's why he would have turned me out to starve if my Katriane'd not made him give his promise! That's what I swore I'd not tell a living soul, so long as he kept *her* in his memory.' Malice lit her expression. 'But if he's broken his word, there's nothing to make me keep mine, not now. Not if he's untrue to *her.*'

'Tell me about Menna,' Asher invited softly; her inspired suggestion had certainly opened the gates with a vengeance. 'When did she come to live with you?'

'When she was – what? – five or six. It's hard to tell at that age. *He* told my mistress a lie, that he'd had another woman and this was their child and he wanted to adopt the girl. She, like the gentle creature she was, agreed, for she believed him when he

272

said it was down to *her* they'd no children, and she wanted to please him so he'd not put her aside; she took in the girl and was good to her.' Alys was still too angry at the insult to her mistress for caution. 'A nice child, but none of his getting, I'd swear to it.'

'When was this?'

Alys leaned back, closing her eyes to facilitate memory. 'It would be after the war – after Omen fell. I remember that, because my mistress lost a brother in the city and was worn out with weeping, and I thought it a good thing she should have a child to care for, to take her mind from her own grief.'

Then it was true. Menna was Vallis! Although it was what she had hoped, it was still a shock to find proof of it. Asher exchanged a look with Mylura. 'Did Menna ever speak of her own mother, of any other family?'

'Did she?' The old woman's voice sounded weaker, worn thin by emotion or weariness. 'She cried, poor mite, I remember that. Night after night they'd dose her with poppy-juice to make her sleep. Dreams she had, too. I sat up with her, for she'd wake, crying as if her heart would break, until at last the Councillor had to ask his diviner to take a hand, for the poor thing was growing thin and pale. That was a man called Truin, not this one.' Alys gave a dismissive sniff. 'After that she was better, but she still had dreams.'

'Can you remember *what* she dreamed?'

Alys wiped her eyes with the back of her hand. 'A bird, I think.' She nodded, plainly pleased to recall so much after the intervening years. 'That was it – she said she dreamed about a big bird, and that she wanted to fly, but had no wings.' A note of reminiscence entered her voice. 'A hawk.'

Asher felt a hard jolt run through her. 'Mylla, we must go.' The warning was too strong to ignore, patterns crowding to the forefront of her mind.

'But we can't.' Mylura gestured at Alys, who had closed her eyes and looked nearly asleep.

'Now. Don't argue.' Her voice sharpened with tension. 'We have to get out of here. *Now.*'

Mylura removed the empty wine cup from Alys' lax grasp and put it on the table; the delay was torture to Asher, who could *see* patterns of warning in her mind, choices being closed off.

'Farewell, Mistress Alys, and thank you.' She stepped back, pulling Mylla with her.

'What is it?' Mylura asked, as she closed the outer door to the apartment. 'What's so urgent.'

'We have to leave.' She struggled to stay calm. 'Mylla, Lassar was *watching* us. I felt it. We have to get away, at once. Mistress Alys will be safe enough.'

'Where?' Mylura made no further protest.

'Carob's. It's closest.'

At the foot of the stairs Asher hesitated, then passed the portress's open door and peered out into the street. There was no one there.

'Quickly. I don't like it here. It's much too quiet,' she whispered.

The prickling of her skin told her Lassar still had her under observation, but for the moment Asher was less afraid of that than of the prospect of other watchers close by, of physical danger. The *sight* was of short duration, requiring great concentration, or so Omond said; but where was Lassar? Near, or far off on the other side of the city?

Then the prickly feeling was gone, but the oppressive silence of the street remained, making Asher feel that behind the closed shutters hid a pair of sharp eyes, keeping them under secret observation. Taking Mylura's hand, she began to run; it might be nowhere was safe for them now, but Carob's was at least near.

It seemed a long way to the inn; as she opened the door to the women's room and stepped inside, Asher quickly scanned the faces of the women present, but most were familiar.

'Cass, have you paper and ink?' she asked urgently. The slave-woman nodded and departed in search of both.

Mylla raised an inquisitive eyebrow. 'What are you going to do?'

'I'm going to write to Mallory and tell him what we've learned. Just in case.' She found her hands were shaking, and here, in the inn, felt no safer than in the old nurse's apartment; all the patterns in her mind were still set at *warning, warning*. 'Someone else should know what Alys told us.'

She sat at a corner table and waited for Cass, who appeared shortly bearing paper, a block of ink, and a pen.

'Is there anything else I can get you?' she asked helpfully. 'You've only to ask.'

'Yes.' Asher was already wetting the ink. 'Could you deliver this letter – not tonight, but in the morning?'

Cass frowned. 'Well, surely, Carob won't mind. Is something wrong, Asher?'

'I don't know. This is only a precaution. I'll put the name of the person I want it sent to on the front, but please – don't mention this to anyone but Carob.'

'I won't.' She hesitated. 'You look very pale. Can I get you some ale?'

'No, thank you.' She was already writing a verbatim account of the interview with Alys, eager to get it all down on paper before Lassar should seek her out once more. Cass and Mylura let her be, talking quietly together, for business was slow and there were few customers waiting to be served.

Avorian knows. The thought was terrifying in its implications; Asher steadied her shaking hand and continued her account. Before, they had suspected, but now they *knew.* She did not share Mallory's hope that he had taken Vallis for any noble motive; he had no reason to continue to conceal her when all Darrian was looking for her, and none to keep her ignorant of her own identity. *'Wings bound and flightless, layered in forgetfulness.'* Avorian's diviner had made the girl forget who she was, forget everything except what he told her. While she was a child, it could have been done for her own safety, but not now, with her father the Dominus dying, and herself a woman grown.

He will try to kill us.

It was a certainty that kept her writing for a long time, adding her own feelings of doubt to the epistle. This was Avorian's city; if he wanted them disposed of, it would be simple enough.

She waved the last sheet of paper to dry it and realized the warning patterns in her mind had not altered, despite her precautions; frustratingly, she could not *see* precisely where the promise of danger lay, only that it was almost impossible to avoid. Should they stay at the inn? But that would place Cass, and Carob too, in danger, for the inn was by no means impregnable, and there was the letter to consider. But if they left the shelter of the women's room, they were all too vulnerable.

She cut off that line of thought; there was no profit in panic. Mentally, she tallied the counts against Avorian from the information she and Mylla had gathered: he had adopted Vallis, he had stolen her, he was making up the Tribute shortfall, he was ambitious but had no children of his own, and could have none.

He means to marry her.

Her impulsive observation to Mistress Alys had been the truth, not the lie she had thought it. Nothing else explained his actions. He intended to marry Vallis. He meant her to fulfil the prophecy, but for his own ends, to rule through her authority. Swiftly, she added her conclusion to the bottom of her last page to Mallory. She felt ice-cold. *Fourteen years he'd waited.* If he had meant well, he would have told Vallis who she was and allowed her to grow up in full knowledge of her destiny. The meaning of the Oracle became crystal clear to her. Avorian had bound Vallis, to himself, and would bind her closer still unless he could be stopped.

'Finished?'

She looked up to find Cass and Mylura standing over her. 'Yes.' She folded the pieces of paper and wrote Mallory's name on the blank side. 'Do you know where to take this?'

Cass peered at the name. 'I'll go first thing in the morning,' she promised. 'Do you want me and Carob to know what's in it?'

'No!' Asher said vehemently. 'And I wouldn't even ask you to do this if I had any alternative. Mylla, we must go. Are you ready?'

She nodded. 'If you want. Come with me to Jan's house; it's closer than the hostel.'

'I hadn't thought of that.' Asher bit her lip. 'I don't want to bring trouble to your cousin.' Her gift had deserted her, but not before she *saw* that there was no greater safety in leaving than in staying where they were.

'He won't mind.' Mylla seemed calm, but Asher could tell she, too, was nervous, lowering her voice. 'You were right, weren't you, in what you said to Mistress Alys? He wants to marry her.'

'Yes. Or it makes no sense.'

'Then we'd better hope he can't find us.'

Outside, it had grown dark. Again, Asher looked warily from side to side in the light spilling from the open door, but the only man loitering in front of the inn paid them no attention, and when a young female voice called from the upper floor of a nearby tenement he looked up and shouted back, plainly a local.

Mylla and Asher began the descent of the long flight of steps which was the quickest way to Jan's house, but when they were only halfway down Asher looked back, alerted by some sound, to find three men coming slowly towards them. She turned forward to speak a warning to Mylura, and as she did so three more men appeared, as if from nowhere, at the foot of the stair. The trio stood, side by side, waiting.

'Ash,' Mylura whispered, sounding unexpectedly frightened, 'that one, the one in grey – that's Jerr. He's one of Avorian's men.'

For a moment, her legs would not move. Asher stared in frozen disbelief at the men before and behind, seeing how easily and completely they had been trapped. The stair was too narrow to slip past whether they went up or down, and the odds were enormously against them in a fight. She went down one more stair, then stopped and screamed, as loudly as she could, the only thing she could think of doing; but the waiting men made no move, and no response came, no sound of running steps or hope of rescue. In the old quarter, many screams went unregarded after dark, when the residents knew it was wisest to ignore concerns not their own.

All six men carried knives, held point outwards; Asher could now feel one at her back, digging into her ribs. The three at the foot of the stair waited until the others joined them, then the man Mylura had named jerked his head sideways; at once the two women were hustled down an empty street and left, into a doorway and along a short passage. It was all accomplished with quick efficiency and in an absolute silence more daunting than whispered threats or open violence.

'Get down here.' The man in grey pointed with his foot to a ladder emerging from a hole in the floor, obviously leading to a cellar. Asher hesitated, and he brought his knife up to her neck. '*Now!* Or die here.' She descended, Mylura following, into an empty, damp, windowless room some twenty feet square, with a mud floor lit by two lanterns hanging from the ceiling beam.

'I'm sorry,' she managed to whisper as Mylura set foot on the floor. 'This is my fault.'

'Not yours – Avorian's.' Mylura was chalk-white but composed, watching as the six men made a swift descent.

'Split them up. Tie the older one to that beam, but don't hurt her!' The grey-suited man gave the instructions in a crisp voice; where the other assailants were almost indistinguishable in the drab waistcoats, loose shirts and breeches of labouring men, he was dressed in grey velvet, and his hands, in contrast to those of his companions, were elegant, the nails neatly clipped. His hair shone a bright gold in the lanternlight, and his long face was handsome, the nose thin and well-shaped, the mouth wide and upward-curving.

Asher was drawn away from Mylura towards one of two wooden posts that supported the ceiling beam; rough hands bound her arms together around the post, immobilizing her. Mylura, looking suddenly very young, stood in a circle formed by the remaining four men, two staying by Asher.

'If you want money,' Asher called out, 'take it. We've not much, but you're welcome to it.'

'Money?' The man named Jerr smiled in her direction, as if surprised she could speak. 'But if you have it, we'll take it.' She felt a hand at her side, seeking her purse and taking it from the pocket of her skirts.

Jerr gestured again to his men, and one moved behind Mylura, taking her neck in his hands; the other two stood to either side, each taking an arm and holding it out at shoulder height so that she stood in the form of a cross. She struggled, and Jerr laughed.

'You stepped in too many shadows tonight. What is it they say: "Four may keep a secret, if three of them are dead"?' He turned to face Asher. 'You're lucky tonight. You get to watch. But if there's another time, this will be *you*.' He whirled, knife in hand, and took the neck of Mylura's dress, slitting it and tearing it from top to bottom so that it hung loosely at her sides; leaning forward, he ripped away the wolf's head badge and put it in his pocket. Mylura did not flinch but she wet her lips, owning a quiet form of courage that should have earned respect; in her place, Asher thought she could never have been half so composed.

'Let her go.'

Jerr swivelled his head slowly back to Asher. 'Why?'

'Because this was my idea, not hers. I can pay you – any amount you ask, if you let her – us – go.' She had no qualms about promising Mallory's gold; he would pay gladly for their release.

'Ah, yes, your friend the Councillor.' He nodded, raising her hopes, only to dash them a moment later. 'He's not rich enough, not to buy me. Not enough for me to betray my master.'

'What is enough?'

It was plain her persistence amused him, for he moved away from Mylura, much to Asher's relief. 'Nothing you can offer me, my pretty,' he said softly. '"Near's my shirt, but nearer's my skin", or so they say. I'd not cross my master, not for all the gold in Darrian; not if I want to live to enjoy it. He's not a forgiving man.'

'"Fish always stink from the head down",' Asher said, as disdainfully as she could, desperate to keep his attention on herself. 'By my guess, you must be the tail!'

His head jerked up viciously. 'Gag her!' he ordered one of the men. Obediently, the one on her left took out a filthy rag from a pocket and stuffed it in her mouth, half-choking her; it tasted vile. Jerr moved until he was standing in front of her, then put the point of his knife to her face.

'I know what you're trying. You hope to keep me from your friend here. But it hasn't worked. I have orders not to hurt you, but none to prevent me harming *her*. Every word you've said, *she'll* pay. And you'll watch, and know.' There was no expression at all in his eyes; to him, this was only a day's work. 'Watch,' he whispered slowly. 'Watch, and *remember*!'

Asher tugged at her bonds, desperate to free herself, but could make no impression on them. Jerr returned to Mylura, waiting only an instant before lifting the tip of his knife and drawing it quickly down in a semicircle on one side of her face, then repeating the detail on the other. Blood began to stream from the shallow wounds, and Mylura let out a brief sigh. She kept her eyes on Asher, refusing to look at Jerr, who wiped his blade fastidiously on Mylura's dress.

Let that be all, Asher thought, trembling. It's bad, but she can bear it; she's the bravest person I know. Please, let that be all.

'They say a woman cares most about her face,' Jerr observed clinically. 'But you don't seem to. Why is that?'

'What good would it do?' Mylura answered stiffly. A drop of blood dripped from her chin on to Jerr's hand, and again he wiped it away on her dress.

'None,' he agreed, moving the point of the knife down to her small breasts. 'Perhaps here?' The knife dug and curved, and Mylura cried out.

No more! Asher choked. It was intolerable to be forced to observe another's pain, an impossibility.

'Better.' Jerr stepped back to inspect his handiwork, seeming pleased with the effect. 'And now, I wonder, where next?' He fingered the tip of the knife. 'Perhaps here?' He aimed the blade at Mylura's flat stomach, and laughed as she tried to move back out of range, pulling his hand at the last moment.

'Kill me, Jerr, if that's what you're going to do.' His laughter sent Mylura's head back; eyes glittering brightly, she straightened. 'If that's what you're paid to do. Who am I to deny the Fates, if this is their will? I'm not afraid of death . . .'

'Ah, but death is easy. It's dying you fear,' he said softly, interrupting her. 'I can see it in you. Because you know, don't you, that you don't matter here? You're only an object lesson for your friend, to teach her the value of silence.' Mylura's expression went stiff with the effort to hide her dismay, but Asher, who knew her well, saw her fear and was consumed by overwhelming guilt; it was her fault, hers not Mylura's. She understood how Mallory must have felt when she was in Lewes' hands, unable to halt the inevitable, powerless, as she was, to save a friend from pain. She kept her eyes on Mylura's face, willing her to survive, to bear the unbearable, to let her know she was *there*, which was all she could do for her now.

Jerr put up a hand to trace one of the cuts on Mylura's face, almost a caress. 'You're not a beauty, girl, and never were. But that doesn't matter to me or these men here.' She went rigid, understanding him too well. 'It's what all women fear, isn't it? You should be glad you won't live long enough to care.' He reached to grasp the top of her undershirt to tear it down, but she was ready for him and kicked out, catching him between the legs with her right booted foot, all her strength behind the blow. He screamed and doubled up.

'Asher – make it worth it!' Mylura was sweating, Asher saw, but knew exactly what she was doing; a quick death rather than rape and a slow one. She wished she could speak, any words at all, and found she was crying. She nodded, swallowing, a vile taste in her throat.

Jerr straightened himself with an effort, still in obvious agony and with no further desire for his prey; Mylla had won herself so much. With one quick movement, he raised the blade and slashed it across her neck, slicing the main artery. Mylura's face had time to register shock, but Asher, forcing herself to watch, saw that it was only brief; death was very quick, the light fading from her eyes in seconds.

No.

It was impossible to believe it had happened; that one moment she should be alive, the next gone. Sickness and guilt rose in Asher, and a hatred that burned more strongly than either. *Avorian.* She let the word burn a path to her will; he would pay, no matter what the cost, hatred taking root in her heart. *He would pay.* Even Jerr, his instrument, was less loathsome to her than the master, a secondary evil.

Jerr removed his jacket, for the front was soaked with Mylura's blood; he dabbed at it ineffectually, then gave up and turned it inside out, hiding the stains. Signalling the men to let the body drop to the dirty floor, he came across to Asher.

'This was for you, so you should see what will happen if you speak a single word of the lie you have concocted. My master would know of it in the same instant.' He looked straight into her eyes as she spoke, and she was chilled by his expression. 'Take this warning. It is the only one you will be given. If you keep silence, you will be spared. Even your real name and background will be lost – for I know who you really are, as does my master. But if you speak, or if you continue on your present path, you die. Not even your friend the Councillor will be able to save you, or himself, or anyone else to whom you tell this lie. Do you hear?'

Asher bent her head.

'My master has chosen to give you this lesson rather than kill you. Consider and be grateful.' It was plain Jerr found such generosity incomprehensible. 'And you – you'd not die so easily as this one, I give you my word on it. Is that clear to you?'

Again, Asher bent her head, glad to be absolved from any necessity to reply. She looked over Jerr's shoulder and saw one of the men lift Mylura and sling her body over his shoulder, as if she were only so much dead meat. He moved to the ladder and began to climb. She felt cold.

Jerr, seeing where her attention lay, said curtly: 'She's for the river tonight. Don't bother looking for her. And now, we'll let you go. Straight back to that hostel and nowhere else, and not a word to anyone. If you speak, I'll come for you. There's nowhere in this city you can run I can't find you, no door that will keep me from you.' He touched the bloodied knife he still held in his hand, then reached behind Asher and slit her bonds, freeing her arms to hang limply at her sides. She was trembling so violently she could hardly stand. 'Remember,' he added softly, 'not a word.'

His companions were gone, and they were alone in the cellar. With a last look, Jerr put his foot on the first rung of the ladder, then the second. Asher spat out the rag, her mouth dry and bitter-tasting, clinging desperately to the wooden post, unable to stop shaking.

'Farewell, girl, and hope, for your own sake that you never see me again.'

Jerr disappeared from view then Asher was alone with the lanterns and the floor, stained with Mylura's blood, and was sick suddenly, retching in endless spasms until she could hardly breathe, falling to the floor and moaning to herself a stream of mindless denials.

She stayed there for a long time.

She never knew how she managed to find her way back to the hostel; she was not aware of where she walked until she found herself at the door of the hostel, and heard the first bell of curfew toll, and knew she must go in.

I can't, not looking like this.

It was her first rational thought for some time. She could not go in until she was in control of herself; no one must know or guess what had happened, or they would be in the same danger as herself. With trembling fingers, she smoothed her hair and wiped her face on her sleeve, biting her lips to give them some colour. She practised a smile, and when she was sure she could keep it in place for the minute or so she would need, she knocked on the door for admittance. To her relief, neither Margit nor Essa answered, and somehow she reached the privacy of her own room without encountering her closest friends.

Once in that sanctuary, she could not control her hands sufficiently to hold the key, which dropped from her fingers to the floor; she stared at it, not really seeing it. It seemed too much trouble to bend and pick it up, and she let it lie until she heard movement on the stairs. Then she stooped for it and locked her door, barely in time; someone knocked, then tried the handle. She ignored the sound of Essa's voice calling her. She stood motionless, unable to summon the energy to move, feeling a lead weight settle in the pit of her stomach. The room was dark, but she did not want light; she did not want anything at all except to be left alone.

The second curfew bell rang and the hostel was suddenly filled with noise as the women made their way to bed, laughing and joking with one another. Their voices did not sound real to Asher. Another knock at her door. A voice calling. She ignored that, too. Guilt dripped like acid through the protective numbness in which she had surrounded herself, corroding the fragile shell in which she hid, bringing with it such mental anguish that Asher gasped aloud.

My fault, my fault, mine.

She thought she might go mad as the words repeated themselves over and over again in her head. Time passed, but she was not aware of it, nor of anything else but her guilt.

Was there a hollow place in her mind, as there was in the world, without Mylla? Her stomach felt tight and empty, the acid of guilt dripping slowly down, each drop a flare of agony. In the dark, Asher knew she had never been so utterly alone as she was that night.

It was a little before dawn when a sense of reason returned, and another thought stirred.

Not me, not the Fates, but Avorian.

She gulped in air, filling her lungs. She could not, would not rid herself of the guilt of responsibility, but it was Avorian who was the cause of Mylura's murder, who was its instigator. It was the worst form of arrogance for Asher to take to herself all the blame, to imply that Mylura had only acted as her surrogate. She would not use her own pain as an excuse to hide herself and give way; Mylura's death was Avorian's open admission of guilt, making their suspicions fact. It was *he* who had stolen Vallis, who held her in a prison of his making, who would kill rather than let his secret be known. That killer was the real man behind the mask.

Mallory. In the morning he, too, would know, when he read the letter, unless . . . but she could not let herself believe Jerr or Avorian knew about Cass, or Carob, or the letter. She had experienced no sensation of being watched during the short time she had spent at the inn; no need, with Jerr keeping them under physical surveillance.

He will know, and he'll come. She knew a fierce desire for the comfort of his physical presence; she wanted to share with him the lust for vengeance that burned in her heart, the sharpness of her loss. She had not mourned Lewes, and there had been no time to mourn even her parents, for the events of the night they had died had left no time for such a luxury, but she would pay Mylla the tribute she deserved. Mallory would understand her helplessness and guilt and despair. Mylla, he'll pay, Avorian will pay, I swear it! she promised passionately; that vengeance was worth living for.

Time went by. Hollow-eyed, Asher sat and waited behind her locked door. She could not sleep and did not weep; there would have been no relief in either. Morning came, and several times someone tried her door, and voices called out to her, but she did not answer them; they were an irrelevance that had nothing to do with her life. They had nothing to do with the cellar, and Mylura, and the real secret only she, and now perhaps Mallory, knew. Essa and Margit and the others might speculate on her whereabouts, and on Mylla's, but they would know nothing, which was as it must be.

When she was sure the others had all gone to work, and the hostel was empty, she unlocked her door and went downstairs to the main salon from where she could watch for Mallory. She trusted him to come; he had to come. If Jerr were watching, she did not care.

As she waited, she wondered why Avorian had let her live. There seemed no sense in it. Did he hold her in such contempt that he believed she would keep silence from fear? Except that even if he had enjoined her death, it would already have been too late, for before Mylla had died, she herself had already written to Mallory, telling him the truth. Was it that, that choice, which had saved her life? Could Mylla's, too, have been saved, if she had been able to use her gift to look at the future, to understand its possibilities? My fault – mine! She curled up, trying to get rid of the pain. In denying the gift's existence, had she ensured it should be useless to her when she needed it most?

The pain of loss was unendurable, but it had to be endured. She must find the courage to bear it.

She returned to the question of her own survival; it was easier to think about that than to remember.

Asher stood by the window and waited, watching, seeing nothing, wondering: Why?

Chapter Fifteen

Kirin had discovered his attic eyrie the previous year, when he was only seven, before his father had died and his Uncle Mallory had come to live with them; it was a wonderful place from which to watch the comings and goings on the hill because it had windows on three of its four sides, so he could see from the front and back of the house as well as the road along the side.

Yesterday, there had been movement higher up the hill; the house which stood behind their own belonged, he knew, to Chief Councillor Avorian, and there were always carts and wagons coming and going, although rarely so early. This time their cargo was wine-casks which he guessed had been sent downriver from the Councillor's estates; that was how their own were dispatched, the empty ones taken away and sent back overland by the slow route. He had counted at least a dozen or more before he had to leave the window.

This morning the excitement was someone coming in through their own gate – a slave-woman, and Gormese by her dark colouring. Intrigued, Kirin watched as she stood for a moment looking up at the house, obviously unsure where to go; then she disappeared along the side and Kirin heard a loud knocking at one of the doors at the rear. He could not hear what was being said as a maid responded to the summons, for he had not thought to open the windows, but he waited until the woman reappeared soon after, still watching as she walked out of the gates and back down the hill and out of sight.

He considered whether he should go downstairs, for his nurse was angry if he was late for meals, but instinct held him by the window and he was rewarded when, a short time later, he saw his Uncle Mallory appear, followed by several of their menservants. Horses were brought, and the party – at least ten, although they were so close together it was difficult to count them all – mounted and left by the main gate, heading downhill. Since this was an entirely new departure, Kirin spent some time wondering where they were going and why, wishing he could go with them. No one *ever* told him what was going on, even though he was the heir to the house, and he debated running downstairs and following them; but they were mounted and he was not, and he was probably already too late. Reluctantly, he abandoned his watch to join his brother and sister for nursery breakfast.

After a hasty meal, Kirin ran back up the attic stairs to his post, for there was still time before lessons. It was early, but already the fishing fleet down by the harbour was making its way out to sea and he sighed. His mother refused to let him go with them, no matter how often he asked, even in the calmest weather. Perhaps he could ask his uncle? But he was a little in awe of his tall uncle, who had spent so many years sailing the world, and who might not think much of an ambition merely to go fishing.

And there he was, coming back. Peering carefully, for his eyesight was excellent, Kirin thought he saw a woman among the group, a woman he had never seen before. Was that all? He made a face, having hoped for something more exciting. He moved to the rear window to watch them dismount, but there was nothing, really, to be interested in, for his uncle and the strange woman had already entered the house, and the rest was dull and overfamiliar.

Abruptly, he remembered he had left his pocket knife in the garden the previous day – he had been throwing at a target with Lake – and decided to fetch it before lessons. Bored, now, with his vigil, he ran down the three flights of back stairs, then, with more caution – for he was now late, which he had promised not to be, and he was not supposed to run about the ground-floor rooms in case he broke things or bumped into any of his uncle's visitors or customers – he opened the door to a small waiting room behind the main hall and let himself out into the garden through the window.

The gardens ascended the hillside in a series of terraces, the lower more formally designed than those higher up, with strict borders and patterned paths. Kirin thought the knife would be on the uppermost terrace, which was only grass and trees, for that was where he had been throwing it. He kept low as he made his way up towards the wall bordering the property to the west. No one saw him and he straightened up as he reached the place, the small ornamental garden sufficiently secluded by trees and bushes to hide him from sight of the house, which is why he and Lake and Crisa used it to play in. Carefully, he began to search the ground.

'Hello.'

Kirin looked up, startled. The voice came from the ash tree beside the wall. There was a man perched in it, leaning comfortably against the trunk, arms behind his head; he was fair-haired and dressed in a grey livery – not their own – but Kirin knew him by sight. He was one of the Chief Councillor's servants.

'What are you doing there?' he asked stiffly, very much the son of the house, for the man had no right to be in *their* gardens.

'Oh, nothing in particular.' The man smiled broadly. 'Are you looking for something? Can I help?' He swung down from his perch to land lightly and neatly on the ground.

Kirin hesitated for this was *his* garden, although impressed by the servant's agility; but the man was not a complete stranger, and Kirin was now very late for his lessons. 'I lost my knife,' he said doubtfully. 'Somewhere round here, I think. It's a good one.'

'I'll help you look.' The man moved closer, apparently scouring the ground for the missing object. Kirin relaxed and went on looking, paying the stranger no more attention.

He was still bending down when an arm came round his throat, his head was forced back and, when he opened his mouth to cry out, a vile-tasting liquid was poured into it. He had no choice but to swallow or choke. Almost at once he felt weak and dizzy, and his eyes closed, his body relaxed.

The man picked him up, placed him over his shoulder, then went back to the tree leaning against the wall. With slow, lazy movements he began to climb, disappearing on the far side.

Kirin did not stir; he breathed in long, slow breaths. Oblivious to anything, he slept.

'Asher,' he began, 'I'm sorry.' But she turned to look at him with a face so hard and angry that the words of sympathy died on his lips.

'Don't.' Even her voice sounded brittle. 'I can't bear it yet.'

Mallory sighed, wishing she would do something as feminine as burst into tears; that would have been easier to cope with than her bitter self-reproach.

'It was my fault,' she said, ice-cold. 'I didn't pay enough heed to the warnings, because I didn't understand. I thought we were cleverer than Avorian.'

'I wish – '

She finished the sentence for him. 'That you'd been involved? Do you really think you would have made a difference?' Her red-rimmed eyes stared the challenge.

Since it was exactly what he had been thinking, he denied it instantly, guiltily aware it was, in fact, probably untrue; she and Mylura had been more than competent, and it was arrogance to believe he would have managed better against such odds and such numbers. 'I liked her, too, Ash, even if I didn't know her very well,' he said gently. 'And it's not your fault, not in any way.'

'Thank you.' But the words were automatic; he had made no impression on her.

'Would you consider going down to Kepesake and leaving me to deal with the rest?' He made the suggestion with inner trepidation, and was relieved she answered him quite calmly.

'This is not a physical battle, Mallory, or not in the sense that strength is what matters. It's a war against a single man, where wits will count for as much as the force of his army of servants. And it's my battle, even more than yours now.'

'Very well.' Left to himself, he knew he would not have given her the choice, but he was learning to stifle such instincts. Her life belonged to herself, not to him, and he had no right to make any decisions on her behalf.

'What do you intend to do?' he asked at last.

'Do?' She looked at him sharply. 'Go on, of course.'

'How?' The signs of exhaustion were obvious in her face, but she seemed to burn from within.

'We *know*. Now we have to find her, and tell her who she is. We have to stop Avorian from marrying her.' Her voice sounded hard, unforgiving.

'But he's threatened to kill you.'

'Does it matter?' Her eyes flashed with sudden rage. 'He'll know I've told you. You know now. I've involved you, without your agreement, for which I'm sorry.' She did not look apologetic. 'Before she died, Mylla said I had to make it worth it.'

'I was already involved.'

'I've nothing else now, Mallory.' She did not speak from self-pity, merely making a statement of fact. 'I can't go back to the hostel, or I risk the lives of my other friends; it would be easy for Avorian to arrange their deaths. And you must say if you want to draw back now. That's your choice.'

He realized, with shock, that she was trying to protect *him*. 'I've made mine, Asher, you know that,' he said stiffly, half-offended.

'Then there's only us. Only we know the truth about Avorian. He'll try to kill us both, he has no other option. We have to find the girl before he succeeds.'

288

'She can't be far away, not if he means to marry her. And he has to do so before the Dominus dies.'

Concentrating on the task in hand was evidently easier for Asher than dealing with her emotions, for she sounded more like herself when she next spoke. 'We don't know *when* he intends to marry, but it must be soon, so that his popularity is still high when he announces Menna is Vallis, and no one will protest too loudly.'

'We'd have a riot on our hands if we spoke out against him now, especially before the tribute ships sail.'

'And he'll have to get rid of you,' she pointed out. 'I'm no one, but you're a councillor of Venture, an equal. You're the real danger.'

'He can't dispose of me easily. Our clan has powerful connections in the capital.'

'He'll find a weapon to use against you. That's the way he works,' Asher said bitterly. 'Anyone connected with either of us is in danger. We don't know what he can *see*, or how much he knows.' A note of despair entered her voice. 'How can we even find the girl without help? She could be anywhere in the city, or beyond.'

'And what do we do with her when we *do* find her?' Mallory said, speaking the question aloud.

'We take her north.'

'To Saffra?' Mallory was surprised. 'Why there?'

'Because while her father Lykon is still alive, her life won't be worth a copper coin once it's known who she is. Amrist and the grey men would find a way to kill her, Mallory. The only safe place is north, out of his reach. And I know the way.'

He nodded pensively. 'She would be safe from Avorian, too. But, as you say, first we have to find her.' But Asher was looking not at but past him, towards the doorway where a tall, thin woman stood listening. 'Oramen?' he asked sharply, for he had not heard her come in. 'Why are you here? I gave orders we were not to be disturbed!'

'No, but I came.' The seeress looked perfectly composed as she shut the door. 'I have, as you know, small talent for divination which does not concern the weather or the tides, yet even I can hardly remain unaware of significant events occurring in this house, disrupting the balances. I think you have need of my services, such as they are. They are yours.'

Mallory saw Asher frown a refusal, but he hesitated. 'Oramen, if we involve you, we risk your life,' he said bluntly.

'*That* I had already gathered.' There was an underlying note of excitement in her voice. 'But my service is to your clan, as it has always been; and for the moment, you are that clan. It seems to me that the fortunes of your house are closely bound to that of your own life, which is at some risk at this moment. Unless I read the signs wrongly, which I do not believe.'

'Mistress,' Asher began hesitantly, 'the danger to yourself is great, for our enemy has a powerful diviner. I would not wish you to take such a risk without knowing the odds.'

Unexpectedly, Oramen smiled. 'I see the future is clearer to you than to me, Mistress Asher – yes, I know your name. Not, I fear through *sight* but because I asked young Pars the clerk. But your gift is undeveloped where mine is at full strength, and I am willing to take a chance. Which is my choice, I think.'

Their eyes met; Mallory felt uncomfortably excluded, wondering what piece of knowledge was being kept from him.

'Oramen, we are looking for a girl,' he said abruptly, interrupting their silent accord. 'Can you *see* for us?'

'Do you have a talisman, or any object belonging to her?'

'Nothing.'

'Do you know her well enough to visualize her, in your mind, to serve as a focus?'

Mallory glanced at Asher. 'Neither of us knows the girl well, I only by sight, but Mistress Asher has met and spoken to her.'

Oramen frowned. 'Perhaps it will serve. And may I know the identity of this person?' There was a moment of silence while both Asher and Mallory pondered the question. 'It may be,' the seeress went on, 'that I have guessed it in part. Some crucial turning point in the balance of luck in our world is building, with good or ill results to ourselves here in Darrian; there is only one person, I believe, upon whose life so powerful an alteration could depend. But if you choose to be silent, I will not question you further.'

An uneasy look crossed Asher's face, but Mallory, watching the seeress, did not see it. 'For your own safety,' he murmured, 'you had better remain in ignorance.'

'But – ' Asher had got up from her chair. Before she could continue, Oramen interrupted her brusquely.

'Then I shall prepare myself. I will be ready presently.' She looked steadily at Asher. 'There comes a time when each and every one of us must make a choice; even when that choice may not be what others would choose for us. At this moment, the balance in our world is askew, the odds against our good far outweighing those in our favour.' Asher made a brief inclination of her head, and Oramen, saying no more, turned and left the room, leaving Mallory staring after her with deep suspicion.

'What did she mean?'

At first he thought Asher had not heard, but before he could repeat the question, she answered: 'Nothing, Mallory. It was just her way of saying she wanted to help us.'

It struck him forcibly that he had inadvertently wandered on to forbidden territory and was being warned off. Not for the first time, it occurred to him to wonder whether men and women were really members of the same species, or whether their inability to understand one another was some form of great cosmic joke at their expense. Asher and Oramen had never met before, but they seemed to understand one another well. Mallory was aware of the stirrings of an illogical jealousy; Oramen was *his* seeress, and Asher, too, belonged to him on some primitive level. He had saved her life, and they had drunk from the same cup, their lives were intertwined.

The strength of his feelings shook him; knowing Asher, he was only glad he had not been foolish enough to speak them aloud.

'Sit one on either side and concentrate your will upon the mirror. You must look towards it, not into it, and show me the face you seek,' Oramen instructed.

Asher complied. The seeress's chamber bore no relation to Omond's apartments at Kepesake; there were no rows of vials, no jars of unidentifiable specimens. Instead, the walls of the square room were covered with charts of all the seas from Darrian east to Petormin, the full extent of the Dominion, and tables showing the relative positions of both moons at any given point of the year, presumably all used to divine the most favourable tides and winds, which Mallory told her was Oramen's special gift. For the rest it was a bare, plain room, the wooden floor uncovered, the only furniture a large round table and several high-backed chairs; the single window was shuttered and it was gloomily dark, although the seeress had lit two grey candles which stood in silver holders on the table to either side of a large, square mirror, giving off a familiar metallic smell.

'It is unfortunate you have nothing belonging to the girl. It will make it more difficult, for I must rely on your own impressions.'

'I'm afraid this is up to you rather than me,' Mallory murmured to Asher. 'I barely remember her face.'

'I remember her.' Asher sought and found a clear recollection of the scene in Avorian's private office, with Lassar and Menna

291

and – Koris? – the Asiri slave-boy; Menna's serene, intelligent face came back to her in surprisingly sharp detail.

'Do you have a little of this gift also, Mistress Asher?' Oramen asked her.

She was beginning to say: 'I don't know . . .' when Mallory said loudly: 'No!'

Oramen looked at him in some surprise. 'But how can you be so certain?'

Seeing him at a loss, Asher found herself smiling. 'I think, mistress, he means that, because I have married, I'm no longer a virgin.'

'Ahh!' Oramen, too, smiled her amusement. 'What a curious notion.'

'What do you mean?' Mallory looked displeased.

'Only that I sometimes think you men regard women rather as sealed letters, if you understand me. That is, that until the seal is broken, the letter has not been read; then the first person breaks the seal and reads the letter, but thereafter any number of people may do so.' Mallory said nothing, sitting tightlipped while Asher hid a smile.

'Is it not true, then?' she asked. 'There's no need to remain virgin for the *sight*?'

'Not in my experience.' Oramen kept her expression perfectly blank; Asher bit her lip. 'I fail to see why such a small thing should make any difference,' she went on innocently. 'That is just – if I may put it so – an old wives' saying.'

Mallory cleared his throat. 'Perhaps we could continue this discussion at another time?' he suggested.

'Indeed.' Serious now, Oramen fixed her gaze on the mirror.

Should I stop her? Asher, aware of a strong respect for the older woman, was unsure how to proceed. Should she speak, or remain silent?

'Concentrate on the mirror,' Oramen repeated in her beautiful voice. 'Show me this girl.'

The scent from the candles began to make Asher dizzy in a way that was becoming familiar; she forced her will towards the mirror, trying to impose Menna's – *no, Vallis's* – face on its silvered surface, but could see only Oramen's own reflection and the weaving flames of the candles.

'It is not enough.'

The seeress's voice was beginning to sound harsher; Asher, risking a look at the older woman, saw she was quite rigid with effort. She tried to shut from her mind everything else, everything she did not want to remember, and to think of Vallis as she had seen her, bending to gather the slave-boy's logs, listening to her father – *no, to Avorian* – as he spoke of the Fates. Asher could see the girl's expression most clearly, blurring the outlines of her face, but more a part of her than her clothes or her looks, surprised at how strong an impression of her personality she retained.

'Better. Continue so.'

Asher was aware of Mallory opposite, of the flickering of the candles and of Oramen's strain; another awareness struggled to force its way through to her mind, but she cut it off. It was not for her to make the choice for another, although Mallory would not see it so. Responsibility, she thought briefly, means something different to him. To take command, to take control. But not to me, nor to Oramen; my duty to her, not for her. She put the thought aside and made herself concentrate again, feeling, in the stillness of the room, the pulses in mind and heart beating in apparent tandem with a steady rhythm, a regular, soporific throbbing.

'Mists – there are mists surrounding, hiding her from *sight*.' Oramen moaned slightly. 'It is not natural; she is well warded.'

'But you are strong and can *see*. Look, and tell us.' Mallory, too, looked drawn.

Sweat beaded Oramen's brow. 'I – ' The seeress placed her hands flat on the table, fingers splayed and rigid; Asher felt her own body grow stiff in unconscious imitation of the other woman's extreme tension. 'I – feel he *sees* me,' she said hoarsely.

'Can you continue? Or shall we stop?' Mallory asked quickly.

'I will continue.' Asher made a convulsive gesture, but neither Oramen nor Mallory noticed. The seeress's voice grew deeper, more strained. '*I see a house – the house where she sleeps.*'

'Can you see where. In the city or outside it?' Mallory said, keeping his voice low.

'*Inside.*' Oramen was gasping for breath. '*The house lies near water. There is a bridge.*'

'The sea or the river?'

'*Running water – it is the river. It runs from left to right.*'

From her knowledge of the city, Asher guessed the house must stand somewhere in the old quarter, either near the Sair Gate to the north or Fishermen's Quay to the east; certainly, Avorian's own house was out of the question, since it was nowhere near the river.

'*There is an inn beside it, and on the doorway of the house I can see a bunch of leaves – no, ivy.*' It was a struggle to hear what Oramen said, her voice had sunk so low. *'The girl sleeps high – high up – warded!'*

'Oramen?' Some element of face or voice must have struck Mallory as disturbing, for he put a hand to her shoulder. 'Oramen?' he repeated more loudly. 'Let go!'

'I – cannot. He sees. He holds me – '

'Stop, Oramen!' Mallory was shaking her, trying to turn her away from the mirror, desperate to break the semi-trance. 'Free yourself – *now.*'

'He won't let me go!' Oramen's neck arched back, but her eyes remained fixed to the mirror's now-clouded surface; whatever terrified her was visible to her alone.

The next few moments seemed to Asher to pass in slow motion; she remembered rising from her chair with the intention of breaking the mirror with one of the silver candlesticks, and Mallory, too, was on his feet, standing behind Oramen. Then the seeress screamed, and at the same time the mirror exploded in a violent storm of glass as Asher dropped to the floor, raising her hands to protect her face and eyes from the sudden blast of deadly fragments.

For a time there was no sound at all in the room, only an ugly, frightening silence. Shakily, Asher took her hands from her face, releasing a shower of tiny splinters which had pierced the skin. Her hands were bleeding. She waited tremulously to see if there was more to come, but nothing happened and slowly she got to her feet, her left foot treading on a sliver of glass which cracked with a sound like a bell being rung.

'Mallory?'

'I'm here.' She blinked, turning towards him. There was blood on his face, but only from superficial cuts like her own.

'Oramen?'

The seeress was still sitting in her chair, head slumped low against her chest, much of her face hidden in the darkness. Asher reached out a tentative hand, then drew it back; Mallory put a finger to Oramen's throat, feeling for a pulse.

'She's dead,' he said dully.

'Her eyes!' The candles showed her the horror of needle-sharp splinters of glass piercing Oramen's eyes and face, an obscene vision.

'She died from shock, I think.'

'How did this happen? Lassar – '

He turned on her suddenly. 'You knew she was taking a risk, didn't you? So did she. Why did you let her do it? Why didn't you

294

tell me, or stop her yourself?'

Asher's own emotions, raw from shock, reeled under the injustice of the accusation. 'It was *her* choice, not mine; this is what she wanted. She knew the risk she ran, and still made up her mind to help us. It was not for me to tell her what she could or couldn't do.'

'Then you should have told me!' He seemed to have a need to blame someone. 'If you weren't prepared to take the responsibility, *I* was.'

'It's not for you to take!' she flung back at him. 'It was *her* life, *her* choice; perhaps this was the right time for her to die. And if you want to apportion blame, chose Lassar or Avorian instead of *me*!'

He was silenced, and she sensed the person he really blamed was himself.

Mylla had chosen to die quickly, with some dignity remaining to her, a rational choice. Oramen, too, had understood that choice. Asher glanced at the body of the seeress, wondering with what force Lassar had shattered the mirror. Was it the strength of the battle of wills between two diviners, Lassar and Oramen?

Her hands were shaking, and she quickly crossed her arms so that Mallory should not see them.

'She was a good and faithful servant to our clan, and a friend,' Mallory said stiffly, putting a hand on Oramen's still shoulder. 'Not you, Asher. Not you, but Avorian. I'm sorry.'

'We can find Vallis. Oramen *saw* enough.'

He, too, seemed to find the prospect of action less painful than coping with loss. 'We can go through the lists of his properties I made. The girl must be in one of them. I've a plan of the city.'

'But first we must prepare Oramen for the burning grounds,' Asher reminded him gently. 'She deserves greater dignity than this.'

'Stay with her.' Mallory touched Oramen's face, his own displaying the same icy determination Asher had seen on it when he rescued her from Lewes, then he moved away. 'She will receive the honour that is due to her.'

'What have you done with him?' Honora demanded, her voice rising dangerously as she took a step forward. '*What have you done with my son?*' She gave Asher a sharp look. 'Send her away!'

Mallory hesitated, but Asher shook her head and tactfully retreated from the room, leaving him alone in the office with his sister-in-law. 'What are you talking about, Honora?' he asked, with less than his usual patience.

'Kirin – he's disappeared! No one has seen him since the morning meal.'

'Not again! Surely he's just avoiding a dull morning with his tutor?' Mallory suggested wearily. 'Have the grounds been searched?'

'He promised me he would not!' She turned to make sure the door of the office was shut, then went on: '*What have you done with him?*'

'Honora, calm yourself,' he began, trying to avert the threatened storm.

She turned a tear-ravaged face to his, her tongue no longer constrained by convention in the face of her loss. 'Who is *she*?' she demanded. 'And what is she doing here? Have you brought your mistress to this house to supplant me, and at the same time you take my son so *you* can take his father's place? Is that what you want?'

Mallory bit back the retort he wanted to make. 'You must know what you say is nonsense,' he said calmly. 'Your anxiety makes you unreasonable, which I understand and can make allowances for, but you *must* not say such things.'

'Why not?' She was shaking from the force of her emotions. 'You care nothing for me, nor for my sons; you want us gone from here, out of your sight, so that you can do what you will, without hindrance. My family warned me it would be so when Kelham was gone, but I tried not to believe it.'

'*Enough!*' Impatience made him sharper than he intended, but the single word was effective; Honora was silenced. 'Believe me,' he carried on, 'I wish my brother were alive – more so than you, if such a thing were possible. I have no desire to take your son's inheritance, whatever you may prefer to think.' The incredulous look she gave him was hardly complimentary. 'And these accusations do not help us find him, if he is really lost. Have you any idea where he might have gone?'

She struggled to control herself. 'None. He was here, in the house – '

'Then he must have left it. Did no one see him – not his brother or sister?' She shook her head mutely and Mallory felt himself grow cold; if the boy really had disappeared and was not hiding somewhere, if he was in Avorian's hands . . .

Honora began to cry and Mallory suppressed a sigh, wishing she had more restraint; her tears seemed to bring her no relief, and he found himself unable to offer the words of consolation she required. What was it Asher had said: 'He'll find a weapon to use against you.' Had Avorian already done so?

'Honora, stop, please.' He was growing angry in the face of her continued tears, helpless to halt them. 'Tell me, have you asked the servants to search for him?'

She swallowed, gulping back sobs. 'In the house, the grounds, and on the hill. No one has seen anything, and Crisa and Lake tell me he said nothing to them about running off.'

'Then all is being done that can be, at this stage.' He eyed her warily, but she seemed to have stopped crying, at least for now. 'Has this happened before? I mean has he gone missing for more than just an hour or so?'

'No.' She looked up resentfully.

'Tell me, why do you have this conviction that I want to take Kelham's place?' He had had enough of her accusations, and decided the time had come for plain speaking.

The question shocked her from her misery. 'Because my family said you would – and Kirin is only a child,' she burst out rather incomprehensibly.

'Then listen to me for a change.' He had her full attention. 'First, I have no desire for this life in Venture; it was forced on me by Kelham's death, and I regret it deeply. Second, I believe I owe you an apology, for I know you offered to discuss the business of our clan but I was less than tactful, not understanding your interest.' Her mouth opened in stunned surprise, but he went on: 'They tell me you are more than competent in the trade. Is that the case?'

'I – Kelham always said so. My father taught me all he knew.'

'Then why, given that intelligence, do you waste your time and mine in this ridiculous fashion?'

'How dare you?' she began. A change came over her face. 'Mallory, did you mean what you said? Swear it to me – about Kirin.'

'You have my word.'

Her eyes searched his face, then she nodded. Mallory saw, to his own surprise, that at last she believed him. 'Then I must apologize also, brother,' she said carefully. 'I thought, from your manner, you wanted to be rid of us all, so you could take what we had. But,' and the anxiety was back in her voice, 'then where is Kirin?'

'I will find him.' Awkwardly, he took her hands between his, liking her more for her honesty than he had till now. 'I will do everything I can.'

She sniffed, making herself seem much younger. 'I shall leave and not delay you.' But at the door she looked back, her fine eyes filled with pain. 'Please, brother, find him!'

Mallory could only repeat his assurances, but a cold hand clutched his heart. Had Avorian taken the boy?

'We've asked at every house on the hill, but no one has seen him,' Pars answered nervously, several hours later. 'I've sent down to the harbour, in case he should have gone there, and to the warehouse.'

'Keep trying.' Even though the search seemed futile, Mallory felt a need to make the attempt. 'And thank you, Pars.'

The clerk hesitated, then said anxiously: 'Councillor, it is impossible he left the grounds; the gatekeeper says he did not leave his post for a moment, and the boy did not pass the gate.'

'Then he must have climbed a wall.' Pars' face brightened. 'Have the house searched again. Perhaps he's found a hiding place somewhere – some cupboard.'

'Certainly, Councillor.' Pars retreated to give the orders. Mallory, however, slumped down at his desk, uncertain for once what course of action was still open to him. If Avorian meant to force him to abandon the search for Vallis, on pain of Kirin's life, what would he do? What *could* he do? Where did his main responsibility lie? Kirin was his brother's son, in his care, and he could not abandon that duty.

What if it had been Asher?

It was an impossible choice. Duty might argue he should ignore the personal in pursuit of the greater good, but the cost was too high; he did not think he could live with himself if Kirin died, simply because he had the misfortune to be Mallory's nephew.

Night fell with no word of the boy. Sedated, Honora slept, but Mallory permitted himself no such luxury; it was not a sentimental affection for Kirin that moved him – if it came to it, he preferred the boy's sister and younger brother – but that Kelham had consigned his family to Mallory's care, to be his first duty. Which was more important: their lives, at any price, or his duty to the Dominus and his country? Either way, he would fail one of them, and he must live with himself whichever he chose.

And if I give in, choosing that duty, what will Asher do? Will she, too, submit, and let Avorian have his way, or will she fight? But he knew the answer already; she had given her word to Mylura and would not break it. If he chose Kirin, he would lose Asher, too. Unfairly, he contrasted her with his sister-in-law, wishing Honora had one-tenth of Asher's courage, until he realized that he had been thinking of Honora as little more than a piece of property bequeathed to him against his will, *his* to command. Her children made her subject, having to rely on him and his goodwill for their inheritance, for their very existence; why, then, should she trust him or in his good faith? Her independent life had ended with the death of her husband – small wonder she resented his own existence.

He was still at his desk when the morning bell tolled the end of curfew, but despite the long night he had come to no firm decision. As the sun rose, he was tempted to ask Asher for her help, if only to discuss the problem, but that was the coward's way, to make her responsible for his own choice.

This was a choice that only he could make.

Asher pored over the city plan looking for Cavern Street, found it, and shook her head.

It was nowhere near the river. That could not be it. She looked down the list of Avorian's properties, relieved to find she was nearing the end at last; since she was unable to help Mallory in the search for the missing Kirin – she could not even leave the house with any degree of safety – she intended to reap some benefit from Oramen's sacrifice and discover the house she had *seen*, but so far without success.

The Street of Gifts – hardly! Even Avorian would not keep his intended wife among those dens of prostitution. It would not be safe. She was no longer surprised to find Avorian owned a large investment in the street; doubtless he employed slave labour to better his returns. From the man she now knew him to be, anything was possible.

A building in the fish market looked more promising, but the plan showed it could not be the place she sought; there was no inn near, and it was too far from the river.

A bunch of ivy . . . of course, a shop-sign! A vintner's! She sighed, realized she could have saved herself several hours of searching if she had remembered it before. There were two such properties on the remaining list, and she sought the first, only to find it on the wrong side of the city.

Then this must be it. She ran a finger over the plan, looking for the Street of Approach, and found it; the vintner's shop *was* beside an inn, marked clearly on the plan. It was high in the north-west of the city, near the Sair Gate, on the borders of the old quarter, overlooking the river and the bridge. She sat back on her heels, flushed with temporary success.

'What are you doing?'

'Oh – Mallory!' Asher jumped to her feet. 'Is there any news?'

The small parlour was at the rear of the house on the ground floor, out of the way. He came in and shut the door behind him, shaking his head. 'None. Asher?' She looked at him enquiringly. 'Have you any suggestions?'

It was obvious he had not slept; she felt a stab of sympathy for him, understanding his dilemma. 'I sent word to Essa and the others, to keep their eyes open for the boy,' she said. 'Just in case.'

'Won't that put them in danger?'

'Why should it? This has nothing to do with Vallis, and in any case I had to let them know I was safe. Besides,' she went on reluctantly, 'we – I – may need their help.'

Mallory frowned. 'For what?'

'I think I've found where Vallis is hidden.'

He looked as if she had struck him.

'Don't worry,' she said quickly. 'I won't tell you; I wouldn't put you in that position. But I had to know.'

'So I may lose you, too?'

Silence descended. Asher, searching Mallory's face, wondered if she had misunderstood the implications of his last remark, then knew, with sudden certainty, that she had not. 'What if I leave your house?' she said awkwardly. 'Then you'd have one less worry.'

'And give Avorian another weapon to use against me?'

'I thought . . .' Asher began. Then, suddenly, 'What was that?'

'I don't know.' Mallory was already out of the room and heading towards the great hall. Asher followed at a run, hearing raised voices.

Had they found Kirin? She hoped, without much belief, that the boy was still alive. She reached the hall, then stopped.

Two men stood in the centre, surrounded by a group of household servants. Incredulously, Asher recognized first Lassar, as was his habit a pace behind his master, then, belatedly, Avorian. The Chief Councillor was smiling amiably at the crowd of onlookers, apparently enjoying their interested attention, looking over their heads to greet Mallory's arrival with every evidence of good humour.

'Chief Councillor.' Mallory's greeting was void of any emotion as he looked at the small, limp body supported in Avorian's arms.

'Councillor Mallory.' Avorian inclined his head, then held the boy out to the younger man. 'I think this is your missing nephew. Lassar discovered him. We were all most anxious to hear of his disappearance.'

Mallory took the slack body. The boy lay unnaturally still but Asher, watching, was first to observe the slow rise and fall of his boy's chest, and to note the relaxation of Mallory's lips as he, too, understood that Kirin was only asleep.

'I think he must have been given something to make him sleep,' Avorian continued easily. 'But Lassar assured me he will soon wake and recover.'

'Where did you find him?' Mallory asked.

'Lassar *saw* him in an empty house in the old quarter; naturally, knowing how anxious you would be, I asked him to search as soon as I was informed of your distress, and this was the result. Doubtless thieves took him, hoping for a heavy ransom.'

Mallory handed Kirin to one of the servants. 'Take him to his mother,' he ordered curtly. 'Tell her he will wake soon, and to stay with him. I will come and see how he is shortly.'

The bemused servant hurried away with his precious burden, but not before he shot his master a look of shocked surprise for his lack of gratitude to the Chief Councillor. Mallory recovered sufficiently to turn back to Avorian and speak a few words of thanks.

'Don't mention it. But I should be glad of a word with you in private, if you are not otherwise occupied?' Avorian's gaze flicked across to Asher. 'I shall, of course, understand if it is not possible.'

'It is convenient.' The servants were melting away now the excitement was at an end; only Pars and another clerk were left in the hall. Mallory gestured in the direction of the office. 'If you will come with me?'

Asher followed behind Lassar, watching Avorian's back with cold hatred, determined not to be excluded from the coming confrontation, but her grasp of events seemed to her tenuous in the extreme. Why should Avorian have Kirin abducted, only to return him in person? Had the whole scene been designed simply to prove to Mallory he had no defence against the Chief Councillor, like herself and Mylla?

She entered the office to find Lassar's bulging eyes upon her.

Chapter Sixteen

'What have you come to say?'

Avorian seated himself opposite Mallory, the desk between them; Lassar stood at his back and Asher moved to take up a similar position behind Mallory, letting her hand drop to his shoulder.

'I thought perhaps it was time we reached some agreement,' Avorian answered pleasantly. 'It is foolish for us to fight unnecessary battles, wasting our time and our energies.'

'Why did you abduct my nephew? To silence me?'

'I have returned him to you unharmed. Does that not speak for me?' Avorian leaned forward confidentially. 'He will remember nothing of where he has been. Yet I hope his disappearance was sufficient warning to you not to interest yourself too deeply in my affairs.'

Mallory wondered, briefly, if the easiest solution to the problem was simply to kill Avorian; he bore no weapon, but was familiar with other methods of killing drawn from the lands of the Dominion, and physically Lassar would be no sort of opponent. There was a flabbiness to him that bespoke indolence.

'I think not.' Avorian seemed to have read his thoughts, for he smiled. 'If you move a hand against me, you would live to regret it; not only is my presence here public knowledge, but several of my men wait outside the gates. I am, I believe, quite popular in this city for the present, while you are little known. Must I tell you what would happen in the event of my death?'

'No.' Mallory felt the pressure of Asher's fingers on his shoulder and forced himself to relax; he dared not endanger the lives of everyone in the household by a false move. 'Tell me,' he went on, changing the subject, 'where is the girl?'

'Quite safe, my dear Councillor.'

'From whom?'

Avorian inclined his head. 'From you and your friends.'

'Then hardly *safe*.'

'That, I think, is a matter of opinion. It occurs to me, Councillor, that you may be labouring under a misapprehension. You believe I have stolen the girl away for my own evil ends, but I know I have rescued her from certain death. I am our country's deliverer, not its destroyer.'

'No.'

He gave Mallory a look of pained surprise. 'How can you be so certain? Have you proof, then, of my evil intentions? Show me them, if you can.'

'If you believed what you say, you would not have ordered the murders of two of my friends. You could have told me the situation and bound me to keep silence; instead you use threats and violence to enforce your will. Your actions speak where your words would mislead.'

Avorian paused, considering the contention. 'Or it may be that we place a different value on those lives you mention,' he suggested at last. 'Who were they – a spying servant girl, and a seeress? What weight do their lives carry compared with the future, the destruction of Amrist's empire? Surely their destiny was to die, that we might win our freedom?'

Mallory was in no mood for verbal fencing. 'And Asher and myself? Do you see that as our destiny, too? All of us mere pawns in the game of the Fates?'

'Yes! If need be.' Mallory was startled by his obvious sincerity; the man believed what he was saying. 'I would regret your death, Councillor. I even spared this woman here because you value her, and so I, too, assign her worth.' Behind him, Mallory felt Asher stiffen. 'My destiny has always been to save our country, and I can allow no one to step in my shadow. You have been favoured by the Fates, and your woman, too, despite her sex; Lassar has *seen* this for me, but also that you represent a potential impediment to my design.'

'What gives you the right to determine the will of the Fates?' Asher asked, in a cold voice. 'You are only a man.'

'Did you speak?' Avorian looked at her in surprise and irritation, much, Mallory thought, as he might observe a dog standing on its hind legs. 'If I address you, you may respond, but otherwise you will remain silent.'

'You do not command me, Councillor. Not here, nor in any other place. I asked you a question. What is your answer?'

Avorian's eyes narrowed, and for a moment Mallory thought it easy to believe the man guilty of dealing death with a casual hand.

'Do not think, mistress, that because you still live you retain a value to me. On the contrary, your purpose is exhausted. You may think yourself one of Fortune's children by reason of the circumstances of your birth, of which my servants have told me, yet to me those such as you should not be permitted to live; you are anti-Fates. However,' he went on, returning his attention to Mallory, 'I will explain myself to *you*, for I shall require your support in the future. You are a lucky man, Councillor, almost as fortunate as myself, and everything I touch turns to gold.'

Mallory could think of several responses to this arrogant boast, but voiced none of them. 'Why, then?'

Avorian's eyes glowed with a curious inner exultation as he began to speak. 'When I was a young man like yourself, before the invasion, like so many in the city I climbed to the citadel to consult the Oracle. Even at my birth the omens were seen to be favourable, and I was a rich man before I was twenty, but I had no heir, the one impediment to my happiness, for I loved my wife and had no desire to put her from me. I wished to know whether I should have a son.'

'And?'

A shadow crossed Avorian's face. 'The Oracle promised me no children by Katriane; that was my sorrow. But nonetheless I was vouchsafed more – much more. For while she might bear me no living child, it was given to me to be father of our country.'

Again, it was plain he spoke the truth, or the truth as he saw it, and Mallory experienced a momentary qualm. 'What was this prophecy?'

'You shall hear.' Avorian closed his eyes for a moment. 'Rarely has the Oracle spoken so plainly as in my case, or shown so clearly what I must do. It was the same year that Vallis was born, shortly before the Oracle itself proclaimed her our hope against the Kamiri. Even then I knew that it was *I* who must preserve her from Amrist, that it was *I* who would save us all! Listen:

"*Destroying and preserving both,*
The wolf, through cunning, not through strength,
Sustains the sleeping Bear.
He mingles with the coming dark,
Invisible; he gathers up
The only fruitful seed and nutures it –"

Is that not plain enough for you? My clan symbol is the wolf, myself therefore the preserver. When Omen fell to the Kamiri, I had long been ready, and it was I who took the girl from her father's house, I who have hidden her all these years while her brothers died and her father's luck failed him. Thus the prophecy that she will save us will be fulfilled through me.'

'What do you intend to do with her?'

Avorian frowned as if he did not care for the question. 'I shall marry her and father a dynasty. I will rule in her name, as the Fates intended.'

'That's a lie!' Asher said angrily. 'There will be no children. Instead of saving us, you will bring further destruction on us all! What else did the Oracle say? Tell us that.'

Avorian did not reply. Mallory asked: 'Was there more?'

The Chief Councillor made a dismissive gesture. 'There was, but of no relevance.'

'I should like to know it, nonetheless.'

'Very well.' Avorian was tightlipped. 'Then hear:

"The grey mask shrouds her from all sight.
Yet, wolf, beware, lest hunger turn to greed;
The cub must wake itself and shed its furry skin
Before it spreads its wings and flies aloft."

It is meaningless – a mere warning.'

'Greed,' Asher whispered, and Mallory remembered the words the Oracle had said to him: *'The leopard hunts for hunger, not for greed.'* Not for self-interest, but for the common good. It was true that Avorian had saved Vallis from Amrist, but the course on which he was determined would destroy her; his hunger had become greed for the sake of ambition. His seed was barren, and if he married Vallis the line would die with her, and the imbalance of luck in the world would never be righted.

'And you, Lassar, what is your interpretation?' Mallory asked, looking beyond Avorian to the diviner, who stirred uneasily.

'There is no Fate so definite it may not be altered, save death,' he said softly. 'Yet my master is a man of great good fortune, and it is not for me to question the sayings of the Oracle.'

'Quite so. It was the Oracle who named the first Dominus, in whose line runs the good fortune of our country. How can you say it is *right* that a man who can father no children should wed into the last of that direct line?' Mallory demanded. 'When in that seed lies our future?'

Avorian's expression no longer held any hint of amiability. His was a cold anger that expressed itself in eyes and voice, not in physical manifestations, but was no less dangerous for that. He held himself very still, and Mallory was disturbed by what he saw in the man, the determination born of self-deception that was the mark of the fanatic.

'It was Katriane, not I, who was barren,' he said coolly. 'The Fates willed it so, that when I marry again there should be no son of mine to argue his share of our inheritance. Vallis will be the mother of my children, my will her will. She has been trained to obey the dictates of the Fates and will not repine when I reveal her true parentage; she will understand what must be.'

'Are you sure?' Mallory saw a smile briefly lighten Asher's thin face.

'A woman's place in this world is to live through her husband and her children; that is the reason for which she was created, that we, not bound by nature, should thus be free to assume the greater cares,' Avorian answered her shortly. 'A lesson you have failed to learn, mistress. Better for you you had stayed on the land with your true husband than interest yourself in the affairs of men!'

'"The grey mare is often the better horse",' Asher quoted calmly. 'From the words of the Oracle, it sounds as if Vallis must remember for herself who she really is: "*The cub must wake itself*".' Mallory recognized the campaigning glint in her eye and hastily elected to intervene.

'What do you intend to do now?'

'With you?' Avorian relaxed again. 'For the moment, nothing. Why should I? I bear you no ill-will, Councillor, you have no power to upset my design, nor cause. You have heard *why* I told the girl. You will not find her.' Asher's hand tightened on his shoulder; Mallory said nothing. 'Not even another diviner could locate her, warded as she is by Lassar who is best of them all, as your seeress discovered to her cost. Do not waste another in searching.'

'Then why all this – *charade*? The abduction of my nephew?'

'Lassar tells me you continue to represent a possible complication.' Avorian frowned. 'And I have a proposition to put to you.'

'Which is?'

'To you, I am willing to offer a position in my new government, once our land is free from the shadow of the Dominion.' Avorian allowed Mallory a moment to contemplate his good fortune, without result. 'We will need men of your calibre, those who have proven themselves able and gifted by the Fates. I will even offer you a choice.'

'I see. And in exchange I say nothing and cease to search for the girl? What if I refuse?'

'Then I will ruin you, and your clan with you.'

It was not the response Mallory expected, and he looked up

sharply.

'It can be done, with Lassar's help,' Avorian continued indifferently. 'He can read the tides of fortune more ably than any, most of all those concerning the flows of gold – I could forestall you in any trade. And there would be assistance from my men. Ships sink; warehouses burn. You have a day in which to make your decision.'

'And Asher?' Mallory was careful not to show how shaken he felt.

Avorian's gaze flickered to her, then back to Mallory. 'You may be unaware that a warrant for her arrest was issued today, for embezzlement of city funds. I myself signed it this morning after an anonymous informant suggested a careful investigation of her Treasury ledgers. It seems there were a few – shall we say – irregularities.' Mallory glanced at Asher, but she displayed no surprise at the news; inwardly he sighed, wondering what else she had failed to tell him. 'If she leaves the city I give my word I will not pursue her, nor inform as to her whereabouts, so long as she does not return. She, too, may have one day in which to decide.'

Asher remained uncharacteristically silent, looking at Lassar. Mallory rose to his feet. 'Then if that is your final word,' he said stiffly, 'we will give you our responses in the morning.'

'Think long and hard, Councillor,' Avorian advised, rising also. 'Such a chance will never come your way again.'

Signalling Lassar to precede him, he took his departure without a backward glance. Asher leaned against the desk as if her legs would no longer support her weight; Mallory knew how she felt.

'So, we only have tonight,' she said quietly. 'If we have that.'

'Don't you want to consider the alternative?'

'There is none, you know that.'

'You said you knew where the girl was hidden,' Mallory commented abruptly. 'Could we get her away tonight?'

Asher smiled. 'I think so, if we can hire helpers. Are you willing to spend rather a lot of money?'

'Of course, but on what? Which reminds me – what is this about a warrant for your arrest?' The news should have shocked him deeply, but now it seemed a relatively minor inconvenience. 'What have you been doing?'

'That was one of the things I wanted to talk to you about.' She looked a little embarrassed. 'But first we need to make arrangements to leave the city tonight, or at first light tomorrow. If we can get a message to Essa, she and Margit can make the arrangements for us, and get the travel passes too.' Listening to her outline her plans, Mallory's mood brightened; it might, after all, be possible. 'Essa will need money as well – about twenty gold pieces – for a covered cart and four horses; we can't take any from your stables. She can organize supplies for us. The only other problem is that we need a diversion for Avorian and Lassar tonight, some method of keeping their attention away from us.'

He thought for a moment. 'I have an idea. Will you risk telling Essa what the passes and so on are for? Wouldn't that put her in danger?'

'She'll guess at some of the truth, but I won't tell her about Avorian. I must speak to her before we leave Venture.' For a moment bleak sorrow surfaced in her face. 'I have to tell her about Mylla.'

Quickly Mallory asked: 'What other help are you suggesting we need?'

'I was coming to that.' She bit her lip. 'I never told you about Stern, did I? He's one of my Treasury colleagues – the one who informed against me. But if you're willing to pay, I think he and his friends could be very useful to us tonight.'

Mallory could no longer restrain his curiosity. 'Tell me more,' he suggested. 'What are these irregularities Avorian mentioned?' Having made his decision, he found himself oddly free from doubt. All the anxiety and indecision he had suffered while Kirin was missing had gone, leaving him to deal, as Asher was, with the practical points resulting from his decision – the need to arrange for Pars to manage the day-to-day running of the business until he should return; he had developed a high opinion of the young man's capability. Perhaps he should give some authority to his sister-in-law, too, to encourage her to continue to believe in his good intentions.

Asher was embarrassed as she explained, her face rather pink. 'I should have told you before,' she began awkwardly, 'how I helped Stern and the others steal from Avorian's warehouse . . .' She went on with her tale, with occasional prompting, detailing the events of a night which filled Mallory, listening, with a combination of hilarity and horror.

'And so I thought,' she concluded, carefully not looking at him, 'that if we paid them, they might help us. A pick-lock and two fighters are just what we need. If you don't mind?' she added quickly.

'Mind? Why should I mind?' He was only just managing not to laugh. 'It's an excellent plan. I'm only glad your acquaintance in

Venture extends to so many useful and interesting people!'

Her lips quivered. 'I shall be only too happy to introduce them.'

'Just tell me how much I'm going to have to pay for the privilege!' And when she told him, he did laugh out loud; only Asher would have worked out so carefully the precise sum needed to bribe a pack of bandits. He wiped his eyes, feeling considerably better. 'I used to think coming to Venture would be dull. Whatever else, you certainly have a talent for making life interesting.'

She grinned, but sobered instantly. 'We must get on. There's a lot to arrange before tonight.'

'Lead on.' He waved a casual hand. He had never worked with a partner before; a ship was no place for joint ventures. It was coming as a pleasant surprise to him to discover just how enjoyable and effective such a relationship could be.

Haravist, the Kamiri governor, held out the offending paper between thumb and forefinger, his expression filled with distaste; he raised his head to an arrogant height and gave a signal to the waiting guard. 'Let him enter.'

Avorian strode forward, stiff with fury at the peremptory summons to the governor's residence. Lassar followed in his wake, a mere shadow of his master. Avorian's gaze flicked sideways from wall to wall, observing the twin lines of watching guards, then settled finally on the stately grey man who occupied the chair in the elevated section of the room, three steep steps separating his exalted person from those of lesser, and lower, status. 'You wished to see me?' he asked abruptly.

Haravist's nostrils flared briefly at the insolent tone. 'I have received certain information,' he said ponderously, waving the piece of paper in his hand, grey skin dark against white. 'Concerning the tribute. That your own contribution of fifteen thousand pieces has not, and will not, be included when the ships sail for Javarin in thirteen days. What have you to say?'

'What nonsense is this?' Avorian reached for the paper, but it was withdrawn before he could take it; furious, he let his hand drop and stepped back. 'From what quarter did you receive this information?'

'It bears the seal of this city.' Haravist sounded bored, but his expression was cold. 'You told me the tribute was already gathered, but I have no proof this is so.'

'You had my word!' Avorian's eyes glittered angrily. 'In this city, that is sufficient, I believe.'

'Do you so?' The tone was even more offensive than the words. 'But I desire proof, Chief Councillor. As you are aware, if any part of the tribute is not delivered in full, the treaty with our Lord Amrist fails. Thus I cannot neglect this warning; it is my duty to demand proof from you. I am governor here, and such is my right.'

'This is a trick, the work of an enemy.' Avorian managed to sound calmer, perhaps remembering where he was. 'If you wish to count the monies for yourself, it may be arranged in the morning, if that will satisfy you?'

Haravist gave him a contemptuous, empty smile. 'I am almost convinced, Councillor. Yet – not quite. Why should an enemy do this, when it can so easily be disproved? It would not be the first time one of your rank has taken advantage of his position. No, I think the task is best begun now, as this letter suggests.' He tapped a line on the paper with a pointed nail. 'There are, I presume, scales in the Treasury, and I have an assayer among my staff.'

'But it will take at least two hours, even using scales. Why such haste?'

'My order disturbs you?' Haravist did not attempt to disguise his satisfaction. 'It is by no means late; the curfew bell will not sound for three more hours. Is there some reason for your hesitation, one you have neglected to tell me?'

Trapped, Avorian could only bow his head. 'Very well, Governor. It shall be done,' he said coldly. 'The Treasurer will be summoned. And now, if I have your permission to retire? I shall await the outcome with interest, but no anxiety.'

'No.' The flat negative made Avorian look up sharply, but the governor's bland face told him nothing. 'I have decided you will accompany us.'

'*When*,' and Avorian emphasized his use of the word, 'the count is complete, and is seen to be accurate, I shall request your assistance to move against the instigator of this libel!' He turned to Lassar, but the diviner only shook his head.

'*If* that is so, you may have all the aid you require.' Haravist placed his hands on the arms of his chair and rose to his feet in a smooth movement; the waiting guard was instantly at attention, forming columns to either side as he stepped down from the platform, gesturing with a casual forefinger for Avorian to follow. After a moment's resistance he did so, falling angrily into step behind the tall governor, a surprisingly slight figure amongst the Kamiri.

Lassar blinked; he, too, was certain who had made the

accusation, and his gift had already revealed to him what alteration in the odds resulted from the move. These revelations, however, he kept prudently to himself, for despite the shifts in his master's fortunes, they remained favourable overall.

The outside of the Perseverance Inn was unappealing, even for the old quarter; an old structure, in an area prosperous during the hey-day of the Oracle trade but now showing signs of terminal decay, peeling paint and cracked plaster gave the building a depressingly dingy appearance. A muddy cobbled alley led the way to a stableyard at the rear, and Asher peered down it, wrinkling her nose in disgust at the pungent smell that wafted towards the street. The three storeys of the adjoining wine shop looked hardly more salubrious, in particular since the windows and door facing the street had recently been boarded shut, as if the house was no longer occupied, and Mallory found himself a prey to sudden doubt.

'Do you think anyone could have followed us here?' Asher asked, glancing round at the constant flow of people along the street. Despite the change in her appearance – her hair restored to its natural colour and cut short as any sailor's, her own clothes exchanged for Ish's loose breeches, shirt and jerkin – she felt conspicuous and ill at ease.

'I doubt it, I'm not sure I'd have known you myself.' Mallory, too, looked different; his hair and eyebrows had been powdered white, and he was dressed as a casual labourer, in thick sailcloth trousers and tunic. 'I didn't notice anyone, and with Lassar occupied along with his master, we should have time when even he can't *see* us.'

Asher grinned. 'That was a stroke of genius, but the governor is only likely to keep them an hour or so for the count. Are you ready?'

A particularly loud roaring came from the inn's interior. Mallory shrugged. 'As I'll ever be. This isn't a place I would have chosen to bring you.'

The interior of the inn was, if anything, worse than the exterior; it was plain cleanliness was not a high priority for the landlord. The floor was filthy, littered with discarded pieces of food and other dirt, and the tables were sticky with spilled ale. There was an unpleasant, and fortunately unidentifiable, smell to the taproom, compounded of human sweat and something even less appealing; it was also surprisingly empty, considering the amount of noise still audible.

'Where *is* everyone?'

'In the cellar, I should think. It sounds as if there's a dog-fight going on down there.' Mallory gestured towards an open door towards the rear of the room. 'Can you see your friends?'

'Yes, over in that corner.' Asher pointed discreetly. 'You see that big man? That's Bull, and the small one is Club.'

'They don't seem to have recognized you.'

She was nervous now the moment had come, less certain of Stern's compliance. 'I hope – '

He loosed the sword in its scabbard, hidden in the folds of the cloak he carried over his left arm; the governor had forbidden weapons within the city walls after the last uprising, but Mallory preferred to keep his blade as a private precaution. 'Come on.'

The four men sat with their heads close together at a table facing the door, glancing up when anyone new entered the taproom; only Stern's face registered suitable astonishment as Asher and Mallory approached them and made to sit down.

'I almost didn't know you. And who's he?' Stern cast a wary eye over Mallory's breadth and put a restraining hand on Club's arm. 'It's all right, this is the girl.' Hare turned to stare at Asher, eyes widening; Bull gave a grunt, then nodded.

'A companion,' Asher said briefly.

'Your cashier friend said there'd be something in this for us.' He was evidently suspicious, peering beyond them to see if it was a trap. 'Why'd you want us?'

'I said I needed your help in return for money, and I do.' Asher touched Mallory's arm, and he withdrew a large leather pouch from the pocket of his trousers and laid it on the table. 'This is half. You'll get the rest in the morning, if you agree.'

'How much?' Club asked, fingering the blade in his hands. 'And what for?'

'An hour's work for forty gold apiece.' Mallory kept his right hand on the pouch. 'There's eighty in here, the rest you can collect from my clerk in the morning. It's ready for you, if I give you the word.'

'And why should I trust you?' Club demanded suspiciously. 'What if the girl's informed on us?'

'Why shouldn't we just take her and give her to the guard?' Bull asked, a beefy hand creeping towards the pouch. 'And take this, too.'

'You'd not get more than a few coppers for her; and you'd not get this at all.' Mallory displayed his sword hilt. Bull's questing hand beat a hasty retreat. 'In addition to this, you can have whatever you can steal. What do you say?' Mallory looked at Stern. 'Is it a bargain?'

Stern licked his lips, his gaze drawn to the pouch, narrow features sharp with cupidity. 'Done.' He made a mark like a cross on the table, sealing the bargain, then looked at Asher. 'That's the end of our quarrel, agreed? You hold no grudge against me for informing on you?'

She nodded, placing her fingers flat on the table. 'Agreed. And I've said nothing about the warehouse, and will say nothing.'

'You?' Mallory looked at Club.

'What d'you want done?'

Mallory shook his head. 'Only once you accept.' He gave the bag a shake, producing a satisfyingly heavy clink.

Club held the knife so the point touched the table, then made the same mark with it Stern had drawn. 'Done. There's no quarrel between us.' He shot Asher a look of deep dislike. 'Bull?'

'Deal.' He, too, signed the bargain, Hare following suit after only brief reluctance. Mallory signed to Asher, who leaned forward, keeping her voice low.

'We need to find a way in to the vintner's shop next to this inn; we also need to know how easy it is to get out in a hurry, by the garden if necessary, and we need to know now.'

'Right.' Without another word, Club got to his feet and made for a door to the left of the inn's entrance, disappearing from sight.

'That leads to the stables,' Stern offered. 'He's good, he'll get what you want. What are you after in this shop? It's closed.'

'A girl.' Mallory saw Hare look puzzled. 'We think she's being held in a room at the back, probably the top floor.'

'What is it – a ransom?' Bull asked sullenly. 'You'll not get much from those folk!' He spat. 'There's no money in this quarter, not since the Oracle trade dropped off. And what makes you think she's in there, anyway?'

'It's not a ransom. The girl is a prisoner, and the rest is none of your business.' He hoped the explanation would satisfy Bull, who looked as if he might be having second thoughts.

'Why'd you want us in on this?' Stern asked Asher. 'You've no cause to do us any favours. What's in it for you?'

'You're the only ones I know with the right – shall we say – *skills*?' she suggested. 'You may be thieves, Stern, but no worse. As I said, I'll bear no grudge. I'm leaving Venture tonight in any case.'

Hare, who had been observing Mallory closely for some time,

said suddenly: 'I recognize you. I thought I did. You were down at the harbour when the new governor arrived.'

'Then you can assure your friends they'll be paid.' Hare glanced uncertainly from Mallory to Asher, nodded, and was silent. 'I've made arrangements with my clerk; if I give you a word, speak it to him and he'll pay you the remainder of the money.'

'Swear it?' Bull said, in tones of quiet menace.

'On my life.' The big man nodded, satisfied. 'Asher says you're good in a fight.'

'Fair. Club's better.' The big man chuckled. 'You saw those sleeves of his? They're weighted with metal balls. When he swings them, they go down like ninepins.'

Mallory, who had been intrigued by the extravagantly long sleeves of Club's shirt, raised an enquiring eyebrow. 'Old sailor, is he?'

'Some years back. Said he learned the trick in Petormin.' Bull plainly admired his friend's unusual skill. 'Very useful for a small man like Club.'

'No doubt that explains his name,' Mallory observed blandly.

When he returned soon afterward, it was clear Club had used the time to best advantage; he looked eager as he sat down at the table, eyes glowing.

'There's half a dozen men in the garden of the shop – mostly armed. The wall between the stables and the garden is manageable down by the river, at a push.'

'And how do we get in?' Mallory asked; he had hoped for fewer guards.

Club gave him a nod. 'Easy as wink, with a bit of help from Hare here. There's a door in the inn cellar, see, where the landlord gets in – or got – his supplies from next door. Hare can open it quick as you like. All we need is a bit of disruption downstairs – it's crowded for the fight. Stern can arrange that.' He was enjoying himself, taking a professional pride in the planning. 'There's a boat moored on the river bank at the far end of the garden next door, too. We can use that after if need be.'

'You think it can be done?'

'I'll not say I'm not curious. I never knew guards at a wine shop before, especially not in this quarter.' Club met Mallory's gaze with unusual candour. 'But, yes, it can be done, with our help.'

Asher, who had remained silent, realizing Mallory was better suited to deal with the four than herself, felt a surge of nervous energy; this was their one and only chance. She tried to focus on her gift, to *see* whether it would show her the most likely outcome, but, as so often, she could make little of the tangled strains.

If Stern had never trapped her into his thieving, they would have had no chance at all. It was as if the Fates had planned it all.

'I would guess we've only an hour, Asher,' Mallory murmured. She nodded, her mouth suddenly dry. To the others, he gestured toward the stairs leading down to the cellar. 'Now's the time to earn your fee.'

Club gathered up the heavy pouch, weighing it in his hand, then thrust it down the front of his jacket, ignoring Stern's hasty protest. 'Ready.'

The cellar was crowded, most of the men gathered around a deep pit dug into the floor from which came full-throated baying and a few agonized yelps. There were two dogs in the pit: one massive brute, white, with a flat face and sides covered with old scars, and another, black, as tall in the chest but less solid, plainly the novice of the pair.

'The money's mostly on the white,' Club murmured as they edged forwards, through the crowd, for the door leading to the shop was on the far side of the pit.

'What are you going to do?' Asher asked.

'Leave it to Stern.'

Hare was in position, the rest grouped round him, hiding him from view. At a gesture, Stern turned toward the pit and whispered something in the ear of a tall man watching the fight with an anxious eye; he muttered something in return. Stern moved away and repeated the exercise a few more times as the yelps from the pit increased in volume. Asher was glad she could not see what was happening, finding such entertainment obscene.

A shout went up from one corner.

'The fight's a fix – the black's been doped!'

Other voices took up the cry – mostly, Asher guessed, those who had wagered the black to win – opposed by the larger section of the crowd favouring the white. Within a short space of time a different sort of fight was underway, the crowd transformed from spectators to participants in what was rapidly becoming a riot. Hare pulled at Asher's arm, and she obligingly placed the picklock in the keyhole of the door; a prickling told her it was warded, but the mechanism was easily disarmed and she nodded, then relinquished her place. Hare had the door open in moments. No one paid them any attention as they slipped through in single file, pulling the door to as Stern emerged from the throng, only a little out of breath; he had picked up an oil lantern somewhere on his travels, which he held up triumphantly.

'Where now?' he asked.

The cellar of the wine shop was much as Asher had expected; row upon row of barrels, flanked by racks of empty glass bottles waiting to be filled. The air was cool, the brick floor damp and slippery as she walked carefully toward the stairwell.

'There's a lot of stock here for a shop that's shut,' Bull murmured, testing one of the barrels and finding it full. 'What's our next move?'

'Up. I don't know how many people there'll be on the other floors, and there may be wards. I'd better go first, then Hare.' Mallory put out a protesting hand, then drew it back. Asher gave him a quick, reassuring smile. 'There may be guards, too.'

Club unfurled his sleeves and gave both an experimental whirl, adding another arm length to his own; the weights swished loudly. Deftly, he caught the ends and held them ready, then stepped behind Hare.

The door was locked but not warded, and they emerged on to the next floor into darkness, where there was a smell of cooking and spilled wine, slightly acrid. The shop building was shallow, despite its broad frontage, and the open ground floor offered few hiding places; Club, moving without sound, did a quick survey and pronounced the floor empty, but pointed a hand to the stairs.

'Men up there,' he whispered. 'Can't tell how many.'

Bull was growing impatient. 'Why're we waiting? Let's get on.'

'I'd better lead again.' Asher brushed past him, glad Mallory's presence seemed to have curbed Bull's excess of familiarity. She felt no warning as she set foot on the stairs and gestured the others to follow, then fell victim to over-confidence as her foot encountered a simple trip wire halfway up. Instantly, a bell rang overhead. Heavy footsteps came from along the passage on the upper floor, and a voice called out: 'Ware, intruders!'

I never thought of anything as prosaic as that – stupid of me. Asher stepped back, knowing herself useless in a fight.

'That's torn it,' Club said calmly.

Mallory, Bull and Club barely had time to reach the head of the stairs before their opponents came into view; there were six of them in all, but the narrowness of the passage permitted only three abreast: a tall swordsman, a second man almost the Bull's size, armed with a heavy cudgel, and a knife-fighter whom Club downed with a blow from one of his weighted sleeves before he had time to take up his stance. Behind the first rank posed a second, another swordsman, a longstaff-fighter, and another armed with the short, curved blade used in Asir. Asher, Hare and Stern had perforce to watch, none of them much use against professional soldiers, but Club slipped between the two remaining of the first rank while Mallory engaged the swordsman and Bull, with a look of pleasurable expectation, closed with the large man.

'What about the guard outside?' Asher whispered to Stern, keeping an eye on Mallory, who seemed to be coping with his opponent, despite the disadvantage of having his back to the stairs.

'Bull and Club'll have this finished soon then they can guard the rear. You watch.' Stern's confidence in his associates was justified by Bull's rapid victory over the cudgeller before he moved down the passage to assist Club, to whom the longstaff specialist posed something of a problem. Mallory, having disarmed his opponent, promptly knocked him hard on the head, leaving only two of the guards standing.

'Mallory – that's Jerr!' Asher called out to him, for she had only just seen the second man standing guard in the passage, which was rather dark. At her cry, both men looked up, just as one of Club's whirling sleeves caught Jerr on the side of his head; he fell heavily to the floor and did not stir.

'I can't kill him for you,' Mallory said grimly, as Bull dealt with the last, now demoralized, guard. 'Not unconscious, much though he deserves it.'

'No.' A primitive lust for vengeance swept through her, but Asher struggled not to succumb, not to prove herself as low a creature as the downed man. Let the Fates deal with him, she told herself fiercely; no one so purely evil could play the odds forever.

'Bull, Stern.' Club was beckoning. 'We go down,' and he pointed, 'and keep off the others.'

'All right.' Mallory reached out a hand to Asher. 'You, and Hare – quickly. We've not much time left.'

Asher followed him down the corridor; the floorboards were bare and gave out protesting creaks as they walked. The guards had been engaged in a game before their arrival, evidenced by overturned chairs and a table littered with cards thrown face-down in one of the rooms to the left.

'I'll see if these stairs are passable.' Asher turned the corner, her heart thudding noisily, and put her foot on the first stair, but no prickling of her skin gave warning of Lassar's work. 'All right –

come on,' she called back.

The landing at the top of the flight was narrow, with two doors leading from it, one straight ahead and one to the left; the choice was simplified by the fact that the door to the left stood open, revealing an empty room. Asher put a hand over the keyhole of the second room, the tingling of her fingers giving a warning. 'This one's warded, and I can't do anything with it,' she said quietly. 'Hare, give me your pick.' He handed her the bunch. 'You'll have to tell me how to use it.'

He looked nervously at the lock, then shook himself. 'I can't teach you now. If I hold your hand, perhaps I can work through you.' He had grown very pale, but he shrugged. 'It's worth a try.'

'Thanks.' She inserted the pick he selected into the lock, then let her hand go loose as Hare's fingers enclosed her own.

'Left just a little . . . put the pick further in. No, softer. Don't push.' A spark leaped from the lock on to Asher's hand and Hare drew back, only just in time. More nervously still, he resumed his position as the spark died. 'Nearly there – up a trifle – *that's it!*' A second spark flared into life at the sound of a click; Asher pushed Hare violently back, but not before the lock seemed to explode, sending out a further burst of violet-coloured sparks.

'Keep back, both of you!'

Mallory was several paces away, but Hare, who had no time to retreat, cried out as two of the sparks landed on his right hand; instantly, their flames expanded until the whole of his hand was briefly enveloped in violet fire.

'What is it?' he demanded shrilly, keeping the hand away from his face. 'What will it do to me?'

'I don't know.' The flames flickered, then went out, but not before Asher saw there was already a perceptible change in the hand itself. The skin had turned bluish-white, and the fingers and thumb were stiffly curved and rigid; Hare tried to move them, but could not.

'It's gone numb! What'll I do?' He was shaking.

'Asher, leave him. We haven't time for this. We have to get the girl.' Mallory took the trembling Hare by the arm and moved him out of the way.

'Don't come any nearer,' Asher warned. 'We don't know what else is here!' She turned the handle, and the door opened.

The room thus revealed presented an astonishing sight; where the rest of the house was poor, no luxury had been spared in making this one place fit for Avorian's betrothed. A rich silken carpet, bordered with gold, covered the wooden floor, and costly tapestries hung on two of the walls. The bed was immense, taking up most of the space, both head and base ornately carved and gilded; it was spread with a cloth of gold brocade far too opulent for the scale of the room.

Outside it was dark, but it was bright inside the room, for a dozen or more wax candles burned in a pair of ornate candelabra which stood on a small table by the bed. By their light, Asher could see not only the slight figure lying motionless under the covers, but also her guardian, an immense woman, larger even than Carob, who sat on a stool beside the girl, hands neatly folded in her lap.

Mallory made a move, but Asher stepped in his way. 'No. Don't go in. Who knows what other tricks Lassar has left in here. Stay, and I'll bring her to you.'

'Come in, missy.' The large woman got to her feet, beckoning; her face was a florid moon, her hands almost as big as Bull's. Her vast bulk was wrapped in a mass of white material – too shapeless to be termed a dress – but it was at her hands that Asher looked; they were red and massive. 'Come and get the girl, if you want her,' the woman went on, in a pleasant, country voice, smiling her invitation. 'If you can, that is.'

'Let me take her.' Asher stepped into the room. Despite the presence of Mallory and the others at her back, she found she was very frightened.

'Lassar said it would be a girl who came if anyone did, another child of Fortune like me.' The big woman waggled a reproving finger. 'You were wise not to let the others in; none of your friends can help you here. This is between us two.' She glanced at the still figure on the bed, then back at Asher, adding conversationally: 'And if you try to take the girl, I'll break your neck!'

'Keep back, Mallory.' Asher knew him too well to hope he would keep out if he thought her in danger. She looked at the woman's hands and thought she could easily carry out her threat; they looked horribly strong, quite capable of closing round a neck. She swallowed.

She took two paces forward, at a loss to know what to do; she had no fighting skills, no means to guard herself against the large woman's superior reach and strength. The girl Menna – Vallis – slept, unaware of the conflict of which she was the centre.

The woman stood facing her and the open door, relaxed and ready. Her hands clasped one another loosely, but when she saw Asher looking at them she mimed an unpleasant squeezing motion.

'Asher – left!'

She flung herself to the side at Mallory's shout, then something whistled past her; a heavy grunt came from the big woman, and when Asher looked up she saw the large red hands were now curled about the blade of Mallory's sword, which protruded from her vast stomach. Her face registered extreme shock as she slid to the floor in a kneeling position, pulling ineffectually at the blade as she let out a long wailing cry.

'Asher, get the girl – quickly!'

Asher bent over the sleeping figure and shook her roughly, but Menna did not stir; in her sleep she looked younger than Asher remembered, and her face was very white. Her breathing was slow and shallow, barely perceptible.

'Hurry!' Mallory called.

She could hear various noises coming from outside the house; as she uncovered the sleeping Menna, Asher took a quick look out of the window to her left, but she could make out only the dark shape of the river in the distance and the looming presence of the bridge upstream, just beyond the Sair Gate and city walls, exactly as Oramen had described them. She put an arm under Menna's shoulders and tried to lift her.

She was heavier than Asher expected, and she knew at once she did not have the strength to carry Menna to the door. Careful not to hurt her, Asher pulled her from the bed and laid her on the floor, then had to drag her in an undignified fashion over the rich carpet, the fine stuff of her thin night-gown slipping easily enough across the silk.

'I'll take her now.' Effortlessly, Mallory stooped and lifted Menna into his arms as Asher finally got her to the landing. His ease was almost comic contrasted with her own difficulty, making her feel ridiculous and a little resentful.

'Thank the Fates for a lucky shot. I could easily have missed. No, don't worry about fetching my sword.' Asher was relieved, not least because the big woman was still alive and groaning. 'Downstairs, now. Quickly.'

Hare did not move, his gaze resting intently on Menna's face. 'Who is she?' he breathed.

Asher did not answer him, but to her surprise Hare reached out his left hand and quickly touched Menna's pale cheek. 'For luck,' he whispered. It was obvious the whole of his right arm was now paralysed, the infection spreading from his hand, and he looked terrified as he followed Asher down the stairs.

On the ground floor, they found the door into the garden

standing open, and Club peering out into the darkness. 'Bull?'

'Here.' A large shape emerged from the shadows. 'All done? We've finished here.' Asher noticed a long cut on the big man's face, and blood dripped from a wound on his right arm.

'Take Hare and Stern and get into that boat. We'll go to the docks.' Club turned to Asher, then back to Hare. 'What's the matter with your arm?'

'I can't move it.' Hare was deathly white as he put a protective hand on his injured arm, then started. 'But – '

'What is it?' Asher asked sharply.

'I felt that!' Colour began to return to his cheeks, and as he looked down at his hand one of the fingers flexed. 'Look! The girl – '

'Be silent!' Mallory rounded on him. 'Not another word. Club, where can we get over the wall to the inn's stables.'

They followed him down the garden in darkness, for the night was heavily overcast with no hint of either moon, until they reached a place where the high wall separating the grounds of the shop from those of the inn was only shoulder height. Club took Menna while Mallory straddled the wall, then handed her up before turning to give Asher a boost. Hare watched, still bemused, flexing his right arm at the elbow with evident delight.

'Many thanks, Club,' she whispered down to him. 'Hare, I'm sorry.'

'But it's all right again.' He looked up dazedly at Vallis's still, white figure, but broke off at Asher's quick shake of the head.

'The word is *Esperance*,' Mallory called down. 'Hare knows where to go for the money.'

'So do I, Councillor.' There was more than a hint of a smirk in Club's voice. 'I never forget a face! May Fortune favour you both.'

Asher jumped down on the inn side and helped steady Mallory as he edged himself to the ground. Together they headed for the stable building.

'Asher?' A slight figure slipped out from the doorway and came to meet her.

'Essa!' The women embraced briefly. 'Is everything ready?'

She nodded. 'As you asked. There're clothes and provisions for you all, and here're the passes.' She handed Asher three sealed travel warrants. 'Did you – ?' She broke off, catching sight of Mallory and the girl.

'No questions, Essa. Is the route north still the same?' Asher asked hurriedly. 'No changes to the safe houses?'

'Didn't you ask Mylla?' Essa looked puzzled. 'She's been north most recently.'

A lump rose in Asher's throat, and she found it suddenly hard to speak. 'She's dead, Essa. Jan doesn't know.'

'*Dead?*'

'Don't.' Asher could endure neither sympathy nor explanations. 'I can't tell you now. We have to leave before curfew.'

Essa recovered as best she could, becoming brusque. 'Which gate?'

'The Sair Gate, it's closest.'

'Then come along.' She led them into the stable where a covered wagon, teamed by four horses, stood waiting. 'There's bedding in the rear. It cost two gold to keep them here for you. The innkeeper's an old skinflint.'

Mallory lifted Menna into the back of the wagon and left it to Asher to settle her comfortably. He got down again, saying: 'You'd better stay with her in case she wakes, though it looks as if she's had a heavy dose of something.'

'All right.' Asher leaned out between the curtains at the rear of the wagon, her voice suddenly unsteady. 'Goodbye, Essa. Tell Jan and Margit and the rest about Mylla.'

'Be safe, child, and come back to us one day. May Lady Fortune guard and keep you.' They stared at one another a long moment until Mallory broke the contact by clicking at the horses.

Almost at once the cart began to move. Asher covered Menna's sleeping form with one of the blankets provided by Essa, carefully tucking it round the girl's body. She felt numbed by their success, as well as Hare's extraordinary behaviour and recovery. 'For luck' he had said when he touched Vallis; and somehow her luck had healed him. How? And how had he known?

That Lassar must already be aware of Vallis's loss she knew; the only doubt was whether they had a few moments' head start or a whole night. It would depend on how quickly the governor's men counted the tribute money and released Avorian from the Treasury vaults.

They stopped at the Sair Gate and she passed over their papers for inspection; the guard let them through, although not without questions at the lateness of the hour. Then they were outside the city walls and heading north, across the bridge over the Sair and toward the timberlands bordering the hills that led to Saffra; it was the shorter route, but slower, for they would have to keep to the trails where Avorian and his men would not.

Five days or more; five days for Avorian to catch up with us. Asher looked down at the sleeping girl, aware the hardest part of their long journey lay ahead. Perhaps Lassar already *saw* them in their flight. Her own gift, which had proven so unreliable, gave her a glimpse of a confusion of possibilities; she struggled to understand, realizing dimly that she would need it to show them the safest path. Except that from now on no path would be safe. Luck. They would need far more than their share to outdistance Avorian.

Chapter Seventeen

'She's still asleep.' Asher frowned. 'I'm worried, Mallory. It's been so long – more than a day now.'

'They must have given her too stiff a dose. But she'll wake, Asher, don't fret. In fact, it's easier for us that she *is* asleep, because I can't begin to imagine how she'll react when she comes to.'

'I know.' Huddled in her blanket, Asher shivered. It was a cool night. They had made camp in a wide clearing in what had once been the great Oxister Forest, but which had been so extensively logged it was now little more than a wood. In every direction stretched rows of stumps where the tall trees had been felled, the timber exported to pay for the ever-rising burden of the tribute. This visible impoverishment was a depressing and cheerless sight.

'She must remember who she is of her own accord. I'm sure that's what the Oracle meant: *"The cub must wake itself"*. It's not for us to tell her.'

Asher yawned. 'I don't suppose she'd believe us anyway.'

'How close do you think they are?'

'Much too close for comfort.' Asher was surprised by the rare clarity with which her gift displayed the warning. 'We had a night's start, but that was all; from now on the advantages are all on their side. They're on horseback, can move faster and change mounts. There's little hope we can do the same with a team of four.'

'Which way should we go when we leave the forest?' Mallory rotated his shoulders to relieve the strain of driving most of the day. 'Any preference?'

'I think west, then north again.' She sighed. 'I wish Mylla were here, she always knew which was the safest way.' Her throat tightened, grief still near the surface.

'It'll be light soon. We might as well get on.' Mallory stood up and held out a hand to Asher. 'Come on, sleepyhead.'

They left the forest at noon, emerging into the northernmost section of the Sair Plains, the river now far to the south. North lay the range of low foothills which rose in the extreme distance to become true mountains, white-capped and frozen, their ultimate destination. Mallory, who had never travelled so far north, was stunned by the vista of beauty ahead, but Asher, who had, was increasingly anxious at the slowness of their pace.

'They're coming, Mallory. Lassar can follow Menna – I mean Vallis – much more easily than *seeing* me.'

'What do you suggest?'

She bit her lip. 'There's a smallholding north of here which is part of the underground route. If we can reach it tonight, we might hide out there. It's very out of the way. Avorian can't travel far at night, any more than we can.'

'All right. You direct, I'll drive.' He set the team in motion again, noting a slight hesitation in one of the leaders; he would have to take care they did not go lame. Asher had been right in saying they would find no replacements on their way and he nursed the horses warily along the flattest section of the trail. It had begun to rain, a driving, icy rain that stung his cheeks and eyes and made it hard to see.

'You see where the trail goes up, round the side of that hill? Go there.'

They turned north, heading up into the lowest rank of foothills; the slopes were sparsely wooded, and Asher wondered whether their equipage would stand out too blatantly, so that even now their pursuers could see them with ordinary sight; but there was no point in worrying about it. She tried to concentrate on her surroundings, on the grey-blue granite against the drab land-scape. Several small farms and cottages dotted the slopes, blending in with the stone, although the north of Darrian was less populous than the south and centre, being much colder and less fertile; but herds of goats wandered about freely, and the sloping fields showed the hay well advanced.

In the late-afternoon, Asher directed Mallory down a narrow rocky trail which wound along the side of the hill, descending to a discreet valley through which flowed a thin green river, like a snake.

'The smallholding's tucked into the base of this slope, so it's practically invisible from above. We can spend the night there.'

'The horses need the rest,' Mallory agreed wearily; the leader was now distinctly favouring his off-hind foot. They made the descent to the valley sluggishly, at little more than a slow walk.

'Where is this place?'

'There, do you see?' Asher pointed to what looked like a natural outcrop of rock, regular in shape, a long, low structure right up against the side of the hill. 'It belongs to a woman named Silla. She and her husband dug the house out of the rock. Now he's dead she lives here alone. She's a solitary person, but she's saved many lives in her time.'

'Ours, too, I hope.'

'How far ahead are they?' Avorian snapped.

'Less than half a day, no more.' Lassar had his eyes closed, concentrating on his inner vision. 'They travel slowly.'

'When will we catch up with them?'

'Soon. Before they reach the border, at any rate.'

'Can't you be more specific than *that*?'

Lassar's eyes opened, and he turned in the saddle to face his master. 'There is no *must* in their future,' he observed placidly. 'It might be tonight, or tomorrow, or the next day. But it *will* be.'

Avorian snorted in disgust, then waved a hand to his men, a dozen of them in all. 'We ride on. North, into the hills.'

Lassar followed his master, urging his tired mount into a trot. It would be night soon, and then at last he would be allowed to rest; of all forms of exertion, riding was the one he detested most.

Asher bent over Vallis, watching as a faint colour came back to her cheeks and her eyelashes quivered.

'I think she's waking,' she said to Mallory in a soft voice.

'Stay with her. I'll go and see to the horses.'

Silla, a gaunt old woman with straggling white hair and sharply severe features, hovered unwillingly nearby. 'Do you want me?' she asked coldly. 'It might be better if there were no unfamiliar faces round her.'

'No, leave us alone. I'll call if I need you.' Asher sat on the stone floor beside the pallet; Vallis moaned in her sleep, the first sound she had made in two days.

'Menna?' Asher whispered. 'Are you awake?'

Her eyelids flickered open and dark eyes met Asher's in a bemused expression. 'Awake?'

'You've been sleeping for a long time. How do you feel?'

'Tired.' Her voice was very faint. 'I was ill. I remember . . .' A pause. 'Do I know you? Your face – '

'I'm Asher, from the Treasury. We met once, in the Chief Councillor's house.'

Sudden alarm registered in her face. 'Where am I – why are you here? Have you kidnapped me?'

'Not exactly.' Asher was relieved to see the girl's eyes close again as her alarm faded and she drifted back towards sleep. 'You're quite safe,' she added softly, hoping it was true.

She remained by the pallet all night, sleeping fitfully, afraid the girl would wake again.

They left at daybreak, the horses restored by a night's rest, but instead of guiding Mallory, Asher travelled for a time inside the wagon, keeping a watchful eye on her charge. The reference to kidnapping concerned her, for it was plain Avorian must have mentioned such a possibility to the girl; she would hardly otherwise have jumped to such a conclusion so rapidly. Vallis slept on, but more lightly, and Asher was aware she might wake fully at any time.

The ranks of hills rose higher as they progressed further north, and their pace slowed as the wagon ascended to a pass between two peaks which, in the absence of sun, still bore streaks of frost on the rock to either side. Asher came out to join Mallory on the driver's seat.

'They're getting very close now,' she said anxiously. 'I can feel it.'

'We can't go any faster. The track's not good as it is, and we can't afford for one of the horses to break a leg.' But he flicked his whip across the backs of the leaders, who responded with a desultory increase in pace.

'They'll catch up before sundown at this rate.'

'What do you suggest?'

'We have to go on, this is the shortest route.' Asher frowned suddenly, sensing a warning in the patterns in her mind. 'I think – yes, go on. But faster.'

Mallory glanced at her face. 'What is it?'

'Listen.' He did so, shaking his head, hearing nothing. 'Can you hear birdsong?'

'None.'

'Then I think we'd best hurry.'

They breasted the top of the pass and paused for a moment to stare at the seemingly endless ranks of peak upon peak ahead; it was a breathtakingly clear day, but Asher was consumed by an overwhelming sense of urgency.

'Mallory, get on! Quickly. We have to get away from here.'

He did as she asked, pressing his weary team on to the gradual descent, their hooves slipping on the scree covering the narrow trail. He was conscious of nothing but the rhythm of steady *clop-clopping* until he heard a gasp from Asher, and pulled on the reins to look back.

For a moment there was absolute stillness in the air; then he saw a brownish puff of smoke from high on the left-hand peak drift upward to the skies in a slow, leisurely fashion. There seemed to be movement on the slopes overlooking the trail, but it was not until the sound finally reached him that he realized what was happening. It was a roaring, tearing sound that built in volume until the earth shook, and only Mallory's tight hold on the reins prevented the horses from bolting.

The level of noise rose until it was deafening, and the air filled with dust and the crashing sounds of falling rock; the wagon shook, briefly. Then the worst was over, and the noise began to fade into the distance.

'Was that a landslide?'

He saw Asher's white face peering back at what had been the trail, and nodded. 'Or an earth tremor. Did you *see* it coming?'

'No, I just felt a warning to move on. Mallory, this gives us more time.' Her eyes lit up. 'Avorian will have to go round a different way.'

Where the trail had been was now a mass of broken trees and rock, and near to where they had paused earlier, a wide crack had opened in the earth; too wide to cross. That they had escaped injury was miraculous. 'Perhaps we are meant to get her away, and the balance of fortune is with us,' Mallory said softly. 'Perhaps we will win after all.'

Fate, Asher thought. If they had not been in precisely the right place at the right time, they would have been killed or forced to turn back, straight into Avorian's arms. Instead they were safe, and even granted a respite. She looked at Mallory and smiled.

'One of us is very, very lucky.'

'Idiot! Why didn't you *know* this was going to happen? They might get away!' Avorian stared at the wreckage of the trail, clenching his fists.

'I cannot *see* everything at once; I cannot watch the girl, and guide us, and ride, without some loss of concentration,' Lassar answered, rather crossly. 'This makes no difference. We shall catch them before the border, all the signs are there.'

Avorian turned on him, his normal composure dented by the strength of his frustration. 'You have never failed me, Lassar, so I continue to trust you. So tell me: does the girl still sleep? She has not awakened and remembered?'

'She sleeps, Chief Councillor. Though less deeply. And knows nothing.' He *saw* no alteration in the probability that his master would regain the girl safely.

His confidence heartened Avorian, who remounted and prepared to head back the way they had come.

Luck. It was all down to luck, and his own, like Lassar, had never failed him.

It was soon after dawn of the fourth day that Asher realized Vallis was fully awake and watching her.

'How do you feel? Are you thirsty?' she asked.

'I should like some water.' The girl's face was a more natural colour, but when she tried to sit up it was clear she was still very weak. Asher helped her to an upright position and gave her water in a flask, from which she drank deeply.

'You've been asleep for some days,' she advised. 'Are you hungry?'

'No.' She gave back the now-empty flask. 'I think – I remember waking before. You're Mistress Asher, from the Treasury in Venture. But you look different?'

'It's only the hair.' Asher touched her short, fair locks.

'And who is the other one – the one driving this wagon?'

'You've met him once – Councillor Mallory.'

Menna met this reply with a stare of open disbelief. 'But that's impossible! Why should *he* help you kidnap me?'

'That's not exactly right, Menna.' She remembered to use her other name just in time. 'We're not so much taking you *from* your guardian as *to* safety.'

'Safety? But why should you do such a thing?' Her brow wrinkled in confusion. 'Was it you, then, who fed me this drug? Or – no, that was Lassar, I remember. But I *was* safe, in my guardian's house.'

'That depends on where you think the danger lies,' Asher observed.

'Have you taken me for money? For a ransom? Or do you want some concession from Avorian?'

Asher could not keep all emotion from her voice. 'We want nothing from him,' she said, cold with sudden rage against the man. 'Only to be certain he does not take what does not belong to him.'

'You hate him, I can see it in your face. How strange.' Asher saw she had not overestimated the girl's intelligence. 'He is widely seen, I think, as an honest and kindly man.' Her wording struck Asher as odd, but she did not feel it sensible to ask what it meant. 'What has he done that you should feel so towards him?'

Asher hesitated; there was, after all, no reason for the girl to believe anything she said. Yet any seed of doubt which could be planted was a gain, however small.

'Do you remember a new maid who was with you for a short time recently – young, about the same age as you?'

'Surely.' Menna smiled, as most people did when they thought of Mylura. 'What of her? You're not suggesting my guardian violated her? He would not do so, I assure you.'

'Not in the way you mean, Menna. But she is dead, and by his orders.'

'Dead' she repeated, looking blank. 'But how?'

She doesn't deny it. Not 'why', but 'how'; perhaps she is less sure of him than I thought.

'A man named Jerr, one of your servants, slit her throat.' Her own contracted at the memory. 'I watched him do it.'

'Then this is for vengeance?' The girl's keen eyes inspected Asher's face in some puzzlement. 'But no, I think not. You mean me no harm.' She was reasoning with herself rather than speaking to Asher. Then: 'Where are you taking me?'

'To Saffra.'

'You know, of course, that Avorian will follow and take me back? I am to be his wife.'

'We were aware of it, and yes, he's already in pursuit, but with luck we will reach Saffra before he catches us.'

'He is the luckiest man in Venture, perhaps in all Darrian. I should not trust your own so far, mistress.' The girl frowned. 'You say you knew of our betrothal – how is that? I thought only he and I – '

'First I guessed it, but in any case he told us of it himself.'

'It is true that I am not his daughter but the child of a distant cousin – a bastard, if you like. But he and Katriane cared for me as for their own. He is an honourable man in his way, whatever you may believe.' The girl was still disturbed by Asher's earlier revelation. 'Why else should he wish to wed me? But you, are you married to Councillor Mallory, mistress? Is that why he is here with you?'

'No. I was married once, to an evil man, but thankfully he's dead.' Menna shot her a startled look, and Asher went on: 'Believe me, it can be better to live alone than with someone like him or Avorian.'

'I owe him this at least, after all his care for me,' she retorted with spirit. 'Is it so much for him to ask? Not for love, but for companionship and the hope of children?'

'I think you would discover it was much more than that, but you look tired. Sleep, if you can.' The girl still looked very frail. 'If there is anything you want?'

'Nothing.' She lay back, her eyelids already beginning to close. Asher watched until the slowness of her breathing made it plain she was truly asleep; a girl capable of such control and intelligence in so unexpected a situation was more than able enough to effect her own escape, given an opportunity.

'She has awakened, Councillor. She is well, but still some way off.' Lassar gestured towards the northern hills. 'We must head further west.'

'I thought you said we would catch up with them in a day – not four!' The delay was eating away at Avorian's self-control. 'In two more they will reach the border. What then, Lassar?'

'We shall be there in time. I *see* it.'

'But you said nothing was certain!' Avorian wheeled his horse to face west. 'We seemed plagued by small accidents on this journey – the landslide, a lost shoe, the grey guard! What next?'

'We will find her,' Lassar said confidently. 'Of that there is no doubt. Perhaps she will even find us, now she wakes. I have foreseen such a chance.'

'There must be no *chance*!' Avorian sounded savage. 'Jerr!'

'Yes, master?' The man rode up to receive his orders. A dark bruise discoloured one side of his face.

'We will travel through the first part of the night, if it is clear enough. Tell the others.'

'Yes, master.' Jerr paused, then asked: 'Are we close?'

'Not enough.' But Avorian, seeing the eagerness on Jerr's face, relaxed sufficiently to add: 'I have not forgotten the injury to you, nor your failure. You will have your chance to redeem it.'

Jerr's eyes lit up with savage joy. 'My thanks, master. I, too, have not forgotten.'

They camped the fourth night beside a clear-running stream so cold that it jarred their teeth to drink it; Menna, washing her hands and face, shivered extravagantly.

'It's like ice.'

'Come and sit by the fire, it's warmer here.' The night, too, was much colder, and already frost was forming on the grassy bank.

Asher moved aside to let Menna share the blanket on which she was sitting. 'It's only a day or more now, to Saffra.'

'Under other conditions, I think I would be glad to go.' Menna held out her hands to the flames, looking pensive. 'They say it is a strange land, all ice and snow and frozen seas.'

'It's very beautiful, but different. The Saff don't live like us.' Asher thought of the haunting caverns deep inside the mountains, of the underground lakes stocked with fish, lit by a type of luminous lichen, all she as a stranger had been privileged to be shown. 'Men and women are valued equally there; it's safe to be born a woman in Saffra.'

'But you and Mallory see yourselves as equals, I think,' Menna said shrewdly. 'Are you lovers, that it should be so? For I have never seen a man and woman work so well together, who understand and respect one another so deeply.'

'Better than lovers – we are friends from childhood.' Asher smiled. 'Although he was not always so willing to share as he is now.'

'My guardian would never have it so.' Menna sighed. 'I think I remember you there that day, when poor Koris, our slave-boy, dropped some wood in the office. You must have heard Avorian say how he believes everything in life is Fated, the lot of women an unlucky one because they are not born men.'

'I, too, thought so once.' Asher paused, then changed the subject for one that was puzzling her. 'When the grey guard stopped us today, wanting to see our papers, you said nothing. Why, when you could have freed yourself?'

'With *their* help?' Distaste was written plain in her face. 'I would rather die! But do not mistake me, Asher. If I can free myself, I shall, but not at the expense of having you sent to the Games arena.'

Asher nodded absently, expecting nothing more. 'Tell me, do you remember anything before you went to live in Avorian's house? Your mother, perhaps?'

Menna seemed surprised at the second change of topic, but answered readily enough. 'I sometimes think I do, but then I wonder if it was all a dream. I was five or so when I came to live in Venture, but I only remember because I was told it, not as fact. Why do you ask?'

'Just curiosity.' It was difficult to restrain the impulse to force the girl's memory. 'Do you ever dream – I mean, the same dream again and again – something that might be memory?'

'How strange you should ask, but yes.' Her face clouded. 'I used to dream of a bird – perhaps that I *was* a bird, a hawk, used to travelling far and free, but now I could not fly any more, and I would wake up screaming, and my old nurse would shake her head and tell me not to be so foolish. I still have it at times, but not often.'

Mallory appeared and joined them at the fire, looking grim.

'What is it?' Asher asked.

'It's a clear night, but we can't go on for some time. The horses need to rest.'

'You mean my guardian may come?' Menna commented lightly. 'If he does, I will tell him you treated me well.'

'I doubt that would stay his hand. Asher, which road should we take in the morning?'

'We have a choice; there's a trail due north, which is shorter but climbs higher, or a trail north-west, which is flatter but longer, and involves a rather shaky bridge.' She froze suddenly, a warning manifesting itself clearly in her mind at the prospect, a line wavering. Danger to herself. Equally, she could *see* the probability that if they chose the higher trail Avorian would catch them before they reached the border. It was strange how much easier she found it to read the patterns on this journey, and she wondered if it was only because there were so few choices she could make.

'What's the problem?' Mallory, who knew her too well at times for her comfort, was not deceived by her manner.

'Danger one way, certain capture the other,' she said shortly. Menna gaped.

'I didn't know you could *see*.'

Asher gave her a wry smile. 'Not well, and not so clearly as I might wish.'

Mallory sighed. 'Your choice, Asher.'

'Then the bridge.'

She was surprised to hear Menna burst out laughing, putting a hand to her mouth. 'Oh, I'm sorry, but you're both so terribly careful of each other's feelings.' She giggled again. 'You should see, Asher, poor Councillor Mallory fighting with himself not to tell you which way we should go, and you steeling yourself against him doing any such thing!'

Reluctantly, Mallory smiled. 'You see a great deal too much, Mistress Menna!'

'I meant no insult, I assure you.' She sobered slowly. 'My guardian would never let me make such a decision. He's always sure he is right!'

Asher's eyes met Mallory's in silent challenge. 'It's a common failing, I think,' she said hastily.

'Why have you taken me?'

Both Mallory and Asher turned to look at her, for all amusement was gone from her voice and she sounded both sad and weary.

'We can't tell you,' she answered. 'If we could, we would do so. If you would only remember . . .'

'Asher,' Mallory warned.

'Remember *what*?' Menna looked upset. 'I know by now you don't mean any harm to me, but if only you would tell me what you want!'

Mallory shrugged, and Asher got to her feet. 'We must get some sleep,' she said abruptly, closing the conversation. 'We leave at first light.'

Menna hesitated, then followed her towards the wagon.

'We have them, they're only a short way ahead!' Lassar said, rare excitement colouring his voice. 'But there is danger, for the woman.'

'Not for Menna?'

Lassar shook his head doubtfully. 'Only a small chance, Councillor.'

Avorian looked tired; at just over fifty, he was still a man in his prime, but four days and most of a night in the saddle had tried his energies and his patience to the utmost. 'Then we must hurry. No harm must touch her.'

Prudently, Lassar kept his minor misgivings to himself. 'It will not.'

'Which way?'

'North-west; the trail branches north of our present path. They have gone that way.'

'Come, then.'

The party rode on, restive at the prospect of victory after so many disappointments; Jerr, his bruise now more yellow than purple, dug in his spurs with unusual viciousness, his face set in an ugly smile.

'How high are we now, do you think?' Mallory asked Asher.

'Seven thousand feet – no more. The trail's flat for quite a long way in this direction, following the path of the valley. We should make better time in the long run than by going due north.'

It was late-morning of the fifth day, and the sun shone fiercely down on them as they sat side by side on the driver's seat; Menna lay in the back of the wagon, apparently deeply asleep. The pass they were leaving was bordered to either side by quartz-veined schist rock which was obviously unstable since the trail was littered with many small fragments of stone and there was a steady trickling sound of pebbles falling from higher up. They emerged at the far end and into the open valley with some relief.

'What a view!' Asher wiped her hot forehead as she surveyed the spectacle of the wide, flat plateau, set between two peaks high enough to be called mountainous. At the far end of the valley the vista opened out, to give a tantalizing vision of snow-anointed summits and vertiginous slopes, with a streak of silver flowing west to east which was the River Saff, marking the border between Saffra and Darrian.

'That's the bridge?' Mallory waved his whip towards the centre of the barren valley through which flowed a second river, an offshoot of the Saff. 'Is it safe?' he asked doubtfully.

'We should get out and walk the horses across, but yes, it's safe enough, and when we're over, we set fire to it. There's another bridge like this further south Avorian can take, but it will delay him and give us more time.'

'Is this one much used?'

Asher shook her head. 'Not now. Before the invasion, this was one of the trade routes for furs from Saffra, but now there's no traffic between us, as you know.'

'How far behind do you think they are?'

'Not far enough.'

Mallory drove along the rock-strewn valley floor to its centre; on the far side of the river he could see the trail began again, a wide track leading north, but the river itself was a formidable obstacle. Fed from the mountains, it flowed at a rapid pace, bearing boulders, tree trunks and even blocks of ice in its current, and it was easy to see that any attempt to ford it would be to invite death.

'See if the girl's still asleep. We can't trust her. She might try to make a run for it,' Mallory advised.

Asher did so, returning almost at once. 'She seems dead to the world.'

'Are you sure the bridge will bear our weight? I had wondered about leaving the wagon and riding from here.'

'We can't, Mallory. Not only is the girl too weak, but it would be too easy for her to get away from us.' They had taken to calling her 'the girl' for the sake of convenience, so as not to precipitate the return of remembrance. 'It's not that far across – only a hundred feet or so.'

'I'll take your word for it.' He surveyed the structure with less than total confidence and enthusiasm. Wooden planks formed the base, tied tightly together and about ten feet across, enough for the wagon; they seemed solid and sturdy, but what displeased Mallory most was the way the bridge swayed, for the sides and infrastructure were constructed only from heavy hempen rope, attached at either end to man-made platforms of stone.

'Don't look so anxious. I've been across here before, and it's not as bad as it looks. The weight of the wagon will steady it a bit at any rate.'

'If you say so.' Mallory got down from his seat and took the halter of the near-side leader. 'You hold the other.'

For a time, Asher and Mallory had to concentrate on their task for the horses evidently shared some of Mallory's mistrust, displaying an intelligent unwillingness to set foot on such a treacherously moving surface; at long last, however, they accepted the inevitable, stepping with extreme caution at first, then with greater confidence as the bridge creaked but swayed less as they progressed. Their pace became steadier.

Turning back to see how far they had come, Mallory was dismayed to see a slim figure moving back from the end of the bridge across the valley the way they had come.

'*Asher, she's running off!*' he called, shouting above the noise of the torrent, pointing frantically back.

'You go on, I'll go after her.' Mallory shouted: 'No!' but Asher was already edging round the wagon and striding rapidly back across the bridge, not daring to run for fear of startling the horses. Once on solid ground, however, she took to her heels in pursuit, gaining rapidly as the girl moved much more slowly in her still-weakened condition.

She must have been awake and heard what I said to Mallory about Avorian being so close. Asher cursed herself for being so gullible.

'Menna!' she called, seeing the girl hesitate at the start of the pass; she enjoyed a fair start. '*Come back!*'

Menna must have heard her, but still she moved off into the shadows of the pass; Asher ran on, already envisioning disaster. Warnings of danger throbbed in her mind, but she would not turn back, not when she was within only a hundred feet of her prey.

She called again, hoping against hope, for the girl had slowed her pace, then stopped altogether beside a pile of boulders.

'Menna!'

The girl did not move; she seemed mesmerized by something hidden from sight by the rocks. Asher covered the remaining ground between them at a run, but still Menna neither turned her head nor tried to run.

'Get away.'

She spoke so softly Asher thought she was crying, until she looked where Menna was looking and saw what held her motionless.

A hissing snarl greeted her arrival, and a glimpse of long off-white teeth as the creature widened its jaws in a defiant growl. Angry eyes of gold-green flared as the sleek body tensed to spring, the tip of the tail lashing furiously, the hind-quarters quivering in readiness. The silvery-white fur was dotted with a design of pale spots, but underneath the ribs were too prominent, and one of the large forepaws had an ugly gash which looked new and sore; it was a snow-leopard, but an old beast, strayed down from the high hills in search of food.

And this time there was no Bull with a net. Nor was this a trained Asiri watch-cat, but a wild creature close to starvation.

Even without using her gift, Asher's dilemma was plain; the beast was going to attack Menna or herself. This, then, was the meaning of the warning she had seen, the moment of decision which was, at the same time, already past. Asher tensed at the same moment the beast gave warning of intent to spring; as the leopard leaped, so did she, pushing Menna, who was right in its path, roughly aside as the animal's full weight landed on her, knocking her to her back to the ground, holding up her arms in a desperate attempt to protect her throat.

The leopard's claws pierced her right shoulder and left arm, sharp pain following moments later. The beast's breath was rank as its head nuzzled at her arms, trying to push them aside to get a clear path to her throat; when that failed, it fixed long teeth round her right forearm and bit down hard through the thick wool of her jacket. Asher heard herself scream as her own blood began to drip on to her face, appalling pain spreading up her arm, and she struggled to breathe against the pressure of the leopard's weight full on her chest and stomach. The shadowy patterns in her mind dizzied her as she fought for her life, *seeing* her own death and life fuse together as the number of choices was reduced to three, then two . . .

The locked jaws about her forearm gave suddenly. She heard someone let out a sob, and felt more agony as the claws were unhooked from her arm and shoulder and the heavy weight of the leopard was rolled off her chest. Blood had dripped into her eyes, and she could not see through the haze of pain, but someone was kneeling beside her, wiping her face with a piece of cloth.

'Asher? Are you alive? Asher?'

Menna bent over her, her hands already busy tearing her skirts for makeshift bandages with which to staunch the flow of blood. Her touch was light but nonetheless an agony, and Asher wished, for the first time in her life, that she could faint and not be forced to bear it.

'How?'

'I hit it with a rock while it attacked you.' Menna finished winding a strip of her skirt round Asher's forearm, then sat back on her heels; the leopard lay unheeded, senseless or dead, at her side, its skull a mass of blood. The smell reached Asher, mingled with her own, and she retched. 'Do you think you can stand? I'm not strong enough to carry you.'

The pain made her light-headed. Asher allowed Menna to help her sit up, then, sweating, to kneel; she had not considered how difficult it was to move without the use of her arms, but any movement at all set her muscles aching and the blood flowing.

Rapid footsteps heralded Mallory's arrival; he took in the scene at a glance, then looked at Menna.

'Will you help? Or must I take the time to bind you?'

Menna straightened in unconscious dignity. 'She saved my life. I give my word I will stay with her until she is somewhere she can be cared for.'

'If I take Asher, you'll not run?'

'No. Not even if my guardian were to appear this instant.'

'If Avorian catches us, she has no hope.' Mallory watched her carefully. 'He must be close by.'

'I owe him a great deal, but not so much as this.' Menna put out a tentative hand to Asher. 'I was its prey, not she; if I doubted your intent, she has proved it must be for my good. I only wish I understood the reason.'

Mallory bent and lifted Asher in his arms, anxious at the amount of blood still flowing from the wounds in her shoulder. 'So do we all, Menna.' He knew a stab of pain as he looked down at Asher's thin face, saw the effort not to cry out, even now, and wondered what his choice would have been if it had lain between saving her or Menna. To be with Asher was to be in a constant state of apprehension; yet she had added a new dimension to his

338

existence, a companionship on a deeper level than he had ever imagined possible, and to contemplate life without her now was to lose that which gave him purpose. He had no direct stake in the future, no children, no creative impulse; the trading empire of his clan would go on whether he lived or died, in one way or another. Asher was the only woman he had ever known – or man, if it came to that – he could ever trust, without reserve, because she was loyal to whatever she believed; it was an echo of his own sense of duty, of obligation.

'If you feel like *that*,' Menna said softly at his side, 'then why don't you tell her so?'

It was not the first time he had been caught unawares by her intuitive understanding, but it startled him nonetheless. 'I wish it were so simple,' he answered truthfully.

'Can you not ask her to become your wife?'

'I could ask, but would she agree? And would it be for the best?' He could tell Asher was conscious and listening, but she made no sign she had heard.

They laid her in the rear of the wagon; Menna bathed her wounds a second time with water from the river while Mallory set about firing the bridge. A light wind had got up, easing his task, and the flames spread with satisfying speed along the hempen ropes, soon engulfing the wooden boards. Menna gave a small sigh from her place at Asher's side.

'How hard it is to do the right thing,' she murmured. 'Or even to know what *is* right.'

Mallory nodded, his respect for her increasing. 'I think, from what I've seen, you will find it less hard than most, mistress.'

She made an impatient gesture, but he saw she was pleased by the compliment. 'We must find someone to apply salve to these wounds; the cat's claws were filthy, and they may fester.'

'Indeed.' He climbed up to the driver's seat and urged the horses into motion once more, knowing Asher would feel each bump and every pothole along the trail. She had mentioned a farmhouse further on where they could spend the night; he hoped they would reach it quickly.

'This is ridiculous!' Jerr said acidly, surveying the ruin of the bridge. 'Master, your diviner has lost his gift. He should have foreseen *this*, at least.'

All eyes turned to Lassar, who answered composedly: 'The man and woman between them have a way of disrupting what is most probable, turning the least likely outcome into the *most.*

There is still no doubt we shall take them before they reach the border; the woman is wounded, and they cannot travel far.'

'You are certain it is she, not Menna?' demanded Avorian irritably.

'There is no doubt.'

Jerr's mount reared, kicking out, and he struggled with the reins. 'Why don't we cross here, all the same? The current's strong, but the water's none too deep. We'd save much time.'

Lassar turned and gave him an oddly disconcerting stare. 'Try, if you wish for death.'

'Why should I believe you, when you've been wrong so often these past days?' Jerr challenged, his temper rising. 'Perhaps this is all a trick, and you're in the pay of this man?' He made the accusation in anger, not because he believed it. 'I'll try the river, and *I* will reach them first!'

Avorian, whose expression had displayed a fleeting and quite unfamiliar doubt, nodded his encouragement. Lassar opened his mouth to speak, but at a sign shut it again, understanding Avorian's intent: this was to be another test of his own skills.

'Go, then,' Avorian ordered. 'If you succeed, we will follow.'

Jerr hesitated briefly, staring at the fast-flowing river where he could see chunks of ice amid the current; but the water was clear, and the river bed seemed flat and manageable. He walked his horse down the shallow rocky bank and into the water. Moving slowly, he went further out, towards the main current, feeling the surge of power against his thighs as the water level rose higher, and his horse stumbled on a rock; it recovered, and Jerr turned back to wave encouragement to the party on the bank.

As he did so, his mount put a foot in a deep hole, throwing both itself and Jerr off balance; the current thundered at man and beast, buffeting them with cruel force until the poor animal lost its footing entirely. Jerr could feel the moment when its foreleg snapped and the horse collapsed, submerging him in midstream. He tried to hold on, but the next moment a lump of ice smacked into his side, winding him and breaking at least one of his ribs; the water was too cold, and his hands could no longer grip. With a despairing cry he slipped sideways, and the current, as if sensing no further resistance, took him and his horse, tossing them contemptuously against submerged rocks as if they were no more than driftwood.

Avorian, watching from the shore, inclined his head towards Lassar. 'As ever, you *see* rightly,' he observed with a faint smile.

Lasser received the compliment with some complacency. 'As

you say, Councillor. Jerr was a man who always chose to be blind.'

'Then we go south, to the other bridge. *Holla!*' he called to the waiting men, wheeling his horse, his good humour thoroughly restored.

Chapter Eighteen

Asher roused, blurred vision coming to focus on two candles flickering in an otherwise dark space. Around her was the scent of damp earth. She lay still on her back on a hard wooden cot, but there was nothing else to be seen in the room; it looked familiar, and she was not alarmed. She was distantly aware of the passage of time since her encounter with the leopard, but it was more like a dream than a remembrance. She blinked, bringing Menna instantly to her side.

'You're awake. Good,' she whispered. 'Keep still, and speak low.'

'Where are we?'

'The farmhouse, with Bran and Soraya. Do you remember?'

'Yes.' Warily, Asher raised herself from her prone position, finding her right arm neatly bandaged. 'Thank you for this.'

'The cuts will heal, as long as no infection sets in, and no bones are broken. You were very lucky.'

'Where's Mallory?' Asher knew a momentary panic. 'He's safe?'

'As much as any of us.' His voice came from the darkness, away from the light of the candles. 'I've been checking the other way out from this cellar. Soraya said it came up behind the lean-to at the side of the house, but to make sure it was clear. We can use it if necessary.'

'They're coming.' The calm certainty she experienced told her it was already too late to effect an escape. 'They'll find us.'

'We know.' It was Menna who answered her. 'Bran warned us; he saw them in the distance with a telescope. But at least we'll be able to hear what's going on in the house upstairs when they get here – there's an opening in the roof just by the hearth, see?'

'I remember – ' Asher broke off, hearing Soraya's low voice say: '*What shall we do?*' and Bran answer: '*Let them in. We can't lock the door against so many.*'

'I could leave you here. You'd be safe if my guardian believed you'd gone on without me,' Menna offered.

'He'll know we're here.' Asher looked at Menna. 'Lassar will tell him.'

'Then I'll stay with you. Perhaps – '

'Hush!' Mallory gestured towards the cellar roof. 'Listen.'

Above, a door crashed open and something heavy was overturned. Asher tried to recall the layout of the upstairs room from her last visit. It was a long rectangle covering the entire ground floor of the farmhouse, with a sleeping gallery above the end by the open hearth which was used in the summer; during the long, cold border winters, Bran and Soraya used the cupboard beds lining the walls to either side of the fireplace. She had slept in one herself on her first journey north, and one was also the entrance to the cellar where they were hidden.

'Where is the girl?' Avorian's commanding voice carried clearly to their shelter. 'And the man and woman who were with her?'

'What girl?' Bran protested. 'We're alone here. Who are you, and by what right do you force your way into our house, with a small army at your back?'

'You – search the outbuildings. You four go through this room. They must be here.' There were sounds of movement and more slamming of doors, and for a while it became difficult to hear what was being said.

'What do we do?' Asher whispered to Mallory. 'Stay, or make a bolt for it?'

He shook his head. 'Stay.' He turned to Menna. 'You?'

She would look at neither of them. 'I should go to him. He must be frantic with worry after so many days,' she said, but did not leave her place beside Asher.

'Lassar, is she here?' Avorian sounded coldly furious. 'You said she would be here!'

'She is here.' Lassar's voice was easily recognized. 'Close by.'

'Then where?' There was the sound of a woman's cry, and Menna clenched her fists. 'Where have you hidden them?'

'Leave her be – ' But Bran's protest was abruptly stayed.

'Show me, if you value your wife!' Soraya cried out again. 'Or your farm.'

'There's no one here but yourselves,' Bran said loudly. 'Keep your hands off her!'

There came the sound of a blow, then an uneasy silence overhead. Menna hid her face in her hands.

'Mallory – ' Asher began, but was again interrupted by a

resumption of conversation upstairs.

'They're not in the barn nor the stable, Councillor, but I found their wagon and team.'

'Good.' There was a short intermission, then Avorian spoke again, they guessed to Bran. 'You will tell me where the girl is, or I shall fire your farm.' A gasp of shock came from Menna, as if she had not wanted to believe her guardian capable of such conduct. Neither Bran nor Soraya spoke.

'Very well.' Avorian's voice held no hint of softening. 'You four, tear this place apart, timber by timber, and burn the wreckage; outside, for the moment, in case Menna is hidden here.'

'No – ' Soraya's plea was cut off.

'I cannot allow this to continue.' Menna rose to her feet; her borrowed clothes were torn, and there was blood on her skirts where Asher's arm had lain. A whisker of smoke drifted down to the cellar. Menna paused, then took a pace forward. She seemed to trip then recovered herself, but her hands were trembling, and she was very pale.

'Menna?' Mallory ventured, but she took a violent step back.

'Leave me be!'

'Help me up, Mallory,' Asher said softly. 'I can walk, if you'll give me your arm.'

'Can you see, Ash? What's going to happen?'

She wished she could lie to him, but he deserved better from her than false assurances. 'Nothing good, I think,' she said steadily.

He pulled her to her feet, holding her close for a moment. 'We must hope, then, that in showing Menna Avorian's true nature we've done the best we could. Asher . . .' He hesitated. 'Will you stay down here, or leave by the other door and get away? I'm afraid to have to watch him hurt you.'

For once she did not try to back away, experiencing a bitter pleasure in the contact; his touch was welcome, not constricting. 'I feel the same, Mallory. Or did you believe you had the monopoly on such things?' A dull ache in her heart brought back images of Mylla's death, memories of guilt, of powerlessless. 'For once I wish you could be a coward.'

'Ah, Ash!' He managed a laugh. 'We're too much alike, and I *am* a coward, for I know what fear is.' His arms tightened round her.

'I will lead the way.'

Menna took hold of one of the candles and lit the steps leading to the main room above, from whence came further sounds of rending. Her expression was fiercely determined as she moved aside the planks making up the base of the cupboard bed that hid the entrance to the cellar and climbed up. The doors to the main room were shut as Mallory and Asher joined her. She placed the palms of her hands against the wood, nerving herself.

'Now.' She pushed at the doors, which opened out to crash back against the wall.

The effect of the sound on the inhabitants of the room beyond was remarkable; all activity ceased on the instant, and, as they watched, Avorian's angry expression changed to gratified recognition. Asher saw his pleasure at the sight of his adopted daughter was genuine; the affection she had noted in his manner to her in the past was still there, and her heart sank at the thought Menna might feel the same.

Avorian was standing halfway across the room from them, an imposing figure in grey riding leathers, tall and vigorous despite the long journey north. He reached out an inviting hand to Menna, waiting, expectantly, for her to go to him. She stayed in her place between Asher and Mallory, a stiffly upright figure.

'What have you done here, Avorian?' she asked coldly.

The outstretched arm was not withdrawn. 'I came for you, as you knew I should,' he said, speaking with an intensity that told Asher he had misunderstood her. 'Come to me. Have these people harmed you in any way?'

'They have not.' Still she did not move, and Avorian frowned.

'Come, Menna!' He was impatient with her continued recalcitrance. 'Come to me at once.'

'I asked you a question.' Her manner to him was quite altered from the filial deference Asher remembered. 'What have you done to these people, to their home?' She gestured to where Bran and Soraya stood, close together, then at the broken furnishings, evidence of wanton destruction.

'Nothing they did not bring upon themselves when they refused to tell me where you were hidden.' He met her stare with a look of suppressed irritation. 'What does it matter, now you are safe?'

'Safe? Safe from whom?' Her voice was cold, and Asher, listening to her, remembered Mallory asking Avorian much the same question. 'From what I see here, I am safer with my new friends than with you.'

He took a step toward her, as if he would take her from her companions by force. 'What have they said to you? What lies?' he demanded. 'Surely you aren't afraid of me. You know I would never harm you.'

Menna swayed, recoiling as if he had hit her. 'What did you say?' she whispered. 'Say it again.'

'I asked what lies these two have told you!'

'No.' She shook her head. 'Although they have said nothing, not even why they took me away from you. But from the few questions they asked, I am not so great a fool that I cannot see they wish me to recall something from my past, something I have forgotten, and I have tried. No, say those other words again.'

She was looking at Avorian as if he were a stranger, and, seeing it, he was silent. No one spoke or moved but Asher thought she heard in the distance the screeching cry of an angry bird of prey. The stillness in the farmhouse held a tangible quality, a sense of expectancy that shivered in the air, until Menna stirred and pierced the quiet with a whispered denial.

'No.'

The whole world changed at the word, all possibilities and probabilities altering in a split second of time that yet seemed to endure for hours; Asher was dizzied by a rush of darting images in her mind, showing her unfinished fragments of future time. Where before there had been only two shadowy paths of choice, now there seemed to be thousands, all in constant motion in rainbow shades that blurred together; she felt them as a physical weight, pressing down on her, and might have fallen if Mallory had not held her up. She thought it would be like the landslide they had barely missed, that soon sound would return, and there would be a crash louder than any she had ever heard as the world settled once more in its new balance, and was surprised to find there was still silence.

Lassar, standing behind his master, was deeply shaken; his world, too, had been broken apart in the same moment, but Avorian seemed oblivious to any alteration.

'What's the matter with you?' he demanded shortly. 'Are you ill?'

Menna slowly raised her head, her eyes bright with shock. 'You spoke those same words to me once before, in a garden, many years ago. I had forgotten it until now,' she said quietly.

Avorian stiffened. 'What words? What are you talking about?'

She answered him, speaking in a slow, halting voice, as if each word were new and unfamiliar: 'I heard you say them to me.'

'What nonsense is this?' He strode forward and would have put a hand on her arm, but Mallory stood in his way. Menna drew

346

back.

'It means you came too late, Avorian. It means I have *remembered* – remembered that I have another name.'

'This man and woman have lied to you, if they told you any such thing!' He shot Mallory a furious look. 'You are Menna, my child by adoption, my betrothed by my choice!'

'No.' Her pale face registered sharp pain.

'*No?*' He was unaccustomed to refusal, and her denial plainly shocked him. 'How can you say so?'

'No,' she repeated dully. 'I am neither Menna, nor your betrothed. Neither exists, never existed.'

'Do not believe, my child, that you have the right to refuse my wishes. In law I may dispose of you as I please,' he advised. 'I have protected you all your life, and you owe me this, at least in gratitude if not from affection.' He tried to smile, as if nothing had changed. 'But when we have returned to Venture you will be yourself again, and there will be no more of this!'

'You must believe me a sorry fool,' Menna said, still in the same dull voice. 'You have no rights in law while my true father lives, and no moral right either, though I acknowledge that some of what you say is true: for yes, you have protected me. For that I do thank you, Avorian. But not for the rest. Not when you would have married me, all unknowing, nor that you have lied to me all these years.'

'Tell me, then, who you think you are?' he challenged her. 'What dreams have you made for yourself, to find a reason for failing in your duty? Tell me, and I will tell you your error. Prove to me you are not Menna, whom Katriane and I cherished as our own daughter for so many years.'

Instead of answering him directly, she turned to Asher, speaking to her and to Mallory rather than Avorian.

'This was what you wanted – that I should know my true name, my true birth?'

'It was,' Mallory affirmed.

'Then I do, and much more besides.'

'Give us this dream then,' Avorian said, in scornful tones. 'What has your imagination conjured, child?'

Menna stiffened. 'I am not a child now, although I was then, when first I saw you. When you stole me from my father's house.'

Avorian made an impatient gesture. 'Enough!'

'I was in the gardens with my nurse.' She spoke clearly, over his interruption. 'I remember now, for it was a very still day in summer and there had been comings and goings at the palace all

347

morning. I suppose it was the news that Omen had fallen, but I did not understand that at the time; only that I was to be kept out of the way.' She gave a half-smile. 'I knew, as children do, that something was amiss, and since no one would tell me I plagued my poor nurse, running off from her and hiding until she should be worried enough to come searching. I must have been five years old or more, and she spoiled me dreadfully.'

'Menna – ' Avorian began; she paid him no heed.

'There were many hiding places but I chose the maze because I knew its secret and thought my nurse did not. When I would have entered it, a strange man came and called to me.' She paused. 'There were so many in the palace that day I did not think it odd. I went to him hesitantly, thinking – nothing in particular. My nurse was not far away, and I was safe enough. And he spoke those same words he said just now: "*Surely you aren't afraid of me?*" Then he held out some sweetmeat or other, and I took it. And that is all I remember until I woke in an unknown house with strangers all about me who told me my name was Menna.' She glanced toward Avorian. 'At first I cried each night, until they dosed me with poppy-juice to make me sleep and memories became only dreams of a hawk and a cage. But I remember it now. I am Vallis, daughter to Lykon.'

'You are Vallis,' Mallory said briefly. 'Our fortune.'

'That, too, I remember. How often have I heard the tale and the Oracle's words, and never thought they held any relevance to myself.' She returned her attention to Avorian. 'Did you ever intend that I should?' she asked bitterly. 'Or are you worse than I now believe, not only vicious and a thief but a collaborator, too?'

'I have heard enough!' He turned abruptly to the four of his men who were in the room, all of whom were listening with close attention. 'Menna, I will hear no more of this. Come with me! I have spent five days following you, and my patience is exhausted!'

'You should return to the city. The tribute ships will sail in eight days, and you should be there to see them go. No doubt the people of Venture will be glad of your return,' she said, with bitter scorn. 'You paid a high price for your popularity, and now I see the cause.'

'And what do you propose to do?' Avorian asked angrily.

'Go to Saffra, as was intended. Amrist cannot touch me there.'

'Why?' he challenged her. Even he seemed to have recognized at last that there was no point in continuing his denial. 'Why go there, when you can stay? If you become my wife, my luck will continue to protect you until the Dominus dies, and the prophecy may still be fulfilled.' As she was silent, he went on with greater confidence: 'I would have told you, in time, who you really were. Ask that woman at your side – she can bear witness what I say is true. What difference do a few days or weeks make? It was my destiny to save you, and our country with you. Our son will rule Darrian as a sovereign state, not as a tribute nation.'

Asher would have spoken then, but saw there was no need. Vallis swept Avorian's assurances aside. 'The Oracle did not speak of *you*. You lie, Avorian. You have always lied to me, as well as to yourself. You would have married me, keeping me in ignorance that you might take all Darrian as my dower, and all our good fortune, too; that alone proves you false. Whatever destiny you speak of, I know it and acknowledge it not.'

'You *are* the renewal of the good fortune of our land,' Avorian said stiffly. 'But you are also a woman. You exist to pass on that gift to your sons – to *our* sons. You cannot lead an army, nor even lift a sword. How do you think our liberation is to be accomplished by a mere girl? But with me at your side – '

'You have always said you believed in the Fates. Amrist will fail because the balance of good luck in our world will change and fall to us, weighting the scales against him,' Menna answered impatiently. 'Your prejudice blinds you. It was my survival to inherit my father's place that Amrist and his folk had to fear, not an army, as the Oracle foresaw. That, indeed, you have assured; even if now you seek to betray what you have preserved.'

'He can father no children, an aftermath of disease,' Asher observed dispassionately, savouring her moment of vengeance. Avorian looked murderous. 'Even there he lies.'

'Then his intent is wholly evil. I am the last of my direct line.' At last, she sounded angry. 'For vainglory, Avorian, you would have destroyed us all.'

'That is not the truth!' he answered heatedly. 'It was for *me* to save, to rule in your name; the Oracle spoke of it to *me*.'

'You have been gifted with more than your share of good fortune, it is true,' Vallis went on, more coldly. 'And such men rarely look to their own motives, for they must always imagine themselves in the right when Lady Fortune herself seems to uphold their conduct, good or bad; yet there is still a balance to be maintained between good fortune and ill, that we may never be certain one will not turn and become the other. And that is your fate, Avorian.' She spoke with authority, seemingly attuned to some voice inaudible to the rest. He shivered at the chill finality in her tone. 'Your luck deserts you now. Your ships will sink, and your clan will fail.'

'*It will not be!*' He took another step towards her, half in fury, half imploring. 'My luck has never failed me. It *cannot.*'

'She speaks truly, Avorian.' Mallory stepped into his path, preventing him from coming closer. 'You told us so yourself. The Oracle warned you, but you would not listen, preferring to believe yourself favoured above all others because you wished it to be so. Greed – that was the key. If you had not presumed to try to marry Vallis, unsuspecting, then you would indeed have been honoured by all. But when you sought to go beyond your remit, the Fates take back what they have given, and your luck fails.'

'I don't believe you!' He faced Mallory, the two men much of a height. 'Is this your doing?'

'You should have listened to Lassar. Didn't he say that nothing is certain, save death? The flaw was always in your nature as the Oracle foresaw. You chose wrongly, and yours is the loss. What was it you promised me – that you would ruin my clan? But it is you, Avorian, who will suffer that fate, through your own doing, none of mine.'

'It will be, Avorian,' Asher added softly. 'I can *see* it is true; your charmed life is at an end, now Vallis reclaims what is hers. There never was a way for you to win; and if you had, we would all be the losers. That was what the Oracle meant: "*destroying and preserving both*". That is the nature of Fate, that there are no certainties, that it is we who shape our own future; nothing is written, no path predestined.' It had taken her a long struggle to reach such understanding, but now she wondered why it had not been obvious to her long before. 'Our lives are a chain of accidents from birth to the grave, and though some are favoured above the rest by Lady Fortune, yet it is in fighting against our perceived lot that we have free will, for good or evil.'

'*Lassar!*'

Avorian spun round to discover his diviner edging discreetly backwards. He halted in his flight, finding his way blocked by Bran and Soraya who stood together, listening in frozen fascination to what was going on at the far end of the room.

'Chief Councillor?' he answered nervously.

'What do you *see* now? Do they speak the truth?' Finding an outlet for his frustration, Avorian grabbed the other man by the sleeve. 'And if they do, why have you betrayed me all these years!'

'Betrayed?' Lassar sounded surprised. 'I have foreseen what you

350

required – that the odds were in your favour that you would marry the girl and rule through her. That was always the most probable outcome.' He added stiffly: 'You never asked me if that would fulfil the Oracle's prophecy.'

'Then why has *this* happened – that this man and woman should intervene, when you assured me they would fail and the girl be mine! How should *they* emerge the winners when my luck has always been unrivalled, the odds always in my favour? Tell me *that*!'

'If you recall,' Lassar said smoothly, trying to extricate himself from Avorian's grasp, 'I said the danger lay in that the man and the woman had the effect of making the least likely possibility become a probability; that is something I could not *see* with any clarity. Equally, if you had had them killed when you wished, there was a clear danger to yourself and to your plans.'

'Then is what they say the truth?' Avorian shook him roughly. 'Have the Fates deserted me now, and must I wait and watch while my clan fails? I must know!'

Lassar's protruberant eyes, unblinking, bulged further in their sockets. 'It is true. I *see* only disaster ahead. The death of your nephew, without issue; of yourself, in due course, with no son, nor daughter, and in poverty. Menna was a part of your luck, but no more. Your contribution to the tribute has stretched even your empire too greatly, and your ships will sink far from home – '

With one swift movement, Avorian drew the knife from his belt and stabbed Lassar to the heart, killing him instantly. He then whirled back to face Mallory, bloodied knife in hand, unabated fury in his eyes.

'At least that has put an end to his litany of doom and disaster! And *you* – I should have killed you, and the woman, that anti-Fate, when I first learned you were a threat to me and mine!' He was breathing hard. 'I can *still* do it, and take back the girl. You carry false papers, and no one would ever learn the truth. What does it matter if the girl knows? *She* will be my luck once more, as she has lost me my own.' He glanced round at the four of his men who were still present. 'Well?' he demanded. 'What are you waiting for? Take him – and the woman. Do what you want with them, so long as they die!'

The two in livery who stood in the doorway drew their swords, but not in response to Avorian's commands. Instead, they took up position to front and rear of him, keeping a wary distance; the taller, a lean, grey-haired man, shook his head.

'I may not be a good man, or even an honest one, Councillor, but I take no orders from a filthy traitor!' He kept his eyes on the knife in Avorian's hand. 'And what else're you, when you would've stolen our luck from us! I'd sooner kill *you*.' He made a practice lunge with his sword. Avorian stepped swiftly back, only to meet its fellow between his shoulder blades.

'Leave him.'

Vallis still watched Avorian; Asher wondered what she must feel, to know herself betrayed by the man who had proclaimed himself her rescuer, with whom she had lived most of her life.

'Menna.' There was still a lingering affection in his voice when he spoke her name. 'Come with me. What I have done, it was for *you*, and for our country. Let me guide and protect you, as I have always done.'

The arrogance of the speech demonstrated he had still not allowed himself to accept his plans had gone awry, believing even now that an appeal could re-establish his fortunes; but if Asher feared Vallis would succumb, it was without cause.

'There is no Menna. What was it you always said to me: "Even a man of straw is worth a woman of gold".' There was no pity in her face or voice. 'You place little value on women, I think, until now when you find yourself in need of me. I remember I was to be grateful for your attentions, that you thought me worthy enough to become your wife. But you will have no immortality, Avorian. This you have brought upon yourself, and I would not change it if I could. You believe that strength is right, that the ability confers the right. It is not so. We are given minds that we may learn to restrain our baser instincts, that we may know that what we desire may not be what we should be given. Every gift but one was given to you, but you coveted more than your lot, and would have stolen what you wanted like any petty thief – and worse, for you would have lost us our only hope of freedom from the grey men.'

He stared at her in angry rebuttal, unable to believe she could speak so freely to him, but she held up a hand when he would have spoken. 'Let me finish. I could command your death, but I shall not, because before you allowed your hopes to falsify the truth, you saved my life. Amrist would have had me murdered as he did my brothers. I will let you go free, to return to Venture, and to wait and watch for what will come, the worse for knowing what *must* be. For you, this is a greater punishment than death – although you fear that more than I, you who have ordered death for others.' She paused. 'I *curse* you, Avorian.'

'*No!*' He made a gesture of aversion with his right hand, but the

352

movement was listless; an acknowledgement of despair hid behind the frozen mask of his face. Asher felt no stirring of pity for him.

'For Mylla's sake I wish him dead,' she said stiffly. 'Although in their way both she and Oramen chose their own deaths. But perhaps you are right, and this is the worse punishment for him. I hope it is so, for I shall never find any forgiveness for him.'

'I had not forgotten.' Vallis turned to Mallory, head held high. 'And you? Are you satisfied? You have a right to speak.'

'It was Lassar who murdered my seeress, albeit on his orders.' Mallory looked grave as he considered Avorian. 'But, yes, I will be satisfied with your judgment.'

'Mistress Asher, you said it was Jerr who killed your friend, but I do not see him here.'

Again, it was the tall servant who spoke for the rest, his sword still covering his erstwhile master. 'He was drowned earlier today, lady, trying to cross the river by the burned bridge.'

'Will that suffice you?' As the younger woman spoke, Asher thought of the prophecy of the Oracle: *'She casts aside the Shadow and flies upwards, soaring free'*, and thought Vallis would be a worthy successor to the hawk, her father, when the time came.

'It will suffice, ' Asher answered briefly, and knew it was true, that Mylla had been avenged.

'Then you,' and Vallis spoke to the tall servant, 'gather the rest of your men and take the Chief Councillor south to Venture. But leave him, without horse or valuables, a good two days' walk from the city. Let him learn what it is to be poor and powerless, and let him consider *then* the ways of the Fates.'

'Willingly, lady,' the man answered. 'Though I'll wager he'll have no luck when he gets there, not when we spread this tale. There's not enough gold in Venture to buy back *his* good name!'

'I had not considered that. They may burn his house.' Vallis seemed to reflect. 'Then when you reach the city, find the slave-boy, Koris, and remove him.' She glanced at Mallory. 'Take him to Councillor Mallory's establishment, for I feel certain that there he will be well cared for.'

'He will.' Mallory looked amused.

'What is this, then? Vengeance?' Avorian straightened, con-strained by the presence of a sword at his back, but already recovering from the blow Vallis had dealt him. 'For what? For an error of judgment? I am not an evil man. It was never my intent to injure you, nor our people.'

'Are you not, Avorian?' Vallis did not soften. 'What else is it but evil when you must buy your ambition at the cost of the lives of others? I do not hold life so dear as you, and who knows how heavy a weight of cares may burden a man or woman, so that the hope for peace, for nothingness, is to be preferred to that intolerable affliction? Yet that must be their choice, not mine. How many, Avorian? How many have died because of you? Do you know the number, or their names?'

'Why should that concern me, when what I did was for the greater good?' he answered angrily. 'Politics is expedience, no more; it may not have been *right* in your naive terms, but it was *necessary.*'

'So you say, Avorian, but those you murdered might disagree. It may be better that an evil man or woman die, to safeguard those who might otherwise become their prey, but I should want to be very sure before I dealt the blow.'

'It was their Fate to die, that I should fulfil my destiny.' Even now he did not doubt it. 'Take your vengeance from the Oracle that bespoke their doom, not from me!'

'It spoke your doom not theirs, and your failure was not theirs.' Her self-confidence was startling. 'That is yours alone.'

Avorian looked coldly at Mallory, then at Asher. 'That man and woman – you chose them over me. May you not live to regret it.' It sounded more like a threat than desire for Vallis's safety. 'May the Oracle grant them all it has given me!'

Vallis put out a protective hand to Asher, as if to safeguard her from Avorian's ill-wishing. 'The Fates may deal an uneven hand in the world, and some of us will always sicken and die because the odds against us are too great; perhaps it is a test, that we should learn to conquer ourselves, that we should not take advantage of such tricks to see some as less than human, simply because they are poor or ill-favoured. Or even born women, Avorian,' she added, with a chill smile. 'But I will not bandy words further with you. The actions prove the man, and you have shown yourself in your true colours this day. Go, then, with my curse. And may we never meet again in this world.'

Avorian's shoulders sagged, as if the curse were a heavy demon sitting on his back, but he recovered quickly. He was not yet broken, rather still unaware that he was now bereft of even the hope of hope. Asher watched him go, surrounded by his erstwhile guard, with mixed feelings; the knowledge that he would suffer eased her grief for Mylla, but, perversely, made her hate him more.

The sounds of horses' hooves finally faded into the distance, leaving behind an awkward tranquillity in which no one seemed to know what to do. Vallis sagged against Mallory, looking pale and drawn, and also sad; Asher put her left hand on the girl's shoulder, ignoring a stab of pain from her injuries.

'He's gone, Vallis,' she said softly. 'You're free.'

'Free? When I must go away and never see my true father alive again for fear Amrist should have me killed? When *he* has stolen all those years from me?' But Vallis did not weep, head held stiffly high. 'I want to be alone for a time. Then I would like to talk to you.'

'As you wish.'

A new possibility insinuated itself into Asher's mind as she agreed, and she sighed; sometimes it was a great deal easier not to be confronted by quite so much choice.

It was some time later that Asher left Vallis in the sleeping gallery, descending to the ground floor to rejoin Mallory in a mood of deep contemplation.

'Asher, do you feel up to talking?

They were alone; Bran and Soraya had disappeared outside on some task, and she had no reason to refuse. 'Of course.' She went to sit beside Mallory on a long bench, one of the few unbroken pieces of furniture.

'What was Vallis saying to you?'

'She asked if I would go north with her, and stay until her father dies and she can come back.' Asher looked down at her lap. 'She knows you must return to Venture to take Avorian's place in Council; by the time he reaches the city he'll be outcast, his men will spread the news.'

'Will you go?'

'I don't know.'

He hesitated, then cleared his throat. 'If you came back, with me – Asher, you must have heard what I said, after the leopard attacked you – would you be my wife?'

She sighed inwardly, but forced a smile. 'Mallory, I don't think it would be so simple. What sort of life would be yours and mine in Venture? I would find being the wife of a city councillor intolerable, and be very bad at it; and I'm not sure that you and I could continue on the terms we are now if I became only an adjunct to you.' She saw him nod his understanding, and was much relieved. 'Independence is hard won, and hard to lose, too.'

'What if I were to leave Venture? Would that be easier?'

'Where would you go?'

'To Fate; to the Dominus. I must, in any event, to tell him as much as I can about his daughter. She's a remarkable person.'

'Avorian did so much for her,' Asher agreed readily. 'Despite what came after. But I don't know, Mallory. Who would look after your own clan's concerns?'

He gave her a quizzical look. 'I rather thought I could leave that to Pars and my sister-in-law; she seems more interested in and better suited to the post than I, and together I have no doubt they can manage. At least then she would be sure of my intentions towards her son's inheritance.'

Asher frowned, uncertain of her own feelings. 'If we were younger, it would be easier,' she said slowly. 'I do care for you, more than for anyone, Mallory. I feel at home with you. But I'm not interested in running a household, and to be your wife would constrict my life in a way I won't accept; it wouldn't be your fault, but it would happen.'

'When Vallis rules, custom may change,' he suggested. 'You could start a new fashion.'

'Perhaps.' She shook her head. 'I'm sorry. I don't know what to say.'

He smiled. 'I thought that would be your answer. I know you better than you think. Don't worry, Asher, you don't have to decide now. But at least let me provide for you in some other way. Would you like to go home to Harrows, or to Kepesake? Or even to Fate, to see Callith? Whatever you want, name it.'

'I wish I knew.' She closed her eyes, sensing the myriad possibilities ahead now that she was free: but free to do what? 'All I know is what I *don't* want. I *don't* want to go back to Venture, although I should like to see Essa and the others again, and I *don't* want to go home to Harrows, or not yet. It's as if this – gift – makes it more difficult to choose, not easier; I have no control over it.'

'And what of my wants?' Mallory asked quietly. 'Do they count in the equation?'

'Yes. But not if they're a condition. Don't you see? You ask me to share your life, but what if our positions were reversed? Would you come and share mine, leaving the rest behind?'

He shook his head in some bitterness. 'How could I? I'm not free to make such a choice.' But she thought he did regret it. 'Let me buy Harrows from you; you can buy it back, if you ever want to, at the same price. That would give you financial independence.'

Asher put her hand on his arm. 'You're a poor sort of merchant, but the best kind of friend. But if I accepted money from you, it would never be the same. I would always *know*, and resent it; and so would you, in time.'

'Stiff-necked woman!'

She laughed. 'Would-be autocrat!' He laughed, too, both united in disagreement. 'Seriously, I'm not sure I want anything to change between us yet.' She coloured, embarrassed. 'What we have – what is love between a man and woman? It seems to me so often like a power-game, an endless round of compromise or a battle for domination which no one truly wins. You and I are both strong-willed, both accustomed to having our way. Friendship seems to offer greater potential for acceptance.'

'Friendship is love; more so, I think, than the passion so many mistake for love. But children, Ash,' he asked quietly. 'Have you no desire to be a mother?'

'Not like most women, no,' she said, surprising him. 'I am Asher first, and female only second. One day perhaps. But I have no yearning for children now.' She bit her lip in amusement, finding it surprisingly easy to discuss such matters with him. 'Can you imagine a daughter of ours, Mallory? What a difficult child she would be!'

He nodded. 'I've a dreadful feeling she would take after you,' he said seriously; but when she looked at him his eyes gleamed with humour.

For an instant, Asher had a glimpse into the future possibility of just such a daughter, a girl with Mallory's looks, clear, intelligent eyes and a determined expression; then it faded. Shaken, she said: 'No,' but without conviction; it had been so real.

'Tomorrow morning we reach the border.' He yawned. 'I'm sorry. I suppose every decent diviner in the Dominion will know how events have changed by now, that Vallis has been found.'

'You're not angry? That I haven't said yes?'

'Avorian would say marriage was the only way for a man to have sons, to plant his stake in the future,' Mallory said in answer. 'But for me – I made a mistake when I was young, marrying a woman I didn't love nor even know. In those days I valued a pretty face and figure above liking and respect, never thinking what it would be like to spend a lifetime with a woman for whom I had no real regard. But I forgive Melanna now, and even feel some pity for her. There are other children in my clan – I'm not so arrogant as to believe the world will not survive without a replica of myself.'

Yet behind his outward composure, Asher sensed he was not so very different from other men, that he would like a son, even if he denied it to himself, and she felt herself withdraw from him a little; not because there was anything unreasonable in such a wish, but because of its implications for herself.

A child – something to tie me down, never to be free again; and Mallory would see me as dependent on him, no more his equal and an independent person but a mother.

Bran and Soraya returned at that moment, and Asher was glad of the interruption. She had to make her decision before morning, and she still had no clear idea of which it would be. The only certainty was that whichever path she chose, there would be loss.

Epilogue

A light snow had frosted the land overnight, but the day dawned to a sparkling perfection that lifted the spirits of the trio who rode through the early-morning toward the river. The cold air was intoxicating, and, as the sun rose on a world that was only white and shadow, they might almost have believed themselves the only living creatures stirring in the empty land.

Only a few twisted trees obscured the wide vista of dazzling white; ahead, the river flowed silver and gold in the sunlight, deceptively innocent. Beyond it, the flat plain gave way to the mountains of Saffra, soaring, spiked peaks that had an air of remote indifference, as if they viewed the world from a great distance, removed by time as well as space from the frantic passions that moved those whose lives were measured in mere tens of years and not millennia. The sight was both humbling and uplifting at the same time, possessing an arcane beauty that calmed the mind and senses so it was possible to feel no care could weigh so heavily as to burden the heart unduly; love, hatred, fear, all were ephemeral, less than real.

As they approached the river, in the distance Mallory noticed a troop of grey men patrolling along the nearside bank, their massive horses lifting up their feet fastidiously from the thin layer of snow, but when he pointed them out to Asher, she displayed no undue concern.

'We have papers, and bear no slave-marks. They'll move on soon. This section of the river is supposed to be uncrossable.'

She was proved correct by the time they reached the river, for the troop was gone, their trail leading west, towards the higher reaches of the Saff.

It was the widest river Mallory had ever seen, more than a thousand feet across and, when he descended the bank to dip his fingers in the water, ice-cold. He looked at the far side in bafflement, unable to see how it was possible to get across, for the current was swift, and from the darkness at the centre the river was deep.

'For seven months of the year, the Saff is frozen,' Asher told him. 'We cross on sledges.'

'But now?' There were one or two small rowing boats moored along the bank, obviously for use in fishing the near shallows, but not suitable for the crossing.

'You'll see.' Asher dismounted and stood on the bank, her gaze fixed on the mountains. Vallis joined her.

'It looks deserted,' she said softly. 'As if no one had ever lived there – *could* ever live there.'

'The Saff live deep inside the mountains.' Asher turned to smile at the younger woman. 'They'll know we're here. They keep a constant watch for travellers.'

'But I can't see anyone.'

'Nor any barrier,' agreed Mallory, coming to stand beside them.

'It stretches along the centre of the river,' Asher explained. 'And you can't see it. It's like a barrier of *will*, a sort of protective charm that keeps out anyone the Saff consider unworthy to enter their land.'

'How does it work?' Mallory was intrigued rather than sceptical.

'The Saff are a collective people. I can't explain precisely. They have a kind of aggregate *sight*; they have a communal as well as individual awareness, and use it to maintain this barrier.' She could not explain it more clearly. 'It works. Mylla once told me about a slave-woman who tried to cross, and the barrier didn't lift, though she tried – it was winter – a dozen times. Mylla had to leave her here, and found out later that the Saff had discovered she had murdered a child in her care.'

'How did they know?' Vallis inquired, interested.

'In some fashion the Saff can *see* inside your mind, and know whether you represent a danger to their society. In their country they don't deal with lawbreakers as we do, but put the offender into a kind of tranced sleep until they're cured of whatever illness of mind made them act wrongly.'

Vallis shivered. 'I should hate to be judged so.'

'What's that?' Mallory had noticed something coming towards them from the far bank, a boat such as he had never seen before, drawn by two white-antlered beasts that seemed to pay no heed to the powerful current, bisecting the water in a neat, straight line.

'They're called *alluvair*, a sort of Saff ox, but they have very long forelegs and short hind legs, and are covered in thick white hair,' Asher answered. 'They're immensely strong swimmers, but the Saff use them for travelling on the mountain slopes, too, although they're not very easy to ride.'

'Why are there no people?' Vallis asked again. 'I thought – '

'The Saff keep away from our side; only their ambassadors ever cross the river.'

For a time they watched in silence as the boat drew closer to the bank. It was of no particular design, having a square stern and a high, pointed bow which seemed to serve no specific function. Other than the beasts, it possessed no means of forward movement, for there were no oars, no rudder nor paddles; it was painted white, and had room for perhaps six travellers.

'Where does the wood come from?' Mallory asked, to make conversation.

'From here, before the invasion.' Asher, too, was paying little attention to the boat, aware both Vallis and Mallory were waiting for her decision.

'Well?' Mallory, it seemed, would wait no longer; Vallis, too, turned to her, trying not to appear too eager.

'I have made up my mind,' Asher said slowly. She looked toward the mountains rather than at her companions. 'I will go with Vallis, for a time.'

'I see.' Mallory's face was expressionless.

'Do you remember the Saff girl we met, by the internment camp?' she asked him. 'She said I could come. Perhaps her people can teach me to use this gift, if I must call it that. That's what I want, Mallory. Because I don't want *it*; less now than before, because it seems to me that to *see* any part of the future can be an evil.' She grew silent, remembering Avorian.

'Omond would teach you, at Kepesake.' Mallory's tone was dry, nearly unfriendly.

'But he thinks the gift a good thing.' She hesitated, unwilling to speak frankly in front of Vallis, but there was no choice if she were not to hurt him further. 'Mallory, if we were lovers in fact, I would stay. But because we're friends I can leave you. If I stayed now, I'd never know if it was the right thing to do. I don't want a lifetime of regret.'

Reluctantly, he smiled. 'I should have known you would always take the hardest route.'

'It will only be until Vallis returns.' The younger woman's face grew still and Asher remembered this reference to her father's future death was hardly tactful, but it was more important to her

361

that Mallory should understand. 'Keep in touch with Essa, and whenever anyone comes north, I can send word to you.'

'I will, and I'll do what I can for her. For all your friends.' The boat had almost reached the bank. 'I think there's more to this than you're admitting, Asher. This is your dream, your adventure; your trip to sea that never happened.' He spoke quite seriously, and she was suddenly filled with gladness he should be capable of understanding so well what she found impossible to express.

'Life is an adventure or nothing, Mallory,' she said, eyes glowing. 'To be free, in despite of Fate, to allow only the bonds we choose to bind us. Not our sex, nor any other accident of birth, but free will, according to our abilities.'

'Then go.' He bent and kissed her forehead, lightly, without passion. 'But give me your word you'll come back.'

'I swear it.' And in that moment she could *see* her own return, the probability of her life once more enmeshed with his, though how or when was beyond her skill to read.

'Come, Asher. They're waiting.' Vallis had stood a little apart as they spoke together, but now the boat was alongside the bank and she climbed in, awkwardly, waiting for Asher to follow suit. Mallory held the craft steady, releasing it as Asher moved to sit by Vallis, and the two white beasts at once turned the boat and headed away, back to the further side.

Mallory found it a peculiar sensation to be the one left behind; always, in the past, it had been he who had gone away, travelling to distant lands, while Melanna had stayed behind and waited for his return. It was, he discovered, an extremely uncomfortable feeling, almost one of envy, to imagine Asher exploring an unknown country. Quicksnow and frozen seas. Would she be safe? Would she ever return, once she had tasted her freedom? The freedom which had been, but was no longer, his. Should he have gone with them? He wanted to.

He shook his head, knowing he could not; while she was free, all kinds of responsibilities tied him both to Venture and to the Dominus. Smiling at the thought, he wondered if this was how sailors' wives felt, left at home with the children and drudgery of every day while their husbands lived entirely separate existences, so that when they met once more it was with constraint, because both had changed in the absence of the other.

He watched the boat and saw it reach the centre of the river. Was that a ripple in the air – a breath of hesitation? But if hesitation there was, it was only brief, and the boat forged on. Mallory remounted his horse, holding the other pair on leading reins.

At last, the boat reached the far bank; the two women alighted, and Mallory could just see Asher turn and wave, pointing away towards the mountains, then she and Vallis headed north, soon to become two distant figures too small to identify against the white landscape. With a grimace, Mallory wheeled his horse and rode slowly back in the direction of Bran's farm; he had a long and tiring journey ahead to be back in Venture before the tribute ships sailed.

Yet somehow he could not continue to resent Asher's choice, nor envy her; the day was bright, the future full of hope. There was much for him to do, and he suddenly determined Asher would be surprised at the changes she found when she came back. And she would come back, somehow he was certain of it. What was it she had said? 'Life is an adventure or nothing.'

He burst out laughing. For both of them, that would always prove a true prophecy.